The Magical Painting

The Magical Painting

A novel of the heart

Maliny Moon
(with Stuart G. Yates)

Copyright (C) 2018 Maliny Moon
Layout design and Copyright (C) 2018 Creativia
Published 2018 by Creativia
Cover art by Cover Mint
This book is a work of fiction. Names, characters, places, and incidents are the product of the author's imagination or are used fictitiously. Any resemblance to actual events, locales, or persons, living or dead, is purely coincidental.
All rights reserved. No part of this book may be reproduced or transmitted in any form or by any means, electronic or mechanical, including photocopying, recording, or by any information storage and retrieval system, without the author's permission.

'The world that we perceive is a "presentation" of objects in the theatre of our own mind.' *Schopenhauer.*

1

"It's Mr Miles on the phone for you, sir."

Andrew Lambert groaned, the voice of Sinclair, the last remaining servant of Castle Strythe rumbling down the hallway. This was not the plan he had in mind for his first night back in Scotland, but Miles insisted. He wanted to meet up. No arguments.

A cold shower did little to bring life back to Lambert's body, a whisky not helping to relieve his exhaustion, but here he was, driving through the night towards his friend's castle. Squinting into the developing darkness, the rain starting to fall, with his mouth dry and tongue rough and foul tasting, he wished he'd been firmer, told Miles to wait until tomorrow. But Lambert knew his old university friend was not the man to argue with and now, with his eyes red raw and full of sleep, Lambert strained to keep the car straight, the headlights bouncing back at him from the solid wall of rain. His life, like the Scottish weather, was bleak and filled with trepidation.

Returning from London to his ancestral castle in Scotland had not been a clear-cut decision for Andrew Lambert. With his company facing an uphill struggle for survival, the problems often seeming insurmountable, it became increasingly difficult to choose between reviving his business, and closing it for good. He'd decided on taking the easier course and an inherited castle nestling in the shadows of the Highlands, a place, although seldom visited, he viewed as his eternal shelter. The place where he had grown up, happy memories seeping from every stone. The decision to return lightened the blow of losing almost everything he'd worked for over the last few years. Business, however, was not something which sat comfortably with him and so, with Jennifer's acerbic words ringing in his ears, he set off on the long journey north, driving his car into a new adventure simply to prove to himself this was not the end of the world.

He knew the longer he dawdled, the worse the journey to Miles' home would be, so he'd taken the bag of peaches old Sinclair had thrust into his hand and now, his stomach rumbling louder than the car engine, he picked one out and took a bite.

The sweet, overly ripe flesh erupted in his mouth, the juice spilling down his chin onto his shirtfront. He cursed, held the peach between his teeth as he struggled to pull a paper handkerchief from his trouser pocket. Twisting his body, raising himself off the seat to gain access to the tissue, his foot pressed harder on the accelerator. The car surged forward. As he battled with the wheel, his mobile phone sprang into life.

The details grew hazy from that point, but of one thing, he was completely certain. As he fought to keep control and answer the mobile at the same time, his headlights picked out the figure of a woman in the road. She stood unperturbed by the downpour or by the oncoming vehicle. He screamed, pulled down hard to the left and everything went blank.

They dropped Andrew Lambert off at the castle in the late afternoon of the second day and Megan came bounding down the steps with her tail wagging and her mouth open in as close a thing to a grin as a dog can get. The two ambulance personnel laughed as Lambert tried and failed to keep the big, black Labrador from assaulting him with huge licks of her wet tongue.

The worst journey of his life had brought him finally home.

A few days ago, he'd arrived at his ancestral castle, tired from his journey, and paused to take in the view. The hard, granite walls were as he remembered, every lead-latticed window black, grim, the west tower foreboding. He'd spent his youth here and when he left for university, he hadn't shed a single tear. Childhood was an adventure, adolescence suffocating. Now, standing here and taking it in, a tinge of regret ran through him, a moment's wish for years gone by, a brief return to more innocent times when cares and worries had no place. He should have appreciated it more, but the curse of being a teenager never allowed him such thoughts. He longed to escape; having done so, he wished he never had.

Appearing from nowhere, Sinclair relieved Lambert of his bags, a thin smile splitting his craggy face. "I'll take these to your room, sir."

It was as if he had never been away.

Given the opportunity, he wandered alone around the many rooms, all so silent and empty, the memories flooding back. Little had changed, but in the study, he turned his attention to a series of three paintings he had never seen before, neatly arranged above the fireplace. Scenes from the past, of how the castle might have looked two hundred, four hundred and seven hundred years before. The third, depicting the castle in ruins, gripped him more than the others and he stepped closer to read the inscription running along the bottom of the frame, 'Castle Strythe, 1386'. He frowned, wondering what had happened to cause everything to appear pulled down, or destroyed. The view of the surrounding hillsides, the distant loch, the same as the accompanying pictures, was in sharp contrast to the desolation of the castle. Curious, he decided to ask Sinclair for an explanation; the scene troubled him, the blackened masonry sinister and the vague portrayal of a woman sitting forlorn on an outcrop of rock so sad it caused him to consider something very wrong had happened in the depths of history.

What a difference a matter of days could make.

For now, returned from the hospital with the accident so recent, all previous troubles seemed far away.

He sat in a wheelchair after they'd dropped him off, his right leg covered in a thick plaster cast, took Megan by the collar, and ruffled the great dog's fur. He looked up to see Miles striding towards him across the gravel. Miles sighed, shaking his head. "You don't do things by halves, do you?"

Lambert shrugged, becoming a little hot around the collar, and turned to the first paramedic. "Thanks. I'll see you in around three weeks."

Miles took the handles of the chair and pushed his friend towards the castle entrance as the ambulance drove off, tyres crunching over the hard-packed shale of the sweeping driveway.

At this time of year, the wisteria and ivy clinged to the dappled cream granite walls of the castle like a second skin, breaking up the drab exterior with splashes of violet-blue flowers hanging in clusters from the spreading plant. Lambert hadn't noticed it on his first arrival, and he wondered why this was so. Nevertheless, grateful for the lightness of heart the wisteria brought him, Lambert breathed in the perfume and relaxed for the first time since the accident.

Miles grunted as he pushed the wheelchair up the incline of the makeshift ramp placed over the entrance steps. As he struggled to the double doors, Sinclair appeared. Dressed in a striped black and white apron the manservant beamed, joining with Miles to push the wheelchair into the hallway. "Mr Lambert, good to see you looking so well…given the circumstances."

"It's good to be here," said Lambert as Miles stepped back, breathing hard.

"I was making a late lunch," said Sinclair, wiping his hands on a tea towel. "I trust you are feeling up to eating?"

"I'm always ready to eat, Sinclair." He patted his midriff. "Too much sometimes. And a couple of days of hospital food have made me eager to sample something slightly more imaginative."

"Mr Miles has been very kind and went shopping for some fresh trout, which we will have for dinner, but lunch will be something light and quick."

"Well, whatever it is, I'm sure it will be delicious," said Lambert, threw a smile towards his old retainer and allowed a recovered Miles to wheel him into the dining room, Megan running around enjoying the game, barking with excitement, her thick rope of a tail thwacking anything within close proximity. Lambert rubbed his own arms, "It's cold in here."

"I'll get Sinclair to make the fire," said Miles, positioning Lambert close to the huge, open fireplace. "I should have told him to do it before, but he insisted on making some weird concoction he said was your favourite."

"I think I can guess. Corn-beef hash," said Lambert with a chuckle. "He's a rock that man."

Miles pulled a face and was about to go when he stopped and turned to his friend again. "Andrew, tell me how it happened. From what I heard it sounded a ridiculously stupid thing to do."

"Thanks, Miles, I can always count on you for a kind word."

Miles tilted his head. "You swerved, so you told the police, to avoid a *squirrel*? Is that it?"

"You phoned me as I was driving. I tried to answer, lost control. You knew I was coming, why the hell did you phone?"

"Oh, so it's *my* fault? Sorry, I understood you were the one behind the wheel." He shook his head, "I phoned to see where you'd got to, you surly sod. I was worried. And thanks to me, leaving your phone open, I heard it all. It was me who called the ambulance, even though I had little idea where you were."

"There's only one road to your place."

"Exactly. So you're bloody lucky to be alive, all thanks to me. But don't mention it, you ungrateful bastard." He laughed. "You must have been driving at some speed though, bonny lad. What actually happened?"

Lambert sighed, grimacing as he tried to reposition his leg. "If I told you, you'd think I was drunk or something."

"The 'something' is probably closer to the mark. So tell me."

Lambert gazed into the gaping fireplace, the grate full of ash from the previous blaze. "I saw someone."

Miles came closer, put his elbow on the mantelpiece and frowned. "You mean a person?" Lambert nodded. "So what was this about a squirrel?"

"I had to tell the police something. So, I used the first thing that came into my head."

"I don't understand. If it was a person you saw, why didn't you tell that to the police?"

"Because she was standing in the middle of the road."

"*She?* And you didn't hit her, so did she run away, what? The police made no mention of there being anybody else involved."

"That's because by the time they got me out of the ditch she was nowhere to be seen."

"But who the hell was she?"

"I don't know."

"Was she old or young? How was she dressed? Was she—"

"Miles, please," said Lambert holding up his hand, "You don't understand."

"Andrew, are you certain this is right? You saw a woman standing in the road and you swerved to avoid her, ended up in a ditch with a busted leg and you have no idea who she was or where she went?"

"She was dressed in Edwardian clothes, Miles."

His friend forced a laugh, "This gets weirder by the second. *Had* you been drinking?"

Lambert shook his head. "I lost consciousness for a brief moment, but I don't understand why. An image came into my head, but I can't recollect any part of it. I *think* it was the castle." He pointed to the three studies of the castle on the wall. "I can't remember. Weirder still, I had the wherewithal to switch the engine off and when I glanced back at the road, she had gone. Not a sign."

"She'd run off?"

"No, Miles. She'd disappeared."

2

Bedtime proved the worst, and Lambert wondered if he would ever have a good night's sleep again. Sinclair offered to help put him to bed the first night, but Lambert waved him away, angry, not because of his manservant's offer of assistance, but at his own helplessness. So Sinclair, who had made up a bed of sorts in the study, left him alone and the night was long and extremely uncomfortable.

At around three, Lambert pushed himself out into the hallway to the dining room. Negotiating the table and chairs, he made his way to the drinks cabinet without too many bumps and scrapes, poured himself a large whisky and sat before the impressive French windows. In the far distance, against the smudges of black and grey that made up the sky, the towering shapes of the Highlands dominated everything and as he stared, the memories of the accident descended, darker even than the night.

She stood, a pale white streak of indeterminate age, emerging from the road as if hoisted upright by invisible wires, and he saw her face, clear as day. Consumed by her, unable to resist, the road and the rain forgotten, he focused all of his senses on the loveliness of her features and she smiled, beckoning him to drive straight towards her.

The phone went off at that moment, the call from Miles. It snapped Lambert back to the present, but too late. At a rush, realising where he was, he slammed on the brakes with all his might, tyres squealing as they slithered over the wet tarmac. He grappled with the wheel, the car going into a wild skid, and all the while, the woman's face filled his vision, her soft, open mouth drawing him in.

The world turned over, body buffeting around like a pebble in a bucket as the vehicle careered out of control, hit a bank, pitched and rotated. The night mingled with the rain and her voice, so concerned, full of panic and distress, "*Andrew!*"

The car slammed into a ditch with a bone-jarring shudder and somehow his foot became trapped in the buckled, twisted metal as the bonnet collapsed inwards. Hot, searing pain shot through his leg, but for the moment, he forced aside the excruciating agony as thoughts of exploding petrol tanks leaped into his mind, overwhelming him. Lambert screamed, fighting to free his foot from under the broken brake pedal. He heard rather than felt the snap of his ankle. A moment of disbelief froze his body, followed by a horrible nausea as strength drained from his guts. Soon, mounting waves of pain flowed from his shattered limb, building in intensity until his screams became almost continuous. Nevertheless, despite it all, he had the presence of mind to stretch forward and turn off the ignition.

He turned, and a bizarre sight greeted him – her face beyond the window, arms imploring him, anguish written in her features, the dread concern of a friend, a lover, yet none of it seemed right. Then the realisation caused him to gasp. He was upside down.

The whisky glass fell from his numb fingers, shattering on the floor, and he jumped, for a moment forgetting where he was and went to stand up. As he bore his weight down on his shattered limb, he cried out and immediately sank back into his wheelchair, breathing hard, biting down the pain. He put his shaking hand against his mouth and waited until his raging heartbeat lessened.

He struggled back to bed and lay in the darkness, body exhausted but sleep far, far away.

Through the course of the next few days and weeks, Lambert sleepwalked his way through life, spending time in the garden, trying to read, listen to music, surfing the Internet, anything to relieve the mounting boredom.

Visions of the mysterious woman from the crash became less, but sometimes, when looking out towards the hillside, her face loomed up in his mind and he took to imagining whom she might be and where she had come from. Perhaps a photograph he saw once, a fleeting glance of a pretty face, or the friend of a friend, an introduction lost amongst the stresses and strains of the past few months. He didn't know, but one thing was certain – she was beautiful.

Time seemed to stretch out, every minute lasting an hour and he grew increasingly restless, his current situation so different from his recent past, when he had so much to occupy his mind. The stress of a business spiralling towards disaster, his failed relationship with Jennifer. Now, he felt frozen in a timeless absolute. Intuitively, he wished he had a wiser vision; something beyond his capabilities, to challenge him, stretch his intellect, bring some hope of a more meaningful existence.

Sinclair, ever close, drifted in and out, bringing food, hot drinks. Sometimes Miles would come and talk, cracking jokes and generally being his usual, cheerful self. Lambert sat through these visits without offering up either verbal ripostes or the faintest glimpse of a reaction. The more he sat, the more morose he became. Reading didn't help, nor the daily ritual of sitting watching mindless daytime television. Even the Internet, with its possibility for discovery and exploration of every situation and thought process from around the world – a world that rarely makes sense – couldn't make any inroads. Boredom and inactivity competed to overwhelm him, and he took to wheeling himself out into the grounds of the castle, even when it rained, to sit and breathe in the sweet air rather than the musty, dampness of the interior.

On one such day, Sinclair, whilst bringing him a tray full of oatcakes, malt whisky and coffee, shuffled awkwardly and coughed. "Sir, if I may make a suggestion?"

Lambert did not raise his head as he considered the malt, peering into its amber depths, savouring the moment. The tumbler, heavy crystal-cut glass, seemed to enhance the flavour as he took the first mouthful, closed his eyes and sighed deeply. "God, that is bloody good."

Sinclair grunted, tried again. "Sir, I am somewhat concerned."

The man's rich brogue seemed on edge, as if he were struggling to find the words. "Are you?"

"Yes, sir. You seem so disheartened, depressed perhaps. I am becoming increasingly concerned, sir."

"Well, you needn't be. I'm just fed up. I can't go anywhere, do anything, and my leg's beginning to itch like billy-oh." To give weight to his words, he raised the plaster cast and waggled it. "See, no more pain. The sooner the bloody thing comes off the better."

"Next week, I believe the doctors said? They will re-examine you, perhaps apply a simpler dressing and then—"

"*Six* weeks they said. Compound fracture, ankle and shin crushed. Even then, I won't be able to put much pressure on it. I'll have to exercise, walk with a bloody crutch..." He shook his head and drained the whisky. "Good stuff, Sinclair. Thank you."

"Sir, your disposition, it..." He made a face as if in pain. "Sir, if I might suggest something? To ease the tedium of your situation."

"Anything you can say that will bring some relief would be very welcome indeed, Sinclair. But please don't tell me it's whist, or chess."

Sinclair's mouth hung open for a moment. "Er, no, sir. Nothing of the sort."

"What then?"

"The West Tower, sir. The entrance is blocked, but I do believe I can find a way in, with your permission of course."

"The West Tower? I'm not sure I've ever stepped inside."

"No, sir, I do not believe you have. Your grandfather kept it locked, and even your father only ventured inside somewhat rarely."

"He said it was haunted." Sinclair looked away, a little too sharply, and the action brought a slight stab of alarm to Lambert, who shifted in his chair and frowned. "You don't believe all that rot, do you?"

"Not at all, sir. Your father was a somewhat *fanciful* man, sir, who often conjured up the wildest of fantasies."

"Did him all right for writing novels though, eh? You ever read one, Sinclair?"

"I believe I started 'The Vicar of Castelrig Knoll', but I am ashamed to admit I couldn't get into it, as they say."

"He did most of his writing in here, in the study, didn't he?"

"During the weekends only, sir. You father was a man of peculiar habits. The rest of the time, he worked in the Tower, looking out across the glen. That was after your grandfather passed away, sir."

Lambert nodded and allowed his eyes to wander over the rolling hills until they settled on the distant mountains. "I was five years of age when grandfather died. Father often spoke of him, but I can't even remember what he looked like."

"He looked remarkably like you, sir."

"Did he? No one ever said." Lambert shrugged.

"He could be your twin brother, sir."

Frowning, Lambert looked away.

Silence hung over them both, the only sound the far-off cry of a soaring buzzard, lonely and hauntingly beautiful as if, in that single, plaintive call, the captured souls of the tormented begged for release. As he looked, Lambert thought he saw a couple in the distance. He couldn't quite make them out, but screwing up his eyes in an effort to male out their details, the face of a man turned towards the glen and the woman's slender hand reached out to caress his cheek. "My love…"

Lambert snapped his head towards the servant, seized by an inexplicable dread. "What did you say?"

Sinclair blinked, "Er, I was talking about the Tower, sir."

Lambert quickly scanned the room, saw there was no one, then took another look across the countryside. "Sinclair, this is private property, correct?"

"Sir? Private property? I don't quite—"

"Damn it, man, has the public access to the glen?"

"This is your estate, sir. True, there are several pathways, which give access. The public have right of way, sir, as long as they do not cross into those areas deemed private. There are numerous notices to alert them to those area, however. Why do you ask?"

Keeping his eyes locked on the rolling hills, the valley, the various clumps of woodland, he shook his head. "It doesn't matter, I thought I…" He blew out his cheeks and swung his wheelchair around. "You were saying? The Tower? What about it?"

Sinclair frowned. "Well, only an idea, sir, but I believe your father may have kept unfinished manuscripts, letters and poems there, together with a large collection of old photographs. I thought perhaps you might want to go through them, unearth some forgotten gems, perhaps discover more of your family's history." He shrugged, gave a half smile. "It would give you something to do, sir, and may even shed some light on…"

His voice trailed away, and Lambert considered what he'd heard. "I'll sleep on it," he said.

But that night, he could not sleep. The appearance of the couple bothered him. They might have been simply out on a stroll, but the more he thought about it, the more this explanation seemed unlikely. He went to the dining room once again to drink whisky, more than one glassful, allowing his mind to linger on the buzzard and its cry, the woman's voice floating as if on a breeze. The more he thought, the more the belief grew something very odd was striving to make its presence felt.

3

He woke with his head pounding, tongue thick in his mouth, longing for water. "Jenny, get me something will you, an aspirin, anything to take away this God-awful headache."

Shadows danced around the corners of his eyes and as the room came into focus, the pain in his leg brought him back to reality. No longer lying beneath the covers of his London bed, central heating wrapping him in its warm embrace, the promise of Jennifer's lithe body responding to his gentle caress … Instead, here he was. Castle Strythe. Another world. He groaned, rolled over, and took his time getting to his feet.

Coffee waited for him in the dining room, the pot fresh, steaming hot. Thank God for Sinclair. The man seemed to possess a sixth sense, knowing instinctively what was required, and when.

Afterwards, Lambert waited at the entrance to the Tower, listening to the old retainer clumping up the winding stairway to the uppermost rooms. For all his life Sinclair had wandered around the periphery of Lambert's existence, as much a part of the castle as the ancient stones, first laid down in the Fourteenth Century, permanent like the Highlands, eternal as the glen. His earliest memory of the man was when, after falling from his bicycle and lying in the gravel wailing like a newborn, Sinclair stood over him, warm smile, big hands lifting him, "A young Laird doesn't cry," he said. "A young Laird is strong and brave, as his forefathers were." He'd patted Lambert on the cheek and the pain eased. When Father came and asked, Lambert shrugged, sniffed and said, "Nothing, Father. A mere scrape is all."

"There," said Sinclair, breathing hard.

Lambert blinked and found the servant standing over him, with two large, well-taped cardboard boxes at his feet.

Sinclair straightened his back, wincing a little. "It's damned awkward negotiating those steps, but I'll do my best."

"I'll phone Miles, ask him to come and help. If you can take the boxes to the study. I'll sort them there."

Sinclair smiled, seeing the sense of his master's words. "Very good sir. Whilst you telephone, I shall bring some more boxes down from your father's study."

Lambert wheeled himself to the house, pausing at the rear entrance to take in the scenery of the glen. The sky appeared leaden behind the mountains, the threat of rain thick in the air, a metaphor for a new phase in his life he mused. What secrets lay contained in those boxes, he wondered. His father had made a good living from his writing, twenty-two books published, two film adaptations together with a long-forgotten television series. And now, the promise of more unpublished tomes about to be brought to light. Lambert ruminated with the idea of becoming something of a literary wizard himself but knew, deep down, such a thing could never be. He had inherited his mother's fastidiousness and cold, clear business sense; his father's vibrant and ceaseless imagination was an alien concept to him. Better at analysing the daily performance of stocks and shares than the creation of character and plot, Lambert kept his mind firmly fixed in the real world, not the one of fiction.

Why then the images of the girl?

His eyes were gritty and when he returned to the study, he wheeled himself over to the fire and allowed himself a moment, to rest. He required a few moments, to recharge his spirit. He allowed himself to drift.

A train rattled through his brain, as if he were travelling between two stops, one London, with its colourful, vibrant life, the other dark, threatening, drawing him closer to the night of the accident.

He fought against the darkness, found courage in a memory, a bottle of Moët and Chandon chilling in a bucket of ice, Jenny moving around in the bedroom.

"Come on, darling. You can try your new coat on later, this champagne won't keep."

She appeared in the doorway, wrapped in her new Burberry coat, open to reveal matching black underwear, her toned body shimmering, slim, endless legs in sheer stockings and black, leather boots. The woman of his dreams; a goddess.

"What do you think?"

Her eyes sparkled like the champagne in the glass as she reached out, took his hand and led him into the bedroom, pushing him down upon the cover. She pulled away his shirt without a pause, ripping the material, discarding trousers and pants. He moaned, not wanting to resist, her soft lips wandering over his body, teeth nipping at his nipples. He cried out, arching his back, responding to such sweet torture!

Moments later, her hot breath lava from a volcano, flowing down his body until it reached the most gentle and sensitive area of his being, the gate opening to what he knew would be paradise.

Lambert snapped his eyes open, sucking in a breath. He put the heels of his palms into his eyes, rubbing away the images. Why was he thinking about all of this now? He'd made his choices. So had Jennifer.

Jennifer. Was the dream a memory, or a hope? A longing for something that never was? Was it even her? He struggled to regain her features, to recognise the Jennifer he knew with the one of a few moments before.

Perhaps...

His hands dropped to his lap and he gazed into the fire and saw her, the woman in the road, her shocked look of anguish as he lay entangled inside the car, her helplessness as she reached out her hand and realised she could do nothing. Who was she and to where had she disappeared? When the paramedics came and eased him from out of the wreckage he told them what had happened but, despite the police combing the immediate vicinity, they found no trace of the mystery woman, as if she had never existed.

And yet, he had seen her.

In answer to Lambert's phone call, Miles arrived within twenty minutes, clapping and rubbing his hands with glee, filling the room with his persona as he strode across the floorboards to the fire burning in the grate. "Damned bloody weather," he said, face ruddy with the run to the castle from his car, the rain pelting down with the force of bullets. "Why the hell did you ever come back to this place?" He turned, massaging his backside before the flames. "Not that I'm ungrateful, mind. It's good to have you back, but I'd much prefer to be living it up in your London apartment."

"I've sold it," said Lambert, pouring out two tumblers with whisky. He clinked in ice and turned, offering out his hand to his oldest friend.

"Well, you're bloody stupid." Miles took the drink and downed it in one. "You made a tidy profit, I hope."

"Yes, of course. Enough to keep me comfortable whilst I'm here." Lambert sipped at his own drink, savouring the warming sensation as the malt trickled down his throat to lie and smoulder in his stomach.

Miles gaped. "You need your head testing."

"No. Father's death made me think, Miles. Made me think what to value and care about." He swept his hand around the room. "All this. My family have lived here for generations and I grew up here, running like a mad thing through the corridors and up and down the winding staircases but as soon as I was able, I couldn't wait to get away. Now…" He shook his head, deep in thought, recalling the images, wondering again if they were of Jenny, or someone else. He finished his drink. "It's different now, Miles. *I'm* different now."

"And Jenny? What did you say to her?"

Lambert shrugged, wheeled back to the drinks' cabinet and poured out another glassful of malt. "We hadn't been getting on for a long time. She was seeing someone else. Some guy from the UAE, dripping with money. Who cares?"

"She was seeing someone else? Since when?"

"Since ages. He'd been screwing her for months and I didn't know a damn thing about it. When the business went pear-shaped, she took the opportunity to kick me whilst I was down and tell me all about him, how fantastic he was, so rich, so handsome." He chuckled, took a sip of the whisky. "I sat and listened to her, telling me how useless I was in bed, how I'd never satisfied her, how—"

"Women always say those things when there's a break up."

"True. A lot of friends told me their own 'bad date' experiences. I laughed them off, finding them trivial, never once realising when it comes to your own experience, it's one of the hardest things to accept." He swilled the whisky around the bottom of the glass, deep in thought. "When I was able to provide something akin to a luxury lifestyle, she heaped praises upon me, telling me I was so handsome, such a brilliant lover, but when I reminded about that after our break up, she mimicked the fake orgasm scene done by Meg Ryan in 'When Harry Met Sally'. She told me she'd done the same. I was devastated."

"Jesus Christ, Andrew, that's no measure of—"

"Apparently it was to *her*, Miles. She made very sure I knew *exactly* how fucking wonderful her new lover was between the sheets."

Miles stood in silence, staring down into the bottom of his tumbler. "You're better off out of it by the sound of things. You don't need a woman like that in your life, Andrew, so forget about her! There's no shortage of pretty girls out there, so never ever give up. Look at me, eh?" A boyish impishness twinkled in Miles' eyes.

"But I miss her *so much*. She celebrated life. Every single day I spent with her was like fireworks going off in my heart." Images of Jennifer, her smile, the way she always played with the hem of her dress, coy, sucking in her lip, tossing her flaxen hair, came into his mind.

"You're punishing yourself for something that was not your fault."

"You think so? They say everything happens for a reason, but I'm not so sure. Sometimes, a picture of her pops up in my head, her eyes, the cut of her hair, to remind me of the pain of losing her."

"I think you need time alone to sort your head out. You're here now, in your ancient castle surrounded by majestic hills, breathtaking wildness and the great history behind it all … maybe things will all turn out for the best, in the end. She was always too stuck up anyway." Miles screwed his face into a gargoyle mask and took a large drink.

"She may have been, but she was gorgeous, and I believed…" Lambert looked away, put his finger and thumb into his eyes. "I believed we had a chance. I *hoped* for happiness, a life together, a family. I toyed with the idea of coming back here, of bringing up our child in the castle. I was a bloody fool, wasn't I?"

"Andrew, stop beating yourself up. You have to let it go, look forward not back."

"I suppose. But it's hard, Miles. One moment I'm in the City, the next the shares hit rock bottom, we haemorrhage money and Jennifer sticks her boot in. Within the space of a week, my whole life was turned upside down."

"And you didn't see any of it coming?"

Lambert shrugged. "I don't know. Maybe. I didn't care, I'd lost interest. After Father's death, I'd thought a lot about who I was, the sort of person I'd become and I didn't like it, Miles. I got out some of my old books and I read them through again, listened to the type of music I used to when I started uni." He chuckled. "I rediscovered myself. Corny isn't it."

"Not at all."

"I think Jennifer panicked at what she saw. As my interest for making money waned, she would disappear for a few days. I never took any notice, but of course, I realise now what she was doing. And why."

"It's for the best. You'll come to believe that, Andrew. Honestly. All you need is some time."

"Yes, I suppose you're right."

Miles smiled, seeming relieved as Andrew relaxed. "Talking of the past, I've missed this old place, and your dad. I really liked him. He often used to phone me up, inviting me over, saying, 'I've just got hold of a lovely bottle of Château Margaux, come and help me finish it'. He often showed his penchant for the finest of Bordeaux wines by finishing off a couple of bottles during my visits. I'd drop everything and we'd spend the most precious moments together. He'd be full of stories, about all sorts of things, but usually about wine." He laughed. "He was something of a historian, your old dad, when it came to the ruby nectar. He told me about the earliest known vessels for storing wine – wineskins, containers made from animal hide or bladders, how he'd looked up references going back to Homer's Odyssey, continuing through to Shakespeare's plays…" Miles stopped, lost in the memory. Silence proved more eloquent than words. "He told me that the last time I saw him."

Lambert studied his friend for a long time, determined not to allow grief to overcome him.

"Andrew, he was a great man your old dad. I loved him."

Lambert pressed his lips together and nodded, unable to speak. He drank the malt whilst Miles moved past him, helping himself to a refill before sitting down in a nearby armchair. Both men stared into the flames.

Sometime later, Sinclair arrived with the first of the boxes and Miles, regaining his enthusiasm, helped the old butler to bring more of them up from the Tower. Within half an hour, eight or ten such boxes lay heaped upon the study floor. Miles grinned, hands on hips, the sweat across his brow. "What the hell is inside all of these?"

"Manuscripts and photographs, so I understand," said Sinclair. "Mr Lambert would often abandon projects mid-stream. I sometimes saw him tying up over four-hundred pages and discarding them. He had no qualms about such things, but when he did experience some form of emotional connection with a story he always finished the work. Every day he would write, from the early morning until well into the evening. When Mrs Lambert passed away he became almost obsessed." He smiled across to Andrew Lambert, who sat holding his whisky between his palms, listening to every word. "Apologies, sir. Your mother was an exceptional woman, in so many ways. Her death affected him acutely."

"He soon recovered though, didn't he?"

Sinclair frowned at the sharp tone used and turned to Miles who offered nothing but a slightly raised eyebrow. "It is true they were more friends than lovers, but…" Sinclair's face grew red. "Forgive me, sir, I do not wish to offend the memory of your father. The life he lived with your mother was not *usual* but it worked for them. He grieved for her, sir, I know that much. Always a private man, he rarely revealed his emotions but I could feel his anguish at her passing." He pulled in a raking breath, "I shall fetch some more boxes."

"No, Sinclair, this will be enough to be going on with." Lambert raised his glass. "Thank you."

He watched the manservant go out and when the door closed quietly, he glanced across at Miles. "A private man? Didn't stop him having a rack of affairs though, did it."

"Don't judge your father harshly, Andrew. There's a lot you don't know."

"Oh, and what makes you the expert?"

"Relationships, they're bloody complicated. Look at you and Jenny."

"Life is a great canvas; it's not easy to find your complimentary colour." He frowned, surprised at his own use of such imagery. Perhaps a sense of creativity was beginning to assert itself. He shook his head, continuing, "Jenny immersed herself completely in the material world. My mother possessed something more, the one thing my father needed from her – the one thing he really, truly valued: he needed inspiration. She gave it to him, showed him the way to success and enabled him to grab the possibility. Without her support and ceaseless optimism I doubt he would have continued writing."

Miles said nothing for a moment, preferring to look though the window to the wonders of their natural surroundings. He smiled. "I read almost all of his books. They were sublime, Andrew. Nothing like anything else. Deep, thought-provoking, forcing the reader, *me*, to question what we perceive as truth."

"I'm ashamed to say I've never read any of them."

"Then you should."

They stared at one another for a long time and then Lambert, snapping himself out of his reverie, prodded his friend in the leg and smiled. "You'll stay, help me through this lot?"

"These boxes?" Lambert nodded. "Christ, Andrew, do I have to?"

"No. I thought you might want to help out an old friend, that's all."

"Pompous ass." Miles grinned, threw down the whisky and stood up. "No, I'm off. I have much to do." He clapped his hands together and beamed.

"Really. What's her name?"

"Hah! You know me too well, you boring bastard. I'm off to wine and dine the lovely Natalie down in town. Then, it's back to my place for an evening of wild, unbridled sex."

Lambert blew out his breath in a long stream. "I envy you at times, you know that?"

"Then why not get yourself a girl, eh? I could fix you up, if you want. Nobody like the material girl Jennifer with her limp thighs and her haughty-taughty manner. What you need, my bonny lad is a nubile young thing who will shag you stupid."

"Yeah, and spend all my money, money which I haven't got I hasten to add."

"God, you're boring."

"Careful, more like. It's all right for you, you have two brothers to look after your estate, a private bloody income and enough time on your hands to indulge in every whim and fancy that comes to mind. I've got this place to sort out. Father left a mountain of debts and my responsibility is to get things straight."

"You should hold a party."

"*What?*"

"A party. A get-together. Invite some of the old gang over, lay on a spread. It'll take your mind off everything."

"Don't be bloody stupid, how am I supposed to organise all of that?"

"I'll help." Miles jutted his chin towards the boxes. "After you've been through this little lot, give me a call and I'll start the ball rolling, so to speak."

"I don't want a party, Miles, I'm too—"

"You don't need to do *anything,* old mate. You can leave all the arrangements to me." He came across and punched Lambert playfully in the chest. "It'll bring you out of yourself. And who knows, you might even have a good time."

He breezed out, chuckling softly to himself and Lambert watched him go and wondered if it might work. A party, like the ones he used to know, with Jenny, voices raised in laughter, filling the place with the sound of happiness, replacing the sadness and grief, which draped themselves over every part of the castle. It was time to sweep away the gloom away, bring some cheer to the old stones.

Maliny Moon

The more he thought the more he became convinced what a good idea it was.

4

Lambert sat for a long time, unmoving, considering the boxes before him. They stank of damp and neglect, some stained dark brown in the bottom corners, most buckled and some broken. He did not know where to start, or even why he ever agreed to such an endeavour. Being bored was one thing, but embarking on the sifting through of endless pieces of dirty, decaying sheets of paper was not what he'd signed up for. He should call Sinclair to burn the lot, but such a thing would be tantamount to turning his back on his father's memory.

He rarely saw his father in his youth. A dark, forbidding shape passing by in the corridors, silent, brooding. Sometimes he would listen outside the study, ear pressed to the door, listening to the constant thump of the typewriter, the occasional loud sigh, the clink of the glass as yet another whisky was poured. Sinclair often took him into town and outside the local bookshop window, the manservant would stop and point out the titles his father had created. "One day you might read them," he said. Lambert never did. Somehow, he could never relate the words, even those of the titles, to the father he knew. When his mother called him for lunch or dinner, they would sit in silence. Lambert never asked where his father was, because he knew. Writing. Always writing.

On the day Lambert left for university, his father emerged from the study, as always dressed immaculately in padded, purple smoking jacket and black silk pyjama bottoms. He smoked a Turkish cigarette with his usual elegance, fingertips alone holding onto the burning, white stick. He appeared tired, with dark shadows under his eyes. "Well Andrew," he said and smiled.

There were no other words.

As the years of study sauntered by his father took to writing him letters. Initially a few hastily scratched words but soon they developed into something far more detailed. Page after page of ideas, thoughts, observations. After a while, Lambert began to build up a much fuller appreciation of his father, together with a deeper knowledge of the castle and the family heritage.

And now, here before him, stacked up in untidy piles, more chapters in the life of the man whom he knew best from his letters. He wheeled himself closer to the nearest box, grunted as he picked it up and positioned it on his lap. He made his way to the desk, laid it on the top and, using the letter opener in the mahogany writing set, sliced into the thick tape, which bound the box together.

A waft of dank smelling paper hit him when he pulled back the cardboard flaps and he reeled away, wrinkling his nose, coughing. He waved his hand through the air to disperse the smell before remembering the thin latex fabric gloves Sinclair had provided. He slipped them on, the sensation of the material on his skin setting his teeth on edge. He delved inside the box.

The first few creased and torn papers were of little interest, bearing scattered scrawls in a spider's hand, illegible and faded. His heart sank as he went deeper and discovered much the same with every piece he examined. Pages of scribbles, sometimes complete sentences but mainly a single word here and there. 'Smiles, face, eyes of sultry, smoky grey' and any number of other, mysterious, meaningless jottings.

Over the course of the next hours, he diligently went through each box, only to find similar extracts. He was vaguely aware of Sinclair moving in and out the room, bringing plates of sandwiches and pots of tea but concentration centred on the boxes and the more Lambert rooted around, the more he became convinced something of value lay amongst the heaps of scrawl. Why else keep them all? There had to be a reason for he could never countenance his father being a mere hoarder.

In the afternoon, he asked Sinclair to take him out into the glen.

"I need some fresh air," he explained, gesturing towards the boxes and the collection of curled papers strewn over floor and desk.

On his return, downing his second whisky, Lambert put his head back. All the talk of Jenny, the break-up, it brought nothing but a dark depression. London, with all its hustle and bustle, seemed a million miles away, and yet she remained. Regret, blame, desire. All mingling together.

There was something he recalled, so sharp, so immediate it made his blood freeze. He and Jennifer attended a charity affair, supporting talented young people. Some students from RADA were there, acting out a series of short, one-act plays, and one of them…

Lambert stared into the mist of his memory. How had he not remembered this before now? One scene was of a duchess who had disappeared. Disappeared from an old castle.

Was that why he saw the woman the night of the accident? Were these two dramas interlaced somehow, distorting reality, making his unconscious appear real?

Too much thinking, he decided. He wheeled himself to the drinks' cabinet, poured himself another malt. Sinclair had mentioned something about the internet going down. It seemed all he had was the Scotch, books, and his father's papers.

He swung around to examine a further box. He sighed, delved into it and there, beneath a thick wad of scrawl, he came across a sealed envelope, thick and padded. Inside were a letter and half a dozen or so sepia photographs. He was about to read the letter when something caused him to stop. A tension in his spine. For a moment, he thought some reaction to the accident, a developing problem to do with nerves or tendons, and he pressed his palm into the small of his back and noticed one photograph poking out more prominently than the others. He picked it out and took in the face looking back to him from across the years. And as he stared, his heart grew cold and the ice spread from inside the core of his being, turning thought and sensibility into impenetrable confusion. His dream of Jennifer, the memory of the party. Students, a missing duchess. The accident.

And as he stared, clarity drove away his confusion.

He recognised the face.

The face of the woman in the road.

5

Sinclair took the photograph between finger and thumb, careful not to touch the central part of the image, and stood frowning. Lambert waited whilst the manservant mulled over what he saw but after a few moments he turned to sifting through the last few remaining papers in the same box in which he found the envelope. At the bottom was a list and when he ran his eyes over the words, something stirred inside.

"I don't know her, sir." The manservant said at last and handed the photograph back. "I'm sorry."

Lambert took it without looking, eyes still fixed on the paper in front of him. "What do you make of this, Sinclair?"

Peering over his master's shoulder, he grunted, "A bibliography of some sorts I shouldn't wonder."

"Of course," said Lambert, "I can see that now. Not a random collection of meaningless, jumbled up words, as I first thought, but the titles of books, with authors and dates. Not laid out in the traditional manner, however. Single words, scratched dates, no formed sentences. A hectic, mad record, hastily written, almost as if Father was attempting to get them down before he forgot their names. Do we have any of these books?"

Sinclair pulled a face, "It's possible."

Both men trawled their eyes across the shelves, to the thousands of volumes arranged in subject order, from autobiographies to zoology, and almost every category in between. The largest section was on philosophy and psychology, with history running up a close second.

"My father was so proud of his old library," said Lambert, voice barely above a whisper, as if the collected volumes had only just that moment appeared before him. "When I was a little boy, I was not allowed to enter here without permission so my mother would disappear inside, leaving me standing breathless in the hallway, wondering what wonders she was going to come back with. I still remember my first rush of excitement when Hans Christian Andersen's stories opened a world of unforgettable enchantment." The boy who loved to read, who retained strange quirks or habits and a belief in magic still lived inside Lambert. Looking over the vast array of so many volumes, he realised how much he had missed it all. "Every man's life is a fairy tale, written by God's fingers," he whispered to himself, recalling Anderson's quote. "Throughout my youth, this room was the most sacred place in the entire castle. There's an entire lifetime of learning locked away between these pages. I should have spent more time in here as I grew up, enjoying this remarkable collection." He sighed. " I didn't. I left and became like all the rest, striving to accumulate wealth, thinking a big house and a fast car were the only things that mattered. To *fit in,* frequent the best parties, be seen with the oh-so-rich-and-bloody-famous. Coming back, I've begun to realise none of that matters. Father knew it and through his books, he must have caused his friends to self-combust in pure, bilious envy! They were so shallow, like me, but he was different. He had dreams, not of the material kind, but dreams of the *soul*." He shook his head, lost in his thoughts. "I succumbed to what was expected, I suppose, became like the rest, locking away my hopes and dreams and throwing away the key. It's so hard to find it again. We're fighting a losing battle, all of us wishful thinkers. The pursuit of wealth, the desire to be famous, the baseless belief that getting our face on television somehow makes us a better person. The pathetic and crass celebrity world in which we live is supplanting learning. Nowadays, learning has so little value, but when I look at all these books, the collective knowledge of centuries, I do not understand how I have ignored such wonders for so long."

"Often we ignore those things closest to us. It's like the glen, sir. Have you ever been to the loch, for instance?" Lambert looked, shook his head. "You see. And yet, you have been to how many other, more distant places? Paris, Rome, New York? You have stood outside the Pyramids of Giza, walked the Great Wall of China, gazed in wide-eyed wonder at Niagara Falls, but you never rowed a boat across your own loch." He smiled. "It's not unusual, sir. I lived as a young man in Edinburgh. I never once drank whisky."

Lambert laughed, returned to the list, and then the photograph.

A woman of indeterminable age, sitting in a classic pose, hands clasped together on her lap, long, heavily embroidered dress, hair pulled back and tied, rivulets trailing down to her shoulders. A profile shot of a finely sculptured face, slightly turned to the camera. "Who is she, I wonder. She's beautiful."

"All I can say is, with some certainty, she does not bare any family resemblance."

Lambert turned the photograph around. A sepia image, glued onto a rigid piece of card, smaller than a postcard. And at the foot was an address. "Talking of Edinburgh, the photographer had a studio in the city." He fanned the photograph, staring into space. "You think it might still be there?"

"Hardly likely is it, sir."

"I don't know. It's worth a try, don't you think?" He studied the name, "Richard Brody, photographer. Does that mean anything to you?"

"Not a thing, sir. Edwardian perhaps, turn-of-the-century. Other than that..."

Unconsciously, Lambert slipped the photograph into his jacket pocket before studying the bibliography once again. "I'm going to look for these books. I might need some help with the top shelves."

"Whatever you say, sir."

In less than an hour, the acquired volumes covered the writing desk, all except one. Lambert re-checked the list against the titles of the books and sat back, sighing. "Following 'The Way' from Vézelay." He chuckled. "Sounds like a poem.

"Vézelay is a small town in Burgundy, sir, famous as one of the starting places of the pilgrimage into Spain to Santiago de Compostela."

"You amaze me, Sinclair. How the devil do you know all that?"

"I haven't lived my entire life amongst these walls, sir, no matter how grand they may be. I visited Vézelay, many years ago. With your father, in actual fact. I remember him telling me he would one day wish to walk the Way, but I do not believe he ever did. We stood outside the old abbey one morning, a huge church for such a small town, and he got down on his haunches and ran his finger over one of the many gold scallop shells embedded in the paving and he looked at me and I could see the tears in his eyes. He never explained why."

"So, this book, it might be somewhere else in the house? Perhaps it's a guide, or a history of the town."

"I couldn't say, sir."

"But…" Lambert reached across to one of the volumes and absently flicked it open. "All of this must mean *something*, Sinclair. And the town, what was it called again?"

"Vézelay, sir. In Burgundy, France."

"Why did he go there, did he say?"

"I assumed it was because he wanted to see where the pilgrimage began. He never said."

"And you didn't think to ask?"

A smile. "Your father was not the sort of person you asked too many questions of, sir. His mind was forever drifting off, creating stories. He often locked himself away in his thoughts, if you understand me, sir."

"Did he ever write whilst he was there?"

"He had a notebook, *always* the notebook, and he would scribble endlessly inside it. Ideas, observations, snippets of conversations, descriptions of people he met or saw. Tools of the trade, so to speak."

"This notebook, do you know where it is now?"

"Your father had many notebooks sir, some filled, some barely touched."

"Yes, but where are they?"

Sinclair shrugged. "I assume…" He looked around the study. "They must be in here, somewhere. When your father passed away, he left instructions that all of his un-completed work should be burned, any notes or—"

"I never knew that!" Lambert's stomach rolled over, gripped by a sudden, unexpected wave of anguish, and he swung around and wheeled himself over to the drink cabinet. He poured a healthy measure of malt and took a gulp. "I never … Why would he consent to such a thing, do you think?"

"Who can say? Perhaps he was concerned someone might plagiarise his words. His last published novel had met with considerable success, what with the film and all. There were rumours a trip to Hollywood was in the offing, but of course nothing ever came of it."

"He died before he got there."

Sinclair nodded, mood changing, becoming darker. "I never read the book sir. As I said before, the subject matter was not of my liking. However, I do know, and it is strange how this has come to me, but there was a passage in his last book. A most intriguing thing, sir."

"Intriguing? In what way? I understood *all* of his books were do with the paranormal, the unexplained?"

"Indeed they were sir, but no, this last novel of his was different. I remember when we returned from Burgundy, how affected he was by the visit. I can see him now, walking over to the fire," he pointed towards the silent, black grate, "standing there with his back to me, his hands stretched out, gripping the mantel, saying, 'That place, Sinclair, it's eating away at me. What I saw'. But I didn't understand. And then he wrote the passage."

"In the book? He wrote something about Vézelay?"

"Yes, sir. And the woman your grandfather met there."

"My grandfather?" Lambert rubbed his chin. "Do you think my father went there to find clues about his own father?"

"I really couldn't say, sir. Your father kept his thoughts to himself."

"Even so, don't you find it curious both members of my own family visit this place? There has to be a link."

Sinclair shrugged and Lambert realised he was wasting his time attempting to prise anything more out of the old servant. Nevertheless, there was no shifting the developing thought that Sinclair was not telling the entire story; not lying exactly, but being somewhat 'economical with the truth'.

"I've never read my father's books," said Lambert. "Why is that do you think?"

"Perhaps the genre didn't interest you?"

Lambert shook his head, questioning his reasons for never opening a single volume of his father's work. An act of protest against his father, the way he seemed to exist in his own, unreal world, far away from anyone, those who cared for him? "No, I think it is more simple than that. He was never interested in my life, so why should I be interested in his, or anything to do with him? He'd rattle out his fantasies for all the world to read and his fans would come to believe they *knew* him. But he couldn't care less. Do you know, he never once asked me if I was happy? All he ever wanted to hear was what I'd achieved. Miles spoke of my father being 'sublime', but Miles didn't know the *real* man. He only knew the fiction." Lambert looked away, eyes growing moist, his heart filled with despair. He became so engrossed in his own thoughts he did not hear Sinclair leave.

When Miles arrived, he found Lambert deep in thought, the fire lit as the late afternoon chill gripped hard. He came into the study, clamped his hand on his friend's shoulder, and sat down next to him. "Well, bonny lad, it's all done."

Lambert studied him as if from a distance, nothing registering on his face. "Miles," he said, "do you know anything about Vézelay?"

A slight pause before Miles laughed, shaking his head. "Never heard of it. Why, is it important?" He nodded towards the many books, strewn over the desk and the floor. "What have you been doing?"

"Reading about my family, its history." His confession of never having read any of his father's books still irked him. So he decided to pretend he had more than a passing knowledge. "You know, my father always put little hints and half-forgotten titbits about us in all of his books. Save one. The very last one."

"I wouldn't know. That's the one I never read."

"Interesting. Sinclair told me he'd never read any at all, only a few passages, the forewords. I wonder if anyone we know has read anything he wrote."

"I doubt it. Friends, *real* friends I mean, they seem reluctant. Almost as if they believe someone they know couldn't possibly be an artist. Not of any description. It was the same with my brother, Alistair. Went to art college, studied hard, began to produce the most extraordinary paintings, even got one or two exhibited down in London. But nobody from our family took any interest, apart from Mother of course." He gazed at the flames. "I don't know where he got it from, his artistic flair. The rest of us don't possess the slightest leaning towards anything arty or creative. Vézelay… No, nothing springs to mind. Sorry."

"I want to go, Miles."

"What? Go where? Vézelay?" Lambert nodded. "Well, I suppose … But listen, my poor, convalescing soldier, before we arrange any foreign adventures, whilst you've been moping around with your nose stuck inside these books, I have been working."

"Working? I never thought I'd hear such a word coming out of your mouth."

"Damn your pious, sanctimonious uttering, you fart filled cad, I have been organising our party!"

Lambert gawped. "Oh Christ, Miles. *Please*."

"No objections," cried Miles, slapping his knees, "the deed is done. The weekend after next, bonny lad, we are going to drink ourselves stupid, and hopefully shaft at least two girls each."

"You can't be serious. Please, Miles, I don't want—"

"Too late. First of all, I've ordered several kilts as well as other products from France and…

" France? Have I heard you correctly? What the hell has France got to do with kilts?"

Miles tapped the side of his nose. "Quite a lot actually. Ever been to Brittany?" Lambert shook his head. "Well, Brittany, my book-worming friend, is Celtic. Yes?" Lambert pulled a face, bemused. "God, you're bloody ignorant. The Celts spread right across Europe, settled in all sorts of places, including Britain, parts of Spain, France… They were an amazing people, and they have left the world two of the most wonderful legacies – plaid, otherwise known as tartan, and bagpipes."

"Miles, you can't be serious."

"I am! The Scots called it tartan, but they don't have the monopoly. The Cornish wear kilts. Did you know that? *And*, they play bag-pipes."

"That's not true."

"Yes it is, you ignoramus! Anyway, I researched kilt-making companies and chose one in France. Lady Chrystel has impeccable taste. Her kilts are beyond compare."

"They're probably beyond my pocket too."

"Forget about that, it's all taken care of."

Lambert made a weak attempt to interrupt, but Miles held up his hand, closing off any further objections. "I'm organising the whole thing, so you can sit back and soak it all up." He grinned, "I got in touch with Peter and Mandy and they're coming over, together with—"

"No, please. I can't bear the thought of having them here, not now." Lambert threw his arms out, "For God's sake, Miles, look at the damned place!"

"We don't have to have the party in this room, you ass. The dining room is fine. And the bedrooms, of course!" He winked. "Don't be such a bloody square, Andrew. There's plenty of time to get everything ready. You need light relief, a chance to let your hair down. Peter will bring some draw and we will have the most wonderful time. I promise."

"I can't think of anything worse."

"Well, you'll just have to suffer it, won't you? The curtain rises at eight o'clock, a week on Saturday night."

"Curtain? What the hell are you talking about?"

"You know what Peter's like. He came up with some wild idea about Roman togas and all of us running round as if we're in an ancient orgy."

Lambert put his face in his hand, massaging his forehead. "Jesus. I'm so fucking fed up with everything. Don't you get it, Miles? In London, we had all sorts of parties and get-togethers, but now ... Do you want to make me a laughing stock, riding around like an invalid in my wheelchair?"

"Hey, I told Peter about your leg. He offered to make up some wild dances with everyone gyrating around your wheelchair, with you in the centre, clapping your hands, semi-naked, high on drugs." He went into a fit of laughter. "I can see it now, you sitting like a little Buddha. It'll definitely work, but not in the way you're thinking. I'm wondering if he could arrange a cabaret show like Le Crazy Horse de Paris – imagine the excitement of seeing beautiful topless woman cavorting before your eyes!"

"This isn't Paris, my dear friend."

Ignoring Lambert's dripping sarcasm, Miles lifted his hands in dismay. "You can hardly meet up with a crazy horse here, but Peter can find a few fat cows who might scream and yelp while performing the cancan after a bottle of whisky."

"I've never been into fat cows. Lithe panthers maybe."

They both trilled with laughter.

"Come on, don't be so picky! After all, with your gammy leg you can't be too choosey." Miles couldn't help but joke. "I just want to entertain you."

At last, the semblance of a smile broke out across Lambert's face. "Okay, I give in. Fat cows it is."

Miles beamed, "What did you say? Jesus, Andrew, this is the first time since the accident I've seen you looking up beat. It warms me, my friend. Truly it does. And don't worry, Peter will come up with something original and fun. He's a great one for parties is old Peter."

"I hope he's not a crazy horse himself?"

"No, he's all right. In small doses." Miles clapped his hands. "So, you've surrounded yourself with books and reading and..." He absently picked up a sheaf of paper, frowned. "What's this? Something of your father's?"

"A few ideas, a sketch for a story."

"Is this how he did it?" He waved the paper. "Jumbled up words, a few names?" He read again. "He's made mention of it here, this place, this Vézelay? Where is it?"

"France. Burgundy."

"And why the sudden interest?"

Lambert shrugged, sitting back in his chair, grown tired all of a sudden. "My father visited, together with Sinclair. Something affected him during the visit, and he put a passage in his last book about what happened to him. My grandfather also went, so I want to read this book, or at least the passage and go there myself, Miles. As soon as my damned leg is out of this bloody cast." To give weight to his words, he struck the plaster with the side of his fist. "Damned, bloody thing."

"What's this book called, the one your father wrote?"

"The title is that of a girl." He reached inside his pocket, pulled out the photograph, and handed it to his friend. "Her."

"Bloody hell," said Miles, voice low in a sort of hushed reverence, "She's incredibly beautiful. Your father had an exclusive taste, that's for sure. And the strangest thing is her features; they don't appear to belong to any century. She's at once from a bygone age and yet, with her coy, sexy smile, it's as if she were from today. Any clues as to who she is?"

"I have no idea. But I'm guessing her name is the same as the book. A simple title, but one which might mean quite a lot." He smiled. "Lorna."

Miles frowned, chewing his lip. "There's something I recognise in her eyes. What's that quote? 'A rose by any other name would smell as sweet'? It's as if I already know her and yet … nobody comes to mind."

"I feel exactly the same," said Lambert and the both of them stared at the photograph for a long time, deep in their own thoughts.

6

The following day, Lambert rose early and struggled into his clothes, the plaster cast continuing to make life difficult. He often found the first few moments of waking were the worst, the pain returning to his shattered limb as soon as he swung out of bed, perhaps caused by the blood rushing into his foot. He clinged on to the edge of the mattress and waited until the waves of agony receded.

Sinclair had created a temporary bedroom for Lambert on the ground floor from one of the small anterooms off the main lounge. Megan assaulted him as soon as he wheeled himself through the door. He could do little but sit and allow her to give him a good wash with her loping tongue and when at last she bounded away, he went to the bathroom and washed properly.

He paused to look in the mirror above the sink. He had to push himself up from his wheelchair in order to do this, and staring back at him, he found a tired, somewhat sad face. He slumped back down and a sudden rush of depression hit him. Only a few years ago, the castle rang with the sound of raised voices, excited, happy. There were always people coming and going, mother having such an active social life. Father, rarely seen during the day, often emerged from his study in the evening and be like a different person. Vibrant, charming, inviting guests around for dinner parties and get-togethers. Whenever Lambert returned from university, the same goings-on always confronted him and made him look forward to the warm, welcoming glow of his family, which awaited him.

Not now. The castle oozed sadness, every stone weeping for the loss of so those carefree times. Within the space of a few years, everything had changed. The only living link to the past was Sinclair and sometimes Lambert wondered what would become of the place once the old retainer passed away, or ended up in a home. Not a cheery idea.

He went into the lounge and wheeled himself over to the massive bay windows. Across the gravelled driveway, he watched Megan rolling in the grass, sneezing and shaking herself. The sheer pleasure she received from such a simple act lifted his spirits and he pushed his morbid thoughts to the back of his mind. Smiling he turned to go to the kitchen and get some breakfast when he caught sight of several notebooks strewn out across the coffee table. Curious, he went over and next to them found a note from Sinclair.

'I have gone to town, sir, to purchase some food and other bits and pieces. I shall not be long, but I remembered where your father left his notebooks. Here they are and I hope you find them interesting. S.'

Not only were the notebooks there, but a copy of his father's last book, 'Finding Lorna'.

He picked the book up and turned it over to read the blurb. 'On a trip to the Yonne region of France, James discovers much more than he bargained for. Seduced by a beautiful woman, who immediately disappears, James, distraught but determined to find her once again, is plunged into a series of haunting and inexplicable experiences. As his search continues, he uncovers not only who the woman is but the secrets of his own desires.'

Intrigued, Lambert took the book with him, first to the kitchen where he made himself some toast and coffee that Sinclair, with his usual consideration, had placed on the worktop within easy reach, then to the library.

The fire crackled in the grate and Lambert wished he could sink down into one of the sumptuous sofas and really enjoy the book, rather than the hard-backed wheelchair. In a few days, his next visit to the hospital might see the damned caste removed, so at least at the party, he would be relatively mobile, having need for only a pair of crutches.

He hoped.

He settled down and flicked through the opening pages, thinking he would scan the chapters and pick out the parts he believed relevant. However, within the space of a few sentences, the narrative gripped him and soon he found himself slipping into the world created by his father's words.

During the late afternoon, Sinclair came into the room with tea and sandwiches. Lambert put the book down and stared towards the fire, now nothing more than a few miserable embers. He hadn't even noticed. He watched Sinclair get down on his haunches to rake away the ash before stacking up some additional logs.

"What time is it?" asked Lambert, thoughts locked into the imagery of the book.

"Almost four o'clock, sir. I didn't want to disturb you when I first popped my head around the door, you seemed consumed with your reading."

Lambert nodded, took the proffered cup, and sipped the tea. "Have you read it, Sinclair?"

"No. I told you, sir, a few passages, but nothing of any substance. I'm not a great reader of fiction, preferring more esoteric topics."

Lambert munched on a sandwich. "What does that mean?"

"Tracts on the human psyche, spiritualism, mandalas."

Lambert shifted uncomfortably in his chair and put the teacup down on the writing desk with extreme care. "Mandalas … Sinclair, the more I discover about you, the more intriguing you become. I have no idea what mandalas are. I know Nelson Mandela, of course, but I'm sure—"

"No, sir that is absolutely not the right connection. Mandalas are religious symbols, intricate designs which represent the endless possibilities of the universe."

Lambert frowned. "Sounds Indian. The word, I mean. Are they Hindu things?"

"Yes, sir. Buddhists use them too."

Reaching across for the book, Lambert flipped through the pages, "I'm sure father mentions something very similar in here…" He shook his head, "No, I'll never find it again. He didn't call them by that name, but I'm certain he mentions symbols of some sort."

"A pentagram perhaps?"

Lambert gaped at the manservant. "How did you … That is *exactly* the word he used!"

"It is nothing unusual sir, not in a work with supernatural leanings."

"But you said you have never read it."

"I haven't, sir, but I know the themes explored in your father's work. Certain strands run through all of his novels, the supernatural being one of them. Unexplained experiences, strange quirks of fate. He believed everyone is linked, sir, our lives, former and future, inexorably entwined."

"And you believe in all of that?"

"I'm not fanatic in my beliefs, but I have a certain penchant for the extraordinary."

"It seems such a penchant could be contagious, especially nowadays. People are always looking to believe in something beyond their own experiences. Crop-circles, ghosts caught on camera, all of that. Do you recall the April Fool's prank Dimbleby did about spaghetti growing from trees? And when Patrick Moore announced over the BBC radio that due to a rare astronomical event, the earth would temporarily suffer a lessening in gravity. If those listening jumped in the air at approximately 9:47, they would experience a 'strange floating sensation'. One woman even swore she floated around her room like a character out of Peter Pan!" Laughing aloud, Lambert waited for Sinclair's reaction.

"Are you saying people believe what they're told, if it's told by somebody trusted, well known? I don't subscribe to such a view sir. Only the foolish and shallow believe the rumours."

"People prefer to believe rumours, Sinclair. They are so much more exciting than the truth. That's what novelists do, don't they? Like my father? They take a few strands of the truth and twist them together into something far more entertaining."

"I believe the greatest works of fiction are essentially truthful, sir."

"Things like the Bible, perhaps? Or the Bhagavad Gita?"

"Well, I wouldn't go quite that far. They are spiritual works, something different entirely." He smiled, as one might do to a small child.

"Do you suppose I'm not spiritual enough, is that it?" Lambert shook his head. "I'm only joking. Promise. Taking time to read these books, I'm beginning to unlock so much from my own imagination it's hard to keep it all inside." He picked up the same paper Miles had found earlier. "I've actually begun to consider ideas for something of my own."

"Really? I didn't think you had such interests."

"Neither did I." He chuckled, going over his writing. "Strange, but reading my father's last book, our stories are virtually the same."

"Clearly, your father's work has given you a spark of inspiration, sir. They do say imitation is the purest form of flattery."

Lambert shook his head. "But there's the thing, Sinclair. I jotted down my ideas before I ever set eyes upon Father's book."

There followed a long silence before Sinclair accented his head a little and took to clearing away the remains of the tea. "Will there be anything more, sir?"

"Yes. You mentioned pentagrams. I looked it up. The "five corners" are where the seeds of Chronos were placed within the Earth in order for the cosmos to appear."

"You'll find any number of references to them amongst your father's books, sir."

Lambert blew out his breath. "I've got enough reading to do to last me a life time. Family history, diaries, symbols…" He nodded towards the open novel on the desk. "Father's last book. To be fair, I've almost finished it. Hard to put down, Sinclair. It's difficult to think my own father created it all. Honestly, his ability to follow through a line of inquiry and embroider it within a work of fiction astounds me. I wish I knew about all of this much earlier. It's a pity I didn't." Disappointment permeated every word.

"Yes, sir. He was an amazing man in so many ways." A look of sorrow crossed Sinclair's face.

"How does it happen that a manservant who has given up his entire life to this place is more interested in something beyond present reality than me, with all my so-called university education?" Trying to hide a growing sense of inadequacy, he mumbled, "I definitely should make more searches though the Internet." He took a deep breath, "Can you give me some insight into what the symbol of the pentagram might have in common with you?"

For a moment Lambert thought he had gone too far as he noticed a dark look cross the manservant's face. It passed, however, almost as quickly as it had come. "I'm not certain if they have anything 'in common', but I have been drawn to such things for many years. Pentagrams have otherworldly properties. It's a well know fact that mystics use such symbols, as do those attracted to the occult."

"What, for worshipping Satan, that sort of thing?"

"You shouldn't joke about such things, sir."

"I'm not joking. I don't believe anything to do with Satan is a joke."

"I am certain your father thought of it the same way."

"I've offended you." Lambert held up his hands, "Sinclair, please trust me, I'm *not* joking. After my parents' deaths, the terrible car accident … If there is a connection, well, that sort of stuff scares the crap out of me."

"It needn't, sir. One simply needs to know how to control it. Your father had a deep interest in the spiritual aspect of being, which has as much usage for good as for evil. Everything depends on the individual." Sinclair shuffled his feet. "Why did you mention the accident? I know you say you saw somebody, sir, but I have a feeling there is something more."

Lambert turned away, still holding his paper. "I can't explain. I had dreams, if you like. I saw things, things I don't understand. Flashing images of this castle, flames, medieval soldiers, the sound of horses, the screams of women. I've never been a great one for imaginary story-telling, but since that night it's as if a light has been switched on in my head."

"Hence your interest in mysticism. Your search for answers, for meaning, sir, it's perfectly understandable when you have diced with death."

Lambert chewed at his lip as he swung the wheelchair around. "And what about my father? Did he truly believe in sacred symbolism?"

Sinclair arched an eyebrow, "Your father, if I interpret your inference correctly sir, was not into demonology or Satanism – he was of the good variety."

"I'm relieved to hear it." Lambert stumbled around in a world he knew little about. His reading had merely scratched the surface and he needed to understand more. "Did he ever conduct a séance here?" He held his breath, eyes pleading with the manservant to go further.

The man's mood changed, his jaw line tightening. "I'm not at all sure where this is leading, sir."

Lambert shrugged, "I'm just trying to get to know the man a little more. Something happened in Vézelay, I understand that much. When he came back, he was an altered man. I know it, from his words. He returned delighted, inspired and eager to write that mysterious last book." He pointed towards the novel. "I'm just getting to the part where he describes an inexplicable meeting with a woman. A woman who seems to know a great deal about the protagonist, a guy she knew many, many years before. Then, when he returns home, she reappears to him, having disappeared in the Yonne Valley. You know where that is, don't you?"

"I do, sir. Burgundy."

"Vézelay. That's a strange coincidence, don't you think?"

"The town is mentioned in your father's book, sir?"

"Not by name, no, but it is clear by the way he describes the place it is the same. What happened to him there, Sinclair? You went with him, you must have noticed something."

"I don't know anything, sir. I've told you so already, your father was a secretive man. He would leave me alone in the guesthouse where we stayed and I wouldn't see him until the evening."

"And you never thought to ask?" Sinclair shook his head. Lambert studied the old retainer and pondered, not for the first time, over the idea of telling him about the woman in the road, the same one in the photograph. As he struggled, he formed his next few words with care. "I want to go into Edinburgh, Sinclair. Miles was pleased to look up the photographer's on the Internet. Possibly you remember … Richard Brady"

"I don't recall the name, sir, but I do remember you—"

"Miles found it for me on his computer, as we haven't got a signal all the way out here. And guess what? It's still there, Sinclair."

"I don't see how it can be the same business, sir. The photograph was from a plate, taken perhaps two generations ago."

"Yes, my thoughts exactly. But if it's a family run firm, they may still have records."

"Sir, I wouldn't place too much hope on such a thing. And besides, what possible good could it do?"

"I'll tell you, Sinclair." He swung around in the chair and scooped up the novel. "The woman in here, this Lorna. She first appears a hundred years ago, to this protagonist's father. Now, whilst he is there, in the Yonne Valley, she materialises again. Not only does she do so, but she follows him to his home where once more she reveals herself."

"But she would be too old, sir. It's not possible."

"It might be. If she were reincarnated."

The servant's eyes grew moist. He looked away.

"In a novel, Sinclair, anything is possible. But in real life…" Lambert pushed his tongue between his teeth. "Sinclair, this is art imitating life, because this is Father's story. He went to Vézelay and saw that woman and when he realized she was the same one his own father had seen, he became haunted."

"*Haunted*? Sir, I think that is somewhat extreme. Your father was a novelist, true enough, but in reality he was an extremely sensible and—"

"I'm sure he was, Sinclair. Until my mother's death. That changed him, didn't it?"

Sinclair shifted his weight from one foot to the next, "I really must get these dishes cleaned up, sir. If you'll excuse me…"

He turned to go, a little too fast for Lambert's liking. "I'm going to Edinburgh. Miles is taking me there tomorrow. I'm going to find out who the woman was, Sinclair." But the manservant was already closing the door, leaving Lambert wondering why his last few questions had caused the man so much consternation. He felt certain the visit to the photographers could lead him to the answer.

7

Lambert dreamed that night. He ran along a narrow twisting path through a deep, dark wood. The cold bit into his flesh, the rough-hewn ground painful underneath his bare feet. For he was naked and as he ran he searched the undergrowth to hide from any prying eyes and listen out for mocking laughter. There was none, only the persistent pounding of someone, or something, following him and drawing ever closer.

Running, head down, he came to a clearing and slowed down, the hard earth giving way to lush grass. The sweat stung his eyes and after he dried them with the back of his hand he spotted a curious ornamental fountain, topped by a water nymph holding a jug, and he stumbled towards it, heart pounding. Why would such an ornate piece be standing here in the middle of a wood? He leaned on its side and all at once the water began to pour. "Oh Andrew," said a voice and he turned around and saw her.

Lorna. She glided towards him, the thin white robe she wore transparent, revealing every curve of her lovely body, bronze limbs slipping out from between the folds. He eased himself back against the fountain as she drew closer. The water splashed over his neck and shoulders but even that did not cool his surging ardour. Close now he smelled her perfume, light and fresh, and his vision blurred, head spinning, and then her hand closed around his pulsing member, moving forwards and back.

Lambert sat bolt upright and instantly cried out as a shot of pain raced through his leg. "*Jesus,*" he spat and waited, face in his hands, the image of her more potent than the agony in his broken limb. As the pain receded, he became aware of his burning erection pressing against the bedclothes. He threw them back and stared, swallowing down the urge to reach down and touch, to bring himself to sweet, swift relief. The thought of her legs and arms, the slim hips, the way she moved, almost glided and ... He moaned, lay back down and with those pictures dancing in front of his eyes, his fingers eased down between his legs to caress himself, slowly at first but increasing the speed. As he conjured up images of making love to her the burning became intolerable and uncontrollable, until at last he gave a stifled cry and found the relief he so longed for.

Later he struggled into the bathroom and managed to stand under the shower. The hospital had told him not to get the cast wet, but he cared for none of that now, all of his thoughts consumed by the images, which had made him do what he had done.

Over coffee, brought to him in silence by Sinclair, he mused over this woman who had entered his life and seemed to be establishing a hold over him, an invisible power which he could not understand. In the library, he picked out her photograph again and stared. The whole thing was impossible, of course. But then, if that were the case, who was the woman in the road? They were the same. What he could not fathom, more than anything else, was how he had imagined her, if imagined her he really had, *before* setting eyes upon the photograph?

He put his fingers into his eyes, squeezed hard, tried to force her face from his mind. He failed, and when he turned his thoughts to the dream, again the stirring in his loins.

Angry, he swung around and wheeled himself over to the bookshelves. Where to begin? The books were arraigned in Dewey order so no difficult task to find first the history, then the family section. A lot of them, however, were beyond his reach and as he was about to call for Sinclair, when he noticed one such title ,'The Ancient Families of the Highlands' by someone called 'F.R.Montrose' and he managed to reach for it. A hefty tomb, brown leather cover, aged bindings. He went over to the desk and opened it.

The details on the first page confirmed this was old. First published in Eighteen hundred and eighty-seven, by a company with offices in Glasgow. He leafed through the first few thick and stiff pages, yellow with age. Nobody had read these pages for some considerable time.

With great care, he came to the section beginning with 'L' but did not find his family listed. He sighed and sat back, wondering what to do now.

In the distance, the telephone rang, reminding him his mobile required charging. He fished it out of his jacket pocket and searched around for the adaptor and realised it was in his room. He wheeled himself over to the door and was about to go out when Sinclair appeared, the phone in his hand.

"Apologies, sir, but Mr Miles is on the line."

Relief washed over Lambert like a soothing bath and he took the receiver and listened to the plans his closest friend had organised for the day.

"It's good to be out of that damned castle," said Lambert, gazing at the rolling hills flashing by. Beside him, Miles, one hand on the steering wheel, the other hanging out the side window, breathed deeply.

"It's not at all damned, Andrew. It's beautiful."

"You know what I mean."

"Do I? What I *know*, bonny lad, is you are becoming increasingly more depressed. You're not yourself and I'm worried."

"It's my leg, Miles. Moping around with nothing to do, Sinclair always there like a mother hen, driving me up the bloody wall."

"What were you talking to him about when we left, it seemed very serious."

"Nothing of the sort. I asked him to pull out any old volumes relating to the history of the family. You know, there are editions in that library that pre-date the Reformation."

"Must be worth a pretty penny then, eh?" He turned and winked at his friend.

"I've no intention of selling them, if that's what you mean. I need to find answers, Miles." He took out the photograph and gazed at her face. "This woman, I have no idea who she was, but I can't seem to get her out of mind."

"Well, who wouldn't? There's certainly something very *tantalising* about her."

"So, you feel it too?"

"Andrew, my friend," his voice sounded serious, taking on a schoolmaster's tone as if he were about to deliver a piece of heartfelt advice to a wayward pupil, "whoever she was and whatever she was, she has long since departed from this world. A sultry beauty from one hundred years ago is not my idea of a fantasy. Try and think about it seriously." He blew out a breath. "Clearly she was known, probably to your grandfather, but I doubt—"

"That's it, you see, Miles. Grandfather. He's the link, I'm certain. But unlike my father, he never kept anything relating to her. I can't find any letters or diaries, whereas father seemed obsessed. Perhaps all writers are, I don't know, but what's curious are the cryptic messages he left behind. Jottings, half-finished sentences, and this…" he brandished the photograph between finger and thumb, "why keep this?"

Miles shrugged, "Well, perhaps this photographic studio will shed some light on it, but quickly I hope as my stomach will not last the day, bonny lad. I need a good lunch to make this journey properly worthwhile!"

Miles parked the car, pulled the wheelchair out of the boot and helped Lambert into it. Together, they moved along Princess Street before finding the address on the back of the photograph, a photographer's studio set between a pizza restaurant and a jewellery shop. They stopped and studied the front window, a canvas blind covering it. Miles pressed his nose up against the glass. "I can't see a damned thing. It must be closed, or closed *down*."

"Perhaps we should try knocking?"

Miles gave him a look. "You wait here, I'll go and ask next door, see if they know anything."

Lambert watched his friend saunter off down the road. He turned to the door and tried a tentative knock.

He sighed and was about to wheel himself away when the door eased open.

Lambert frowned, not knowing what to do for a moment. Something moved to his right and the blind slowly drew upwards to reveal two enormous wedding portraits, lit by the soft glow of warm lights, flanking a display of old-fashioned cameras and light sensitive plates, a haphazard collection of old bromide prints scattered around them. Smiling, Lambert pushed himself through the door, knocking it further open. A bell sounded, adding to the sense of stepping back in time.

The interior was small, softly lit, the walls decorated with a selection of different sized photographs, all of them in frames of one type or another. Between these a collection of cameras for sale, cases, holdalls, batteries, memory cards and numerous books and magazines to do with photography. Warm and welcoming, designed to put prospective customers at their ease, Lambert breathed in the atmosphere of calm before he wheeled himself over to where a large, ancient camera stood, sporting a bellows lens, and supported by a heavy looking wooden tripod.

"Magnificent, isn't it?"

Lambert turned to face a small bespectacled man, dressed in well-pressed white shirt, black trousers and red dickybow, appearing from between the beaded curtain, which separated the interior from the shop space. Lambert grinned in agreement, "It certainly is. How old is it?"

"Eighteen-eighties." He rubbed his hands together, "How can I help you, sir?" His voice sang with the soft, lilting brogue of the native Scot.

"It's more in the way of a question really," continued Lambert, pulling out the photograph. "I found this amongst my father's old possessions and, as you can see," he turned it over, "your business address is on the back."

The man took it with the deference of one well used to handling such items and narrowed his eyes as he read the inscription on the back. "This is certainly us, but..." He shook his head, "Well before my time, I'm afraid."

"I wondered if you might have a record of who the subject was?"

The man pursed his lips, "I doubt it. Our archive is somewhat haphazard and many of the old ledgers are missing. I've been meaning to get it sorted for any numbers of years now, but you know how these things are..." His voice drifted away and he smiled awkwardly as he handed the photograph back to Lambert. "I'm sorry."

"I'd be willing to pay for your time," said Lambert quickly, studying Lorna's face once more. "It really is very important."

The man frowned, considering the offer, and held out his hand again to look at the photograph more closely. "There's a serial number," he said to himself. "It might be possible." He turned the print over and for the first time focused upon the woman's face. A curious change took hold, his body growing rigid, mouth open, eyes glazed, almost as if he were slipping into some sort of catatonic state.

Lambert studied him, intrigued. He was about to speak when the man beat him to it.

"It's Lorna," he said, voice small and distant. "I can see her now ... Beguiling and sensual, with the power to make men willingly carry out her wishes. Anything she desired would be given." His smile broadened. "*Anything.*"

Lambert felt crushed, as if the very walls themselves were pressing in all around him. How could this stranger possibly know the woman's name? Struck by a growing sense of detachment, as if he were viewing a dream from afar, an outsider looking in, Lambert suppressed the desire to snatch back the photograph. Instead, he hesitated, hardly daring to breathe.

After some moments, the mood past, the air grew lighter and the man, blinking repeatedly, seemed to return to the present. He thrust out his hand to return the picture, a hand that shook. "I'm sorry, sir but I'm not sure. Come back in two days and see what I have found. No promises mind," and he swung around and disappeared through the beaded curtain.

"What the bloody hell..." Lambert left the sentence unfinished. He gazed at the photograph in his hand. Whoever this woman was, she had the power to seduce from across the years. Almost as if... His breathing grew more shallow, her face filling his mind, controlling his senses, the heat rising from beneath his collar, "It's almost as if she were still alive."

He went outside and watched the shoppers passing by, the normality of everyday life such a contrast to what had occurred inside the shop. The door slammed shut behind him and he jumped, turning to see Miles approaching, shaking his head. "It's closed," he said.

Lambert frowned as Miles studied the window again, with the canvas blind once more obscuring the display. "I think they might be able to trace her, Miles."

It was Miles's turn to frown. "What are you talking about? Who might be able to trace her?"

With his head thumping, Lambert didn't have the energy to explain. Instead, he allowed Miles to push him back to the car, lapsing into quiet, aware of the sounds all around, but not concentrating on anything.

The shopkeeper knew her name.

8

Over the next few days, Andrew studied the books Sinclair fetched down from the top shelves. Combined with the papers, letters and diary extracts he already had, a picture was beginning to form. The more he read, the more fascinated he became but by the time he came to the final volume – a beast of a book, with a broken spine and dog-eared pages – his eyes ached and his head throbbed.

All this changed when he carefully opened up the fragile volume.

There, in the inside cover, was a handwritten letter, signed by Andrew's grandfather.

For a moment he sat, staring in disbelief. Throughout all of his searching, he hadn't come across one piece of written evidence from his grandfather. Now he held in his hand an actual letter, a spidery scrawl recording feelings and thoughts. And as he read, his heart pulsed, throat grew dry and he knew, finally, some of the pieces were falling into place.

'My dearest love.

I commit these words with unseemly haste, but know, as with all things, I am sincere in everything I do and say.

Our first meeting left me breathless and bewildered, as if I had lost my way and stumbled along an unknown path. All I knew was the love I felt for you. For you came into my life, unlooked for, and have captured my heart. And with your departure, I feel such emptiness, such a weight of sadness and grief that I do not believe I can continue.

For a life without you is no life at all.

I know not if my words will find their way to you, but the moments we had – no matter how brief – were some of the happiest I have known. On the fateful night of your disappearance, with the storm raging, I did not have any opportunity to explain my situation. My wife, returning from the continent, and my young son coming upon us, all of it so unnecessary, so painful. For you to flee into the night, to run barefoot through the grass, leaving myself and the castle far-behind, what was I to do? I searched for you, in the first light of dawn, and at the loch, I came across your shawl. The despair I felt at that moment is beyond words.

By the time I informed the local procurator my wife had returned. Nevertheless, I have never given up hope. For I know you did not enter the loch and when I received the note from Richard Brody, my heart leaped with a newfound hope.

I would give the world to you, my love. Come back to me, from wherever you are, and I will leave everything I have. For you are all I desire and all I need. I beg you. Return and give your love to me once more.'

Lambert's hand trembled as he groped for his mobile and punched out Miles' number. He waited as it connected, tapping the side of his wheelchair with impatience. "Miles," he said, his voice barely above a croak when his friend answered, "listen. I've found something, a letter. We need to go back to the photographer's, Miles, and we need to go back now. It's her, Miles. And I know what happened."

Within the hour, Lambert sat once again in the passenger seat as Miles took the road away from the Highlands towards the city of Edinburgh. The sun was out for a change but did nothing to lighten the mood.

"Andrew," said Miles after he had again listened to the story of Lambert's discovery, "there's something I need to tell you about the photographer."

"Something you *need* to tell me? I don't like the sound of that."

"I phoned a friend of mine in the Chamber of Commerce. The photographer is not run by the same family. It was taken over almost half a century ago, but the new owner's kept the name."

"So, from what you're saying, it's highly unlikely they have any records." Lambert hit his knee, "Damn! Just when I thought we were getting closer."

"Apparently, the family moved down to Annan, so all is not lost."

"Well, all we can hope for is that some record still does remain as to who that woman was and where she came from."

But not so very long afterwards, the two men stared at the front of the photographer's shop in dismay, the window shuttered up. Miles rattled the handle, which remained firmly locked. He stepped back and tilted his head to get a good view of the upper storey, but blanked out windows peered down at him, empty, lonely. "This is weird," he muttered. He went to the boards covering the front window and attempted to steal a look between the cracks, but no matter what angle he tried it from, he failed, as his face revealed when he leaned against the boards and shook his head. "It's almost as if it was never here."

"But that's ridiculous. Two days have past … "Lambert bit his lip, "Wait, Miles. You phoned them, remember? Phone them again, now."

Miles shrugged but did as Lambert asked, waited, pulled a face and stared at the screen. "I don't understand."

"What?" Lambert reached over and tore the mobile from his friend's grasp.

"It's unobtainable. Out of service."

"But that can't be Miles." Lambert pressed the 'recall' button and listened. Icy tendrils spread out from inside the very core of his being. "Jesus. What the fuck is going on?"

"I don't know," said Miles in a low voice.

A visit to the same pub they visited a few days ago brought some sense of relief but when Miles returned to their table with two pints, he looked more troubled than ever.

"I spoke to the barman. Landlord, to be precise." He took a sip of his beer. "I asked him about the photographer's, as it's only a couple of doors down."

"Yes? *And?*" Lambert wasn't sure if he wanted to hear Miles' words. He gripped the side of the table, face set hard, the pulse in his temple growing stronger.

"It's been empty for at least a year, possibly more."

Lambert's felt his bowels slacken and a sudden lightness overcame his senses. He held onto the table as his vision blurred and an awful sound of roaring wind erupted in his ears. He gritted his teeth, struggling to control himself, fighting off the urge to keel over, fall to the ground and sleep.

"Andrew? Jesus, are you all right?"

But no, he was far from all right. He wanted to leap up and scream it out to the world. None of this was possible, all of it a sickening nightmare, spiralling out of control. Because he stood in that shop and spoke to the man. It was real, it *had to be real!*

What terrified him more, what brought with it a sense of utter despair, was the fact the identity of the woman in the photograph was now lost.

Perhaps forever.

9

The amber liquid came almost to the rim before Lambert held up his hand, picked up the heavy tumbler and took a large mouthful. He spluttered, holding onto the arm of his wheelchair, eyes squeezed shut and Miles laughed, raised his own glass, and downed it in one.

Sinclair, standing a little way off, had an amused look on his face. "You should sip a good Islay malt, Mr Lambert. Savour its aroma, allow it to linger on the palette, *feel* its velvet path down to your guts."

"Very poetic," murmured Miles as he poured out a second glassful. "I'll stay here tonight, bonny lad. That way I can have a few more of these. What's for supper, Sinclair?"

"Mrs Malone is serving grilled sole this evening, sir. With boiled new potatoes and a green salad."

"I hate salad."

"Not Mrs Malone's, sir. It's like nothing you'd have ever tasted before."

"Sinclair," said Lambert, taking his second mouthful with far more reverence, "tell me about the letter."

The manservant shifted position, curling down the corners of his mouth. Lambert thought he saw the darkness returning to the old man's eyes and as he watched him pick up the letter, unfold it and study the words, he felt for certain Sinclair was trembling.

"Your grandfather was very old when I first came here, sir," he said without lifting his face from the paper, "I remember him, sitting at the window, looking out across the glen. For hours, he would do that, very rarely did he speak. I took up my position here in the year of his death. Your grandfather was ninety-six years of age, sir. You yourself were five."

"I remember him, as silent as a piece of stone," said Lambert, swirling his whisky around the bottom of the glass. "I can't ever recall him talking."

"Mr Lambert told me your grandfather had not spoken for many years. In fact, as far as I understand, the last words he uttered were on his death bed."

Lambert clutched his glass, not daring to take his eyes from the manservant, knowing what the answer to the question he needed to ask would be, but dreading it all the same. "What words, Sinclair?"

Sinclair pursed his lips, neatly folded up the letter again and sighed, "Lorna."

Sometime in the late evening, with the fire roaring and the two of them sat in front of the flames with Pink Floyd playing in the background and Meg asleep on the mat, Lambert aired something he had suspected ever since his accident, "Do you think Sinclair knows more than he's telling?"

Miles, half-asleep, the whiskey and the fire both causing his cheeks to be much redder than usual, gave a chuckle, "Of course! He's always been secretive that one. The way he stares at you, with that look on his face, so bloody superior."

"How old is here, do you think?"

"God knows. Nine hundred?"

"Be serious, Miles!" He drained his glass, considered a refill but decided against it. There was a warm glow ruminating in the centre of his being and he didn't wish it to develop into the first stages of nausea. "He must be getting on. He said he knew my grandfather. He died back in Seventy-six, when I was five."

"Your grand pappy was quite an age by then." Miles leaned forward. "I've often believed Sinclair was some form of vampire. You know, *nosferatu*." He laughed, threw back the whisky. "I wouldn't be surprised if he's got all sorts of papers and photographs stashed away somewhere."

"Since my accident, I've felt the urge to ask him about it. I'm convinced he knows more than he's telling."

"Andrew, my old friend, you're still not sticking to this whimsical story of the girl on the road trying to save you?"

"And why not? It's true."

"All right, let's suppose, for one small moment, it is true. *Why would she do such a thing*? Eh, you tell me that? Why would she choose to appear to you on that particular night?"

Lambert pressed his lips together, frowning deeply, and, unable to catch his friend's questioning look, chose to stare at the floor instead. "Because, dearest

Miles, the date. It was the anniversary of my grandfather's death." He looked up, and the ice spread, and the tendrils of fear, of anxiety, of disbelief, wrapped themselves around his throat, constricting him, making his voice not much more than a hoarse whisper. "There's something more. This party you've arranged, the date of it. This time last year, Miles. One year ago. My father died."

And Miles, for one of the few times in his life, appeared to have lost the power of speech.

From where he sat, Lambert heard Miles stomping around in the guest room overhead, sighing loudly before the bed groaned under his weight. Lambert smiled and wheeled himself over to the sink, swilled his face with ice-cold water, shook his head as a dog might, attempting to wash away the last vestiges of whisky racing through his blood stream. He stared into the mirror before closing his eyes, spinning around and returning to his bed. He heaved himself out of the chair and slumped into the bed, cursing his leg and wishing to God it were the day after the morrow, for then he would be at the hospital preparing for them to cut the damn plaster off. One more day, he was certain he'd get through. So, for now, he lay down, stared at the ceiling, and tried to work out how he could broach the subject of how long the servant had worked in the castle, running through any number of scenarios, rehearsed speeches. He did not want Sinclair to feel in any way put out, or insulted. The man had been a rock, especially since Father's death. A delicate path needed to be trodden so Lambert tried to answer his own question, adding up the years to work out how long the man had been in the house. Certainly, before Lambert could remember, perhaps since Seventy-two. Even a conservative guess would put him in his early sixties, but he might be a lot older, of course.

He frowned, squeezing out the earliest memories he had of the tall, laconic Scot with his serious frown and his dutiful, easy manner. Fleeting pictures, like curled up black and white snapshots, floated by, but nothing of any substance. Nothing he could put a year to, all of the memories vague, ephemeral.

On the bedside table was one of the notebooks he'd come across. Different to the others as not one page held a single word, so he decided to use it for himself. Earlier he'd sketched out the ideas for a story, with little idea where the scenes or the characters came from. Using a stub of a pencil, he crossed out some of his words, added others, and went over the plan until the page blurred and his eyelids grew heavy.

He put his back and sank into the pillow, the notebook and pencil slipping from his grasp and before long the black veil of sleep descended.

He dreamed. He saw her, eyes shining, full of longing and desire. Scenes, as if from a beautifully rendered film, flashed through his unconscious. Long, sun-drenched days relaxing on a small, deserted beach, swimming in the clear water, endless nights spent watching the stars, forgetting their previous lives before they found each other. Soon, the images melded, becoming fixed. They lay in a secluded cove, overlooked by a tiny whitewashed village, listening to the sound of waves lapping against the shoreline. Her soft hands crept over his thighs, butterfly fingers barely caressing the skin as they traced their journey across his body. He moaned, stretched out his legs, spread his thighs to allow her hand easier access. The weight of the body next to him pressed closer. He reached out his hands and gasped at the warmth of the flesh, soft and undulating. He ran his hands over the smooth curve of her hips, the slimness of her waist, and the firmness of her breasts. In darkness, he moved his head to her throat, his lips sliding over the vibrant flesh towards those full mounds and he enclosed his mouth over her. She responded with deep moans of her own, as her back arched and she clawed at his hair, urging him to move into her, which he did. "Oh Andrew. Love me; melt inside me like delicious honey."

Her words brought a surge of energy and he lost all control, mind in a whirl as if indeed he slowly melted into smooth ductile honey, the mixture sticking them together forever. When the earthquake of lust surged through his loins, he roared and collapsed breathless upon her.

She held him, kissing his neck, her fingers massaging his scalp though the hair, her lips moving to his ear to whisper, "My hero, I want you endlessly."

His eyes sprang open and he lay there, in the dark, heart pounding like a steam-hammer, hair, face, and lower body drenched in sweat. A pulse of warmth dispelled the vision forming in his brain, of a dream so realistic it simply had to be true.

A breeze blew through the room, lifting the curtains to reveal the open window. The bed moved, a presence lifting itself from the mattress and he thought he heard a sigh. Unable to move, not daring to look, he waited in the darkness and fought to bring back the realisation, the belief he was in his own room, the dream over. But then came her breath and his body froze, muscles calcified as if they were locked rigid by steel bars. His breathing grew difficult, pulse throbbing in his throat, tongue too large in his mouth.

Through sheer force of will, he reached out with his hand towards the bedside lamp, groped for the switch, stomach churning, bowels now liquid, and he flicked on the light and waited before daring to look.

He craned his neck and looked towards the door. On the carpet, half pressed through the tiny crack, was an envelope. With his limbs shaky, muscles barely able to move, he managed to clamber out of bed and he hopped across the room. The pain stabbed at his leg, but he got down on his haunches, picked up the envelope and, without hesitation, ripped it open.

It sat in his hand. As it had before. As it had in the photographer's shop.

The photograph of Lorna, exactly the same as it had been except for one slight difference.

Her smile was broader.

10

He sat in the kitchen, having tried to make as little noise as possible, conscious of Sinclair and Miles sleeping a few doors away. The worst thing would be for them to wake and bombard him with questions. He needed peace, some quiet time to reflect and try to understand what had happened to him. The dawn, still some way off, made no impression upon the gloom of his room, but he did not care. Nothing but the experiences of just a few moments ago troubled his thoughts. He knew as certain as anything, somebody had shared his bed. The photograph, pushed under his door, may confirm the identity of the person, but such a thought was so outlandish, so fantastic, he did not dare to ponder it. Instead, he sat and gazed into nothing and tried to come up with a satisfactory explanation. For the moment, there did not appear to be one.

Sometime during those long, blank moments, he must have drifted off to sleep because from nowhere a strong hand shook him by the shoulder; he sprang up, startled and disorientated. He looked about and Sinclair hovered close by, filling the kettle, dropping tea bags into the pot.

"I'm bloody freezing," said Lambert, holding himself. "What time is it?"

"A little after six, sir."

"Jesus. Do you always get up at this time?"

"Old habits die hard, sir." He smiled, splashed milk into cups, "How many sugars does Mr Miles have, sir?"

"I've no idea, but he won't be up for a few more hours yet." He shifted in his chair, scratched his chin and tried to make himself seems serious. Dread, however, brought a shrill to his voice. "Sinclair, I need to ask you something."

"Seems you are full of questions recently, sir."

"I found this under my door." He pulled out the envelope from under his pullover. "Have you any idea when it arrived?"

"In the late afternoon, sir, whilst you and Mr Miles were in Edinburgh. I would have told you, but by then you and he were feeling much the better for whisky."

Lambert smiled, despite the trepidation he felt. He ran his finger and thumb along the top of the envelope, and turned it over, squinting at the postmark. "Christ."

"What concerns you, sir?" Sinclair moved closer.

"It's from Annan. Posted from there the day before yesterday."

"I fail to see the significance."

"No, it's nothing…" Lambert put the envelope on the table and stared at it for some time. The photographer's family hailed from Annan. What were the chances the shopkeeper had taken the photograph to his home, and not returned? A possibility, but what about the boarded-up windows? He put his face in his hands and rubbed himself back to something close to being awake.

Sinclair placed a steaming hot cup of tea next to his elbow and Lambert smiled his thanks and took a sip. "I'm confused, Sinclair."

"If there's anything I can help you with, sir, I'll do my best."

He turned to go, and Lambert swung his wheelchair around quickly. "There is actually, Sinclair. Please, sit down." The manservant frowned, face clouding with uncertainty. "It'll only take a minute."

The old retainer nodded, pulled out a chair from under the table and sat down. "Like I said, sir, I'll do my best."

"The letter from my grandfather, the one I found in the book. The date written on it was Nineteen hundred and four. Do you believe it to be genuine?"

"I have no reason to *doubt* its authenticity."

"All right, let us assume then that it is genuine. Can you shed any light on the impossibility of my father witnessing my grandfather with this mysterious woman?"

Sinclair blinked. "Your *father*, sir."

"Yes. My grandfather writes that his son came across them. He doesn't say what they were doing, but it's fairly obvious. But that cannot be. My father was born in Nineteen Thirty-six."

"The boy was not your father, sir."

At that moment, it seemed as if the very walls themselves had fallen in around his ears. Lambert heard, but he did not believe, only conscious of a dreadful, growing presence in the room, thick and impenetrable. Ensnared, with no place to run to, he struggled to come to terms with Sinclair's words.

"Mr Andrew," Sinclair continued, his voice taking on the tone of a patient, understanding schoolteacher, "it is not something I've ever wanted to advertise, not something your father himself wanted me to divulge. There was, there *is* no need to go into all the details, but suffice to say—"

"Sinclair," said Lambert, forcing the words out of his constricted throat, "I want you to tell me everything. I want you to make it all make sense."

"That might be difficult, sir. I don't want to cause you anymore upset."

"I'm not upset, I'm confused. Since my accident…" He shook his head.

"Very well. I'll try to be brief. The boy in the letter was the son of your grandfather and his first wife. Apparently, so I understand, their union was not a happy one. As far as the story goes, your grandfather met and fell in love with another woman—"

"Lorna. The girl in the letter?"

"I believe so, sir, although I never did know her name. He went to France, so I believe, to undertake the Pilgrimage of Santiago de Compostella. You may have heard of it."

"My father went there. Sinclair," Lambert leaned forward, tension mounting. The uncertainty, the desperate notion of a whirlpool of twisting, confused dates and facts overwhelming him. "I know all this, we've been through it. My father went to the same place. In France."

"Vézelay? Yes sir, so he did. I accompanied him."

Lambert massaged his forehead with finger and thumb, frowning, finding it increasingly difficult to stay on course. "Yes. It's coming back. All right, all right. Listen. My grandfather went there, and my father also. For the same reason?" He dropped his hand and stared at the manservant.

"Sir, let me tell you what I know. It may become clearer, but I'm not at all sure. Your grandfather visited Vézelay with the prime reason of going on the pilgrimage. This was not long after Edward the Seventh had ascended the throne. Europe was a very different place then, and the region he went to was rural, remote, but Vézelay was and still is one of main starting places for the Pilgrimage. It was there he first met this woman." He held up his hand as Lambert opened his mouth to speak. "I do not know the details, but something passed between them. A spark, a shared attraction, I know not. Whatever it was, after he returned home, she must have followed him for they took up the affair once more. His wife had given him a son and their life fell into the usual round of mundane, uninteresting experiences. Your grandfather had always been somewhat reclusive so his wife took to travelling. Your grandfather did not complain. When this woman arrived from France, your grandfather's wife was away in Italy."

"Convenient."

Sinclair pressed his lips together, a pained expression crossing his face. "Yes, sir. I believe this woman had a greater goal in mind."

"What do you mean by that?"

"In Nineteen Hundred and Four, the King, Edward the Seventh, visited Edinburgh for the first time. Something happened, sir. The previous year, he came here in secret to speak to your grandfather about something."

"Came *here*? You mean, to the castle?"

"Yes. By then, your grandfather was estranged. The woman had come back, you see. The night mentioned in the letter, when she disappeared? Well, the reason the letter was never sent was because she returned to the castle. Your grandfather believed she came to see him, but that was not the case."

"It was to see the King?"

"Yes sir. When your grandfather discovered the truth he was beside himself with grief, and years later, when he met another woman – your grandmother, sir – even then his pain was beyond endurance."

"So, this Lorna and the King. They were lovers?"

"I cannot be certain, but I do not believe so. There was a reason for her attachment, but what it was I have no idea. However, I am certain it was not of the sexual variety."

"Okay, let me get this straight Sinclair. My grandfather meets this woman, he falls in love with her. She follows him here and they have some sort of a dispute?"

"I don't know. I think 'dispute' is putting it too strongly. I believe she might have been looking for something."

"So she runs off, into the arms of the King, to find whatever it is, presumably?"

"Perhaps not into his arms, sir, but yes, close enough."

"What did she do then?"

"She disappeared, and your grandfather went looking for her once again. To Vézelay I assume."

"This whole bloody thing is going round and round in circles, Sinclair!" Lambert ran his hand through his hair. "You think my father knew everything?"

"I believe his brother must have told him."

"His *brother*?" Lambert paused in the act of lowering his hand to his lap. "Wait. My father had a brother?"

"Half-brother, yes sir. The child I told you about, sir, from your grandfather's first marriage. The boy who saw your grandfather and this woman making love," he pointed his finger vaguely in the direction of the open door, "in the study."

Lambert sat and stared, random facts, thoughts, figures, all of them vying for prominence in his brain. "Whatever became of him?"

"He took his own life, sir. One night, just after your parents held a party here. A party for your seventh birthday. Apparently, they sent out all sorts of invitations and one of them was to your uncle. I believe the thinking behind it was to try and build some bridges, after your grandfather's death." He shrugged. "Well, as things would have it, on the night of the party he wandered down to the loch and threw himself under the icy waters."

"Christ, that's awful! Did anybody ever discover the reason?"

Sinclair's face grew ashen and he looked away, his bottom lip trembling.

"Sinclair, for the love of God, tell me."

The manservant brought up his face, eyes welling up. "Sir. It is not something I have ever wanted..." He sniffed, pulled out a handkerchief and dabbed at his eyes. "He saw you, the birthday boy, as your mother brought you down the hallway, showing you off to everyone. Have you no recollection of it, sir?"

Lambert struggled, forcing his thoughts to his youth, of birthdays, anniversaries, family get-togethers. Nothing was certain, a thick mist hanging over everything. "Not of that particular party, no. What happened when I was introduced, Sinclair?

"Your uncle, his face... Dear God, I'll never forget the look on his face."

"What about his face, Sinclair?"

"Not only his face, sir, but what he said."

Lambert drew closer, gripped the manservant by the sleeve, becoming angry, "Tell me, God damn you, tell me what he said."

Sinclair pulled in a deep breath, "He said that you were the spitting image of his father. Your grandfather."

"Is that all?"

Sinclair shook his head, "He looked into your mother's eyes and said, loud enough for everyone to hear, 'She'll come again. You know it and so do I.' Then he went outside and nobody ever saw him alive again."

The sky was white, not one single gap in the cloud cover. With no breeze, it would continue this way for days, unless something dramatic happened, as it often did this close to the Highlands. In the distance, those solid, eternal mountain peaks dominated the horizon, some of them continuing to wear a slight scattering of snow on the peaks. Early April, usually a time of promise with the sun out, the air warm. The peculiarities of this part of the world, sometimes warmer than the Mediterranean. All too rare those moments. Lambert looked and his heart grew heavy, with Sinclair's words darker than the mountains themselves, with no promise of any form of change. *She would come again.*

The words stung like slaps, not because of what the manservant said but that nobody had ever once, in all his life, deemed to tell him. He was the spitting image of his grandfather, and his grandfather had fallen in love with another woman, a woman with peculiar powers.

Father, living his entire life, locked away in the library, bashing at his infernal typewriter, lost within his own imagination, never giving a single second to consider the implications. His own brother, seeing their father making love, keeping the secret for so long. And Sinclair, loyal, hard working, a pillar which held up the family, never speaking of grandfather siring sons from two women, the years between them long. Too long for them to have ever had much in common. Hence the rift. Father, living like a hermit, his brother, uncle... Lambert threw himself back in his wheelchair, pressing both hands against his face, "*What a fucking family,*" he breathed and turned the wheelchair to face the castle, realising for the first time he never asked Sinclair for his uncle's name.

The honey-coloured granite stared back at him, solid and dependable, the wisteria growing thick. Along the top of the west turret, a vine wrapped itself around the crenellations, breaking up the harsh face of the stone. Once it would have been a formidable structure, now it looked more like something out of an advertising brochure offering romantic weekends for lovers. He sighed and wondered what life must have been like all those years ago. Thirteen hundred and something. He couldn't be sure. Perhaps a little more research would give him the answer, but with Sinclair's disclosure so recent in his mind, research was the last thing he wanted to do.

A wind gathered and it came running through the glen, a curious moaning sound, a lament sung by vague, detached voices. It built up in strength and volume until Lambert's wheelchair shuddered and when he tried to push himself towards the castle, the wind changed direction, becoming an invisible barrier in front of him, preventing him from further movement.

As the moan became clearer words formed, not vague noises wafting from the ether. A woman's voice, crystal clear, soothing yet alarming that in this wide-open space with nothing or anyone in close proximity, she should speak as if she were standing at his shoulder, "Andrew. Are you looking for me, Andrew?"

When he snapped his head from left to right, there was no one, and in that instant, the wind disappeared, leaving him alone with nothing but the glen and the sky so very white.

11

Miles came across Sinclair in the kitchen, the aroma of sizzling bacon irresistible. "Any coffee," he asked through a stifled yawn.

"I've made a pot of tea, sir."

"I prefer a cup of coffee."

"I'll put some water on to boil and—"

"I'll do it." Miles went to the sink and filled the kettle. "Where's Andrew, still in bed?"

"Mr Andrew is in the grounds, sir. I wheeled him outside as he wanted to spend some time alone."

Miles grunted, settled the kettle into its base, and turned on the electricity. "Hung over is he?"

"Something like that, yes sir."

The almost melancholic tone of Sinclair's voice caused Miles to stop and frown. He sat down at the table, pressing his hands together as if in prayer. "You've been with this family a long time, haven't you Sinclair."

"Almost all of my life, yes sir."

"And would it be fair to say throughout those years, you've grown quite close to the family?"

"I think that is fairly self evident, Mr Miles."

"No, I meant in a *personal* way. You care for them, or cared, in the case of Andrew's father."

Sinclair turned away from stacking plates and cups and regarded Miles with a quizzical frown. "They are my family, sir and always will be. My deepest regret is Mr Andrew has not yet found a wife."

Miles shrugged, the idea of leading down the aisle causing him not so much humour as disbelief. "I'm not sure Andrew wants to."

"I do hope you are mistaken, sir. Mr Andrew is the last of the line. If he were to die without issue…" His voice trailed away and for a few moments, a silence fell over them, oppressive and heavy.

"I'm worried," said Miles slowly. "This talk of a woman, the *obsession* he's developed for finding out about her…" He shook his head. "It's not healthy, Sinclair. Has he spoken to you about his dreams?"

"A little, sir."

"They're happening too often for my liking. And this story he tells, the reason for the crash, some woman standing in the middle of the road forcing him to swerve to avoid hitting her. He could have died, Sinclair."

The manservant glanced away, the line around his jaw tensing. "Yes. The doctors informed me how close he was to breaking his neck."

"Exactly. And he hadn't been drinking, I know that much, so this *hallucination* … Has anything like it happened before?" Sinclair pursed his lips and Miles sensed the man's reluctance. He waited, but when nothing was forthcoming, he pulled in a breath and continued, "So, would you like to tell me when? Recently?"

Sinclair's face grew grim but as he was about to speak, the kettle came to the boil and the moment past. He swung around, busied himself with preparing a cafétierre of coffee whilst Miles hesitated in pursuing his line of thought. Something in Sinclair's manner struck him as unusual. The manservant always seemed so unaffected, calm, tranquil almost. However, the mention of the woman in the road brought about a change to the man's mood. No longer the relaxed and gentile persona of a man whose only concern was for his duty, but something deeper. Troubled.

Armed with his coffee, Miles wandered outside, lifted his head skyward and breathed in the clean, fresh air. On such a morning, he experienced overwhelming relief he no longer lived in the stink and rush of the City. Those years, for the most part enjoyable, brought him success and financial security, but almost every day he would wake and yearn for the mountains. And now, here he was at last. He knew it would take something extraordinary for him to leave again.

"Morning Miles."

He jumped and cursed as coffee splashed over the rim of the cup to pebbledash his trousers. Lambert grunted as he wheeled himself alongside his friend.

"Bloody hell, Andrew!"

"Sorry, you haven't scalded yourself have you?"

Miles pulled out a handkerchief and dabbed away at his trousers, "No, I'm okay. These things needed washing anyway." He smiled. "Are you all right?"

Andrew frowned. "Yes. Why do you ask?"

"I've been talking to Sinclair." Andrew's head snapped up, eyes wide with alarm and something more. Fear? "Andrew, what the hell is going on?"

"What do you mean? What did Sinclair say?"

"Nothing. Why are you so nervous all of a sudden?"

"I'm not nervous." He pushed himself away from Mile's gaze and sat with his back to his friend, facing the distant mountains, laboured breathing revealing his irritation.

"Have you had another dream?"

Andrew whirled around. Again, the reaction. Startled, a rabbit caught in the headlights, fists bunching, veins in the neck straining. "Sinclair did say something, didn't he? Damn his eyes!"

"Andrew, you need to calm down. Sinclair hasn't said a word to me about anything. What is the matter with you?" Miles got down on his haunches, hands gripping the arms of the wheelchair. "You need to rest. Since the accident you've done nothing but trawl through dusty books and then that photograph … I don't understand any of it, but you have to take some steps back, Andrew. It's taking over you, your obsession for this woman."

"Lorna."

"Yes, whatever her name is. You have to give it up."

"I can't, Miles. She's … I can't explain, but you must trust me. It's like she's here," he slammed his fist against his chest, "you understand? In my heart, my soul. Every time I close my eyes to sleep, her face comes to me and last night…" He put fingers into his eyes and squeezed. "The night of the accident, she was there. I saw her, no mistake. And as I lay in the ditch she reached out to me, so full of concern, wanting to help me but unable to do so."

"Because she isn't real, Andrew. She's a figment of your—"

"No, she's *not*!" His hands came down, knotted into fists again and he slammed them against the arms of the chair, causing Miles to reel back in alarm.

"This is the thing you don't understand, Miles. How can you? If you'd seen her that night, you'd know. Her *power,* it's intoxicating."

Miles stood up and swallowed hard. He studied his friend, the way his body trembled, the intensity of his gaze, and the concern he felt deepened. "All right, Andrew. We'll say no more about it, okay? We'll take you down to the hospital, get that damned cast off your leg, then we can turn our mind to the party. Yes?"

Andrew nodded, a faraway look clouding his face. He sat that way for some time before he seemed to haul himself from his thoughts and he smiled. "Please don't worry about me, Miles. I'm not going mad."

Miles wasn't convinced. "If you say so."

"I'm … confused, that's all. I haven't been myself, I know that. Perhaps you're right. I've been too long surrounded with books and letters and…" He frowned, reached inside his jacket and brought out a neatly folded piece of paper. "This letter, from my grandfather. At first, I believed it to be overly sentimental, the wanderings of a tortured mind, but now … Now I see it for what it is. He's pleading, crying out his love for this woman. A woman, who entered his life, took hold of his heart and then disappeared. Can you imagine his despair, his anguish? To have met and fallen under her spell, and then for her to leave? He must have been close to taking his own life."

"So why didn't he?"

"I don't know. She came back." He held the paper as if it were precious which, Miles mused, for him it must have been. "After the hospital, I want us to go to Annan. I want to go and visit the photographer's."

"Oh Jesus, *please* Andrew, haven't you—"

"Miles. I have to find out who the woman in the photograph was. They're bound to keep records."

"It's clear they haven't, Andrew. And why the hell do you want to go to Annan?"

"Because they sent the photograph back to me. It was waiting for me this morning. The postmark was from Arran. No explanation, nothing. Just the photograph. So, I'm going there. You can take me if you want, but if not Sinclair will."

Miles held up his hands, "Okay, Andrew. I'll do it, but I can't see it doing any good."

"I think it will, Miles."

They drove down to the Western General hospital and after he wheeled Andrew into a small ward to have the cast removed, Miles wandered down the corridors, found a drink dispenser and bought himself a coffee. He stood and stared out of a window and watched the cars coming and going, the people wandering around, the sick, the aged, staff and visitors. He wondered, not for the first time, if he should make an appointment with a consultant, or someone, and discuss his fears regarding Andrew's bizarre behaviour. He'd attempted to press his friend about his latest dream, but Andrew proved reluctant to divulge the details, simply saying it was 'intense'.

Perhaps, after the party, things might get easier. He'd been talking to Peter again, who seemed particularly interested in the 'disappearance' of the mystery woman, as detailed in the letter written by Andrew's grandfather. When Miles gave him the gist, the response was enthusiastic. Peter always was so damned theatrical, constantly thinking up ways to bring something unique to any gathering. He could be incredibly boorish when he wanted, but at least, no matter what he came up with, he did his best to provide a fine selection of attractive ladies!

Miles chuckled into his coffee. Perhaps the answer lay right there. Find a nubile young thing for Andrew. Such a find would certainly take his friend's mind off the mystery woman. He drained his cup and smiled to himself with all the self-congratulation he could muster, because he had the solution, at last, to Andrew's obsession. Sex.

12

Lambert appeared as if reborn, face alive with joy, limping along the corridor with a single crutch, the lower part of his foot wrapped in a bandage but the cast well and truly gone.

"At last I'm free of that damned wheelchair," he said, grinning broadly, as Miles came up to him and clamped his hands over his shoulders. "You can't imagine how I feel, Miles. I thought I'd never get out of the bloody thing. To think, I can at last sleep in my own bed!"

The two friends strolled down the corridor, oblivious to the bustle of the hospital wards, and when they got to the exit they both stopped and breathed in the air.

"You seem almost like a new man," said Miles."

"I feel like one." His face grew serious. "Miles, I'm sorry for the way I've been lately. I should never have spoken to you the way I did; it was unforgiveable and—"

"Please," said Miles holding up his hand, "I understand. These last few days haven't been easy."

"It's not just that. I've been struggling to come to terms with what happened, and why. The accident. I know you think I imagined everything, but when she appeared the way she did, from nowhere, there was nothing I could do. Before I could think, it happened. I over-reacted, swerved, panicked."

"Well, it's all over now, Andrew. Now you're back on your feet, literally back on your feet, we can—"

"Miles, I want to go to Annan. I need to find out if they have any information. Then, I'll forget about it."

From the look, which came over Miles' face, it was clear he did not believe his friend's words.

Andrew sighed, "*If* she is real, Miles, it will bring some sense of meaning to what happened."

"And if there are no records, what then? Andrew, it's not likely is it, to be honest. The guy in the shop, he didn't seem too confident, then they send the photograph back to you. None of it is promising, to be fair."

"Fair or honest, I don't care. I want an answer, nothing more."

They drove through the twisting streets, leaving Edinburgh and the Highlands far behind, motoring down into Dumfries and Galloway, the countryside changing, the rolling landscape more gentle. Andrew sat in silence whilst Miles swapped CDs, eventually finding something suitable to reflect their moods. With the sounds of 'The Handsome Family' filling the car, enigmatic lyrics mixed with sublime musicianship, Andrew, his hand involuntarily closing around the photograph of Lorna, drifted off into a far and distant place…

The castle echoed to the pounding of marching feet and raised voices and the king threw back the bedclothes, stumbling across to a crude, clay bowl sitting atop a worm-eaten cabinet and splashed icy water over his face. He gasped at the cold, pressed a grubby cloth against his skin and waited until he became fully awake.

Something hammered against the door and he sighed, stretched and groaned. His joints did not respond well to the damp of this infernal place. When his brother returned from the East not so long ago, with tales of the burning sun, golden beaches, and lithe legged beauties, he experienced such a yearning to take a ship and sail away. Instead, he sat cramped upon his hard-backed throne and did what he could to combat the cold. Nothing helped. It never would.

He shuffled over to the door and pulled back the bolt. "*What* ?" His voice cracked like a whip and the armoured man-at-arms before him bent from the waist whilst the others a few steps behind fell to their knees.

"Forgive me, sire, to wake you this way, but there is news."

"News? What damnable news is so urgent you see it fit to disturb my rest?"

"Incursions, sire. Border reivers, pressing further north than ever before. They have over-run some of the watch-forts and are building their own bastle houses in their stead."

King Robert of Scotland, the second of that name, felt his mouth fall open and for a moment, the strength left his legs. He slumped against the door well and the man-at-arms reached forward to offer support, but the king had not slipped into unconsciousness. Not yet. He dashed away the man's hand. "How have you come by this news?"

The man stood bolt upright. "Locals cattle farmers, sire. They fled, in fear of their lives, and sought shelter in the royal bailey."

"There are many of them?"

The man shrugged, "No more than eight."

"Bring their spokesman to me."

The man's face blanched. "Sire. The person who speaks for them is a woman."

Robert arched a single eyebrow. "All the better. I doubt she is high-borne, but she must have some fire in her belly to speak for these people."

The man looked askance at his fellow soldiers, who appeared uncertain, eyes faltering. "She is … I can put it no other way, sire. She is unlike any other woman I have ever known."

Intrigued, and with the strength returning, Robert stood up, rubbing his own arms. "Well, bring me this mysterious woman, the like of whom you have never seen before, and I'll listen to what she says. In the meantime, prepare the men. I've suffered the insolence of these reivers for too long. It's time I put a stop to them."

"The woman says there were over a hundred of them."

"And she would know?" He snarled, "For God's sake man, just bring her to me. She sounds more a witch than … Than *what*, I wonder?"

"A beauty ,sire. The most beautiful woman I have ever seen."

"Well, there we have it. Bring her hither, and in the meantime muster the men."

He swung around as the men-at-arms bowed lower still and slammed the door in their face. His bare fleet slid across the stone floor and when he reached the great oak bed, he slumped down on the edge, the cold biting deep, and drew a quilted cover over his shoulders to keep the worst of his shivering at bay.

Perhaps he slept, he could not be sure, but the repeated pounding on his door raised him with a start and he snapped his head around and barked, "*Enter!*"

The door creaked open and a nervous face appeared through the crack. "Pardons, majesty, but I have the woman."

Robert sighed, "Bring her in, for God's sake!"

The soldier accented his head and disappeared for a moment. The door opened wider and the woman came in.

And Robert gasped…

"We're here," said Miles in a loud voice.

Lambert jumped awake, heart thumping, and he looked around, startled. Miles parked the car and Lambert put his fists into his eyes and rubbed hard.

"Are you all right? You look like you've had another nightmare."

"No, no I'm okay."

"You were mumbling in your sleep, something about the cold." Miles laughed. "I hope to Christ we get some answers from these people, Andrew. You're really beginning to freak me out."

"Miles, I'm perfectly fine. I was dreaming, nothing more. How long was I asleep?"

"Almost the whole trip." He shook his head, "Gave me the chance to put on the type of music I like, which was a bonus. I can't be doing with your taste, bonny lad."

"There's nothing wrong with Mahler. In fact, for me, Mahler is the most—"

"Andrew," said Miles quickly, pulling a face, "I don't want to know, okay? I'm not into any of that." He blew out his breath loudly. "Let's just get this over with."

He got out, came around the front of the car, and helped Lambert onto the pavement.

"Beautiful day," said Lambert, feeling the warmth of the spring sun on his face. "About time."

Miles grunted. "Have you any clue where this place is?"

"Yes," said Lambert, going to his pocket. He realised he still held the photograph and he stole a glance before replacing it with the hastily made note he had prepared earlier. "Sinclair did some ringing around. I feel like a bloody hermit living out there with no Internet, but sometimes the old methods work." He brandished the note. "Here it is. We'll need to go into a local shop, see if anybody knows the street."

It took them visits to three shops before somebody knew the directions. Fortunately, it was not too far, but Lambert struggled nevertheless. Unused to the crutch, he made heavy going of the way and was forced to stop more than once. His foot throbbed with the effort and after the sixth or seventh such pause, Miles ushered him into a nearby pub, sat him down at a table closest to the door, and ordered drinks and sandwiches.

"Do you know anything about Border Reivers?"

Miles blinked, the suddenness of the question taking him by surprise. "Border *what?*"

"*Reivers.* I suspect it means raiders, but I can't be sure."

"Never heard of them. What's it from, a film?"

"No. History, Miles, *our* history." Lambert took a bite of his sandwich and stared into his beer. "There's so much I don't know, Miles. The history of our family, the castle. Don't you ever stop to think about who we are, where we came from?"

"I spend too much of my time wondering about where I'm going, not where I've come from."

"Yeah, but it's different for you, isn't it? You're family, they're English, so you must have a different sense of identity."

"Yes, in a way, but I was born here. I feel as much a Scot as ... Andrew, you've spent more time in England than you have here. You're more bloody Sassenach than I am!" He chuckled and took a mouthful of his bitter. "I've never been into family history and all that. I had a great uncle, I think, who fell in the Great War, but that's all I know."

"You should research things like that, Miles. Our links to the past, they give us a sense of our own identity, our roots. Don't you ever think about things like that? *Who we are?*"

Miles folded his arms and studied his friend, becoming serious. "This is about *her*, isn't it? The mysterious woman in the road? You think you're connected in some way, that she's someone from your family's past?"

Lambert shrugged, brought out the photograph and stared. "Have you no curiosity, Miles? She existed, this photograph proves it. But who was she, that's the crux of it all. When I dozed in the car, the dream I had was about an old king in a drafty castle. A group of messengers came to him, to bring him news of Border Reivers attacking his realm. The person who'd brought the news was a woman..."

"Don't tell me," Miles came forward, drank, and jabbed his finger towards the photograph, "her?"

"I don't know. I woke up before I saw her face."

"Well that's convenient. You've probably read something and it's got stuck in your head."

"Miles, for Christ's sake, I know nothing about Scottish kings, or Border Reivers, or anything remotely similar. None of the reading I've done mentions a single word. Why the hell would I dream of it now?"

"I don't know, but I can't see it being anything else. With all the bloody reading you've been doing lately, you've probably come across it without even thinking."

"You think so? You think that might be it?"

"Of course, you bloody numbskull! That's why the party will blow all of those cobwebs out of your head. You'll feel a hundred times better afterwards, I promise."

Lambert stared at Lorna's face, her subtle smile, the eyes wide, a slight hint of amusement playing around at the edges … a beautiful face, enigmatic, finely honed with high cheekbones, full lips, smooth, rounded chin, a girl from out of a dream. Was that it? Was it all a dream?

"If there was a girl, Andrew, at the party? Would you be interested?"

Miles' voice was low, soft, almost soothing. So in contrast to the question itself. Lambert chuckled and slipped the photograph inside his jacket. "Depends."

"On what?"

"On whether she can cook a good breakfast!"

Miles roared with laughter, threw himself back into his chair, and drained his glass whilst Lambert breathed in relief. He wanted no more questions about Lorna, who she was, where she had come from. The one certain thing was his absolute conviction she still lived. And until he found her, no other woman held the slightest interest for him.

13

The house was a lumbering, redbrick fronted Victorian affair, with bay windows and steps leading up to the front door. Coloured green, in the centre of the woodwork a large, ornate brass knocker, with letterbox beneath. With no sign of any bell, Miles, giving a shrug, went straight to the metal knocker and brought down the clapper hard.

They both stood and waited. Behind the net curtains, grey and impenetrable, nothing stirred. They exchanged glances and Miles knocked for a second time, harder than before.

From somewhere deep within the building a door creaked, footsteps approached. Andrew experienced a curious tingling sensation at the nape of his neck, trepidation as to what he might confront when the door opened.

And then it did.

She stood there, a slightly built woman dressed in black, white hair pulled back in a bun in sharp contrast to the austere cut of her clothes. Her eyes creased, mouth a thin line, unmoving. Her tongue slipped out, moistening her bottom lip and the voice, when it came, was high and tinged with suspicion, "Yes?"

Miles coughed and looked to Lambert for guidance. But Lambert wasn't concerned with politeness or proprietary, he wanted answers. He pushed past his friend, the photograph in his hand and thrust it forward, allowing the woman little chance to avert her gaze.

"I gave this to somebody in your shop in Edinburgh," he began, perhaps a little too aggressively. He heard Miles' shocked breath. "You know the shop you have in the City?"

"I'm sorry," she said, her eyes flittering from the photograph to Lambert, "but I'm not sure I understand."

"I do apologise," said Miles quickly, gripping Lambert by the elbow and pulling him slightly to the side, "we should have telephoned, but we are very anxious to discover the identity of this woman. My friend here, he is a little…" He smiled.

Miles's face, when he smiled this way, took on an almost boyish innocence, which most people found disarming and quite attractive. This woman proved no exception. She spread her hands, her cheeks colouring slightly. "If you wait for one moment, I shall fetch my husband."

The door closed and Lambert sighed, turned and made his way down the steps with great care. "This isn't a good idea, Miles. We should have telephoned ahead, as you said. Imagine two men such as us appearing out of the blue. If I were her I'd be calling the police right this moment."

Miles joined his friend. "You could be right, but if the police do come, we'll simply explain. We have nothing to hide."

"True enough, but … God, Miles, I feel a complete ass. Forcing you to bring me all the way down here, only to have the door slammed shut in our faces. I'm a bloody idiot." He reached out and took firm hold of Miles' forearm. "I'm so sorry."

"Don't be daft." Miles forced a smile, face becoming red. "We've been through a lot, you and me. When Father died, you were there, to help. I'll never forget your kindness."

"You did the same for me."

"Yes, yes I did, but…" He shrugged, blew out his cheeks. "Christ, I think we should go. Maybe you could write them a letter?"

"I'll do it now." Lambert patted his pockets, struggling to maintain his balance with one foot lifted off the ground. "I'll buy something from a shop, drop my address through the letterbox and we'll see what—"

The door wheezed open again and this time, replacing the stark vision of the woman, stood a heavy-set man, canvas trousers, damp patches at the knees, tweed trilby perched at an angle on his head, and holy cardigan open to the waist. He was cleaning his hands on a large green cloth. "Can I help your two gentlemen?"

Again, the exchange, but this time Lambert decided on a much more gracious approach. "We're sorry to disturb you, but you see…" He smiled, and produced the photograph again. "I took this to your shop, in Edinburgh. The man I spoke to, who I assumed was the—"

"One moment," said the man, shaking his head before putting the cloth into his trouser pocket. "My shop closed down some six months ago. I retired. If you gentlemen are looking to have any wedding work done, then I'll gladly recommend another studio."

Lambert, unable to formulate a response, managed a tiny whimper whilst Miles, eyes on stalks, made a tentative move on the first step. "I'm sorry, you closed down six *months* ago?"

"Well, give or take. Gentlemen, if it's not a wedding portfolio you're after, what exactly do you want?"

Lambert, as if in a trance, passed the photograph over to Miles who, after a fleeting glance, showed it to the man in the doorway. "My friend he, er, he was wondering if you might have any records of this woman. It was taken at your studio, you see. A long time ago."

"Nineteen hundred and four," said Lambert, putting his crutch under his arm and limping closer. "Anything you can tell us, the slightest detail, would be amazingly helpful. I'll gladly pay."

The man frowned, appearing not to listen, his face intense, studying Lorna's portrait. He flipped the photograph over, scanned the writing and the date and screwed up his mouth in deep thought. "Nineteen hundred and four..." He turned it and looked at the face for a second time. "I have no records whatsoever of any individuals..." His lips moved as he silently read again the inscription. "There's no doubting this was taken at Richard Brady's studio, probably by the man himself. But my family bought the business, you see. If any of Brady's plates survived, I'm sorry to have to tell you none of them passed into our possession."

He handed the photograph over to Miles and smiled somewhat apologetically. "Strange it should be Nineteen Hundred and Four, being such a significant year for Edinburgh."

"I had no idea," said Miles, looking down at Lorna. "Why was that?"

"The king, Edward the Seventh, made his first official visit to the city. He was very warmly greeted and became something of a celebrity." He chuckled. "You know, I have photographs from the visit, taken by Brady. Would you care to see them?"

The lump in Lambert's throat grew larger. He reached out a trembling hand and gripped Mile's by the coat tails. "That would be most kind," he said in a croak.

He showed them into a small, tidy parlour, large glass-fronted cabinets against two of the walls, ornaments on top, art-deco sculptures of dancers captured in mid-flight, long legged, wearing classic Twenties flapper-girl hats. Two chintz covered armchairs and a bookcase. A wall-mounted clock ticked away the time, its pendulum gently swinging, the face clean and simple. No other sound. A room to while away the days, to sit in silent contemplation, or to read. Lambert limped to the window. The street, with a few cars passing by, was quiet, sedate almost. This place must have remained unchanged for a hundred years or more.

"Why do you think he said what he said about the shop?" asked Lambert, gazing out into the street.

"God knows. Perhaps he made a mistake."

"A mistake?" Lambert gave a wry smile as he turned to look at his friend. "Don't be bloody stupid, Miles. We both set foot inside the place, we saw it all laid out. A working shop, with cameras and everything. And the man. Who the devil was he?"

"I've no idea, perhaps an assistant."

"All right, that might be the case, but ... Strange this old guy shouldn't say anything about our visit, don't you think?"

"We never told him we went inside, did we? Perhaps if we had he might have—"

"I should ask him how he got my address. Miles, aren't you in any way *curious* about any of this? To be told there are no records and to send it back without a single word of explanation?"

"So what the hell are you saying, Andrew? That we imagined it all, you and me both?"

"No, of course I'm not saying any such thing, but you have to admit the whole episode is bizarre. If this guy didn't send me the photograph, then who did? The postmark said Annan, not Edinburgh, so it must have come from here. There has to be a reasonable explanation, don't you think?"

Before Miles could voice a suitable retort the door opened and the man returned, a black bound file under his arm, and several large sepia photographs in his hand. "I'm so sorry," he said, "but I haven't introduced myself. Harvey.

Thomas Harvey." He held out his right hand and first Miles, then Lambert took it. His grip was firm, strong.

"My name is Andrew Lambert, this is my friend, Miles Frazer. I'm sorry for such an inconvenience, to call upon you this way."

"It's perfectly all right, young man." Harvey gestured with his free hand towards the armchair, "Take a seat whilst I sort through these."

As they sat, Harvey set the folder and the photographs down on top of one of the cabinets, carefully pushing to one side the statuettes of the dancers. He flipped through the leaves of the book, blowing a low whistle, peering at each page before moving to the next. "A pity we didn't think to keep any of the records or plates. I assume some of them must be fairly valuable by now. Especially those of celebrities. Not that the cult of the celebrity was anything like it is today. Ah," he stabbed at a page with a forefinger. "Here he is." He turned the book in triumph and held it up so Lambert and Miles could see.

Edward the Seventh , jovial face and thinning hair, his small beady eyes gazing into the distance, sat in semi-profile, just as Lorna had done, but without her alluring smile.

"This was taken in the same studio as your lady friend. Probably around the same time, I shouldn't wonder. The plate exists. I've often considered passing it over to a museum, but time moves on," he laughed, "and I forget."

He went over and gave the album to Miles, then picked up the other photographs. "These, however, are not from the studio. Brady took them during the king's visit, so they are not quite of the same quality. Photography was nothing like as spontaneous as it is nowadays, what with all of that digital palaver." Shaking his head, he passed them over to Lambert. "I'm sorry there's nothing more I can do for you, but … I say, young man, are you all right?"

But Lambert was far from all right and Miles, sensing the change, leaned over to hold onto his friend's shoulder and at that point saw it too.

The photograph, held by Lambert in hands shaking uncontrollably, was a street scene. The king, closest to the camera, was in a royal coach, hand raised, waving back to the countless smiling faces lined all along the route.

But it was not the king who caught the attention of the two friends. In the background, standing out clearly amongst the onlookers in the front row, was Lorna.

14

In the driveway, Lambert stood and watched the taillights of Miles' car disappearing into the murkiness of the dusk. He had refused Miles' offer of help, to support him up the castle steps, preferring to be alone with his thoughts. The journey home seemed so long, so painful, conflicting images racing through his head, pulling him in every direction. Sometimes he felt like a squash ball, slammed constantly against this wall and then that, not knowing where he was going to end up next. Bruised and battered, his mind scrambled by the question, how could Lorna be in the photograph? Nineteen-hundred and four?

He went into the castle as if in a dream, only vaguely aware of Sinclair fussing around him, offering him drinks and snacks, all of which Lambert refused. He slumped in front of the fire and played through the remote control, flicking from one television station to the next. Nothing registered. When he went to bed, he didn't even bother to check the clock.

The darkness enveloped him like a warm blanket, but he chose to lie on top of the covers, naked save for his pants. He stared at the ceiling and conjured up images in the cracks. If he tried hard enough he could make out Lorna's face.

Lorna's face ... and images from the past.

Robert hobbled over to her, and drew her inside, a gnarled fist seizing her slim, warm hand, leading her to a chair. "Sit, my dear," he said.

She had never been this close to a king before. As a child she remembered her mother telling her of the fabled 'king's touch', said to cure terrible afflictions of the skin. Robert's touch, however, brought nothing but revulsion and she pulled away. He was an aged, twisted man of indeterminate age, flesh grey and sunken, body crooked and worn out having spent too many years in cold, dank castles.

He listened with interest to her story, of the reivers coming out of the night to burn, rape, and steal.

"They raped you," he asked, and she saw the spittle on his lower lip.

"I hid," she said, "if I had not, I would be dead."

"You are no serving girl," he said having studied her face. "You are high-born, of that I am clear."

"My family came over with the Conqueror, my great-great grandfather marrying a local Thegn from Northumbria. I have the blood of Saxons running through my veins."

Robert cackled, turned and spat into the fireplace. He watched the globule bubble and sizzle in the flames. "Saxons. Bastards more like." He grinned. "I have enough damned bloody problems in the north without tales of reivers crossing the borders. What would you have me do?"

"My husband was granted land north of the border, and has built a fine castle not so far from—"

"Then why are you not there? Reivers attack homesteads, not defended sites which might cause them effort."

"Whilst I was visiting such a homestead, the attack came."

"Visiting? Dear God girl, you travel the land as if you were blessed with some sort of immunity. We have been fighting English and reivers all along the borders for years. Who were you visiting?"

"Close friends, family. I came here to beg your protection, sire. We are desperate. Every family along the border lives in fear of the night, of what might happen. All we ask is you send some men, to run the reivers off our land. To send a signal."

"I'm too damned old for chasing after bastards like them, but not too old to be warmed in my bed," he leaned forward, cackling, his hand running up her thigh.

She gasped, knocked away his hand and stood up. "For the love of God, have you no shame?"

"Watch your tongue you arrogant bitch! Highborn or not, if you speak to me that way again, I'll cut off your pretty head. I am your king, and you'll do as you're bid."

"As God is my witness I will not! My friend's father lies dead, the mother Lord alone knows where, and his sister—"

"*His* sister?" Robert cackled again, running his tongue along his bottom lip. "So you friend is a man, eh? A lover perhaps? Does your husband know?"

She turned away, biting down the tears. "I thought you would help. You are our *king*."

"Aye, I'm your king," said Robert, climbing to his feet and moving closer, "and you are the most desirable wench I've ever laid eyes on. If you would grant me but a moment of your precious time, I will show you what a wonderful thing a king's appreciation can be, my sweet. All you have to do—"

The door swung open and a young, barrel-chested man strode in, ruddy-faced and wide-eyed, rubbing his gloved hands together and making straight for the fire. "Dear Christ, it is cold!"

Lorna gaped at him as he spread out his palms towards the flames and when he turned he stopped, as if in shock, mouth trying to form words, but without much success.

"This is Lorna," said Robert, "a high-born princess of Northumbria."

Lorna gasped, "Sire, you honour me with such praise, but I—"

"Lorna?" The young man moved closer and, without a pause, took her hand in his own, and bent his head to kiss the soft skin. When he brought up his eyes again, he stepped back and grinned. "By God, if you are not a princess, you ought to be!"

Robert laughed and slumped down into his chair. "This is my son, John, Earl of Carrick. You've come at a most opportune moment, John. Lorna here has suffered the most heinous of crimes against her friend's family – attacked by reivers."

"Christ save us," said John, still holding her hand and staring into her eyes. "They come when we least expect. You suffered much?"

"My friend's father killed, mother taken … cattle and other livestock carried off, together with horses. After eating and drinking their fill, they torched the homes. I survived by sliding into a pit, covering myself with thatch and lying still."

"Sensible, and brave." He brushed his lips across her hand again then turned to the fire. "It will take me less than half a day to gather together enough men to send out a scouting party. Men-at-arms will follow, if you say it can be so, father."

"I suppose," the old man gathered his cover around him and stretched out his legs. "We've been meaning to strike at them, for some time. Perhaps this is the moment."

Lorna looked from one to the other. "The Lord our God takes care of us, sire. Whatever our actions, they will be the right ones."

Robert and his son exchanged a look before the old king shuddered, smacked his lips, and grinned. "So be it. John, you will take a detachment of armed troops with this girl, follow her lead and drive the reivers off. But don't be too long. I have need of you here."

"Aye. We will prepare enough provisions for three days. If we are longer—"

"If you are longer," cut in Lorna, "you can find rest at my husband's castle, where a warm welcome awaits our friends."

John beamed, "An honour to be your friend, my lady."

The king coughed, John reddened around the jaw line and Lorna stood and smiled.

* * *

Lambert went straight to the library as soon as he woke, without pausing to wash or drink coffee, the images of Lorna, John, the king still fresh in his mind. He trawled through the many books Sinclair had brought down from the high shelves and searched every reference, no matter how vague, until he was able to gather together enough information to make sense of his dream.

He sank into a threadbare armchair, his thoughts percolating whilst waiting for breakfast, a more appropriate place to eat than the dining room he now found. Since the accident, he'd found his lack of mobility was more of an issue, the pain often unbearable. Stoically he worked through it, swallowed handfuls of pills, taking the opportunity whenever he could to immerse himself in further study. The smell of freshly made coffee wafting through the open door brought him back to the present and he remembered, with a start, how his father rarely appeared for breakfast, finding the early mornings the most productive times for his writing. His imagination was far too important to be broken by mere breakfast.

He looked around and there, on the writing desk, sat a silver tray with coffee pot, cream and sugar. Lambert wondered how long it had been there. Sinclair's voice whispered from somewhere over by the door, "Have you finished, sir?"

Lambert nodded. "Why did my father write in the west tower?"

Sinclair frowned, caught off-balance by the question. "I believe he found it quieter, sir. Less chance of interruption."

"But he wrote in here too?"

"Yes. I suppose it would depend upon his mood. He'd work in the library to make use of the books, of course, but quite often he would wander into the tower, armed with notes and references."

"I want to go up there. I want to see where he wrote his novels. Perhaps the ambiance aided his imagination, do you think?"

The manservant disappeared with the tray and the untouched coffee and toast without another word. Lambert gazed through the window, returning to his dreams. They were becoming more vivid, as if he were a living witness to what occurred, standing in the room, watching. The last held no horrors, but Lorna's face, so real he could almost reach out and touch it, was an impossibility. And yet, the more he brought the disparate pieces together, the more incredulous he became. She appeared in the photograph of Edward the Seventh's visit to Edinburgh, and in the small portrait. There was no mistake – he saw her plainly. She was the same woman who stood in the road the night of the accident. By coming into his dreams, slipping inside his consciousness, she grew more real with every passing day. The entire situation, just like the woman herself, was an enigma.

He put his face in his hands and rubbed himself vigorously. The dreams were set in an earlier time so he must be mixing the details, all his reading and studying of letters twisting together to create any number of distorted, confused images in his brain.

"I took the liberty of making you some more coffee, sir."

Lambert jumped and focused in on the silver tray. He couldn't remember asking for more coffee. In fact, he had no idea how long he'd sat, thoughts and ideas branching out in a myriad of directions. He massaged his temples, easing some of the pressure. He was compelled to go on, to find out who this mysterious woman was, why she tormented him so. Nothing else mattered any more.

"Thank you Sinclair." He smiled, this time forcing himself to pour the coffee into a cup. As he spooned in sugar, he said, "Have you a key to the tower?"

"Yes, sir. I found it when I cleared it of all those boxes. I cannot remember the last time the place was opened up before then."

"I see. But the tower is original, is it not?"

"As far as I am aware there has always been a tower."

"Do you have any idea how old this castle is?"

Sinclair turned and pursed his lips, "I believe it was originally laid down in the mid-fourteenth century, sir. Your family took it over much later, so I understand. I'm not sure of the correct dates."

"Mid-fourteenth century, so that would be ... during the reign of Robert the Second?"

Sinclair smiled, unable to disguise his surprise, "Yes, indeed. Robert the Second."

"Do you know if my father took an interest in him?"

Sinclair shrugged. "Only the well-known parts. Robert came to the throne late, married twice, sired any number of children, and not all of them in wedlock." He sniggered. "Something of a randy old man was Robert. At least your father said so. However, he was more interested in the history of Robert's eldest son—"

"Earl of Carrick." Andrew surprised himself how quickly the name jumped into his mind.

"Indeed, sir. Something of a tragic figure."

"Aren't they all? So much pain, and anguish, often brought on by mistakes, errors of judgement." He knew now he needed to find out more facts concerning John, Earl of Carrick, later Robert the Third of Scotland. Here was a link, a lost piece to the puzzle and, once found, some of the mystery might become less clouded.

Sinclair interrupted Lambert's thoughts with a cough, "I sincerely hope all this research and the emotions they conjure are not causing you too much strain, sir."

"No, no I'm perfectly fine."

"It's just that, I called you, you see. But you were so lost in your thoughts ... Almost as if you were somewhere else, sir."

"You *called* me?" Lambert shrugged. "I don't recall. Was it important?"

"Sir Henry McKenzie wanted to have a word, sir."

"Sir Henry? My God, I haven't seen him since the funeral. How did he know I was back?"

A slight colouring spreads across Sinclair's jaw. "Your triumphal return is at the centre of local news, sir."

"Is it, by God? That, or the collapse of my business? It graced the inside pages of the Financial Times for a brief moment. I think they managed two sentences, bless their hearts." He smirked. "I wonder why nobody from the local rag has called to interview me."

"This was the reason for Sir Henry's visit, sir. Well, one of them. I think he wanted to speak with you more generally, sir, to see how your convalescence is coming along. He was your father's closest friend. I think he feels somewhat *responsible*. He mentioned something about his daughter wanting to—"

Lambert sat up. "Kathleen? Is she here?" Sinclair looked blank. "She left Scotland for the warmer climes of Queensland in Australia." He shook his head, smiling as the memories came flooding back. "I think she married a musician over there, took to developing her own career as a singer. Bird song is one thing, but when I first heard her CD I was overwhelmed how someone I only knew as a sweet little girl could have developed such a clear and powerful voice." Vaguely aware of Sinclair gathering the coffee pot and going out, Lambert looked back to his years of innocence. Within seconds, Lambert returned to his childhood, a golden time when Kathleen and he played and talked of their dreams and hopes for the future. As they grew older, Lambert's feelings changed, aware of another hidden, more alluring side to her nature. Sometimes he would leave the castle grounds and take long walks through hills, often alone, sometimes accompanied by Kathleen. And as they walked, she would sing, as a reply to his more intimate questions. It became her special way of avoiding the answers and the more she did so, the more he liked it. Soon, he used this device at every opportunity, captivated by her wonderful voice, which like the birds, seemed gifted by God.

The sweet memories brought a smile to his face and the thought of seeing Kathleen again, after so many years, lightened his heart. He stood up, leaning upon his crutches, and moved over to the mirror to check out his physique. His slight potbelly brought a brief wave of depression, knowing how the sight of him going to seed would upset her. He sucked in his stomach and saw it brought little change. He blew out his breath and groaned, "Oh my God."

A soft footfall caused him to swing around and, before he could speak, he lost his balance, grabbed for the worktop edge as the crutch crashed to the floor. Sinclair rushed forward and held him and the two men smiled at one another. "Apologies, sir," said the manservant, helping Lambert to a chair. "I didn't mean to startle you."

"No, don't worry. I keep forgetting." As if to emphasise the fact, he lifted up his bandaged foot and settled it on top of another chair. He hissed as numerous stabs of pain ran through the limb.

"You still need to take it easy, sir. Another week or two the hospital said, so Mr Miles told me."

"Well, we'll see. Sinclair. We'll see."

Later, after an arduous climb to the small, gnarled door, Lambert let himself into the cramped confines of the room at the top of the tower. A heavy covering of dust lay over everything and Lambert hobbled across to the tiny, leaded window, struggled with the latch and pushed it open. The ancient hinges screamed their defiance and Lambert managed to force it ajar by mere inches. He stepped back, defeated and glanced around the interior.

A desk, under which was shoved a tired looking chair with a cracked seat, stuffing oozing from broken seams. Strewn with papers, a black, heavy typewriter dominated the surface. Across to the right, a bookcase jammed with books and magazines and, on the top shelf, a brown-stained decanter, contents long since evaporated, and an empty glass misted with grime.

Lambert leaned on the desk, sifted through some of the papers, noticed the name Suzanne Valadon a number of times and wondered who she might be. He eased out the chair and sat, the leather creaking but remaining intact and set to reading his father's long forgotten words.

The next day, Sinclair came in with news Sir Henry wished to visit, eager to see his late friend's son after so many years. Lambert agreed, spent some time shaving with a disposable razor, pulling on a freshly ironed shirt, as if it were Kathleen herself coming to see him. He sat in the library and waited. As soon as he came through the door, Sir Henry seemed at once to read Lambert's mind, pumping his hand and saying, "It's so good to see you, Andrew. Kathleen sends her best wishes. She's in London right now, recording her latest album with a Covent Garden based tenor. She thought you might be there too, but I suppose you could both catch up when you're on your feet, so to speak."

Lambert forced a thin smile, his hopes Kathleen herself might appear dashed. "I'm looking forward to seeing her very soon. I've taken to listening to some of her old songs whilst cooped up in here with all these books. Her voice is as lovely as ever. I'm more than honoured to have one of her signed CDs in my collection."

Sir Henry's face brightened and he sat down. He glanced behind him as Sinclair arrived with drinks and a plate of sandwiches. Both men waited patiently whilst Sinclair poured the tea. As Sinclair closed the door quietly, Sir Henry gave a tiny chuckle. "Strange he should stay here after all these years. I've packed away all of my servants now. The world is a very different place to what it was, even twenty years ago."

"I asked him the same thing. In many respects this is more his home than it is mine."

"Don't say that, Andrew. It's wonderful to have you here. Memories come flooding back, of good times spent with loving friends."

Lambert studied his father's friend over the rim of his teacup, blowing across the surface before taking a sip. "It's true I should have visited more often, but the business tended to take up almost all of my time. I became blind to the peace of this place, and its beauty."

"So what has changed?"

"Plenty. The business is going into receivership and..." He allowed his words to drift away and put his concentration in drinking his tea.

Never one to linger on any negative aspects, Sir Henry turned his attention to some of the books and papers strewn across the desk. He pursed his lips.

"Seems you've been busy." He leaned over and studied some of Lambert's research. "John, Earl of Carrick, King Robert the Second's eldest son? Well, well ... A very different man to his father and a most tragic figure."

Lambert, intrigued, looked at Sir Henry in a new way. "You know about him?"

"Oh yes, very much so. No disrespect, Andrew, but I never took you for a scholar. What is your interest?"

"I'm trying to understand his connections with the castle. Tragic, you said. In what way?"

"He was involved in an accident with a horse, which rendered him disabled. Unable to rule effectively, his brother took over the throne and, some say, murdered the Earl's son, his own nephew, to ensure his own continuance on the throne after John's death."

"He murdered his own brother's son? Bloody hell, nice bunch weren't they."

"I don't think they had a monopoly on cruelty. One only has to look at the family feuds of the Conqueror's sons or those of Henry the Second, known as The Devil's Brood. There is a rich vein of violence running through every royal family."

"Yes, I suppose you're right. Did he ever come here, do you know, to our lands hereabouts?"

"John Carrick? I wouldn't know. Possibly. Why do you ask? Looking for traces of him in your family's history? Funnily enough, your father had a certain obsession with this idea." Sir Henry remained silent for a moment, lost in his own personal thoughts. "I was never completely sure of the real reason. No doubt research for one of his books."

Lambert repositioned his foot, wincing. "There could be a reason for him to have come here, though? In pursuit of Border Reivers perhaps?"

"*Border…*" Sir Henry shook his head. "There is always the chance, I suppose. The raiders operated all along the border, hence their name. They brought despair to both English and Scots alike. Something of a blight, in my opinion."

Lambert nodded. "Would you like another cup of tea, sir? Sinclair said he was slipping down to town, to do some shopping, so I'll have to prepare it myself." He held up his hand as he struggled to his feet, "I'm determined to become more active. Sitting around is making me soft." He laughed somewhat self-consciously, desperate to demonstrate his physicality, if not for sir Henry's sake, then for Kathleen's who, he hoped, would receive a favourable report from her father.

But Sir Henry was on his feet first. "You needn't worry about any of that, my dearest boy. It's something of a strain for you, as I can see, and I dare say there is a much more agreeable method of refuelling." He turned a hopeful eye towards the drinks' cabinet, filled with a selection of fine malts. Lambert grunted and fell back into his chair whilst Sir Henry poured out two generous measures of Islay Mist. He closed his eyes in relish as the first drop rolled over his tongue, then passed a tumbler to Lambert before sitting down to continue his narration. "It is well known Border Reivers operated in this area, raiding, driving off cattle, killing and burning. They were a constant problem for well over two hundred years. Carrick may well have utilised this castle as a base, to strike out at them whenever operations demanded, but I can't be certain. Nobody, neither your father nor your grandfather ever mentioned such a thing, and I doubt if there is any record."

"So it is all conjecture?"

"Yes, but not beyond possibilities." His eyes wrinkled over the rim of his glass. "You intrigue me, Andrew. I fail to understand your interest, or how you have come to acquire such knowledge."

"I've got plenty of time on my hands, Sir Henry."

"Yes." He grinned, raising his glass. "And a wonderful way to spend it!"

"I can't allow myself to drink too much," he patted his stomach. "I've got more than reading to do. As soon as my leg is healed, I'm going to have to get myself back to full fitness."

"Full fitness is not something which has interested me too much, I have to admit." His eyes twinkled with boyish impishness. "I take the Winston Churchill view towards keeping fit, and it didn't do him any harm." He drained his glass, looked through the papers again, screwing up his eyes in concentration. "You've been doing such a lot of work here, Andrew. Suzanne Valadon?" He picked up a single sheet between finger and thumb. "I don't understand the link. What do the Earl of Carrick and Suzanne Valadon have in common?"

"I have no idea. Perhaps my father was playing around with ideas for a novel."

"Valadon has some intriguing similarities I suppose. She too had an accident, falling from a trapeze whilst working in a circus. She turned her hand to painting, modelled for Lautrec and struggled on in a world dominated by men to make her mark. She had affairs with some of the most famous Impressionists, notably Renoir. He painted her a number of times."

"How do you know all this stuff?"

Sir Henry laughed at Lambert's look. "My dear boy, I have all the time in the world to nurture all of my interests."

"You think my father was planning out a new novel about these two?" Lambert leaned forward, all of his attention focused on this old friend of the family, a man whose encyclopaedic knowledge fascinated him. "What might be the link? Painting?"

"Painting? I'm not sure if Carrick was a painter."

"There's a painting in the study, of this castle, depicting it in Thirteen Eighty-Six and it is in ruins."

"Yes. The castle was burned to the ground."

Lambert held his breath. "By Carrick?"

"No, by Richard the Second of England."

Lambert shook his head, eyes not focusing on anything, trying to piece together these seemingly unconnected pieces of history. "There's so much I don't know, so many threads running through the story of this place. Father must have struggled with it too, and perhaps this got his imagination working?"

"It seems to be doing something similar for you."

Lambert smiled. The old man's words struck a chord, for Lambert had, almost unconsciously, begun to jot down ideas for a story, something which he had never done before in his life. Could creativity be inherited, he wondered.

They talked through the afternoon, leaving history behind as the discussion turned to the estates in the local area, how holidaymakers seemed less this year than ever before, despite the promise of good weather. With ever decreasing revenues, the need to find other means of maintaining incomes grew more imperative. "I'd open it up for visitations," mused Lambert, "but it's not so very impressive."

"Some of the private estates have opened their houses for wedding receptions, some even utilising their chapels to do the actual service. You need a website, Andrew. Get this place out into the modern world. I doubt many people even know of its existence."

"I'll talk to Sinclair and Miles." Lambert screwed up his face. "Not sure if I want to do all that work, I have to say. Maybe later."

As the afternoon drew on, Sir Henry made his excuses, and Lambert accompanied him to the main entrance. "It was so good to see you again, Sir Henry."

"I miss your father, Andrew. We would often meet, chew the cud, put the world to rights." He smile, a distant look crossing his face.

"Please let Kathleen know I'm looking forward to seeing her again."

Sir Henry blinked a few times. "Yes, yes I will Andrew. I'm sure she'll be in touch, when she gets a moment. Her life is somewhat *hectic* nowadays. But I'm sure..." His voice trailed away and he went down the broad steps and crossed the gravel driveway to his waiting car.

Lambert stood in the doorway long after his father's old friend had driven away and knew Kathleen, like almost everything else, was part of his past and would continue to remain so.

"I'm so sorry for being out for so long, sir," said Sinclair later on, returning armed with carrier bags from one of the out-of-town supermarkets. "I hope you enjoyed your time with Sir Henry?"

"Yes, very much so. We discussed John Carrick."

Sinclair busied himself with putting items in the freezer and various cupboards. "I fail to understand your obsession with Carrick, sir."

"If I told you you'd think I was going out of my mind."

"Sir, I think nothing of the sort. I do believe you are confused about certain things; your accident, perhaps caused some form of concussion, who knows."

"I'm not concussed, Sinclair. The hospital did all the checks."

"Yes, sir. I know they did." His eyes expressed his deep anxiety. "But you experienced a dreadful shock, which can cause many different failures to our way of thinking, sir, often leading to mind-altering complications."

"You're talking about the woman I saw, aren't you? Lorna?"

Sinclair slowly turned. "Forgive me, sir, I do not doubt what you saw, but you are confused. These *obsessions* you have developed, I do not believe they are particularly healthy. I apologise for being so blunt."

"I'm not offended, Sinclair. I respect your honesty and I'm grateful for it. But as to the girl, I'm not obsessed, I simply need to know who she is." He shrugged. "I'm having dreams, Sinclair, dreams so real I can smell and touch everything I experience. I had another last night, and it took place in the royal castle of Robert the Second. I saw everything, as if I was standing as close to them as you are to me now. The king, his son, Lorna … All of them, so distinct."

Sinclair stared down to the floor, "Sir, I really think you should speak to somebody about this. You're confused and—"

"A shrink, you mean Sinclair? A psychiatrist?"

"Psychologist, sir. To try to discover the reasons why you are having these dreams. It's not doing you any good, no good at all."

"In the tower, in the desk drawers, I came across mountains of notes my father made. All sorts of scribbles about Carrick and a woman painter."

"Suzanne Valadon. Yes, I know of your father's interest. He spoke to me about it one afternoon, one of those rare occasions when he felt compelled to speak at length of a project he was formulating. Your father was so often embroiled in stories, reality and fiction tended to blur."

"He spoke to you about a story, to do with Valadon?"

"Ideas for a story. I do not think he ever wrote anything concrete, sir. He asked me my opinion of whether a woman could be a painter, as Valadon was, in another, earlier age."

"Medieval times, you mean?" Lambert clenched his fist in a demonstration of triumph. "That's it! The link."

"Link, sir? I don't understand the inference. Link about what?"

But Lambert didn't answer. Instead, he turned and shuffled out on his crutches, wondering who else he might talk to in order to find the answers to the questions running around in his head. Of the identity of a medieval woman who longed to paint and whether or not John, Earl of Carrick, ever came to his family castle and a hundred other things. Only then might he find some peace of mind and, hopefully, a good night's sleep. For he needed rest as a powerful and tantalising desire gripped every sinew, a desire he did not realise, until now, for which he possessed the ability to fulfil.

15

He woke refreshed, his mind full of ideas. Even the simple act of swinging his legs out from under his bedclothes caused him no concern, for the pain seemed to have eased. He smiled back at himself from the mirror and went downstairs, the rain hammering against the roof. But he didn't care. Not now. He dived into his research and two hours or so later, the sun broke through the clouds and Lambert's mood lightened still further. He closed the book he was studying, took up his crutch, and made his way out into the day. He paused at the top of the steps, eyes shut, and breathed in the warm air. For too long the cold and the damp seeped into everything, himself included, but now a new energy sprang up from deep inside, and he went down to the shingle driveway and crossed to the fields.

He set his mind on reaching one of the small clumps of trees, which hyphenated the landscape as beyond stood an old summerhouse. By the time he reached the rickety steps, his foot was singing with pain. He hobbled up to the entrance, found it be locked, and cursed. After a swift glance back to the castle, he put his shoulder against the door and pushed through, the rotten, worm-infested woodwork offering little resistance. The framework rattled and groaned as he shuffled inside and sat down on a part of the bench running around the interior that appeared not to be in danger of collapse.

Since his talk with both Sir Henry and Sinclair he spent his time picking out what he could about the castle, together with anything relating to John, Earl of Carrick. There was nothing to link the two, so why had he conjured up such an idea in the dream? He knew for certain none of his studies hinted at John meeting a woman called Lorna either. Perhaps, in some bizarre, unfathomable way, he must have inherited his father's boundless imagination. He sighed, stretched out his legs and tried to clear his mind. At such moments, he wished he practised a form of meditation. He needed quiet, rest, a prolonged period of stress-free relaxation, which might help him escape from images of castles, Robert the Second, John Carrick, reivers, photographs … Lorna.

No, everything except Lorna. There was no denying his mind more and more often turned towards thoughts of her. She came unwarranted, invading both his waking and sleeping moments. What if Miles and Sinclair were right? What if this obsession was indeed the onset of madness? His uncle's words came to mind, uttered before he committed suicide, 'She'll be back'. Why had not anyone told him the story before? He'd had to drag it out of Sinclair, as if the manservant feared a repetition of that terrible event, brought about by Lorna's monopolising Lambert's life in the way she did.

Thoughts of Lorna lightened his heart, filled him with enormous energy, gave him a purpose, the opposite to what those around him believed. Finding the right woman with whom to settle down was never far from his mind, but finding a woman such as Lorna was going to prove damned near impossible. If he could meet such a woman, with her strength and beauty, a woman who would set him on the right path, teach him to understand the hidden secrets of this world and live in harmony with it. Never before had such images invaded his dreams, causing him to realise in Lorna he had the possibility to fuse physical and mental needs, bringing the two together in one desire.

In the past, the few women he knew were both unadventurous and quiet, deprived of any kind of imagination, or they were firebrands, good-time girls whose lives only ever blossomed through all nightlong clubbing. He never gave up believing in finding true love, even when he remained involved in all forms of vapid entertainments, for no other reasons than to be seen doing so. Corporate events, private parties, clubs, awards ceremonies, theatres, concerts, jazz festivals, sports events, endless dining and wining with sex sometimes punctuating it all. So many gatherings, so much euphoria from those around him whilst he only ever experienced dissatisfaction. Jennifer, his last girlfriend, proved a real gem: pretty, well educated and spoiled rotten. Blessed with an envious figure and a vivid imagination, she played him like a violin. Being preoccupied with her career, she gave little time for Lambert's romantic advances and he harboured suspicions she was secretly dating someone else. When he confronted her about his ideas, she exploded in fury, accusing him of being overly suspicious, of not trusting her, patronising and, most hurtful of all, acting like a self-appointed feudal despot.

As things transpired, she *was* seeing someone else, a man belonging to the world of the super-rich, as far removed from Lambert as anyone could ever be.

He sat on the edge of the bed the night she admitted it all to him, his world crumbling, a coldness spreading throughout his body as her words spat out from her sneering mouth.

"He gives me everything I need, Andrew. You understand? *Everything.*"

"So, now when you've explained it all so plainly, making it as clear as day, you're expecting me to do what? Beg you to stay? To get down on my knees and cry, 'Please, don't leave me, please, please, with a cherry on top?'"

In response, Jennifer walked out at that very moment, her few possessions already packed, leaving him when life was dealing him the worst hand he'd ever been dealt. The receivers arrived as the business collapsed. Perfect timing, he mused, for Jenny to escape the sinking ship. Well, perhaps he didn't deserve her. He should have put his energy into getting his business back on track, but as with everything to do with Andrew Lambert, his heart got in the way. He lacked that ruthless streak, where being determined and decisive in business accomplishes so much. Emotions forever clouded his judgment. He did not possess the unique insight into what it takes to develop a well-coordinated team. As a result the business drifted but, in a curious way, he came to realise he'd made the right decision by leaving everything behind. His destiny lay in other areas, the path less trodden the right choice.

He recalled another wise quote from someone, 'You never find yourself until you face the truth.' He believed everything in life happened for a purpose. Jennifer's leaving, the accident, his uncovering of so much knowledge about the castle, his family history. All for a purpose. Lorna's apparition wasn't a random act of nature, it meant so much more.

But, despite his best efforts, he couldn't shift the thought of why a woman like Lorna could find anything remotely attractive about him. What had he to offer? His ancient castle, the links to the past, his honesty, sense of honour? None of those things could be enough for her.

He leaned his head against the wall and put the heels of his hands in his eyes. He couldn't deny the dramatic way his life had changed since leaving London. Before, the extent of his imagination focused on how to spend his money. Now, fantasies burst forth like flowers in springtime and the most powerful centred on an intangible named Lorna. How could he embrace a life based on nothing more than dreams? He should be strong, strong enough to rid himself of such wishful thoughts.

But even as he gritted his teeth to try and push thoughts of her away, images arrived; her auburn hair, smooth, silken skin, well muscled limbs combining to conquer him, to transport him to the limits of ecstasy. Her body danced before him, graceful, energetic, demanding. He groaned, his erection growing and he surrendered to his thoughts and dreams, and mostly to his desires. "Oh dear God..." Wasn't there a way to bridle his feelings, to put them to more positive use? He laughed at his own shallowness, knowing one thought alone influenced all others. Thoughts of her.

He saw her again in the darkness of the road in the night of the accident. This time, however, he recalled her words, "There is not a future, only possible futures. The 'now' is like the palm of a hand, each finger pointing to what might be. As with all things, one shall prove the most powerful, one, which will surely take us on the main course and lead us to our destiny."

Destiny. But is not my future linked to the past? He closed his eyes, the years opening up once again, to a world long gone, but never forgotten and his mind filled once more with images from the Fourteenth century...

They rode out of the royal castle in the early hours, the plan to travel through the night whilst the reivers slept, and attempt to cut them off before they slipped back over the border into England. Robert, with no intention of incurring the suspicion and possible wrath of the English, gave his instructions to John as Lorna listened. To be cautious, not intimidate or cause alarm to any he came across, to use force only against reivers and no one else.

Lorna, astride a grey dappled mare, travelled beside the solid figure of the king's son. She handled her mount with the assuredness of one well used to horses and John smiled as he handed her a goatskin gourd, "You ride like a princess, my lady. Perhaps you really are one?"

She took the gourd and drank from it. The wine tasted warm and sweet and was no doubt expensive. Trade with Mediterranean lands was hazardous and arduous. Such luxuries did not come cheap. "I am not a princess," she said, passing back the wine to the Earl of Carrick. "I am of noble birth, as I explained to your father, but not royalty, my lord. My husband is a minor earl whose lands are somewhat negligible."

"Yet he owns a castle."

"As do many along the border. His household is small, no more than a dozen acres or so. The reivers are a constant threat."

"His loyalty lies with the English?"

"In these uncertain times, can anyone be sure of loyalty from anyone?"

John nodded, face growing serious. "You're true enough there, my lady. My father's kingdom is hard pressed on all sides. Perhaps the greater threat lies in the north and that is why I have been in negotiations with Scandinavian friends, to forge an alliance."

"Scandinavians?"

"Aye. Swedes. An alliance would do both our countries good, sure up trade routes, strengthen security. The Swedes are a powerful ally, my lady. Let me show you how powerful." He swivelled around in his saddle and lifted his head, "Karl, my good friend. Draw closer"

Within a few moments Lorna heard the approaching tread of hooves and turned to find a young, lean looking man with the most piercing blue eyes she believed she had ever seen, beaming at her. She took in his fine physique, the smooth, alabaster skin of his face, and the rippling muscles in his bare arms. But more than anything, his great mane of white blond hair captured most of her attention.

"This is Karl Portenson, an emissary from the royal court of Sweden."

The giant Scandinavian grinned, revealing a fine set of gleaming teeth, and bowed from his waist. "I speak little of your language," he said, and then he took her hand and kissed it.

Lorna gazed at him, his whole body brimming with health and strength. And as he held her hand in his, a warm glow developed inside, slowly spreading out as if she were taking in the most glorious of summer sunshine. In something of a daze, vaguely aware of John's laughter, of horses neighing, the distant clatter of swords and armour, she focused on this new man's features. The urge to press herself against his magnificent frame caused her heartbeat to hammer in her bosom as the mystical allure of his body became almost irresistible.

A cry shattered her reverie and Lorna turned. A rider approached, storming towards them from across the plain. He reigned in his heaving steed, breathing hard, face streaked in sweat. The dawn had barely begun to break across the horizon, but there was light enough to recognise the urgency in the messenger's face as his eyes bulged with excitement. "We have them," he squawked, "their camp lies in a small valley beyond the rise."

John struggled to control his mount, spooked by the sudden arrival of the scout. "How many?"

The man shrugged, no doubt illiterate and unable to count, but he nodded his head towards the troop of men strung out in a long line behind the Earl of Carrick, "not as many as us, my lord."

"By Christ, we will have justice this day," said John. He grimaced at Lorna. "You will remain here, my lady and when we return we shall—"

"No," she snapped, setting her mouth in a hard line, "I want to see this." She turned her gaze to Karl Portenson, "If it please you, my lord, you will accompany me to a safe place where we can observe the fight."

"It will not be pleasant, my lady," said John.

"Nor was what they did to my friend's family. And I witnessed that."

John nodded, relenting. "So be it. Karl, stay close, and keep her safe!" He drew his sword, raised his arm and thundered, "To arms, lads. And give no quarter."

A great cry sprang out as over forty spurs touched flanks, weapons rang from scabbards, and horses broke out into a determined gallop.

"Mr Andrew, sir?"

Lambert sat up, blinking repeatedly, and saw Sinclair in the entrance to the summerhouse, his angular frame blocking out the sunlight. "Christ, Sinclair. I wish you would stop doing that."

"Apologies, Mr Andrew, sir, but you have a visitor."

"A visitor?" Lambert reached for his crutch and hauled himself to his feet. "What the devil is the time?"

"Almost four, sir."

"Bloody hell," he rubbed his eyes with his free hand, "How long have I been out here?"

"I assume since this morning?"

"You should have called me earlier. Damn it, I've wasted the whole bloody day." He hobbled forward and Sinclair stepped aside, holding onto his younger master's arm to guide him into the open. "Who is this visitor?"

"Someone Mr Miles has sent, sir."

"Mr Miles?" Lambert chuckled, "Not a woman, is it?"

"Sir?"

"Never mind. A joke." He took a few nervous steps across the grass, "I'm starving hungry, Sinclair. You couldn't make me something, could you?"

"Sir," Sinclair looked grim and Lambert stopped. "Your visitor, sir ... It is not a friendly call, sir."

"What do you mean by that?"

"I'll leave it for Mr Miles to explain, sir."

"So he's here too?" Lambert frowned, a queasiness beginning to develop in the pit of his stomach. "What the hell is going on, Sinclair?"

But as the manservant's reluctance to answer stretched out, Lambert's unease turned to anger and he whirled away and strode out across the grass as fast as his bandaged foot and crutch would allow.

He found them in the reception room and as soon as he came through the door, Miles was already crossing the floor, both arms outstretched, "Here you are at last! Sinclair's been looking all over the damned castle for you."

Lambert nodded, but looked beyond his friend's shoulder to the other man, dressed in a grey tweed jacket and dark trousers, who stood next to the fire, smiling. Lambert had not met him before.

"Who's this?"

"Andrew, don't get all uptight," said Miles quickly, his easy voice just starting to fray a little at the edges, "this is Neal Franklyn. An old friend of the family."

Franklyn came closer, right hand held out, "*Doctor* Neal Franklyn Andrew."

Time seemed to freeze for a moment as Lambert stared at the proffered hand, not daring to believe the evidence of his ears. When he finally spoke, his voice was little more than a croak. "Doctor? What sort of doctor?"

Franklyn's arm dropped and before anyone could speak, Miles stepped in, slapping Lambert around the shoulder, "Andrew, for Christ's sake. I told you, Neal is a friend of the family. I've been talking to him about—"

"About me?" Lambert's eyes narrowed. "Is that what you're saying, Miles? You've been discussing me, what happened, the accident, the dreams?"

"Mr Lambert," interjected Franklyn, using his very best beside manner, "perhaps if you would allow me to—"

Lambert held up his hand. "It was nice of you to come, Dr. Franklyn. Sinclair will serve some drinks, but I won't be joining you – I'm really *very* busy right now." Struggling to keep his growing rage out of his voice, Lambert went to leave.

"Miles told me you haven't been quite yourself lately."

Franklyn's voice took on the ever-so-sincere tone of the clinical psychologist, one which Lambert knew so well, listening as he so often did to the many visits his mother received from a small, mild-mannered man from Edinburgh. '*Here's here to talk to Mummy, dear. Don't look so worried.*' But Lambert did worry. And now, here it was again, only this time it was he receiving the very finest bedside manner. He turned his gaze to his friend. "Miles, I'd really appreciate it if you'd leave me alone. I don't need a shrink ."

Stunned, Miles gaped at his friend, before turning to Franklyn, who merely shrugged. "Andrew," said Miles, using the tone of a man deep in shock, "I know you've been under pressure but—"

"I'm under no pressure," said Lambert and he pushed past the two men and made his way over to the drinks' cabinet. "You know what we saw, Miles. The photographs, the letter. And yet you insist on believing I'm cracking up, that I'm out of my mind." He leaned the crutch against the side of the cabinet and selected a decanter of brandy. He poured himself a healthy measure and drank, doing his level best to control his breathing.

Franklyn cleared his throat. "I think Miles is more concerned with your dreams, Mr Lambert."

"Is he?" Lambert swung around, the heat rising from under his collar, and he reached up and loosened it. "And what is he so concerned about, exactly?"

Franklyn shot a glance across to Lambert's friend before any answer came, "Perhaps if we could just talk, Mr Lambert? It might help."

"I've given you my answer to that, perhaps I should tell you again?" The glass clinked on his teeth as he drained it. "I have no intention of talking to you or anybody else. I have dreams. So what? I thought Freud was big on dreams, but I had no idea he believed them an indication of insanity."

"Mr Lambert," said Franklyn, shaking his head, bemused, "nobody, certainly not Miles, is suggesting you are *insane*. Perhaps if you could give an indication of how you feel when you experience these dreams? It might throw some light on why they seem so real, so intense?"

Miles gave a tiny cough. "Andrew, Sinclair said he could hear you shouting when you were in the summerhouse."

"Oh he did, did he? Well he has no bloody right to be telling you anything about me."

"Why the hell are you so angry," said Miles, taking another step forward, "we're only trying to help. We're your friends."

But Lambert was having none of it. He turned his back and poured another brandy. "I'd like you to go now, Miles. And take your *friend* with you."

He waited until he heard the door close before he picked up the glass and took a mouthful of the Hennessy, allowing it lie across his tongue before swallowing it, feeling its warmth slide down his throat to simmer in his stomach. He enjoyed the sensation and it brought him a slow sense of relaxation. By his fourth glass, he was beyond relaxation and when he hit the sofa, ignoring the pain, his only thought was to sleep.

16

The fire crackled and spat making it dangerous for anyone to move too close, which was unfortunate as the night was cold, the sky clear, the stars twinkling in the frosty air. Most of the men wore padded jackets, some with fur collars, and all with thick trews, the bottom halves covered with tightly bound sheepskin, but not Lorna who sat in her tent shivering, longing to go to the fire and allow the warmth to seep into her frozen joints. She knew, however, she dared not show the men the slightest weakness; it was she who had insisted on coming on this foray into the wilderness, to seek out the reivers who had murdered her friends and levelled their village. The king, for his part, remained in the depth of his royal castle, tucked up in bed and full of wine. Thank God for John who, through his valour and determination, had hunted the reivers down and launched the attack. The memories of the ensuing slaughter, so vivid, raced through her mind, no matter how hard she tried to push them aside.

They rode, both her and Portenson, to a ridge and dismounted. The big Swede gestured for her to get down onto her knees, and she followed his lead without a word of protest. The ground was hard, compacted, and bitterly cold. Portenson seemed to ignore any discomfort and scrambled forward. Lorna struggled behind him, gritting her teeth, determined to see what became of the murderers who had attacked her friend's homestead and carried out such horrors.

She sighted their camp, several fires lighting up the immediate area. Men lay spread out on the ground, most of them covered in blankets, whilst dozing guards sat on outcrops of rocks, propped up by their spears, unaware of the impending attack.

When John's soldiers burst through the trees, screaming their fury, the raiders exploded into confused, startled action, crossbows and bows coming up, swords and axes swinging. But all of it proved too late. The riders bore down with tremendous speed, catching most of their quarry unaware, and as the first head left the shoulders of one of the reivers, Lorna groaned and turned away.

"You must look."

Lorna felt cold on the inside. She was sure she'd never be warm again. The fires of hell would be welcome at that moment. She snapped her head to the Swede's, frowning. "I've seen enough."

"No," he said, his voice mellow, almost soothing, "you have your friends to think of. For them, for the pain they suffered, look."

He held her eyes and despite the mayhem erupting below, her stomach lurched. When he drew her close, she almost swooned.

"Be brave," he said and placed his finger and thumb on either side of her mouth, and gently turned her head to the scene of the attack.

She lay flat, aware of his body pressing against her so close, witnessing what went on below, glancing away every time a blade struck home and a victim screamed. With each death, she kept her mouth clamped shut and forced herself to watch.

The Earl of Carrick whirled in the midst of the disorientated and desperate reivers, his sword sweeping through the air, smiting those who stood, running down those who attempted to flee. He seemed seized by bloodlust and Lorna could clearly see how his face appeared consumed with wild, almost maniacal glee. He laughed as he cleaved heads, sliced through limbs, basking in the outpouring of blood. His men too relished the opportunity to dole out death, vengeance and retribution their driving force. They showed no mercy, not even to those threw up their arms in surrender.

Soon the struggle ended and silence fell over the camp. John's men dismounted, strolling amongst the fallen, prodding the bodies with the toes of their boots, despatching any who stirred. John stood in the centre, blowing out his breath, stroking the neck of his horse. He held his sword and it dripped blood. Even from the safety of her vantage point, Lorna was close enough to sense the elation of the victors, and viewed the carnage with mixed emotions; relief it was over and grateful the guilty were despatched, but horrified at the carnage. When the final reiver breathed his last, she rolled away and stared to the sky.

"Is it always like that?" She turned her head to face Portenson as he propped himself up on one elbow. "So swift, so violent?"

"What do you expect? It is battle, and battle is always terrible."

"You have fought in such horrors?"

He nodded and, without a word, he reached forward and brushed away the hair from her face. She did not resist. With the cruelty she had witnessed receding, she allowed a warm thrill to course through her body.

"There must be someone waiting for you, anxious for your return?" A lust filled smile spread over his lips.

"We all live in the hope someone needs us. Don't we?" She looked at him, her throat, growing dry, made her voice sound strained. She frowned, wondering what meaning lay within his words.

"I've been drawn to fighting all my life," he said, "fear nothing but a stranger to me. A life without fighting is beyond imagination and victory…" He smiled. "Victory is the prize for which I strive."

"And am I to be your prize?"

He reached out, taking her face in his hands and leaned towards her. "The most precious one of all," he exhaled into her ear.

Now, sitting alone in her tent, the muffled laughter of the men around the campfire the only sound, she wondered if Karl Portenson's words held the truth. With the reivers despatched, she needed to turn her thoughts to her husband's castle. John had intimated he would send a small scouting party deeper into the woods to search for any evidence of Lorna's kidnapped friends, but they may be away for days. Duty demanded she return to the castle.

She fell down amongst the blankets, salvaged from the reivers' camp, and tried her best to get comfortable. The ground was hard and the cold bitter. Almost at once she realised she would be unable to fall into any kind of meaningful sleep.

When the entrance to the tent gaped open, she sat up, frantic, believing the enemy had returned, but before she could cry out a large, strong hand pressed itself over her mouth and a voice she knew whispered in her ear, "Be still, my lady."

Breathless she allowed the covers to fall from her as Karl Portenson knelt before her, his features disguised by the night. "You cannot—"

He pressed his finger against her lips, "Yes. I can." His hand fell away from her face and drifted towards her bodice, tugging at the thin cords holding her clothing together.

"Ah," his fingers wandered over her breast, like feathers, floating across her skin.

He pressed her down amongst the blankets and she did not resist, locking onto his eyes. She gasped, the heat rising, as if this magnificent man was filling her entire spirit. She clung onto his shoulders, intent on keeping her moans as low as possible, but finding such a course impossible to follow as she became lost in the fires of passion.

She awoke to the sound of birds singing in the surrounding trees and she sat up and took a glance outside. A cold mist clung to the ground and the camp still slept. She turned and saw where he had lay and for a moment, her thoughts returned to the night before. Never had any man loved her the way he had, at once powerful and yet gentle. The last thing she remembered was his deep black eyes. Reassuring her, dispelling pictures of warriors with insane faces, blood streaming, the ragged air filled with the cries of the slain. All of it disappeared, replaced by relief, the pain inside her chest lost as the horrors retreated to other, far away worlds.

Lorna sighed and returned to her blanket. She rolled herself up into a tight ball and closed her eyes, the exquisite warmth of the memory causing ripples of pleasure to flow through her stomach and thighs, convulsing muscles, bringing such sweet joy to every fibre of her being. She drifted off to sleep smiling.

"Jesus Christ!"

Lambert rolled over, burying his face hard into the back of the sofa desperate to blank out the images of Lorna's face, in rapture as the Swede made love to her. He could not. He saw her eyes, wide with desire, lips full and ready and his own passion invaded his senses, and he gripped a cushion, bit into the material and waited for the flames to subside.

He grabbed crutches and got to his feet, groaning with the effort. The room was in darkness and his body stiff with cold. He eased himself forward, still disorientated from the dream, light-headed, throat dry. He needed a drink and, as his stomach rumbled, he realised how hungry he was.

With one hand stretched out before him, he made his way towards where he thought the door was, but then he collided with a solid object, an armchair, something big and heavy, and he fell over it, hitting the floor with a jarring jolt.

"Andrew?"

Someone was there with him in the room, close. He tried to move, but his foot was screaming, wrapped in flames.

"Andrew, lie still."

He wanted to shout out, to fend away whoever it was, but her voice ... *Her voice! Oh sweet Christ, her voice!*

17

Miles came off the phone to Peter after visiting the off-license. He stood on the pavement, staring at his mobile, hoping his words had made sense. Peter agreed to the idea of re-enacting the various ways Lorna may have disappeared. Miles gave him the scant outline for each scene, but even before the conversation had ceased, Peter's imagination took over. Now, alone in the street, the drinks' order completed, Miles hoped Andrew's mood would return to how it was pre-accident. Since then, his friend's personality had grown more serious and intense. The constant searching and dreaming of the woman Lorna did him no good whatsoever. Miles turned his mind to how to placate Andrew, apologise, and get the uptight little sod to relax and agree to them all having a bloody good time.

He called into a small café and ordered a latte and Panini, took a free newspaper from the rack and sat. A particular story grabbed him but a sudden exhaustion overcame him. He yawned. He thought the waitress returned with his order, but he couldn't be sure. His eyes grew so heavy.

He glanced up and was surprised to find a woman sitting opposite him across the table.

No one spoke. The waitress hovered close by with his coffee, placing it carefully on the table before moving away. Miles barely acknowledge her, all of his attention centred on the woman before him. Auburn haired, skin bronzed by the sun, eyes so large they could swallow him up whole, she was utterly ravishing. She seemed to exude a latent sexuality, which Miles immediately picked up. Before he uttered a word, she leaned forward, smiling, and said, "You're a friend of Andrew's, yes? Miles?"

If her sudden appearance shocked him, her words brought a sense of complete bewilderment. His mouth dropped, brain disengaged and he sat as if struck dumb.

"Please," she said, her voice soft, mellow, the tiniest hint of an accent, but not one he recognised, "I didn't mean to startle you. I'm an old friend of the family." Her eyes sparkled with every utterance. "He may not have mentioned me as I was more a friend of Andrew's father. If you understand the inference."

He did, but he continued to struggle to bring his jumbled thoughts together. To give him a moment, he took his coffee and sipped. As he moved to return the cup to the table, she reached out and with the index finger of her right hand, stroked his upper lip.

Miles gaped as she took her finger and licked away the smatterings of cream.

For a long drawn out moment, no more words followed and Miles sank into her gaze. Then, when she sighed, the silence splintered and he snapped his eyes open and shut a few times. "I'm sorry," he began, "but I didn't—"

"He hasn't been himself," she continued, leaning forward on her elbows. He gasped. She wore a sleeveless dress of white cotton, a delicate pattern of repeated flowers descending vertically to the waist. Her full breasts strained against the partially open bodice, sun-kissed flesh glistening with health. Miles did not think he had ever set eyes upon a woman more beautiful in all of his life. "I'm here to ask you something."

He pulled his stare from her breasts to her face again and forced a single, "Yes?" through a throat constricted and dry.

"Don't question him too much."

Miles frowned, his sense of bemusement growing. "Question him? I... I don't understand."

"You will," she said with a smile and laid her hand over his. "Can you order me a coffee? Espresso?"

He sat, staring, her words coming from far away. She remained still and silent, eyes never blinking, until at last he found the strength to stand. "Yes, of course" he mumbled but before doing so, he pressed his hands into his eyes, eyes which had become sore and gritty and he realised how exhausted he was. Bright flashes of blue and violate danced before him and he yawned loudly.

"You wanted an Espresso, sir?"

He snapped his eyes open and jerked his head around to find the waitress standing at the table, smiling. "Er, yes. Thank you."

She placed the coffee in front of him. "I think you must have dropped off. Are you feeling okay?"

He shook his head, blinking and was about to answer when he turned to speak to the mysterious stranger once more. His throat closed up, gripped by shock.

The place where she sat was empty. The woman had gone.

* * *

Lambert finished off the lunch Sinclair had prepared and dabbed at his mouth with a serviette. "I'll have to go down to see Miles."

"So, you're still talking to him, sir?"

Lambert blinked in surprise, "Of course. We had a disagreement, nothing more. Sometimes we have to accept the idea of being wrong."

Sinclair removed the empty plate. "It is not my business, sir, but I couldn't help noticing that this morning you seem … *different*. More at ease."

"I didn't dream, that was why. I fell over a chair, in the dark. It did me some good."

The manservant turned a quizzical face towards his young master. "You knocked yourself out? I fail to see how such an event could make you feel better."

Lambert smiled. "I think I've been too wrapped up in worries, Sinclair, allowing events which I have no control to cause me stress and anxiety. I am more accepting of the situation now."

"I'm so glad to hear that, sir."

"I've got a lot to do today, after I've gone down to Miles's. I need to start getting ready for the party. It will bring a sense of fun to these old walls." He waved his arm in a wide arc. "Music, laughter, it'll do the place good."

"Yes, no doubt." Sinclair returned to finishing off his chore. "I have prepared the dining room sir, cleared away most of the ornaments and furniture. I hope it will suffice."

"I'm sure it will. You know, I'm actually looking forward to tonight. I can't remember the last time we had friends here."

"Not since your parents were alive, sir. Happy times they were. I would very much like the castle to be happy again."

"Aye, me too." He stretched out his foot and waggled it. "You know, the pain has almost completely gone, so I'm going to drive down to visit Miles myself."

"Are you sure that's wise, sir?"

"Don't worry, Sinclair, I'm perfectly fine." And to prove his point he stood up without the aid of the crutch. "You see. I'm almost reborn." He laughed and limped out with more energy than he had had at any time since the accident. At the door, he paused. "What about Megan?"

"I'm taking her down to the kennels for the night. I don't think she will relish a bunch of new people surrounding her."

"Oh, I don't know. I have an idea she secretly enjoys the idea of dancing. I often envisage her creeping down here at night to watch late-night movies." Sinclair's face took on a wild, concerned look and Lambert burst out laughing, "Take it easy, Sinclair, *I'm joking!*"

The manservant relaxed and Lambert, chuckling, went to fetch his coat.

He took the drive across to Fort William at a steady speed, sometimes a little too steadily as impatient drivers hooted horns and waved fists, desperate to overtake. Lambert smiled in return, never allowing himself to be intimidated. He found if he pressed down too hard on the accelerator, the pain soon returned; even keeping his foot at a constant pressure caused significant discomfort, forcing him to pull over on several occasions to rest.

His plan was to visit Miles, tender his apologies, and contact his regional business office from there by internet. However, the day was so warm, spring sunshine lighting up everything with the promise of rebirth, he decided to enjoy his solitude, take in the glorious scenery and breathe deep. He parked in a lay-by and wound down the window. The air, sweet with the smell of heather, brought instant refreshment to his senses. This truly was a beautiful country, so unspoilt, a land where one could forget all the worries and concerns the modern world brought. Here, time stood still. It must have been the same for Lorna, all those centuries ago. She too must have stopped and looked out across the endless, rolling hills and drank in the wonders.

He continued with his drive to the office. He parked the car and got out without the use of his crutch, which he left behind in the back seat. A sudden, sharp pain reminded him his good leg now had the sole responsibility of supporting all of his weight and this was going to prove a long and difficult visit. So, reluctantly, he tore open the door and brought out the crutch.

Taking his time, he limped over to the glass door, punched in the key code and went inside.

The coolness of the small, intimate foyer greeted him and from behind the reception desk, a uniformed man gave him a nod. "Anyone here, Norman?"

Norman trailed a finger down a print out and pursed his lips. "Mr Monroe and Miss Sullivan. I believe most have gone out for lunch sir. How are you feeling?"

"Better," and Lambert went to the lift, waited, and then travelled up to the main suite of office.

The lift doors opened and he stepped out and the bright sunshine hit him like a sledgehammer between the eyes. He staggered backwards, covering his face with his arm, groping with the other for support.

There was none.

His hand struck air and he whirled around, fearful, confused, wondering where he was and what had happened.

With a swirling mist before his eyes, he took a moment before he felt confident enough to move forward. As he did he realised, with building terror, he no longer stood inside the office, but on an open moor, filled with the chaos of medieval fighting men rushing here and there, barking orders, all confusion and haste.

Unable to come to terms with anything happening around him, his bowels loosened and he stumbled to a rock and collapsed on top of it. He took in huge gulps of air, not believing what he observed.

Men. Hundreds of them, dressed in chain mail hauberks, some with reinforced plate at elbows and knees, many of them in twos or threes sweating and struggling with massive boulders towards three huge wooden machines stretched out across the flat plain.

"Move your arse!"

He looked up and gasped at the sight of a burly, fully armoured man-at-arms standing before him, clad in quilted blue jacket, sword at his side, and horrific looking halberd clutched in leather bound hands. His helmet was open at the face, hinged guard pushed back. For some reason due almost certainly from his hours of reading recently, Lambert recognised it as a pig-faced helm, or basinet. The man, however, did not strike Lambert as being the type of person he would wish to engage in conversation, especially when he struck out and waggled a finger in his general direction. "Fucking move!"

"Aye sergeant!"

Lambert almost fell over as a much shorter soldier staggered past, gripping a large stone in his gloved hands.

"Sorry sergeant, I couldn't get it out the ground."

"Idle bloody layabout," snarled the sergeant and he launched a tremendous kick at the soldier, who squawked as the boot struck him on the backside.

Lambert stood up and at last was able to pick out the details. It was a siege, the giant machines he knew as trebuchets, which used a counterweight to launch rocks and stones to strike at defences. He heard the great moan of the wooden arms as the nearest machine swung into action, and he followed the trajectory of the enormous stone as it arced through the air and headed towards…

He knew at that point, if any doubts remained, he was indeed insane.

The giant stone streaked onwards with almost silken ease and smashed against the walls of the castle, which stood some hundreds of paces away, and well out of bow range. A castle Lambert knew all too well.

His own.

His head whirled, sky spinning, blending with earth, rocks and grass. A kaleidoscope of colours, nothing tangible, discernible, all a swirling mass of confusion and bewilderment. He teetered forward, a drunkard, control gone. He hit the ground, hard, compacted, and his knees screamed as they took the full force of his collapse. Fog whirled around him, an envelope of cold…

Hands were lifting him, voices soothing, concerned, "Andrew…"

"It's his foot," someone else said. A deeper voice, more authoritarian.

He didn't need authority. He only needed sleep.

Wet, cold. His lips tingled. Eyes opened. Nothing, a featureless, motionless blob, grey and indistinct, invading his senses.

And he saw them.

Two faces, frowning, serious. A woman and a man, leaning too close, features distorted.

"Andrew?"

The mist receded at a terrifying speed, disappearing into the far distance, leaving a perfect face, almond eyes, ruby lips filling his field of vision. "Are you all right, Andrew?"

A pretty girl smiled and he realised with a start he sat on a stool in his office, staring at the girl's concerned face. "Yes, thank you Alice," he said, and shook his head. "I blacked out for a moment."

"Crutches aren't meant for slippery surfaces, like this floor," said a young man whom Lambert recognised as Clive Monroe. "You need to be so careful to avoid any secondary injuries caused by a crutch slip."

"Thanks for your friendly tip, Clive. You're right, of course – I need to be more attentive." He bent down to massage his foot. The bandage was thin, the bones underneath prominent, swollen. Sinclair's words rang true. He *had* done too much, the drive over, the attempt to walk without a crutch, which brought such a blinding stab of pain, all combining to cause confusion, light-headedness, and ultimately hallucinations.

They helped him back to his car, and this time he didn't object, not even when Miles arrived. Someone, thankfully, had phoned him and he watched his old friend run across the forecourt, face etched with concern. Lambert smiled, tried to do the best he could, but slipped away into the warm embrace of sleep.

18

Returning from the raid, they escorted her to the castle and waited, still mounted, as she climbed the narrow steps to the great, heavy door and pounded on it with her fist. Lorna shot a glance towards Karl and then the bolt from within drew back and ancient hinges screamed as the wooden entrance eased open.

Castle Strythe was a modest affair, a single tower set on the east wing, the semi-circular keep forming the main defences, with no gatehouse only this doorway, wide enough to allow two men abreast to enter. In many ways, the simplicity of the design gave added strength to the edifice when attacked. Easy to defend, so far it had remained untouched by war or raids. But for how much longer, Lorna could not say.

The wizened servant by the door bowed from the waist, "My lady," he said and stepped aside.

She turned again before entering and smiled to John, Earl of Carrick, who sat grinning from astride his horse. "Thank you, my lord, for all you have done."

"Don't thank me, sweet lady," he returned, throwing a mischievous glance towards the Swede some two or three paces away, "we are here to serve."

Karl nodded and, giving her a wink, he turned his mount and moved away, with his companions following.

She stood in the doorway and watched them riding away, hoping he would turn and give her one, last wave. He did not, but she waited until they receded into the distance and were lost from her sight. She thought something moved within the early morning mist, but then it too was lost and only silence remained.

She wiped away the tear threatening to spill, and went into the cold, unwelcoming bleakness of the castle.

The great hall opened up before her, the floor covered with rush mats and dust. It required sweeping, the shutters pulled open, light to come streaming in to bring freshness and hope to the drab, stark interior.

She had been away for little more than a week and already she hated it.

"I shall go to my room," she said, "to change."

"I presume my Lord Strythe would wish to know of your return, my lady, at once."

"And where is he at this moment?"

"Asleep, my lady."

"Ah," she cast her eye around the hall, went across to a large trestle table, and prodded through the scraps of bread and cheese, which lay strewn over the surface. A half-empty jug of wine took her attention and she tipped it into a nearby goblet and sampled a mouthful. "Dear God, this is almost vinegar." She swung around. "There has been some sort of celebration?"

"A guest, my lady, a man of most gracious charm and prodigious talents."

"Really?" She arched a single eyebrow. "What sort of guest?"

"A painter, so I understand."

She tilted her head, ran her tongue over lips wet with wine. A visitor always broke up the monotony of the castle, but a visit by a painter was by far the most interesting event to have occurred for a long time. Her heartbeat quickened at the prospect of being in his company, of sharing his experiences, for in secret she had often put brush to board and dabbled in the art of painting. "And where is he, asleep as well?"

"I believe he is to the rear, my lady, in the grounds. He has recently returned from the east, from the great city of Constantinople itself. My Lord Strythe learned of him from our liege lord, Sir John Swinton. I shall announce you."

"I need to get out of these filthy clothes first," she said, draining the wine. "But yes, inform our distinguished guest of my arrival, and tell him I shall meet him in the garden as soon as I am ready. As for my husband, let him sleep."

The servant bowed, turned on his heels, and scurried away.

Lorna stood leaning against the table, cradling the goblet in both hands, and pondered who this mysterious man might be. But even as she thought, images of Karl reared up in her mind, the memory of him, the way he held her and loved her. She squeezed her eyes shut. Would she ever know such a man as he ever again? And, having sampled such delights, what next with her husband? Lord Strythe, a good and gentle man, giving her this home, this way of life she should value, but which held nothing but a routine she now loathed. And where Strythe was kind, he was nonetheless reclusive, a shadow flitting in and out of her life, more concerned with walking in the grounds, ruminating over the past. Her suspicion was he was slipping into melancholy, harking back to a life he once knew, now forgotten, a life which did not include her. Where she was vibrant, adventurous, alive, Strythe was falling deeper and deeper into himself. No excuses for the changes developing inside her, but Portenson had brought the hopes of a new, exciting path, one that traversed her own longings whilst allowing her to remain loyal to the Strythe family home. It may prove an arduous task to balance the two, but she had her duty, and duty was everything for a lady such as she.

She opened her eyes and put the goblet down. If anything was certain, she decided to assign her former life to memory, replacing it with new and fulfilling experiences. She smiled and made her way to her rooms with a lightness of being and a dance to her step.

Lambert's joints ached and he groaned as he pushed himself up by his hands. He took a moment to look around him. Low mist clung to the ground like a blanket, but the fields were empty, nothing but the occasional outcrop of rock and clusters of trees to break up the plain. The huge mangonels had gone, nothing remaining to give any hint of them ever standing there. He sat up, rubbed his eyes with the back of his fists and breathed deep. The air tasted fresh and clean, restoring his senses, and he looked over to his left to the castle and saw it intact and peaceful.

He stood up, dusted down his clothes, and slowly made his way over the fields. Almost at once there came the mighty pounding of hooves and he swung around wildly, desperate to seek out some cover. Before he could take another strep, a dozen or so riders thundered by, men clad in chainmail and metal helmets, shield slung on their backs, some with lances, all of them streaked with sweat. One, more than the others, took his attention. A giant of man, long blond hair streaming behind him, the flesh from his bare arms pearly white, rippling with muscles. None of them gave him so much as a glance and he watched them until the mist swallowed them up. He stood and waited, the silence hung over him like a shroud, cold and wet and he realised his own clothes were dry and unstained. Frowning, he turned and made his way once more towards the castle.

Drawing closer he identified the familiar parts of the structure, but taken as a whole there were surprising differences between this and the home he knew. He stopped, studied the parapets and the tower, the walls covered in plaster, gleaming white. He never would have thought such a thing possible. His own castle presented bare granite to the world, and the transformation was marked. Uneasiness stirred and he decided it would be best to go to the rear. Indeed, as he contemplated the move, he became aware of an overpowering urge to follow it through. Something , an unseen force, pulling him. He shook his head, nothing making any sense. Why was he here, how had he arrived? And the attack? What was that?

"I'm going mad," he muttered and tramped across the field to the walls, and skirted around them to where the gardens stood in the castle he knew.

They were there, but not the same. Instead of serried rows of roses, and masses of azaleas, a profusion of lilies interlaced between dwarf hedges of box replaced them. He tried to seek out the ornamental fountain, but it did not seem to be there, so he went to move closer and froze.

A man and woman sat under the shade of a poplar tree, their voices low. Lambert, trying not to make too much noise, took a step backward and dropped down to his knee. He did not believe either had seen him, so he crept forward, making his way to another tree, this time a yew, and craned his neck around the solid trunk.

He almost cried out.

It was she. As sure as the sun shone in the sky. Lorna. There could be no mistaking her rich auburn hair, the swan neck, the fine features carved from purest alabaster.

He shook his head in an attempt to rid himself of the image. He must be imagining things. Impossible. In a dream perhaps, but here, before him, a matter of a few paces away? He sat down and leaned back against the tree.

What if it was an illusion? He did not remember falling asleep and the last thing he recalled were the soldiers, the huge siege engines, the rush of stones arcing through the air ... No, this had to be a dream and if he pinched himself, he might wake up. That is what they said, wasn't it? To bring yourself out of a dream?

She laughed, and all thoughts of leaving this imaginary world evaporated at that point. The sound of her, light, happy, filled with unbridled joy, instilled within him a warm glow, to sit and listen forever would be the most wonderful of gifts.

"Master Devoir, it's magical and mesmerizing," she said, voice child-like, over-excited.

"I paint the world no one can see and would ask you to be my Muse. I will depict you beyond time and space."

His words brought a visible change to her, and she grew vibrant and passionate, her face alive with expectation. Clearly in agreement, she took to discussing the details. "Would it not take a lot of time to sit for you? I'm not sure I'm patient enough and would surely become bored."

"No, no, Madame, I promise you – but one look at my magic brush and you will be captivated!"

Both of them laughed this time, and Lambert edged around the tree to enable himself to listen more closely.

"You tease me, Monsieur. I wonder what magic brush you mean."

"Well, Madame, if I were to stand, you might gain a more advantageous position from which to view the effect you have on me."

"Monsieur, your ardour is flattering, but perhaps if we keep to the business in hand. The painting?"

"Ah, Madame, you shatter the moment…"

"No, I return to reality, Monsieur. Whatever your desires towards me, they can never be fulfilled. My husband is kind, but jealous. It would not serve you well to give him cause for suspicion."

There was a rustle of material and Lambert stretched upwards, supporting himself by his hands and saw the man revealing a rolled-up piece of canvas from out of a cloth bag. He unfurled it, and Lorna snapped her palm over her mouth and whimpered.

"This technique," continued Monsieur Devoir, "was taught me by an old mystic whilst I was visiting the most ancient city of Constantinople. By the use of specially prepared paints, the artist can create a virtual optical illusion, and hide the true meaning of a work through the clever use of light and shadow. There is something in the pigment which creates an unreal image, as if it were a dream, at once temporary and powerful."

"How so powerful?"

"It is said that the sitter takes on some of the mystical properties and them self becomes captured within the painting itself."

"Captured? Monsieur, you intrigue me. How can a painting do such a thing?"

"Madame, there are wonders in this world which have yet to be revealed. This painting will be one of them."

"It sounds incredible. I wonder..." Her fingers floated across the canvas. "Monsieur, can I reveal something to you, something which no one else knows?"

"Madame, I would want you to reveal *everything* about yourself to me."

She giggled, "Monsieur, you joust with your words and give them meaning which I did not intend!"

"My sweet lady," he said, grinning, and he took her hand and held it lightly in his own. "You may not intend them, but I do."

She gasped, but her hand remained where it was. "I am flattered by your attentions. Truly."

"So tell me what this secret is."

She bit her lip. "I have a desire to be a painter myself. Once, not so many years ago, Lord Swinton came to the castle and brought with him the most wonderful portrait of the Holy Mother, which he said had come into his possession whilst on Crusade."

"An icon, madam. Such things are common in the east."

"I have never seen anything so beautiful! I attempted to reproduce it in the quiet of my room, using ground up minerals and oil. I did my best, failed miserably but have never lost the desire to try again. Nobody knows about my passion, of course."

"A painter's life is the most difficult of all. Some appreciate us, but our work is seldom valued. And for a woman..." He shook his head and smiled. "A woman would never be accepted as having talent, no matter how proficient she is."

Lambert's hand slipped on the wet grass and his chin hit the ground. He cursed, slammed his eyes shut and kept as still as stone.

"There is something here," said Lorna sitting up, her voice becoming low. "Did you hear it?"

"No, Madame. There is no one. Come, take another look at this painting and tell me what you can see."

Lambert let out his breath in a long, low sigh, and managed to sit up, rubbing his chin.

Lorna peered at the picture. "I can see a few smudges of paint on the white canvas," she looked hesitatingly, "but nothing more."

"Let me hold it up, and try ... Yes! Yes, there, you see, as the sunlight hits the surface?"

"Oh dear Lord, yes! But that is astonishing. It appeared so ordinary, so flat, and now ... Now I can see two people, a couple, sitting hand in hand beneath a tree. But they were not there a moment before, Monsieur."

"No, for the reasons I have stated. So, my lady, you agree to sit for me?"

"I'm not sure. This process, the mystical aspect ... A frightening idea, Monsieur, to be sure."

"Nonsense! I note the sadness in your eyes, my lady, and in the way you walk, forever searching. Searching for someone, I think?"

She smiled, "You are perceptive, Monsieur."

"If I were to paint you, your soul would remain within the paint, and whatever dreams and hopes you have, will be there too. Perhaps ... The ancient mystic told me that often such dreams can transcend centuries, that what we seek remains in a state of limbo until we have found it, no matter how long the search."

"And you believe such a thing?"

"I believe what the mystic told me has substance, my lady. Perhaps our arrangement will prove its authenticity?"

"So, you have these paints, imbued with the properties you described?"

"Yes, I purchased them from the mystic. All we require, my lady, is the opportunity."

"I will need to speak to my husband. I have to be careful, Monsieur. He must unearth no knowledge of our discussion; for him it will be a normal painting, nothing more."

"As you so desire, my lady. When can we begin?"

"As soon as possible. Tonight, after our evening meal." She turned her wide eyes to his. "Monsieur, I wonder if in return for my sitting, you would do something for me."

Again, the twinkle in his eyes. "You have only to ask."

"I wonder if you might give me some instruction on how to paint?"

His other hand joined his first and squeezed hers. "My lady, nothing would give me more pleasure." A wink of an eye and a flash of teeth before he breathed, "Well, perhaps there *is* something more."

They both laughed and Lambert smiled to himself. It appeared the sitter and aspiring artist had found the right way to a new adventure.

He heard the rustling of material and knew Lorna was on her feet. He gathered up his knees and, putting his back hard against the trunk, forced himself up.

They came by within a pace. He closed his eyes, concentrating on keeping his breathing shallow, but he felt certain they would see him.

He sensed Lorna stopping. He opened his eyes and there she stood, not six feet from him.

"Monsieur, can you feel something?"

"My lady?"

Lambert observed Devoir turning his head, frowning and shaking his head.

"There is something here..." She edged closer, her eyes looking right through Lambert. If he wished, he had merely to reach out his hand and touch her. "Something or someone." She titled her head. "I feel such ... such passion, Monsieur."

"You do, my lady?" The Frenchman beamed. "Yours will be the most wondrous portrait ever put to canvas, and when we have finished..." He sighed.

She swung away from Lambert. "Monsieur Devoir, you are incorrigible. But you're also... quite sweet." She leaned forward and kissed his nose. He dropped his arms in shock and she whirled around, laughing with total abandon. But when she faced Lambert again, she stopped, abruptly. She frowned, her eyes seeming to bore into him. "He is still here, I know it. I wonder..." Her hand stretched towards him. Lambert sucked in a breath, closed his eyes and waited, knowing once she touched him the illusion would shatter and reality would return. But what reality would it be?

"And here we are," said a voice, which was not Lorna's, and the hand shaking him did not strike Lambert as being in any way feminine. He snapped his head around and found himself in the passenger seat of Miles' car as the tyres crunched over the shingle of the castle drive.

"Bloody hell," said Lambert, shaking his head and rubbing his eyes. "I must have been out for hours."

"Yes. You barely have time for a shower. All being well, the caterers have been and the food is ready. Sinclair told me he'll take the night off, so the place is ours, bonny lad, until the wee hours!"

"Do we have to do this, Miles? Couldn't we just have a few drinks, a quiet evening? Please?"

"Too late, everything is prepared. I gave Sinclair orders to lay out your best worsted suit, so get yourself showered and shaved and be down on the steps by eight-thirty. Got it?"

"How many are coming?"

"About fifteen. And," Miles dug his friend in the ribs with his elbow, "there's a very nice young thing joining our evening, Andrew old mate, who has expressed more than a passing interest. Her name is Evelyn, and she absolutely bloody gorgeous."

"I don't think I really want to—"

"Like I said, too late! Now get ready and I'll see you in about two hours."

Lambert clambered out of the car and watched Miles swing around and drive off in a great shower of dust and thrown up pebbles.

He groaned, squeezed his finger and thumb into the corners of his eyes, and wondered if this girl, Evelyn, would be anything like as beguiling as Lorna. He blew out a breath. Somehow, he doubted it.

19

In the end, the number of guests topped the twenty mark. Sinclair, having slipped out almost as soon as the first people arrived, had done an excellent job at preparing the place for the party. The caterers too, whoever they were, had supplied a good spread of food and when Lambert came down from getting ready he succumbed to temptation and sampled some of the hors d'oeuvres. Smacking his lips he stood and surveyed and knew it would be a good night.

Miles was one of the first to arrive, but not alone. He came walking up the drive, grinning, with a girl on each arm.

"All set, Andrew, bonny lad?"

Lambert grunted, stepping aside to allow the girls to move inside. He couldn't help but follow them with his eyes, both wearing skin-tight jeans and tiny cropped-tops. Miles slapped him on the arm. "Blonde one is mine. Name of Cheryl. The other one is the girl I spoke to you about. Evelyn. You'll be in there, old man."

"Miles, I'm still not exactly—"

"Fix them some drinks, bonny lad. Peter will be here soon."

And sure enough, Peter arrived within ten minutes, together with a bevy of others. Miles had cast his net wide, inviting not only some old, well-established friends, but several from university and others whom Lambert had never set eyes on before.

With the music playing and the wine flowing, barriers tumbled and, as the evening progressed, more and more guests arrived, filling out the room. The food too proved popular and all in all Lambert found himself enjoying the gathering more and more.

Evelyn kept a discreet distance for most of the time, much to the annoyance of Miles who came up to Lambert's elbow at close to eleven and took him aside. "For Christ's sake," he shouted above the din of the pulsing music, "why the bloody hell don't you go over and talk to her?"

Lambert's stomach lurched with the idea of opening a conversation with such a gorgeous looking woman. He leaned into Miles, speaking down his ear, "I'm not sure she even wants me to."

"Don't be so bloody prudish, Andrew! Of course she bloody wants to. Look at her for God's sake."

And Lambert did look at her. Gloriously slim, tight top of sky blue, bronzed arms with white bracelets, and her jeans tighter than he ever imagined possible. He fantasised over taking her upstairs and peeling away the denim. He wished he had the self-confidence to do so. Her face was smooth, a cute chin, chiselled cheekbones, thin nose, huge brown eyes and mousy coloured hair curled inwards at the ends. He tried to gain her attention more than once, but she always seemed so much more interested in what her companions were saying, her laughter reaching him above the music more than once. A thought developed. A curious one. Evelyn, so desirable and available … despite conjuring up images of taking her to bed, nothing stirred in his loins. An automatic response to a pretty girl, nothing concrete or certain. He knew why this was. She may well be pretty but she was far cry from the woman whose apparition had chased him ever since that fucking accident. This girl was an intruder.

"The thing is Miles, I'm—"

Before Lambert managed another word of explanation, the music snapped off. In the stunned silence people exchanged looks, some giggles, but all went quiet as Peter stood on top of a table and clapped his hands together. A big man, barrel-chested and thick limbed, his ruddy face topped by a fine mess of mousey brown hair, he appeared to fill the room with his enormous size, great arms like hams waving wildly around. "Oh my beauties," he began in a strange, sing-song manner, "gather around me and listen to tales of recklessness and love, of heroism and despair. For tonight, we will unravel the wonders of the flame-haired beauty, come to haunt the halls of Castle Strythe."

Miles punched Lambert playfully in the arm, "Here's the moment, old friend, Peter's charades."

Lambert groaned.

"All right, all right," boomed Peter as the guests broke into loud conversation, their initial shock giving way to mischievous laughter and bemused questions. "I've collected together some scenes," he produced a wad of neatly typed out pieces of card, "On each is a scenario about why our mysterious beauty—"

"Lorna," shouted across Lambert, immediately becoming self-conscious as every eye turned to him. He gave a sheepish grin, "Well, she is *mine*!"

The guests laughed, all except Evelyn who, it seemed to Lambert, noticed him for the first time that evening. He caught her eyes, held her gaze for a moment but as the heat rose to his jaw line, he looked away, becoming queasy at her self-confident, almost arrogant gaze.

"Yes," boomed Peter, "the lovely *Lorna*! She lived in this very castle, way back in the Fourteenth Century, and then she simply disappeared. There are stories of her husband wandering endlessly across the glen in search of her. Some say his cries of despair can still be heard to this day!"

"That's Andrew crying over his taxes," shouted someone.

Peter waggled a finger, "Joke yee not, my fine friend, for this is a story of lost love! The stories tell of a king who wanted her for his own but she, being of proud lineage and untarnished propriety, refused his advances and so he laid siege to this place and burned it down!" He jabbed his finger towards Lambert, "That man's family rebuilt this place on the original site and it remains standing here to this day. But Lorna, bless her heart, came back. She helped the wounded at Culloden and…"

His voice droned on, recounting various pieces of Lorna's history, and Lambert turned to Miles, leaning into his ear, "How the hell does he know all this?"

Miles shrugged, "His brother is a professor of history at King's College and has access to all sorts of stuff. Andrew, he's dug up some amazing things. I'll tell you, after the party."

Lambert, his shoulders growing tense, had a sudden urge to drink another brandy.

"So, there are four little scenes," continued Peter, "and I want you to get into groups and act each of the scenes out. To the winners…" He jumped down from the table and went to the far corner, returning with a wooden crate cradled in his arms, which he placed with great reverence on the tabletop. He gave a theatrical flurry of his arm, "… a crate of the finest Burgundy wine." He grinned. "From Vézelay!"

Steel fingers gripped Lambert around the throat. For a moment, he thought he would faint, but Miles held onto his arm and helped him to a chair. "Christ, are you all right, Andrew?"

But Lambert could not speak, the thumping of his heart becoming stronger, and he dragged his hand across his face to wipe away the sweat springing out over his brow. Miles thrust a glass of brandy into his hand and Lambert stared at the amber liquid, wanting to run away. "Vézelay," he croaked, and looked up. "Why the hell did he get the wine from there?"

Lambert refused to take part, preferring to sit in the corner, still giddy, and watch. Four scenes, the guests by now much the worse for drink, spending most of their time laughing and pawing at one another's clothes. One girl lost her blouse and then her bra, whilst one of the men dropped his trousers and somebody screamed. It would seem everyone's interpretations of Lorna's disappearances had more to do with sex than reality.

"I want to play strip 'Mousetrap'," somebody said, and everything soon degenerated into blind, confused grappling, with couples falling to the floor to kiss and writhe together under tables and across the hearthrug.

"Ah, the excesses of youth," slurred Peter, coming up to Lambert. He'd lost his coat, his shirt ripped to the waist. A girl clung to his arm, hair dishevelled, a glass of wine slopping over her hand. "I have a little surprise, old friend." He raised a single eyebrow, clinked his teeth with his own glass, and downed it in one.

"A surprise?" Lambert shook his head, "I think I've had enough of those for one night, Peter. Why don't we—"

"Nonsense, old man!" He whirled around, with such a burst of unexpected strength, the girl lost her balance and crashed to the ground, where she broke into uncontrolled laughter. "Boys and girls," roared Peter, ignoring the girl at his feet, "My own wee beauties! We have come to the finale of the charades. You've all done well, but there can be only one winner and our dear host," he threw his hand out towards Lambert, "has chosen the winner."

Lambert frowned and went to speak, but Peter silenced him with a sharp look.

"The winning group is, Claude and Suzanne, Elizabeth and Evelyn!"

Those who could cheered, some applauded, most raised their glasses. Claude, a bespectacled tall, angular individual swung Suzanne to him and kissed her full on the mouth. As his hand delved under her skirt Lambert could clearly see she was naked underneath. He groaned. And then he spotted Evelyn gliding towards him. She pulled up a chair and sat down. Beyond her, Lambert saw the Vézelay Burgundy presented to the so-called winners and then the music began. Evelyn leaned forward and picked up his hand. "You don't say much, do you?"

He blinked and turned to her for the first time, drawn to her full lips. "I'm not feeling too good," he said.

"Oh, that's a shame." She patted his hand. "This castle. Is it really yours?"

Lambert nodded. "It's been in my family for over two hundred and fifty years. We were granted a license by King George the Second to rebuild here, as a reward for fighting on his side during the Forty-Five Rising."

She shook her head and laughed, taking a drink from her glass. "I haven't got a single clue about anything you've just said."

He joined her laughter. "Well, it's not all that important really. I rarely think about it, the history of this place. I spent most of my formative years far away."

"But you've become intrigued, or so Miles told us, about a mystery woman? A woman your father knew?"

Lambert considered launching into a full explanation, but did not wish to change a light-hearted conversation into something more serious. So, he shrugged, pulled a face, "Well, something like that."

"You don't want to talk about it?"

"I'd rather have another drink," he raised his empty glass.

"A dance? Would you like to dance?" She swivelled on her chair and gestured towards the three or four couples who were moving around the space in the centre of the room to the sounds of a group Lambert did not know. "I'd like to dance," she said.

"Very well. Let's see what we can do!"

He welcomed the opportunity to loosen himself up. Besides, his foot was so much better now, the pain almost gone. So they went to join the others and the dancing took over, transporting them to another place, where worries and concerns did not dwell.

When, after over half a dozen songs, he finally returned to his seat, bathed in sweat, shirt unbuttoned to the waist, and more breathless than he had been for a long time. "I am totally unfit," he said, downing a glass of water.

Evelyn grinned and he studied her, realising with a jolt she bore no resemblance whatsoever to the images of Lorna which dominated his thoughts. Perhaps this was why he experienced no desire for her whatsoever. He couldn't fathom it. She was slim, attractive, a wonderful dancer, she filled her jeans spectacularly, and yet … He decided not to pursue this line of reason, putting it down to the drink and was about to say something totally innocuous when Peter once more piped up, climbing onto the table as before, but a little less assuredly this time. The music stopped. He swayed as he spoke. "My lovelies … a short pause in our revelry, but we have with us the lovely Cheryl!"

Some people applauded, but most turned quizzical looks towards the said Cheryl, who nodded, waved her hand a little, and beamed, "Yes, that's me folks."

"Cheryl is somebody a little bit out of the ordinary."

"Please shut up, Peter."

"No, it's true. And I won't have you heckling me. This is my moment, you hussy."

"Dog breath."

"Bless you," said Peter, raising his glass, "that reminds me. The taste of a good malt always improves the palette!" He drained the glass, smacked his lips, and threw out his arms, "Cheryl, my lovelies, is a clairvoyant."

A few gasps, even more sniggers.

"Is this true, Cheryl?" asked another girl, sitting with her legs crossed, revealing a well muscled thigh, which Miles was spending a lot of time stroking.

Cheryl pursed her lips, "Well, I've *heard* things. My mum took me to a séance, and I saw some stuff, which nobody could explain, not even the medium. It was she who told me I had 'the sight'. So…"

"You see," said Peter, "we have a *medium*. So, with all this talk of mysterious disappearances and sightings of weird inexplicable happenings, let us hold a séance."

Lambert groaned and put his head in his hand.

"What's the matter?" asked Evelyn, touching his arm.

He looked up. "Jesus, a fucking séance? This is becoming a farce."

Around him, some of the guests, those still able, were arranging a table and chairs in the centre of the room. People were laughing as they did so, and Cheryl stepped amongst them, clapping her hands to gain attention.

"Listen everyone," she said above the din, "if you're not willing to do this seriously, there really is no point."

"Oh come on, Cheryl," slurred Peter, climbing down from his dais, "it's just a bit of fun."

"Fun or not, there are certain things you have to do in order for it ... Look, it may not even work, but we have no chance unless people are open-minded and can keep themselves focused."

"Well that rules me out," said Evelyn standing up. "I don't believe in it. So ... what do I do?"

"Sit it out," said Peter, becoming serious all of a sudden. "We want this to work, guys. So, come on. Cheryl, what do we need?"

"Change the music. Something soft, calming."

"There's some Brian Eno somewhere," said Lambert and went over to the corner cabinet where he kept his CDs. Technology may have advanced, many preferring to download, but Lambert kept all of his CDs and soon fished out the desired album. He put it into the machine.

"There can't be any flowers, or anything containing minerals in the room. You'll have to take out the food."

"*What?*" Peter laughed, "but there's tons of it. Andrew, is there another room we can use?"

"There's the library," said Miles standing up. "There's no food or anything in there. It's perfect."

Lambert felt his stomach beginning to twist. The library had become his inner sanctum, and he had hoped the party would not spill over into it. He sighed, "All right. There's a table and enough chairs."

"Good," said Cheryl. "We'll go in there, and those of you who are sceptical, you can stay in here."

"And eat the food," put in Peter, and clamping Lambert around the shoulders, steered the host towards the door, "This is going to be great fun, Andrew. Trust me."

But Lambert felt nothing of the sort. As his stomach churned, and his throat became dry, he began to regret ever having agreed to this gathering. Lorna was his property, his fantasy, his desire. To have these *outsiders* attempting to infiltrate was not something to welcome.

Peter gripped his arm, "Andrew. It really is only for fun."

"Let's hope so," replied Lambert, trying to sound enthusiastic.

He failed.

20

They found candles and placed them in brass holders in the centre of the table. There was no other light. The music Lambert chose hummed in the background, soft, lilting sounds designed to set the mind at peace.

Cheryl sat at the head, with Lambert at the opposite side facing her. Around were a number of others, but most of the partygoers had chosen to remain in the other room, an arrangement which suited Lambert just fine. He felt some form of barrier had developed between himself and Evelyn, one which he found unsettling.

"Will we use some sort of pentagram?"

Everyone's eyes turned to Lambert. Only Cheryl spoke. "What do you know about such things, Andrew?"

"Only what Sinclair told me."

"Sinclair? Your … butler?"

"Apparently he's studied such *esoteric* stuff. He mentioned something about mandalas."

"Mystical symbols which represent the power of the universe," continued Cheryl, her eyes focusing on Lambert with a keen intensity. "Carl Jung said once you dreamed of mandalas you had achieved nirvana." She laced her fingers. "Pentagrams are sensed to protect us from evil entities, called up from the pits of hell."

"Holy shit," gasped Miles. "I thought you said this was going to be fun!"

She shot him a scathing glance. "Anything to do with spirits can never be thought of as *fun*, Miles. But rest assured, we're not conjuring up anything bad. At least I hope not."

"No," said Lambert, "it's not going to be bad."

Cheryl smiled. "No. And that's why we won't be needing a pentagram."
Lambert nodded.

"Sit with your palms down on the wooden surface of the table," said Cheryl quietly. "We must all try and keep ourselves calm and quiet. If you don't think you can do this, please leave."

"This is all a bit heavy," mumbled Miles, who received a volley of scathing looks from the others, especially Peter whose whole persona had altered, becoming far more serious. He scowled and Miles forced a smile. "All right, point taken. Let's try…"

Lambert closed his eyes, doing his best to blank out images from the party. Unconsciously, an image of Sinclair came into his head, the manservant with his arms crossed, standing at the top of the steps leading to the house. "I'm not here to criticise, sir," he said, his voice taking on a tone of sadness, "but I have found these last few weeks particularly difficult."

Lambert blinked at the hazy light of the candles. The far corners were in total darkness, the night well advanced, and a definite chill settled over the room, one that he had not noticed just a few moments ago. Why would he think of Sinclair, and those words? He knew Sinclair had never said anything remotely similar to him recently, if ever.

"We're here to listen, to understand," said Cheryl. Her eyes remained closed, mouth partly opened. Lambert studied her. Another attractive girl, but so unlike Evelyn. Her features were round, almost elfin like. A small girl, short blonde hair and, when they were opened, dazzling blue eyes. There was an innocence about her, which made her strangely alluring. If Lambert had the choice, and the courage, he might even ask her for a date. He suspected she was with Peter, but he couldn't be sure.

Next to her, Cheryl had a piece of paper and pencil. With her eyes still closed, she began to write, repeating the words for all to hear, "Tell us your name, who you are. We're friends."

No one moved, the mood growing ever more sombre. Lambert chanced a glance towards Miles, whose head was hanging down. He appeared to be snoozing. The others too seemed subdued, as if overcome for the moment by the deepening ambience. Not frightening in any way, but unlike anything Lambert had experienced before.

Something moved in the corner. He tensed. He couldn't be sure, as the shadow was so black, but certainly, there was a presence. Someone else, perhaps, who had come to join the group.

"We are not here to judge or condemn," said Cheryl, her voice light, almost as if she were falling into some form of trance, her words detached. Indeed, the more Lambert concentrated, the more convinced he became her voice was undergoing some surreal change, both in volume and intonation.

"We wish no harm," she continued. "We are friends."

"Friends?"

Lambert almost cried out. The word, uttered with heavy disbelief, was that of a woman. Lambert's hands pressed down hard on the table. Another glance around assured him nobody else had stirred. Even Cheryl seemed to be slipping further into her trance.

"I'm so much more than a friend."

Lambert held on, eyes on stalks, drawn towards the far corner, the area where he had first noticed the movement. And there it was again. The slightest stirring, a fluttering of something, like a ripple in the atmosphere.

"Can you see me, Andrew?"

He snapped his head from left to right, mouth open, wanting to speak, to tell everyone, but no words came. Nothing came, except the pounding of his heart, the gripping of every muscle in his body by an invisible force of immense power.

"What a wonderful coincidence. I was visiting my castle and here you are."

She appeared from out of the air, floating from the shadows and Andrew knew he was witnessing something, which simply could not be.

It was Lorna. She stood, as real and as tangible as any other person in the room. Her auburn hair hung heavy to her shoulders, her full lips curled into a smile, and those eyes, drinking him in. She was dressed in a velveteen gown of deepest purple, richly embroidered with a repeating pattern of interlaced flowers and vines and around her slim neck, a necklace of blue beads on a silver chain.

"Do not be afraid, you're on the right path, Andrew."

He could not move. He tried, but nothing worked. So he sat, transfixed, as if the entire world, for that one incredible moment, existed for them, and them alone. No one mattered, the room receding into blackness, the air thick and heavy. Even Cheryl had gone from his sight. The only person remaining was Lorna. She drew nearer and laid her delicate hand upon his shoulder.

"Do not be afraid," she repeated, her voice so soft, cooler than a spring, as light as clouds, "it is only a vision." He longed for her to carry him away, never to return to this place or any other, to remain by her side and feel the glow of her body, the warmth of her spirit forever. She reached over and brushed the back of her hand down his cheek. His head span, eyes becoming heavy, the desire building from deep, deep within.

"Oh Lorna," he managed, eyes now closed.

"I want you to reveal some hidden secrets of the castle. Why I'm here and what you can do to help me… to help us, to be precise."

"To help us?" He looked up, breathing becoming ragged as he struggled against a mounting anger. "Or to get me into that damned wheelchair? You caused the accident, remember."

"Sh…" Lorna leaned into his shoulders "Umm … you're sweet when you're angry."

Andrew moved a little bit back, trying to escape her irresistible power of seduction, but he failed, resistance crumbling.

"I know you love mystery, Andrew. Don't you?"

"Yes, but this mystery is all to do with you. That night, everything that has happened since. Why are you pursuing me?"

"You should unravel the mystery by yourself, Andrew."

Her fingers played with his scalp and he became lost in the sensation of her touch, taking him further and further away…

They travelled to market on the first day of spring on a sturdy cart pulled by two horses. The sky, unsullied by clouds, stretched out before them and offered Lorna a sense of comfort she had not known throughout the long winter months. Snow had imprisoned them within the walls of Castle Strythe and once the store of salted meat and smoked herring depleted, nothing remained to eat but coarse grains, dried peas and beans. The thought of being able to stock up on well-needed supplies made her mouth drool at the prospect.

When they reached Annandale, they discovered English troops billeted there, strutting around the market square as if they owned the place. Given the whispered conversations Lorna and her two servants, Gilbraith and Lewis, noticed when they arrived, this seemed the case.

They tied up the cart and Lewis helped her down. As they made their way towards the market stalls a nearby bunch of soldiers, loitering on the corner, made lewd and suggestive remarks as Lorna past and at one point, she had to restrain Gilbraith from leaping down and confronting them.

"They are base and ignorant," she said softly, patting his arm.

"They are insulting," he said through gritted teeth.

"Calm yourself, good Gilbraith. We will spend money, purchase our wares and be gone. We will have no trouble here."

But trouble did follow.

At an inn some soldiers, drunk beyond measure, stumbled and fell into the street, two of them urinating on the wall, and a third repeating the same action but on an old, wizened beggar huddled up in a shop doorway.

When Gilbraith intervened, they buried a knife into his side, dragged him bleeding into an alleyway and beat him to death.

Lorna, on hearing the news, stood as if struck dumb, eyes gazing into nothing, unable to think clearly. At last, Lewis guided her to the mayor who sat and listened, put his face in his hands, breathing heavily. "I cannot do anything," he said, his voice filled with despair. "The English have the town sealed up as tight as a boar-trap. I am powerless."

"Since when has civil justice deserted the good streets of Annandale," she demanded, leaning over his desk on her fists.

"Since the English arrived," he said, his expression miserable, defeated. "There is nothing I can do."

"So, these men, *animals* more like, they are free to do as they please?"

He spread out his hands, a gesture which implied their conversation was at an end.

She went out into the daylight with Lewis by her side.

"Mistress, we should go home. I will talk to one or two of the local people and see if I can arrange something for Gilbraith, prepare him for burial." He ran a hand through his hair and sighed. "Something, but for the love of God in this damned place, I know not what it shall be."

But Lorna stared at him expressionless, her eyes set hard in her cold, drawn face.

"I shall seek out their commander," she said at last and before Lewis could voice his concerns, she turned on her heels and stormed away.

She found their lord after questioning several groups of men, most of whom leered at her, licking their lips and grabbing hold of their crotches. One man, a burly fellow with a mass of red beard sprouting out from under his chainmail coif, seemed to offer her more than mere lechery, and he bowed from the waist and showed her to the where the commander was barracked.

"We've taken over the Guild Hall," he said as they tramped across the cobbles and up the steps of a large, well-presented building off the main square.

"Why are so many of you here," she asked as he pushed the door open and stepped aside to allow her entry.

"There have been raids all along the borders."

"Reivers?"

"Aye, only this time we suspect they have been aided by Scottish troops. We're here to sort it out, my lady." He shook his head and rubbed his hands together, "I'd sooner be down in Derby than here. Too damned cold, if you'll pardon my language."

"You're a good and gracious man," she said, "I shall make sure your lord knows it."

He dipped his head and she went inside.

A large open space confronted her, rushers on the ground, but little else. A few soldiers milled about, talking in hushed tones, and in the furthest corner, another door with a man-at-arms positioned outside, armed with a large, evil looking halberd.

The soldier, who had accompanied her, grunted and waved her forward. Lorna followed, ignoring the men arching their eyebrows as she crossed the room.

"Is Lord Melling within," the soldier asked the guard.

"He is. Who wants to know?"

"This lady," he turned and gave her a quizzical look.

"I am Lady Strythe, of Strythe manor. I am here to speak with your commander."

The guard did not appear impressed. "And what might be the manner of your business, my lady?"

"Accusations of murder."

Sir Richard Melling, surrounded by fully-armoured men-at-arms, was clad in half-plate, his sword and helmet lying next to a large piece of parchment, upon which was scrawled a detailed map of the area. He paused in the process of tracing a mailed finger along a river when Lorna came in, and his mouth fell open. Three other men, who wore surcoats adorned with family crests denoting their position as knights, stiffened, exchanged looks, and waited.

"Begging you pardon, my lord," said the guard, lowering his head, "an urgent request for an audience."

Melling frowned, allowing his eyes to settle upon Lorna. In an instant, he turned to his companions, and waved them out. They seemed to resent the intrusion, grumbled and groaned, but nevertheless gathered up what equipment they had and sloped out. The guard waited and Melling, pausing for a moment to take in another survey of Lorna's body, came around the table, put his fists on his hips, and smiled towards her. "And what type of audience might that be?"

"Begging your pardon, my lord, but she did not—"

"You are dismissed," said Melling, without taking his eyes from Lorna's face. When the door closed, he grinned. "Well, my lovely, how can I help?"

"You can give me justice."

He cocked his head, "Justice? How so?"

"My servant, a family retainer, was murdered by several of your soldiers down in the market square not two hours ago."

Melling pulled a face, rocking back on his heels, "That's quite an accusation."

"It is the truth."

"Clearly you believe it so, but have you any proof?"

"I have witnesses. My other servant, Lewis, and—"

"*Independent* witnesses, my lady. Nothing less will do."

"There are many who saw it."

He chewed his lip, considered her for a long time, then returned to the table, swept up his sword, and buckled the belt around his waist. "I can't promise anything," he said with his back to her, "I have over five hundred troops billeted here. It may not be so easy to pick these particular men out." He swung around. "But if I can find them, and they admit their action, I'll hang them before nightfall."

"That would suffice, my lord."

He smiled. "Might it? Mm…" He rubbed his chin, "Perhaps afterwards we can think of a way you can pay me for my services."

Lorna frowned, aware of his meaning, but not willing to give him the satisfaction. "I have little money, my lord, but what I have, I will gladly contribute to your—"

An explosion of sound from without caused them both to stop and whirl towards the door. A pounding of boots across the floor, raised voices, the clink and crash of arms. Before Melling could speak, the door burst open and a young man, dressed in exquisitely crafted armour, filled the doorway. Bareheaded, his youthful face lean and bronzed by the sun, he stood with one hand gripping the hilt of his gold-encrusted sword, and his smiled broadened.

"Well, well, Sir Stephen. What have we here?"

"My liege," said Melling, dropping to his knees, head bowed low.

The newcomer, still grinning, turned his keen, intelligent eyes towards Lorna, a single eyebrow arching. "And you, my lady. Do you not kneel?"

Her lips parted, as a simmering wave of curiosity and pleasure mingled within her. "For whom should I kneel, sir?"

The youth threw back his head and laughed. "You have lived too long in these desolate parts, madam," muttered Sir Melling, his head still lowered. "For this is King Richard the Second of England, my lady. The fairest and greatest king that has ever lived."

And when the youth laughed again, Lorna recognised his air of natural superiority and knew she would soon receive justice and perhaps something more.

The candles had burned low, their flames feeble, flickering pathetically as they gave a few, last desperate efforts to emit light. Lambert took some moments to gather his thoughts, allowing his mind to piece together the fragments of his dream. For it had to be a dream, no other explanation were possible. He looked around him, the others dozed, some mumbling incoherently, and even Cheryl, sitting back in her chair, seemed lost in sleep.

"I'm here, Andrew."

He shot a glance to his right and saw her, standing as real as she ever did. As in the road, her face was filled with an expression of warmth, of openness and caring. A stunning face, captivating, alluring. A face to dream of, to long to kiss. She glided forward. "They came to my castle, Andrew. *This* castle. And they burned."

"I ... I don't understand. Who did?"

"The English. I showed you, in your dreams. They came and laid siege, broke down the walls and ran amok inside. They killed the few servants we had and took my husband out into the bailey, where they prepared to cut off his head."

Lambert gasped. "Dear God. Richard did that, the king?"

"Not personally, but by his order. He made advances to me, Andrew. Advances I did not reciprocate, and he became angry. More than angry, unable to comprehend how any woman dare refuse him. But he was arrogant, Andrew. A mere child when it came to love. They said his wife could not bear children, but I know this was not the case. Anne was perfectly capable; it was *he* who was not."

"So he took his revenge by burning this place down?"

She nodded. "When we first met, I respected him, perhaps even in awe of him. A king. Can you imagine? That such a man could look upon me as an equal, such a thing was beyond imagining. I was blind to his longing, thinking he merely wished to help me, help my family and protect us from further raids. I misjudged him. When I told him of my love for another, he turned his anger upon me. I believe it was an anger, which had been brewing for a long time. I was merely the catalyst, or, to be more precise, my rejection of him was. I struck him so hard I knocked him down and I fled, much to my shame. I learned later my husband did not die. They sparred him, setting him adrift."

"The legend, of him wandering the glen in search of you? It is true?"

She bowed her head. "I had no knowledge. I believed him murdered."

Lambert pulled in a breath, cast his eye around the table at his sleeping friends. "Why can they not hear us?"

"We are outside of their world, Andrew. Through your dreams, I have enabled you to experience my presence. I am real." To confirm her words, she reached out and took his hand. "You see? You can feel me, and I you."

"But…" He gazed down at her slim, tapered fingers, "What do you want from me, Lorna?"

"Your help. Your trust. Love."

"But you said you loved another."

She gazed down to the ground. "Andrew, after they burned the castle down, they ransacked the inside and took away many family treasures. But of all things they stole, the most valuable was my portrait, the painting Master Devoir made of me. You remember, in the garden? I sensed your presence. Although I could not see you, I knew you were there."

Lambert pulled his hand away, the fear becoming palpable. "So, Devoir … it was he?"

She did not answer.

"Wait. This cannot be true. I must be dreaming now. I'm going mad."

"No," she took his hand again, squeezing it. "Andrew, your grandfather was exactly the same, forever grappling with the truth of his senses."

He gaped at her, unable for a moment to comprehend the enormity of her words. "You mean, you *knew* him?"

"Yes, Andrew. He helped me, or at least he tried to. He did his very best but something … He was resistant, Andrew. His rejection of the powers which permeate the universe was an obstacle to our future." She smiled at him. "You look so like him, do you know that?"

. "This … none of this can be happening. It *can't* be happening."

"Believe me, Andrew, what you experience at this moment is real. What you have seen in your dreams are memories; they happened. The painting is the conduit. They took it, Andrew." She gripped his hand again, squeezing tight. "I must have it back, and the secrets it holds. And you are going to help me do just that."

21

When Andrew Lambert wandered into the dining room sometime later, head filled with cotton wool, eyes sticky, barely able to focus, his few remaining guests were still asleep. He stood and studied them, most lying with their limbs intertwined, semi-naked, food and spilled glasses of drink all around them. He folded his arms and leaned against the door well.

A shadow moved next to his shoulder and he turned, alarmed, but then relaxed as Miles, dishevelled, hair wild, face red, smacking dried lips, came up close. "Christ," he muttered, "how long were we out for?"

"I don't know," said Lambert, his body growing more alert and light, soon wide-awake. "I have no idea of the time."

Cheryl emerged, similar in her state of exhaustion to Miles, and snaked an arm around his waist. "I'm thirsty," she said. She caught sight of Lambert and forced a smile. "I'm sorry, Andrew."

"Sorry? Why are you sorry?"

"For the séance being so crap."

"Why do you say that?"

"Well…" She gave a tiny shrug, held Miles closer. "Nothing materialised did it? I felt sure we would get something."

Lambert wanted to reveal all, wanted to grab her by the arms and shake her, tell her what a damn, blind fool she was. Of course something had happened – more than something! Lorna. Had she not seen, or heard? He threw his gaze from her to Miles and back again, saw the despondency, and realised in that single moment, he, and he alone, had experienced Lorna's appearance.

Cheryl reached out and lightly took hold of his arm, "I did *feel* something, Andrew."

"You did?"

"Yes, but nothing at all like I expected."

"What was it," interjected Miles, scratching at his scalp, "A Red-Indian? I've heard mediums often use them as some form of spiritual guide. Chief Whopping-big-plums, or something."

Cheryl shot him a furious glance and he paled, looked away. "No," she said, and turned again to Lambert. "It was about you, Andrew."

"*Me*? What about me?"

"I had the most total belief you had lived before, hundreds of years ago."

"Like a reincarnation?" asked Miles.

"Yes," she said with renewed energy, "that's exactly right!" She smiled at Lambert. "Did you feel it, Andrew? During the séance, a huge wave of warmth, love even."

He went to speak, lay out every emotion from the fire which blazed inside, but stopped himself, knowing neither would believe him. So, he smiled. "I've never had the slightest notion of my having lived a previous life. None at all."

"Well I did. I saw you. You were young, and you had a wife. But … you appeared troubled, as if all of the world's problems were on your shoulders. I don't know, but an enormous sense of sadness surrounded you. You seemed lost. Afraid almost."

"Afraid of what?"

"I don't know."

Lambert squeezed his lips together, "Cheryl, I think I'm beginning to understand." He reached out and took her by the shoulders. "You are certain it was me you saw?"

"Yes. It had to be. Your face, your hair, the way you … Who else could it be?"

"My grandfather." Lambert gripped her arms, "Everybody says I am the spitting image of him. It must have been him you saw, because he lived here too. He had a wife, a son. It must have been him, but why on earth would you experience such a thing?"

Cheryl was nodding her head. "Yes, now I come to think of it, I think I've seen a photograph, here in the castle. It must have been its memory which I saw in my mind's eye, but when I tried to focus in on the details, it all blurred."

"Great," cried Miles, clapping his hands together. "It's like waiting for the punch line that never comes. There was an Englishman, Irishman and Scotsman in a bar ... and they all bought each other drinks and became the best of friends. Crap!" He laughed, and Lambert dropped his hands.

Cheryl stared at him. "I got a sense of something more, Andrew. Not merely an image, but other things, another woman. A painter. I received such energy from her, such determination to succeed."

Lambert's mouth went slack. "A *painter?*"

She nodded. "I have no idea why these things came to me. Writing too, lots of words stamping out across a computer screen. Andrew, what the hell does it all mean?"

Before Lambert could offer up an explanation, Miles cut in, "I thought you said you didn't experience anything?" He slapped Cheryl on the bottom, and grabbed hold of her hand. "Come on, let's go to bed."

She giggled and Lambert watched them swerve out of sight, making their way to one of the upstairs rooms. Lambert remained standing for a few moments, considering how to explain the mess of the house to Sinclair. He considered calling a cleaning agency, but it was still far too early. He went back into the library, spotted Peter stretched out on the floor with a girl, arms, and legs entwined, his hand between her thighs, her arm around his neck. Both were asleep. There was no sign of anyone else. His eyes fell on a half-finished glass of whisky. He discovered it to be palatable and threw it down his throat. He went out into the hallway and stopped, an invisible force, a magnet of some sort, drawing him into the study. He gazed at the fireplace, to the paintings of the castle and then, scanning downwards, to the family photographs. He went to them, picked up the first gilded frame. His mother and father stared back at him, smiling, father in his kilt, the castle in the background. The next, his father again only this time with his own father, Andrew's grandfather. The image was blurry, taken at a time before fast shutter speeds. Grandfather must have moved, his face not quite in focus. Andrew put it down, convinced a detached voice was urging him to look again. He resisted and went out, feeling distinctly deflated.

Upstairs, he washed before going into his room. He crossed to the large balcony window, pushed open the doors and went outside. The night air was chill and he peered into the distance to the horizon and noted the first streaks of grey heralding the dawn. He yawned, returned to his room, took off his clothes, and climbed into bed.

As soon as he pulled the cover over him, a massive wave of exhaustion washed over him but he had no recollection of drifting off to sleep. Indeed, his mind became a total blank. Until somebody slipped in beside him.

For a moment, lying in the darkness, he believed he was dreaming again. But this could not be his imagination. The whole bed dipped with the weight of the other person as they got in next to him and when the hand reached over his abdomen and slowly crept down to his groin, he knew this was real.

He turned and every pore, every nerve ending, every part of his body grew alive, as if an over-powering surge of electricity pulsed through him. His erection sprang out hard against his pants and he reached out and gasped to find her naked and so close.

"Andrew," her voice, barely a whisper, seemed to promise so much and as her hand rested on his pulsing erection, all conscious thought left him and he reacted through pure instinct.

Her body was a dream, his fingers sliding over silken flesh, her nipples responding to first his touch and then his lips. He folded his mouth over her breasts and moaned at the luxurious taste of her sweet, perfumed skin.

She whispered, "Let me show you." She took the lead and instructed him, without words, how to touch and tease, finding the centre of her desire. "My pearl," she whispered, throwing back the cover to expose her lithe body, her legs opening, "reach inside my shell, my love. Seek out my pearl... Here, let me guide you..." And he, a willing pupil, followed her, caressing her soft, giving flesh. He was on fire, loins filled with urgent passion. "Slowly, it must be slow."

She gave herself to him completely, becoming as one, an embrace of souls. The exquisite feel of her body, her moans, the way she held onto him with so much desire. Raising himself up he stared into her eyes and smiled, "I love you," he said, kissed her, not wanting it to ever end, the pleasure surging through him intoxicating. Sweet, all consuming, a whirlwind of ecstasy.

It proved too much and he cried out as he came, weeping into her soft flesh, crying like a child with the beauty of their union.

He lay on top of her and she held him close, kissing his ear and neck, tiny moans seeping from her throat. His hands ran down her body and his voice, trembling, hoarse, uncertain, "I've never..." he began.

"Sssh, words will serve only to melt away feeling," she said, caressing his scalp. "We are one now, you and I."

He turned his head, trying to catch the details of her features in the dark, but only her eyes, shining bright, revealed her joy. Lambert grinned and kissed her, long, soft, rolling his mouth over hers, tongues meeting.

"You think you could do that again?" she said when at last he drew back his face, her finger nails tracing snake-like patterns across his buttocks.

"Almost certainly," he said, a surge of energy welling up from within. He knew from where it came as his hands enclosed the firmness of her breasts.

With the morning light streaming through his bedroom windows, Lambert lay on his back, forearm draped over his brow, staring into the distance. His body, although drained, felt more alive than he ever remembered, and such positivity and expectancy gripped him he wanted to jump up, dance around the room and sing so loud the entire house would wake. He rolled over to tell her of his happiness and stared into nothing.

The bed was empty, the indentation in the mattress the only clue of her presence. For a moment, he wondered if it could all be a dream, another vivid, captivating episode of pure imagination. He put his fist in his mouth and bit down hard. Surely, it could not be so.

Despair overwhelmed him and he slumped down on the edge of the bed. His eyes, though moist, settled on the unmistakeable evidence of their love on the sheets, and he grinned, reached across to feel the warmth of her lingering in the cotton, and her perfume on the pillow. He pressed his head into the soft, giving material and whispered a gentle 'thank you' to the Universe.

He dressed quickly, pulling on a t-shirt and chinos, and padded down stairs to try to find her. Instead, he found Miles at the oven, cracking eggs into a pan. "Morning," he grunted, turning the flame down as the water came up to the boil. "I was about to come and wake you."

"Oh?" Andrew went to the cafétierre and tipped out a cupful of coffee.

Miles cast him a glance from the corner of his eye and smirked, "You seem happy."

"So I should be! Where's Evelyn?"

Miles frowned, returning to his eggs and checked the heat once more. He put two slices of brown bread into the toaster. "Why are you asking about her?"

"Because," smiled Andrew, leaning with his back against the worktop, "She is amazing. She came to me last night, Miles. After the séance. I'm not sure—"

"Hold on," said Miles, laughing, "you're telling me Evelyn got into bed with you?"

"Yes!" He drained the coffee. "Christ, you make shit coffee."

"And you, bonny lad, talk nothing but shit. *Evelyn*? So, what did she do, screw your arse off?"

Lambert spluttered, "Absolutely! She was … Christ, Miles, I've *never* made love to such an incredibly gorgeous woman in all my life. She was *amazing*."

"Another dream, Andrew? Jesus."

"*No*, Miles! It was real, I promise you. This was like nothing that had gone on before. She slipped in next to me and, jeez, she just took over. It was … I don't have the words. I came like a fucking train!"

The bread popped up but Miles wasn't interested. He held his friend's gaze. "Okay, Andrew. This girl. Are you sure it was Evelyn. I mean, did she *tell* you?"

"*What*? Well, no, she didn't … But, who the hell else could it be?"

"Because Evelyn went home, Andrew." Lambert gaped at him. "Remember we saw you after the séance, me and Cheryl? I took her upstairs, remember?" Lambert nodded, throat growing dry. "Well, we found Evelyn in the bathroom, throwing her guts up. Cheryl took her home."

"She did *what*?"

"Took her home. Evelyn was in a right bloody state, drunk like you wouldn't believe. So Cheryl took her home, and the shitty thing is, she never fucking well came back! Sent me a fucking text, the bitch." His voice changed to a singsong mockery of Cheryl's, "*Sorry, lovely, but I'm going to stay here with Evie.*" He turned away and started putting far too much butter on the toast. "Bloody cow."

Lambert stood, mouth partly open, staring at the floor, "But … But, if it wasn't Evelyn, then who? I didn't speak to anyone else, and…"

Miles looked up. "Andrew? What the hell's the matter?"

"The séance, Miles."

"Yeah. I was there, remember? Nothing happened, only some jumbled-up pictures in Cheryl's head. Don't you recall her saying—"

"She was wrong, Miles. Something *did* happen. I saw her. Lorna. She came out of the shadows, as real as you are here now. She touched me, spoke to me. I tell you, without a doubt, she was *real*."

"Andrew, you've got to stop doing this to your—"

"Listen to me," he snapped, leaning forward at a rush, gripping his friend by the arms, "it's true, damn you, Miles! I'm not going mad, I swear to you. She materialised and later, she got into bed with me and we made love. It was her, it had to be."

"She couldn't have done, Andrew. For Christ's sake! It must have been somebody else."

"*Who?*" He shook his head. "There is nobody else. Peter's girlfriend? No, that isn't possible. Cheryl and Evelyn had left, there *was nobody else!*"

"Then you must have imagined it."

"You want to see the sheets? She's all over them!"

Miles ripped his arms free of his friend's grip. "I'm not listening to this. I've gone along with everything, but no more, Andrew. If you're not willing to see somebody, to talk all this out, then…" He shrugged. "I can't. I can't have anything to do with it anymore."

Lambert dropped his shoulders and blew out a breath. He turned away and shuffled back to his room, climbing the stairs as a man condemned.

The room was as he left it, her shape on the bed, and he sat down, pressed the pillow into his face, and breathed in her scent. It had happened, everything was real, but despite the realisation of the truth, he nevertheless broke into tears as the despair enveloped him.

22

Sinclair returned sometime after breakfast and found Lambert in the garden, sitting with his foot propped up on a stool, enjoying the sunshine. "Good morning," he said, coming around to face Lambert, who smiled.

"Sorry about the house. I haven't had a chance to clean up yet."

Sinclair shrugged. "You had a good time?"

"Yes. Yes, all very *interesting*. And you?"

Sinclair nodded, looked around for another chair and spotted one over by the shed. He fetched it, eased open the legs and sat down. "I have something for you," he said. "I saw it by sheer chance, in a bookshop." He held up his hand. "I bought this book on Richard the Second. An interesting king, ascended the throne at ten years of age, faced down Wat Tyler at fourteen, lied through his teeth, and eventually was deposed. *But* ..." He flicked open the book where a piece of card kept the place, and ran his finger over the text. "He came to Scotland, to fight. Nothing major, a number of skirmishes. The Scots were asserting themselves, pressing forward claims to this area," he made a sweeping gesture through the air, "all around here. Richard joined some of his troops for a few days—"

"He laid siege to this castle," interjected Lambert, and smiled when Sinclair appeared surprised. "I've done research of my own, but thanks."

"Did you know he set fire to the place? Burnt it to the ground?"

"Yes. I know that."

"Do you know why?"

"Well," Lambert shifted uneasily in his chair, reached down and rubbed his ankle. Memories of how Miles reacted only hours ago troubled him. He didn't wish to cause the same responses from Sinclair. "I can guess."

"It was because of a woman."

Lambert nodded, remembering the dream, the one where he had been a virtual spectator. The siege, the mangonels. "Isn't it always?"

Sinclair turned again to the book, "There is little known, very few contemporary records, but a chronicler notes the king searched for a painting."

Lambert sat up, alert. "A painting?"

"Yes. So not a woman at all." Sinclair closed the book. "Rather, the *image* of one."

Lambert spent most of the day in the study after informing Sinclair he did not wish to be disturbed, under any circumstances. He needn't have bothered, the telephone did not ring once. Later, his dinner proved a sorry affair and he barely touched it. He pushed the plate away and sat back to stare out of the window. A deep developing melancholy settled over him. All through the day, after Miles had driven off in something of a rage, Lambert sat and considered the events of the previous twenty-four hours. No matter how much he tried to convince himself otherwise, he knew Lorna was real. They had made passionate, beautiful love … But where was she now?

He went into the parlour, picked up Sinclair's present and read a few paragraphs. His eyes soon became gritty and he put the book down, flicked through the television channels, pausing every so often to watch snippets of the news, or a panel game. The mindless, physically draining images of strangers laughing inanely at presenters who should know better than to nose-dive their careers into hosting such drivel. He was about to turn the television off when a programme came on which caught his attention. He leaned forward, his heart beginning to thump.

A documentary. All about Border Reivers, and the Battle of Otterburn.

Lambert went to bed, his mind in tatters.

Crows blackened the sky. Or were they rooks? Lambert never could tell the difference. Something about the beak, and a half remembered saying, 'If you see two crows together, they're rooks, and if you see a rook on its own, it's a crow.' He gave a dismissive chuckle, sat with hands on knees and squinted over the field.

He sat on a slight rise, a sort of hummock, and the grass was wet despite the sunshine. Below him, men busied themselves around the machines of war, the occasional stone racing upwards and outwards towards the castle, to smash against the solid looking walls. Lambert winced with every impact. Beside him, a group of knights on horseback waited, growing ever more restless. He could smell the sweat of horses and men, heard the creak of leather, the scream of metal plate.

"We're almost through," said a massive man-at-arms, lance in hand, shield slung over the side of his saddle. He wore a sword at his side, the visor of his iron helm titled back to expose a hard, determined face. "What are you orders, sire, when we break in?"

"Find the girl," said a slim, pasty looking youth. Lambert recognised him from his previous visit to this world of the past. Richard the Second, king of England. "I want her to watch it burn."

"And her father?"

"Tan his arse and set him adrift. He'll lose enough this day without us bringing an end to his sorry existence too."

"By your command, sire." The burly knight kicked at his mount's flanks and guided it down into the field below. An assembled group of spearmen came to attention as he rode past and Lambert strained to see what would happen next.

"Why do you want this damned, bloody painting?"

Another youth spoke, slightly older than Richard. He wore a surcoat emblazoned with his coat of arms in four quarters of blue, red and gold, topped by a crown indicating this was a knight of The Most Noble Order of the Garter.

"I want it, Robert," continued the king staring down at the castle, "because I have never seen such a thing in all my life. This *girl,* she refused me. Did you know that?"

"So all of this because she refused you? I can't believe it. You're married, first of all and besides, you can take any number of mistresses, both official and unofficial. Is this one endowed with a spirit, which might open a door into fellowship with God?"

"I fell in love with her from the first moment. She possesses an incredible power of seduction." He shifted in his saddle, "She is a beauty."

"So, this painting, it reminds you of her, is that it? You'd better imprison her in one of your castles and make love to her whenever you want."

The king's jowls reddened slightly. "Don't be so lewd, Rob. I saw the painting, damn your eyes, and it *moves.*"

"*Moves*? Everything moves, Richard, it depends on how much you've had to drink." He laughed, saw the look on his king's face, and grew serious again.

"Very well, I can see you're in no mood for japes. Tell me what you mean exactly?"

"What I say. In the painting, her face only becomes discernible from a certain angle, under particular lighting. She showed me, when I went visiting her. If you—"

"You mean you've been here before? When was this?"

"Several months ago. I arrived unannounced. Her husband greeted me like a fart; surly, without grace or manners. And she, she came to me wearing a thin wisp of a robe, underneath which her breasts and snatch were clear to see. She seemed pleased to see me, with no shame or coyness."

"So, what did you do? You coupled with her?"

Richard's eyes narrowed. "I took her into the garden and we sat on a bench. Her limbs were shimmering beneath her robe, Rob. I couldn't contain myself. I pulled her to the ground and she struck me."

"She did what? Struck you? And you did nothing?"

Lambert stood up. He'd heard enough, the anger brewing inside, and he strode forward. "You miserable little shit," he shouted, fists bunched. "I know who you are talking about and if I were you—"

The man called Robert was laughing, holding onto the pommel of his saddles, his body racked with convulsions, "Jesus God, Rich, a mere waif of a girl knocked you to the ground, and there's the truth of it."

"Shut your mouth, Robert."

"Tell me it isn't true." Robert leaned across and landed a playful punch on the king's arm, "I dare you. The truth. She hit you and almost knocked you out!"

The king turned away and levelled his gaze directly towards Lambert, who stood not two paces from him. "You're a sorry bastard," said Lambert.

"If you have to know," said the King, eyes closing.

"I do, Rich. Tell me the truth, damn you."

"Very well." He pulled in a breath. "I took her roughly by her dress. She struggled, it ripped, and she hit me, across the face. I have to admit, it brought tears to my eyes, more from shock than pain. And then she laughed." He snapped his head back to his friend. "So *I* struck *her*, Rob. She fell to the ground and I would have had there and then if her poxy husband had not intervened."

"He stopped you?"

"He came out of the castle like a wild boar, frothing at the mouth, telling me to leave his grounds. I took another look at her, with her gown all open and her legs … Christ, Rob. I swear to you now, I would have had her. I was like a piece of iron."

"But, methinks, her mockery brought you nothing but shame, eh?" Robert laughed again. "Poor you!"

"You'll not speak of this to anyone."

Robert swivelled around in his saddle and viewed the array of men-at-arms sitting astride their steeds. "I'll not," he said, "but they might. Keep a silent tongue in your heads, lads, or you'll lose your balls before your heads!"

Lambert staggered backwards, relieved in a way, but troubled also. To think, the youthful King of England, not quite the man he believed himself to be, belittled by a woman. He would never live down the shame. Lambert fell down on the hummock. "What a little shit," he said to nobody in particular, his thoughts turning to Lorna and their lovemaking. If it were real, and not a dream, it proved to be the most wonderful and fulfilling experience of his life. She could not have been play-acting. The Swede, he was man enough for two, but size was not everything. No, there had to be some other, deeper reason why Lorna refused Richard's advances. Why she struck him so hard.

A rider came over the rise at that point, causing Lambert to look up. The man reigned in his horse, which stomped on the ground exhaling ferociously through its nostrils. "By your leave, your Grace."

"What is it," spat Richard.

"We have forced the door, sire. Our men are inside, over-powering the few retainers within. What are your orders?"

Lambert was already racing down the hillside, covering the distance between the hummock and the castle in minutes, all thoughts of his inadequacy, real or imagined, forgotten. Behind him the King's voice rang out, "Find the bitch, and burn the place down whilst she watches."

She was not there. Lambert walked through the rubble, kicking away at pieces of still smouldering timber. The men, like a bunch of banshees, mad with lust and rage, went to the business with great abandon. But she was not there.

Her husband, however, was.

They had Strythe bound hand and foot in what had once been the great hall. Lambert came through a broken entrance and surveyed the scene. Strythe, naked, stood trembling in the centre, whilst Richard and his friend, Robert, studied him, arms folded, laughing loudly.

"By God, Sir Swinton shall hear of this," he said, voice strong, without fear, in sharp contrast to the way his frame shook. "I am a loyal retainer to his majesty King James and what you do here today, is an act of war!"

"Shall I stick him now," hissed Robert, drawing his sword. "He'll not talk to you this way and live, damn his heart."

"Let him be," said Richard, laying his hand upon his friend's arm to restrain him. "The fellow is upset." He sniggered, "I mean, look at him. His little worm is all shrivelled." He went up close to Strythe, cupping the man's chin in his mailed fist. "Sir, it may have escaped your notice, but your castle is destroyed, your men dead and you," he shook his head, "you sir are in mortal danger. Wherever your liege lord is, he is not here. I have heard it said his son, the Earl of Carrick, has taken control of his father's realm. Is it not so?"

Strythe attempted to turn his head, but Richard held him firmly.

"He'll punish you for this day," said Strythe, eyes narrowing. "You think you have impunity, but believe me, you have not."

Richard smiled and looked to his friend. "Brave, isn't he."

"Reckless," spat Robert, took a step forward and slammed his fist into Strythe's midriff. The man's breath gushed from his mouth and he doubled, falling to his knees, wheezing in gulps of air.

"Leave him alone," shouted Lambert, stepping between the king and the whimpering Strythe. "You've done what you came to do, now go."

Richard looked right through him, snarling, "Find the painting," he said and whirled away. Robert bowed and strode over to his men, sheathing his sword as he went.

Lambert bent down to Strythe's level, "Are you all right? Where is Lorna?"

Strythe groaned, but otherwise remained quiet. Lambert stood and, stepping between the shattered masonry, found his way back outside.

Men loitered in small groups, chatting and laughing, some of them chewing on pieces of dried meat, others drinking from stone flagons. Debris lay all around, together with several bodies, but overall the air was relaxed. Victory. Lambert went past them and retraced his steps to where the garden had been, where Lorna first voiced her interest in being painted.

"She's gone," came the King's voice, appearing around the corner with a framed painting in his grip. The expression on his face was one of feverish triumph, eyes so wide the whites flared light beacons.

"What will you do with it," said Lambert, trying to catch a glimpse of the picture.

"We found a stable boy. She rode off. Left her husband to it, the bitch."

"She would never do that," rasped Lambert. "He must have ordered her away, to save her from you, you bastard. She believed him dead and is not to know the truth until…" He stopped, knowing it was useless. He was a shadow, nothing more. They could neither see nor hear him.

"Shall we go in pursuit?"

Lambert swung about and faced Robert, hands on hips, breathing hard.

"No," said Richard, holding up the picture. "I have this. It will suffice. Let her rot in hell."

Robert laughed, clapped his sovereign on the shoulder and together they walked back to their mounts, ignoring Lambert, the fractured castle, and the miserable Strythe who remained on his knees, weeping like a lost child.

23

"Thank you for coming," said Miles, greeting Sinclair at the entrance to the castle.

Sinclair assented his head slightly and stepped over the threshold. He stopped and looked around. The interior was in total contrast, not only to the exterior, but to Castle Strythe. The decor was bright and modern, clean lines and an open-plan arrangement giving such a sense of space Sinclair felt he had stepped inside a completely different building.

"You've never been here before?" asked Miles, gesturing for the manservant to take a seat in what was probably the living room.

"Never," said Sinclair, moving over to a large, L-shaped sofa whilst Miles crossed into the kitchen area and prepared tea. "I had no idea it would be like this."

Miles chuckled, "I'll give you a tour later. We have six bedrooms, with a further two in the annexe. I've let them out for holiday visitors for many years and they provide a steady income, but never enough to keep the old place going. So, I had a rethink, brought designers in, and got the interior transformed. It is now airy and light, well insulated, with temperature-controlled heating and mood lighting. The whole house is run by a computer."

"Really?"

"Yes, really. I've saved hundreds in only one year. Best thing I ever did."

He brought over the drinks and handed one to Sinclair, who took it with a smile.

"Two sugars, as I recall?"

Sinclair smiled again, "Nothing much gets past you, Mr Miles."

Miles sat down opposite in a large armchair, crossed one leg over the other and sipped at his tea. "He's still having dreams."

Sinclair paused, thought, and blew over the surface of his drink. "Yes. I suspected as much."

"Did he tell you what happened at the party?"

"Not in detail, no."

"Well, suffice to say he had some sort of a *vision*. We held a séance, for a bit of fun you understand. I can't remember much, putting my hands on the table, listening to Cheryl droning on and on. Next thing I know, I'm waking up, feeling like shit, and Andrew is telling me the girl came to him."

"Lorna?"

"I'm worried for his sanity, Sinclair. I've tried to get him to talk to a friend of mine, a psychologist from the University of—"

"I overheard the shouting, Mr Miles. Forgive me, but I thought you ill advised to attempt such a thing. Mr Andrew is going through some sort of a crisis, his nerves shredded. You should have come to talk to me."

Miles frowned, drank his tea, and settled the cup with great care on the floor. "I have always had the feeling you know more about this than you let on, Sinclair."

"Really, sir? Why do you say that?"

"Intuition. I know *something* is going on. There have been too many inexplicable happenings. For instance, when we went to the photographer's in Edinburgh, he told me the shop was fully kitted out with all sorts of items. Yet, when I tried the door, it was locked, the shutters down over the window. On our return, the same was true." He sat, unblinking, measuring the manservant as if waiting for some reaction. When there was none, he continued. "Later, during our visit to the former owner of the studio, we were shown a print of Edward the Seventh's visit to Edinburgh. Do you know anything about that?"

"Nineteen Hundred and Four, I believe." Sinclair sat back, cradling his teacup between his palms. "It was a great day for the City." He drank the last of his tea, turned his head to look out of the vast panoramic window that afforded the room so much light, as well as providing a spectacular view. "My family and Mr Andrew's have been linked for generations. We fought at Culloden, on the side of George the Second against the Prince. The forging of our links go way beyond friendship." He smiled, and met Miles' gaze. "We are linked by blood, sir. I may be a servant to Castle Strythe, but the estate means more to me than simply a collection of stone. It is my home too." He leaned forward and placed the cup next to the sofa. "Mr Andrew's father made enormous efforts to try and put the issue to rest, sir. He removed every scrap of evidence, every letter, every photograph. He burnt them all, in a large bonfire in the ornamental garden. Afterwards, he—"

"Just a moment," said Miles, his voice brittle, unsure. "What are you talking about? What *issue*?"

"The woman, sir. The one Mr Andrew calls Lorna."

Miles gaped at the manservant. "I ... Wait, Sinclair. You're telling me, Andrew's father *knew* this woman also?"

Sinclair's face remained impassive. "Sir, if you wish to know the truth, you must suspend your disbelief. What happened, what is *happening* goes far beyond normal experiences. I struggled for many years to grasp the significance, but when I accepted it..." He shrugged. "In the Fourteenth Century, this entire area was one of conflict, terror and murder. Border Reivers roamed right across the region, attacking homesteads, carrying off women and children, cattle. They burned and plundered and both the Scottish and English royal houses went to great lengths to suppress them. Neither succeeded, but in so doing the two nations themselves clashed. Richard the Second sent troops to this area, to crush those lairds whose fealty was in question. One of them was Lord Strythe, of Castle Strythe."

Miles considered the man's words, pursing his lips, becoming confused. "I don't understand what this has got to do with Andrew, or the woman."

"Please, sir. Bear with me. Richard had no need to be here. He was having troubles of his own, numerous barons discontented, problems with the Welsh. He had previously been very successful at defusing the Peasants' Revolt. He lied to them, perhaps he believed this course was the best in all things. Who knows? Whatever the reason, when he came here he met Lorna, who was married to Lord Strythe. Richard became infatuated, to such an extent he went to the castle to beg her to come into his bed. But Lorna refused him, for she was in love with the painter Devoir."

"A painter?"

"Yes. He had come on a visit, invited by Lord Strythe, to paint her portrait."

"But you said she loved him."

"Yes, ironic isn't it. Her husband invites the man with whom she fell madly and passionately in love. When she refused the king, he took his revenge on her. He could not accept a mere woman possessed a power stronger than his own, a power driven by her divine love for Devoir. So, he burned the castle to the ground. She disappeared and Richard stole the painting."

"The painting Devoir made of her."

Sinclair nodded. "Mr Andrew's grandfather left numerous letters and diary entries concerning the matter, sir. According to the evidence unearthed, Richard took the painting with him and placed it in the royal collection."

"You told me Andrew's father burnt everything."

Sinclair smiled. "So he thought. I rescued many of the Grandfather's effects, including some of his diaries."

"*You* did? Why would you do that, Sinclair? Why go against your employer's wishes?"

"Because I had come across the writings before Mr Andrew's father had. Many, many years before. Whilst the old man still lived. I spoke to him about them. He seemed surprised, a little frightened. He believed I would tell the world, but I gave him my word I would not. I never have, but now..." He turned to the window again and the view. "I hoped none of it would occur again, that she would disappear back to wherever she came from. But I was wrong. Something happened on the night of the car-crash. I'm not sure what, but Mr Andrew's consciousness changed. He became *aware*. A lot more than his ankle was affected that night."

"You mean, the accident in some way gave him a kind of... *insight*? Is that what you're saying?"

"I believe so, sir. I think Mr Andrew came close to death at that moment, sir. The paramedics told me his heart stopped twice in the ambulance, the damage to his leg caused internal bleeding, which sent him into shock. He is lucky to be still with us, sir."

Miles fell back into his chair, hand clamped to his mouth, eyes growing moist. "I never knew."

"Nor does Mr Andrew, sir. He lost consciousness for something like thirty minutes. This may seem a strange thing to say, but something similar happened to Henry the Eighth. He was knocked from his horse in a joust, damaged his leg, but more crucially he lost consciousness for almost forty minutes. Afterwards, his personality changed. He became more prone to bouts of anger and, more importantly, depression."

"You think Andrew is suffering depression, because of the accident?"

"I am sure of it. It's true I have not known him for many years, but think about his life prior to returning to the castle. He ran a successful business, had a beautiful girlfriend, an enviable life in London. In the space of a few months, he loses everything. His business collapses, his girlfriend leaves him. And as soon as he arrives here, he is involved in a near-fatal car accident. Such a course of events is enough to change anyone, but the accident ... I believe it accelerated his inevitable fall into depression."

"You might be right. He is certainly different." Miles sank into deep thought, considering the old servant's words. "When depression is so deep, we struggle to find something, *anything* which may lighten the darkness. Perhaps this is what he is doing, with these recurring fantasies of Lorna. Perhaps, searching through all of his father's papers, his mind has conjured her up, made her real?"

Sinclair grunted, nodding. "How is it depression comes without being asked? To where does its dark, satanic path lead ... from where does it spring? I wish I knew."

"If any of us knew, perhaps it wouldn't exist."

"He has no idea about what happened in the crash and that, I think, is where we should leave it."

Miles nodded. "And you seriously believe all of these visions and experiences stem from what happened that night?"

"I do, sir. He has always maintained he swerved to avoid a woman standing in the road. Who can say if he saw her *before* the accident, or if such an idea formulated inside his consciousness afterwards? We may never know."

"My God," Miles blew out his breath, exasperated. "So, let me get this right; you think Andrew is reliving things from the past? His dreams, they are in way a film being replayed in his head?"

"If, from what you say, during the séance you held, Lorna materialised and became real, it is no longer a film, sir. The same happened to Mr Andrew's grandfather." Miles gawped, stunned. "Yes, sir. Many years ago. When the King, Edward the Seventh came to visit."

"Yes, you said. He came on a State visit to Edinburgh, in nineteen Hundred and four."

"Before that sir."

"*Before*? What the devil do you mean?"

"King Edward visited Castle Strythe before his official arrival in Edinburgh. It was during the visit that Lorna revealed herself to Mr Andrew's grandfather."

Miles sat and stared in silence. Opposite him, Sinclair waited, the view of the rolling countryside taking all of his attention.

"I think you'd better tell me everything, Sinclair."

The manservant nodded and smiled. "Yes, sir. I think I should."

24

A single carriage drew up outside, the pair of horse finding the shingle uncomfortable, and they pranced, lifting their hooves in discomfort as tiny stones stabbed into them. The driver reined them in, calling out soothing words and they soon became calm. He clambered down, went to the carriage door and opened it, dropping the folded step to allow the passenger to ascend.

The man was large, wearing a morning suit with a white carnation in his lapel. Small, piggy eyes were in sharp contrast to his full, jovial face. He dusted himself down and surveyed the surroundings. The driver bowed with great reverence.

"My God," said the man, eyes roaming across the exterior of the castle. "It is exactly the same."

The driver stepped aside, closing the door and took a look for himself. "A few modifications, sire. The ramparts, they are not built for defence, rather for decoration."

"You're right, Norris. Well spotted," and he clapped the driver on the shoulder. "Other than that, it's pretty much an exact replica. Who did you say lived here?"

"Lord Strythe, sir. Although he now goes by the name of Lambert."

"Never heard of him. Does he ever visit the House?"

"I do not believe so. The family retain a purely nominal title, sire. The estate is run through private means, agriculture and some speculative interests in the production of malt whisky."

"You've done well, Norris. Forewarned is forearmed, as they say."

"Unfortunately, sire, Mr Melrose, chief archivist at the gallery did the research. I am merely its conduit."

"Conduit? Interesting choice of word. You amaze me sometimes, Norris. Well," he clapped his hands together, "whoever did the work, they did a damned good job. Go and announce me, would you." He took in a deep breath and turned his face skywards, eyes closed. "It is heavenly here."

Norris approached the door, but before he had made even the first step, the large, heavy door, creaked open and a tall, angular man stood, eying them with a slight degree of suspicion. "Can I help you, gentlemen?" His accent was light, the singsong tone of the Lowland Scot.

Norris gave a bow and stepped to his right, swivelling to reveal the gentleman waiting by the carriage. "May I present His Royal Highness, King Edward the Seventh."

Edward chuckled, made a dismissive wave and came forward, brogue shoes crunching over the ground. "No need for all of that, Norris. I'm not here in an official capacity."

The man in the doorway stood as if struck dumb, mouth open, eyes bulging. Edward went right up to him, took his hand and pumped it vigorously. "Good to meet you, sir. Apologies for arriving unannounced, but I have wanted to visit ever since I laid eyes on the painting." He sniffed, threw his head to the sky once more and beamed, "By God this is wonderful you have here. You're a very lucky chap, if I may say so. Lord Strythe I presume?"

The man blinked a few times, focusing on how the King still held his hand, and mumbled, "No … No, I, er, no longer…" He shrugged. "My name is Lambert, *Mister* Lambert. My family has no title, Your Majesty."

Norris smirked.

"Ah, yes, I understand." Edward at last removed his grip from Lambert's hand. He stood, waiting, expression expectant.

Lambert looked from the King to Norris and after a moment's pause, seemed to regain his composure, almost as if a light went on within his eyes. "What am I thinking? Your Majesty," he bowed deep, "Forgive me, but I was so shocked… Please," he took a step away from the door, motioning to the interior, "enter, Sire."

Edward laughed, gave a quick jerk of his head to Norris, who immediately returned to the horses, and went inside Castle Strythe.

They partook of port, with some cheese and bread after Lambert had given Edward a tour of the household. The King took in every facet of the interior, the many paintings and tapestries lining the walls, the impressive library, and

The Magical Painting

the collection of fine French furniture, including a writing desk said to have once belonged to Marie Antoinette. It was certainly of superb quality, slender, tapered legs, decorated with delicate, interlaced fleur-de-lis motifs.

Once outside, strolling through the ornamental gardens, Edward sat beneath a hawthorn and breathed in the clean, crisp air. "Naturally, Balmoral has a particular beauty," he said, "but I love the warmth and simplicity of this place … the sense of *homeliness*."

"Your Majesty does me great honour."

"I believe things have not always been so, am I right?"

Lambert frowned, lowering himself onto the adjacent marble bench. "I'm not quite sure I understand what you mean, your Majesty."

Edward slapped his own thighs. "Well, let me tell you. I have recently retained a quite remarkable gentleman, a Mr Melrose, a former art conservator for Sotheby's of London. A most amiable and hard-working chap, in every sense of the word. I set him to work on the Royal Gallery and he made a quite astonishing discovery." He beamed, sat with his back against the hawthorn and folded his arms. "He came across a painting, not such a grand looking thing at first sight, but then…" He raised a forefinger and waggled it to nobody in particular, "By viewing it from certain angles, with the light just so," he stabbed the air with the finger, "you can see a woman!"

"A woman?"

"Indeed. And a mighty handsome looking one too." He chuckled, dropped his hand to his lap and sighed. "I saw her, you know."

"I'm sorry, I don't understand."

"I saw her in person, is what I mean. The same woman. She was exhibiting some of her paintings at the Galerie Bernheim-Jeune in Paris. The point of all this, Lambert, is that she was painted in the grounds of a castle. Mr Melrose did his research and, low and behold, the castle is *this one*, Mr Lambert! Castle Strythe. How can this be, that is what I want to know. How can I see the figure of a woman from the Twentieth Century in a painting of this castle made in the Fourteenth?"

Lambert shifted position. "I cannot even begin to speculate, Your Highness. I've never heard of any painting of Castle Strythe being part of the royal collection. How fascinating."

"Your family are not the original owners of this castle, so I understand? You retained the name of the lands, but nothing more."

"We were granted this land by George the Second, in recognition of our part in the suppression of the Highlanders at Culloden. Prior to that, the castle was in ruins."

"Yes. Burned down by Richard the Second, way back. Thirteen-Eighty-Six, or thereabouts."

"As far as I know, yes. You have certainly done your research, sire."

"I owe everything to Mr Melrose. According to him, the painting came into the collection at about the same time, so Richard must have stolen it. Who do you think the woman is?"

"I have no idea, sire. The lady of the house, I presume. Perhaps she has a resemblance to this painter you know?"

The King did not appear convinced. "You know nothing of this medieval Lord Strythe?"

"Not a great deal. I understand his lost his lands, became something of a sad figure. I believe he fought on the side of the Scots army at Otterburn and helped defeat the English." He forced a smile, the heat rising to his face. "Forgive me, sire, I do not mean any insult. As far as I am concerned, the English are our friends. The past, well, life was very different then. Intolerance and ignorance, on both sides."

Edward waved him away, "No, no, don't trouble yourself over that, Lambert. What's done is done, eh. Otterburn? I cannot recall anything about such a place. The Scots defeated the English you say?"

"Aye, under the Earls Carrick and Douglas."

A servant appeared from within the castle. He stopped some way off and bowed. Lambert raised an eyebrow and the man nodded, turned and went back inside. Lambert stood up, "If Your Majesty would allow, I have ordered some light refreshment to be served."

"What a splendid idea," said Edward, slapped his thighs again, and got to his feet. He rubbed his stomach, "Light refreshment, eh? Let's hope it's not *too* light."

After their lunch, and a second tour of the castle when Edward insisted on going up to the battlements to take in the view, Lambert walked the King back to his carriage. Norris already had the door open, the little steps pulled down.

At the door, Edward stopped and turned to his host. "Thank you Mr Lambert. When I saw the painting, I simply had to find this place. Now that I have…"

He gave a whimsical smile. "So beautiful." He put out his hand and Lambert clasped it firmly.

"Perhaps one day, sire, I could come down to London and view the original?"

Edward's face clouded over and for a moment, Lambert believed he had overstepped the mark between familiarity and propriety.

"I'm sorry, your Majesty, if I have in any way offended you, but I assure you I—"

"No, no," said Edward quickly, "nothing of the sort, Mr Lambert. Goodness me, no. I'm afraid … A very dear friend of mine arrived from France not long after I came across the painting. He became enthralled, so I gave it to him. As a present."

Lambert, unable to grasp the meaning of the King's words at first, looked away, muttering, "I see. Well … Perhaps…"

"Yes. Mr Lambert, rest assured, I will send you his address. Perhaps you might get the chance to visit him. After all, he lives in a most wonderful part of the world and quite a famous one too. His château is simply majestic."

"Yes, that would be very kind, your Majesty. Whereabouts is it?"

"Burgundy, Mr Lambert." He shook Lambert's hand once more. "In the Yonne valley. A very wonderful little place called Vézelay."

25

Andrew Lambert sat on the grass gazing across the still, silent loch with the distant mountains providing a perfect backdrop. The loch, small and unsullied except for gentle ripples brewed up by the slight breeze, snaked into the distance, its shape something of an elongated hoop. Circumnavigated in less than an hour, nevertheless it was the home for any number of birds and other fauna. Right now, an almost reverential quiet, almost deafening, settled over the place.

He heard a soft footfall and turned, giving a start as Lorna drifted down the hillside, stopped and smiled. He was already getting to his feet as she waved him back down, joining him on the grass.

"Beautiful, isn't it," she said, edging closer.

To reassure himself that this was not another illusion, he put out his hand and brushed his fingers down her bare arm. She wore a thin cotton dress, full length, cut to the thigh. Her bronzed limbs flashed provocatively from between the slits. Around her throat a delicate chain, matching those, which encircled her wrists. He couldn't help but stare at her legs and when he became aware of her eyes, he gave a nervous laugh and looked away.

"You can carry on looking if you want," she said, teasing him even more by running her tongue along her bottom lip.

"Where have you come from?" he said in a rush.

"You know. I've told you."

"But…" He shook his head, his heart throbbing, "I don't understand any of it."

"You don't need to," she said, resting her chin on his shoulder, huge doe eyes gazing at him. "You really are very, very sweet, Andrew."

"Sweet?" he laughed, thinking he should be angry but unable to find the desire. He enjoyed her touch, her closeness, the way her eyes drank him in. "Lorna, where do you go?"

"Where do I go?"

"Yes, when you're not here, with me."

"I'm always with you, Andrew."

"No, I mean *physically*. After the party, you simply melted away and I felt such a whirl of emotion, most notably embarrassment at telling Miles I thought you were somebody else."

"You think someone else could make love to you the way I do?"

"No! No, it's not that at all, but…" He shrugged his shoulders, trapped, pressed against a wall.

"I'm teasing you," she laughed, "of course I understand what you mean, but the truth is, I don't know. Something takes over me, a sudden surge of energy, invisible, all-consuming, frightening in its power. I float, in a whirl of blue crystal, not aware of time or space, only … utter bliss. And when I wake, I am here. With you." She picked up and studied his hand for a moment, "I think what we should do is not question. It began with the painting. As soon as I laid eyes upon its surface and saw myself something indescribable happened to me, as if some great hand had lifted me up, carrying me away to a new understanding."

"But the King took the painting, didn't he."

Her face dropped to the grass between them. "Yes. He came here, burned down the castle and humiliated my husband … The life we once had was destroyed."

"I saw everything – how Devoir made love to you, how the King struck you, the shame at his own inadequacy."

"Anyone is inadequate compared to Devoir. You saw what you wanted to see, Andrew. Devoir was a most wonderful artist, the sort whose genius crosses time, leaping from the past to the future. Such knowledge made the King jealous."

Andrew lowered his eyes. "Yes. Is that why the King struck you, and burned down the castle?"

"Because someone else, beside him, possessed God's power. Perhaps, even more than he, a king! It left him feeling humiliated, but nobody could know. It had to remain a secret." She tiled her head. "Would you have burned down my castle if you harboured the same thoughts, Andrew?"

"No, but then again, I'm not a king." The idea made him laugh. "And besides, it's my castle. Why would I burn my own castle down?"

"Why indeed."

"I'm trying to understand why you chose *me*. What happened to you happened centuries ago. I'm here, in my rebuilt castle, with no connection to the past. What is it you want from me? You have to tell me, reveal your secret, before you drive me mad, as you did my grandfather. Do you want to do the same to me, is that it?"

She smiled. "Your grandfather … Well, perhaps miscalculations were made and I've reappeared at the wrong time. But you, you are so like him, not only in your physicality, but in the way you talk, your manner. You could be him, reborn."

"I can hardly remember him."

"But you have seen photographs? The likeness is uncanny."

"That's not so surprising, is it? Many people have commented on it. But something makes it different for you, more important. Is it simply because you missed a century, got off at the wrong stop? Like a train? Tell me."

A darkness fell across her face and her eyes became moist and almost at once, he regretted his choice of words, their harshness. "Yes, I did love your grandfather. He was so kind, so different to anyone I ever knew. It was as if we were meant to be, a connection so strong it bridged the years, the centuries which separated us. His desire was to possess ne, but he could not. He was not long married, his child but a baby. Your father."

"And what of Devoir? What was it that distinguished him from the rest?"

She turned her face skywards. "He led me to another world."

"Another world?" Lambert's throat went dry, his heartbeat throbbing, "Explain, please."

Her eyes were twinkling when she turned to face Lambert. "Someone sat amongst the nearby brushes. I couldn't help but spot him, and I smiled knowing someone was there, longing to approach and help Devoir cover me with rose petals. At first, the petals fell on my neck and shoulders and their perfume, so intoxicating, seemed to send me into a sort of delirium. Devoir's hands deftly slipped my dress down, exposing my breasts and as his mouth folded over them, I moaned, losing control. The delicious moment overcame me. I caught sight of the stranger caressing himself as Devoir caressed me."

The Magical Painting

Lambert's entire body shuddered with desire, the images created by her words so powerful he became that stranger. "What happened," he gasped.

"Devoir was the greatest master of art, if you understand me."

Lambert fell back into the grass. "Christ. You drive me insane. It's as if the stranger was me!"

"From that moment, we made love whenever we could. Soon, nothing else mattered except to be in his arms, to feel his strength, his total control of my body…"

Andrew gripped his head with both hands, squeezing his eyes shut. "Please, just leave me alone. Disappear, get out of my life!"

But when he opened his eyes, it was as if he had never spoken, as Lorna continued with her story as if he were not even there. "It was this love Devoir gave me that turned Richard into a jealous monster. When he propositioned me with his idea of me becoming his mistress, I tried to tell him the truth, how my love for Devoir was too strong but … No, the destruction of my home has different reasons for the ones you mentioned, Andrew. It is something of a long story, but as you have already seen so much, some more cannot do any harm." She swivelled around to face him, placing the fingers of both hand on either of his face, lightly, a butterfly's wing caress. Within a single breath, his eyelids became heavy.

"Relax my dear," she said, her voice distant but soothing.

"Yes," he whispered."

Yes…

The dense forest gave no hint of its secrets, deep verdant shadows concealing all. Even the largest of creatures, such as deer and boar, found safety and protection within the thick foliage. Nevertheless, when the hunters came, birds set up the cries of danger, and animals scurried away, deeper still into the lush green.

Men came, tramping through as if they rode wild horses, fearless and aloof. They wore leather jerkins, coarse trousers and felt boots. In their arms some held long boar spears, read to be thrust at any animal which ventured close. Others, similarly dressed but without the long polearm, cut swathes through the bush with their swords. Bringing up the rear, lightly armoured men, straight-backed, serious, eyes forever scanning the trees. These were noblemen, out on the hunt, and in their centre, the King of England, Richard the Second.

A cry went up as something large dashed from a clump of gorse. Men sprang forward, boar spears rigid, cocked, primed to kill.

Richard whooped with joy, held aloft his own spear, and kicked the flank of his horse. "At 'em lads," he shouted, head down, pressed against his mount's neck, eyes alert, seeking out the prey.

Richard was a fine horseman. Having descended the throne at the age of ten, through necessity a select group of nobles governed the country. Some proved worthy, most not. Jealousy and envy played themselves out in the court whilst Richard spent every available moment honing the skills of the knight. Too small for armour and weapons, he took to riding and within a very short space of time, his natural enthusiasm and eagerness to master the skill turned him to a most efficient rider. At times like this, with over-hanging branches and enough entangled roots spread out across the ground to unhorse the unwary, his skills were tested.

On both flanks, the dismounted men-at-arms kept pace with him. A new sense of urgency coursed through everyone, sensing the close proximity of the quarry, expectation and excitement reaching dizzy heights.

Richard saw the cause. A huge boar, back bristled, eyes burning with red rage. It flexed as Richard turned his horse about, preparing to strike with his spear. He levelled the point towards the beast and then someone came crashing through the trees. The boar pulled back, Richard struck, putting all of his weight into the thrust. But the boar proved too fast, the weapon striking fresh air.

"I have him, sire!"

A flurry of activity as others emerged from the undergrowth, too much noise, too many voices. All at once Richard felt himself surrounded, concentration broken. He thrust for a second time and again missed. His horse reared, front legs striking out, shrieking with terror as the boar made a rush forward, swerved at the last moment before the horse's rapidly descending hooves crushed him, and he was gone.

At that point, a single arrow sang through the air, designed to strike the retreating boar. It missed, for the beast proved too swift, and smacked into Richard's thigh. He screamed, instinctively grabbing at the offending dart.

Men pressed from all angles, anxiety etched on every face. They all knew the story of William Rufus, killed in a hunting accident over two hundred and fifty years before. Or murdered, depending on which theory you accepted. They gabbled and barked, pushed and pulled, and the Richard's eyes rolled and he slid from his saddle into the waiting men's arms.

The Magical Painting

It was the period when Scottish troops and Border Reivers crossed and re-crossed the boundary separating the two kingdoms. Raids and skirmishes became more frequent and Richard, travelling to Chester to lend his presence to ongoing disputes with Parliament and create a loyal power base, news reached him of further troubles on the border. Concerns over invasion from France, with the help of their friends the Scots, meant he needed to see for himself what was happening.

But not before he partook of some hunting.

Now, eyes focusing in on his surroundings, he peered into the gloom and breathed in the heady perfume of dozens of candles. Essence of honey and jasmine competed for dominance, the mix bringing him a sense of calm he rarely experienced.

He sat up and winced as a stab of pain shot through his thigh. He collapsed back into the bed, gripping the wound. He waited, aware of the bandages, the lack of the arrow shaft. He craned his neck and realised someone has cleaned and dressed the wound after cutting out the dart. Whoever the surgeon might be, his skills were beyond compare.

A figure crossed his sight, lost in the shadows, the swish of material dragging across the cold, stone floor the only evidence of its presence. Richard propped himself up on his elbows and squinted into the murkiness.

She came to him, white headgear covering hair, trailing to her shoulders, wearing a long blue dress of heavy cloth, cut into her delicious figure, her breasts firm, waist trim. As she drew closer, it was her eyes, more than any other aspect of this delightful creature that seized most of his attention. They were huge, shining like lanterns in the gloom, brighter even that the candles. He dare not look away in case this vision was a dream, a fantasy.

She smiled, her soft lips barely parting. "My lord. Your men brought you here on a litter. Unconscious, unaware, I hope you are not too surprised by what has happened."

He shook his head, throat constricted. Her voice, a low, gentle whisper, seemed, despite its gentleness, to lift him. Already, within a few seconds, he felt rejuvenated.

"You must thank the kind surgeon who tended to me."

"It was no surgeon, sire. Your wounds were treated with an herbal remedy, the arrow removed with utmost care. Washed and dressed, you were then brought to this room to rest."

"Well," Richard smiled, "how long must I rest for?"

"A day, at the very least. Two would be better."

"But that is preposterous! My duty demands I return to my duties... Where is the surgeon? Send him to me, I wish to question him over what is the best way forward."

She bowed slightly, face creasing up with amusement, "I would beg your pardon, sire, but I have already informed you, there was no surgeon."

"Then whoever it was who bathed my wounds, send for him." Richard looked angry, his face reddening slightly.

"Sire," she bowed deeper still, "as it pleases you, I undressed and cleaned your wound."

Richard gaped at her, steel fingers seizing his throat, squeezing hard enough to bring water to his eyes. He spluttered, "*You?* What the devil do you mean?"

"Forgive me, sire, but there was no one else. My husband has been called away on urgent business with Lord Swinton."

"*You bathed me?* You mean..." He shook his head as the terrible realisation dawned on him, "Dear God Almighty, you *saw me!*"

"Sire, you were asleep!"

"Sleeping or not, you saw me! Damned your eyes woman, I am the King."

"Forgive me, sire. You are King of England, as I have ascertained from your livery, but here, we owe fealty to the King of *Scotland.*"

"Pah! The King of Scotland is a decrepit old man, who abdicates his throne to his son, John, Earl of Carrick. The man has no shame. No *majesty.*" The girl remained with her eyes downcast. Richard, breathing hard, flopped back onto the bed. "Damn them all. A day, in this place?"

"Sire. I will need to redress the wound." Her face came up, the tiniest hint of a smile fluttering across her lips. "And I shall need to do it now."

Richard considered her words and surrendered to them without a fight, knowing the sense of what she suggested. He had seen similar wounds fester, causing the victim pain, even death. Everyone knew the stories of his ancestor, Richard I, how a wound from an arrow took his life. So he acquiesced, nodding his head with approval.

Her hands were a dream, the lightest of touches, the gentlest of movement. Richard lay back, eyes closed, putting away all thoughts who she might be; a mere commoner, albeit a beautiful one. As she slowly pulled away the bandaging, she pulled apart his undershirt, exposing him. Unperturbed, her fingers drifted over the wound, and tendrils of ice cold ran over his flesh. He moaned as both hand floated over his thigh, transmitting a sort of throb. Not unpleasant, the pain caused the king to hiss, sucking in air through clenched teeth. But the pleasure, the sheer, unbridled joy her touch brought him put all such considerations far, far away.

His manhood stirred. He held little hope of controlling himself, her fingers bringing him to fever pitch. He let out a long, low moan of ecstasy. His member sprang up, and she stopped.

His eyes snapped open. "What is wrong?" He looked up. She stood before him, one hand over her mouth, the other playing with her bodice.

"What the hell is wrong with you, woman? Have you never seen a man hard before?"

"Not … Not one of a king. I … "She turned away once more. " I do not mean to offend you."

"Offend me?" He managed to raise himself, ignoring the pain, and slipped his arm around her waist. "How could you *ever* offend me?"

"Sire, I must stop, I am not worthy."

"You are more than worthy. You are like a golden sunrise, a Moon shadow, a humming bird's wing, as beautiful as anything ever known."

"Oh my Lord, you speak truly?"

He took her face in his hands and kissed her lightly on the lips. "More than you can imagine." He held her close, kissing the top of her head, knowing his erection pressed against her, but ignoring it and the raging desire inside. "Tell my guards to attend me. I have something for them to do."

They worked hard to prepare the room, using whatever material they found, draping every piece of furniture with heavy, embroidered blankets, sheets, even tapestries. They set candles in metal holders, and when they could find no more, they allowed the wax to form tiny platforms for the candles to stand on. When lit, the room glowed with the haze from over a hundred burning poles of wax, the myriad flames setting off weird, contorting shadows, which danced across the walls. Richard sat on his bed, dressed in a light cotton shift, and he beamed at his men before dismissing them with a small wave of his hand.

He waited, not daring to breathe lest the slightest sound destroyed the magic of the moment. Some invisible presence settled over him, calming him, soothing away the throb in his thigh. He closed his eyes and imagined her standing before him, her full breasts and slim waist, honed to perfection. He sighed and the door whispered shut.

"You came," he said when he saw her, so tiny, as if afraid, a nervous bird caught in a trap. He swung his leg over the bed and stood up, biting back the pain. "Lorna," he said, holding out his hand. "Come to me, sweet girl."

She cast her eyes around the room, the yellow glow spreading over her own skin, causing her to become like gold, her naked forearms shimmering. She crept forward and he caught her, drew her close, and kissed her. She moaned in his embrace, arching her back to stare deep into his eyes. "My Lord, I cannot do this."

"You can! Can you not feel the force drawing us together?"

"I feel it, yes. But, such a thing cannot be so."

"Fate brought us together. My accident, you tending of my wound. Your touch, so wonderful, as if you possess some incredible power to heal those injured or in pain. And when you touched me, not only did the agony melt away, but also something far more powerful replaced it. You have captivated me, in some way beyond my understanding. Never has such desire, such joy seized my heart!"

"Sire," she blushed, breath coming in short, frantic gasps, "we cannot. I am married, and you … Oh my Lord," she flattened her cheek against his chest and he kissed the top of her head.

"You feel it, don't you," he said, "We are linked, you and I. And this night, we shall be as one."

She turned her face to his and he kissed her, their mouths rolling around each other, his desire becoming unbearable. He gently swung her onto the bed, his mouth leaving hers to run over her throat, her breasts. Their bodies seemed to meld into one, a slow, soothing coupling, fiery bodies synchronised, limbs entwined, guided by their yearning. As he drove into her the world retreated and nothing else mattered.

They lay in a tangled heap, drenched in sweat, her breast heaving, his hand caressing the thigh she draped over his own. "Oh my God," he said, "I have never experienced such love, such passion. You are an enchantress, capturing my very heart and soul. I want to spend endless nights with you."

She shook her head, sadness playing around eyes growing moist, "My Lord, this can never be."

"What do you mean, it already *has* been, my beautiful creature. I want you for my own, to repeat this whenever we can. I will send for you and you shall come and live close to my royal residence. A home shall be prepared for you, well furnished, with servants and—"

"Sire, what you ask of me is impossible."

"No, do not say that! If your husband is your concern, I will pay him handsomely. I will settle everything with the utmost deference and compassion. But you will be mine, Lorna. There can be no argument."

"And what of your wife, my Lord?"

"She is nothing but a child. We rarely spend any time together. Besides, she will not even know of your existence."

"You would have me as your mistress?"

"I hate that word, but yes, if you must know, for you to be so is my ultimate desire. I will come to you and we shall couple as often as our love dictates."

Her face darkened and he became aware of a change in the atmosphere. She sat up. "I will not. For many reasons, but I will not be your whore."

"*Whore?* Dear God in heaven, the very thought brings tears to my eyes! You will not be my whore, madam! You will be my lover."

"In your position, the word means the same." She stood up, pulling her dress to cover her naked body, her eyes, red rimmed, welling up with tears. "I enjoyed our coupling, my lord. You are a considerate and pleasing lover, but this arrangement of yours will never be. I cannot. I will not!"

He struggled to understand her refusal. "All I look for in return is love, appreciation and admiration. I *long* for nothing more. It is unbearable to hear your words. They are like knives thrust into my heart."

But his words did not bring the desired response. She swung around and ran from the room. Richard stared towards the closed door, not daring to believe her reaction. He sank back onto the bed and gnawed at his bottom lip. As he did, sorrow turned to something more. Shame. Embarrassment. Betrayal. The anger welled up and he gripped the covers with all his might. "Damn her," he said aloud, battling hard to contain his emotions.

Sometime in the night, Richard rose from his bed, the cold bringing nothing but discomfort to his joints. If he thought about it, every bone in his body ached. His leg, however, did not. The dressing remained dry so he was able, without much difficulty, to make his way out of his room in search of another blanket. Three was not enough.

A slumbering guard lay crumpled up on the floor. Richard felt the urge to reproach him, and was about to when he heard a low moan. He stopped, listening, holding his breath.

The moan came again, quite but full of deep passion and longer this time.

There was no mistaking her moans of pleasure. Richard regarded himself as being emotionally intuitive, able to discern another's intentions and feelings. And now, here he was, listening to her in ecstasy. Who dared to bring more pleasure to her than he, the king? She refused me and now she was making love with someone else?

Furious, he moved down the dimly lit corridor, ignoring the guard who continued to sleep. At the end of the hallway was a small flight of stairs and he put his head to one side, caught the noise again and knew which way to go.

Curiosity mixed with a stirring of desire drove him on. The idea of such passion eclipsed his fury, replacing it with unexpected desire. There was something inherently magical about this woman, her ability to heal by touch, and bring such cravings for sexual gratification.

He turned the corner at the top of the stairs and proceeded along the corridor. The boards creaked terribly, forcing him to stop every few paces. But the closer he moved to the source of the noise, the more reckless he became.

When he reached the door, he no longer cared. Visions of her body, naked, wanton, consumed by desire filled his mind. He pushed the door open, face lathered in sweat.

The man lay upon her, hands clamped beneath, plunging into her. She writhed, face alive with ecstasy, arms flung sideways in surrender whilst he continued with supreme skill, sometimes withdrawing to display his manhood before returning to her inner sanctum.

Richard stood transfixed in the doorway. Her moans grew ever louder and Richard, as if in a daze, drifted closer.

The man noticed him and stopped. The woman gave a shriek, not for Richard's intrusion but for her lover.

"Your majesty," gasped the man, and drew out of her completely, his long member flaccid, hanging between his slim thighs like the neck of a swan. Richard could not take his eyes off it, even when the woman joined him, a thin sheet around her, muttering something, something Richard could not hear, nor wanted to.

He snapped his head to her. "You would cuckold me, madam? Is that your game?"

"Sire?"

The man took a step closer and Richard span, struck him backhanded across the mouth, drawing blood. The man staggered backwards, falling to his knees, "You majesty, I beg your forgiveness."

"Get on the bed," snarled Richard, glaring at the woman. "You are mine."

She gathered the sheet tighter still around her. "I am not, my Lord, and I shall never be."

"You *are not*? How dare you refuse me? If you do not do as I bid, I shall have you flogged."

"And if you so much as touch either of us again," she said, holding his blazing eyes, "I shall tell every man and woman alive how cruel you are, and what your plans were for me. Your repayment after all I did for you? I saved your life. God will never forgive you!"

"No one will ever believe you."

She tilted her head. "You care to test me, sire? Remember, I am a Scottish subject. I owe no allegiance to you, but if you continue on this course I shall tell the world what I know about you and how you planned to use me, despite your marriage!" She looked down to below the king's waist and curled up a corner of her mouth.

"So that was why he returned?" said Lambert, nodding his head, blinking in the light of the dusk, eyes coming back to life. "The story he told to his companion, about him seeing you in the garden, teasing him whilst he was watching you making love with another man. It wasn't completely true, was it?"

"The essence is the same, I suppose. The man wanted nothing more than to maintain his mystique. The power of kings. He begged me to be his mistress and with my refusal he revealed his true nature."

She laughed, and Lambert, hesitant at first, joined her.

"But later on," he said, "Richard came here, burned the castle down, and took your painting."

"Yes. A painting I want back, Andrew. He stole it, placed it in the Royal Collection, and there it festered, all those centuries."

"And the other man, Lorna? Your lover?"

She reddened, turned away. "My most devoted friend."

"More than a friend I think."

"He was a gentle and considerate lover. My husband never suspected, even whilst he kept me in his room for hours upon end." She turned again to face Lambert. "As you could so easily guess, my lover and my painter were one and the same."

"Yes, of course I guessed. So, was Monsieur Devoir your greatest love?"

"Yes. He was everything for me. He taught me the secrets of painting, but his most precious gift was his divine love."

Andrew had yet to see the painting, but he wondered if he wanted to. Thoughts of that most distinguished of men, who could take such a powerful, sensual and mysterious woman to the heights of heaven brought such uncontrolled jealousy to the very fibre of his being he wanted to scream and shout out his rage. On the other hand, he was no alone. The King too shared such intense feelings.

He blew out a loud breath, allowing his hands to drop, and went to speak to her. He gasped for all he saw were the surroundings, empty with no other living person in sight. Lorna had disappeared once again.

26

Lambert slipped his tablet into its protective pouch and was about to move when Sinclair came in. There must have been something in Lambert's expression that made the manservant stop and frown, curiosity burning across his features. 'Are you all right sir?'

"Perfectly," said Lambert, forcing a smile. "I'm just making some notes."

"That's exactly what I wanted to hear." A smile returned. "You facial expression told me the opposite."

"Oh, don't pay attention to my facial expressions. Actually it wasn't me."

"How is that?" Sinclair raised his eyebrows.

"Memories. Never mind," Lambert gave a small, dismissive wave.

"I didn't know you had one of those things, sir." Lowering his head, Sinclair peered at the tablet.

"Oh yes. It's useful for reading my writing whilst I'm out in the garden. Better than being stuck in here. It's a pity, even on the cloudiest days, the reflective screen makes it so damned difficult to read. But overall it's okay."

"Writing you said? I suppose that is what took all your attention this morning. You missed your lunch. I thought perhaps you had planned to have it with someone else."

"No, there is no one else. How could it be that I missed my lunch?"

"I opened the door to bring you something, but you waved me away in refusal."

"Did I? Shit." Lambert shook his head, bemused. "Well, no worries, I'll grab something whilst driving."

Then came a whisper, "Have you forgotten what caused your accident?" Lambert snapped his head up as Lorna's voice drifted from out of nowhere.

He shivered. No, it couldn't be her, he thought, trying to reassure himself, it's only me, my own thoughts.

"You do surprise me sir," continued Sinclair, seemingly unaware of Lambert's change of demeanour. "I never suspected you had developed an interest in writing."

There was a long pause before Lambert gave a forced smile, "Well, letters mainly. You know what I mean. Creditors, lawyers." He held up his hand. "Nothing fictional."

"Why do you say that?"

Lambert went to speak, thought better of it, and shrugged, "Well, I wouldn't want you to think I was dabbling in father's business." He winced, realising his explanation sounded inadequate.

"Your father wrote fiction, sir, of the most engaging kind. If you were to do something similar, it is nothing to be ashamed of."

"No. I suppose you're right. But, he was an expert, wasn't he, been writing for years."

"He was a creative soul, sir. Expert is not the correct term to use."

"Perhaps not, but it's not something I could do half as well. I've never even been to a creative writing class."

"Neither had he, sir."

Lambert frowned. "Really? So, how did he learn to write?"

Sinclair pursed his lips, "Again, I'm not at all sure if that is the correct explanation. Words can be so inadequate sometimes. He *learned* to write by writing, driven by something inside him, intangible, difficult to define. He once told me the stories simply evolved inside his own head, of their own volition."

"Almost as if he had an urge to write, is that it? The very act of writing itself was its own catalyst."

"Very well put, sir. Catalyst. Yes, I think that is exactly how he would describe it, not that he ever tried to. He accepted who he was, came down here every morning and did what he did."

"With great success."

"I believe he would have continued irrespective of that sir. Your father was a writer, it was his life."

Lambert smiled, "Well, I assure you, I'm writing letters, only letters. The bank, they're becoming tetchy."

"Is here something I should worry about?"

Lambert turned away for a moment, the manservant's gaze becoming too penetrative. "No, nothing to worry about, Sinclair. We will survive! Do you remember that song? Gloria Gaynor wasn't it?" He turned again chuckling, before realising the old manservant's face continued to look severe. "I promise you, Sinclair, it's nothing serious. Whatever happens, you will stay here for as long as you want. I know how your life is tied to this castle. You're the one surviving memory in the whole history of our family. And I appreciate it so much. I really do."

Tears appeared in the devoted manservant's eyes. Sinclair gave a knowing nod, "Thank you sir, I'm touched by your words."

"Come on, Sinclair, no need to become all maudlin." He patted the tablet. "Did father ever use anything like this, or was he like you – old fashioned?"

His smile chased away the tears. "I think in the early days the closest he ever got to new technology was an electric golf-ball typewriter. But he had to surrender eventually. Apparently, many agents and publisher are requiring electronic communications with authors nowadays. At least, that is what your father's agent told me when he asked me to go through the files on the computer. It was shortly after your father's death, sir. He was working on a book and must have informed his agent of the fact, but his wishes were for all of his work, notes, jottings, etc to be destroyed. However, no matter where I looked, I couldn't find any evidence of his last manuscript anywhere."

Lambert thought about the west tower and wondered if he should mention the papers he found there. Perhaps Sinclair's search had not included that old, forgotten room. He decided to keep his thoughts to himself, for the time being. "Perhaps he'd already destroyed it himself."

"Yes. Perhaps he had."

Later on, sitting out in the garden, gazing fixedly at a nearby oak, Lambert thought about the book his father had started, of the papers strewn across the desk in the tower. To give him some sense of comfort, Lambert pressed the tablet harder against his midriff. Strange how certain things made their presence felt so strongly.

The day stretched out and Lambert remained in the study for most of it. When he emerged late in the afternoon he saw the manservant through the main door, bending down over one or two of the large potted plants, which ran around the perimeter of the driveway.

"I need to talk to you, Sinclair," he called.

Sinclair, in shirtsleeves, looked ruffled as he entered the study, breathing hard, the sweat smeared across his forehead. Lambert frowned. "Are you all right?"

"Yes, thanks." He slumped into a chair, running his hand through his hair. "Just tired. Before tending to the plants in the drive, I've been raking over the flowerbeds in the garden. I'm finding it difficult. Age. I'm getting older and nothing can stop the inevitable running down of the clock."

Lambert studied the old man's strained features and didn't like what he saw. "You should take things more easy."

"And how am I supposed to do that?"

"I don't know, but you're pushing yourself too hard. You should find a less strenuous means of exercise. How about tai chi?"

Sinclair scowled, clearly not appreciating Lambert's attempt at humour. "Take things easy you say? If I do that, who will do the cleaning, the washing, the shopping?"

"It's the best excuse and always works, eh? When you don't want to do something you can always find reasons not to."

"I did those things for your mother too." He stood up, taking a deep breath. "I'm going for a bath. I'll finish the garden tomorrow, put in some marigolds and sweetpeas ready for the late spring."

"I'll hire a gardener, how about that?"

Sinclair frowned. "You have plans to stay here, permanently?" Lambert shrugged and Sinclair shook his head. "You've surprised me again, sir."

Lambert touched his arm. "I wanted to ask you something, but it can keep."

"No, please, tell me now."

Lambert took in a breath, preparing himself, unable for the moment to look Sinclair straight in the face. "All the years you've been here, Sinclair, I've never actually got to know you. Your family, Sinclair? Where are they from?"

"Why do you need to know anything about them, sir?"

Lambert studied the tabletop. "Curiosity. All the while, I've been sifting through papers and books, trying to piece together the past of a family I barely knew. But no matter where I look, there is nothing about you, despite you having been here forever." He met Sinclair's stare. "Strange."

"Nothing *strange* in it at all, sir. My father was a regimental sergeant major, fought in the Second World War. He'd married a local girl, my mother, and I was born not so very far from here in Kirkcudbright. Nothing very spectacular about any of it."

"But your family fought at Culloden. Were you not granted land, by George the Second, as we were?"

"Squandered, or so I understand. My father never spoke of it and the whole period slipped into obscurity."

"And have you any brothers, or sisters?"

"As you, sir, I am an only child. I am the last of the line, something which has often kept me awake at night, wondering what the future might hold." He licked his bottom lip. "Something you needn't concern yourself with, given how much younger you are to me."

"About what would happen to this place, you mean?"

"Indeed, sir."

"I'm not worrying about the bloody inheritance, for Christ's sake. Besides, this place will probably go to the National Trust when we both finally roll over. No, I..." Lambert pulled in a deep breath, "Sinclair, I wanted to tell you, I'm sorry. That was all."

"Sorry? For what?"

"All the years I abused you. Demanded, expected, taking you for granted. I'm sorry."

"Sir, you don't have to—"

"And don't call me 'sir' any more, as I won't call you 'Sinclair'. It's out-dated and doesn't feel right."

"I'm not concerned with such matters, sir –" He stopped, awkward, face reddening slightly. "I'm sorry, *Mister* Andrew."

"Andrew. Call me Andrew."

Sinclair sat down, a glimmer of a smile playing around his mouth. "All right, *Andrew*. There's something of a generation gap between us; thirty years is a long time. I served your parents, watched them shower you with their love but now..." Megan wandered in, tongue lolling from the corner of her mouth. She made straight for the water bowl and lapped at it noisily. Sinclair stretched out and scratched her behind one floppy ear. "I feel sure, if you were to meet the right girl, there is time enough to get married, have children. The future will be secured."

"You make us sound like the bloody Royals, Sinclair." He turned away. "I was wondering about a few other things." Sinclair waited and Lambert interlaced his fingers, choosing his words carefully, not wishing the manservant to grow overly curious. "The west tower. Why was it in such a state?"

"Well, I assume it is because it hadn't been tidied up." Megan gave a deep groan and rolled over onto her side. Sinclair seemed lost in thought, eyes distant, gazing into a void.

"But you'd been in there, hadn't you, before you brought down the boxes? When you were looking for father's last work?"

Sinclair looked up, eyes alive again. "Strange you should mention that, because I could never find the key."

Lambert frowned. "But you opened up the room for me just the other day."

"Yes, that's true, but previously the key was not on its hook."

"But it was this time?"

Sinclair nodded. "I can't think of any reasonable explanation. All I can assume is that it must have been hidden underneath another set of keys and I simply overlooked it."

Nodding, Lambert whispered, "Keys do become lost and then are found again, but only when they so desire it."

"I beg your pardon, sir?"

Lambert blinked, "Eh? Oh, sorry, I was thinking aloud. No, it doesn't matter, I suppose. So, you never actually checked the west tower for father's last book?"

"Are you telling me you have found it up there?"

"Not as such. Some notes in the desk drawer, a few scribbles. Some are difficult to decipher. Do you know what happened when grandfather left for Vézelay?"

Sinclair frowned and leaned back in his chair. Megan sighed again, stood and took another drink before flopping down onto the cold stone slabs of the kitchen floor. "Why do you ask?"

"Curious. Something I read amongst the papers. He went there looking for something."

"Yes, and from what I gather, he didn't find it."

"I'm going."

Sinclair gaped. "To Vézelay? When?"

"As soon as I can. I need to find the same *something*, but I don't know what."

"It's an awful long way to go if you don't know what you're looking for."

"I have a feeling, a belief, whatever you like to call it, but all I know is when I get there, everything will become clear."

"And if you find what you're looking for, what then?"

Lambert turned his eyes to the old manservant and held his concerned stare. "Then I'll stay and you can have this place."

Sinclair appeared stunned and for a moment couldn't speak. Lambert stood up, put the kettle on to boil again and waited, staring into nothing. So deep in thought did he become he did not even hear Sinclair leave the room, with Megan always so close.

He dreamed in the night, a confused and haphazard collection of images of dark twisting corridors winding through the interior of a dripping, dank castle. He stopped and listened to moans and groans, animal noises, distant but sounding angry. And behind him, footsteps, hobnailed boots crunching across stone flags. A hand, as cold as icicles, gripping his shoulder, breaking through the skin, touching the bone.

He let out a muffled cry and lay, shivering, in bedclothes pulled up to his chin. Bathed in sweat, he stayed quiet, clamped his hands over his face, not daring to believe he remained safe in his own bedroom.

Slowly, with no more noises, he allowed his hands to drop, and peered into the dark.

He saw her, running barefoot across the rolling landscape. She had been for a long time, the soles of her feet shredded and bloody. She wore her thin delicate dress and it trailed behind her, cut to the thigh, exposing her flesh. He reached out, but no sensation of touch followed. This was more a vision than a dream.

A castle appeared, stark, grey stonewalls, narrow arrow slits in the tower, men looking out from the battlements. One soldier hollered down to others to lower the drawbridge. Lorna, slowing to a walk, staggered up to the entrance and collapsed on her face.

Lambert went to throw back his bedclothes, desperate to get to her and help, but something prevented him, a force beyond understanding. This was wrong, not a dream, not reality, something else. Something unknown and confusing. However much he tried to help her, he could not. Fear turned muscles to liquid, sinews to mush. No strength, no possibility of movement. So he sat and watched and fought to suppress the mounting terror that covered everything with a smothering film of uncertainty.

They helped her inside, the Earl Carrick already striding across the open bailey. He was half-dressed, his shirt hanging out of his thick, padded trousers.

Brushing back his long hair, he stooped down and cradled her in his arms. "Lorna?" He whispered, and her eyes fluttered. She smiled but before he could utter another word, she went limp. "Carry her to my chambers," he said.

So they did.

And Lambert found the force to follow, but not with his legs. Sitting on his bed, transported through the maze of narrow corridors by invisible hands carrying him, as real hands lifted and carried Lorna towards a bedchamber where he witnessed all.

The Earl of Carrick held her hand whilst a young serving girl applied cold, wet compresses to her fevered brown. Lorna moaned, opened her eyes again and settled upon him. "John," she said.

"Don't speak," he gripped her hand. With a look, he dismissed the girl, waited until the door closed, then leaned forward and kissed Lorna's forehead. "What in the name of God has happened?"

"They came," she managed, her voice a mere croak.

"Who? Who came, Lorna?"

"The King's men. So many, with huge war engines. They threw down our walls, John, and burned it down."

"The *King*? What the hell are you talking about? Why would the king—"

"Not our own dear Robert," she said, "the King of *England*. Richard the Second. He has crossed the border with soldiers, John. He told me. He moves to Chester, to gather more forces."

"Hush," he said quickly, stroking her brow. "You're all confused, my sweet. The King of England would not come here. There is no reason."

"Yes, John. There is. They want to clear the borders. He told me, John. He told me *everything*."

Light changed, filtering through the arrow slits. A weird, sallow light. Sickly almost. Lambert wrapped his arms around himself, the temperature plummeting.

She sat upright in bed, sipping hot wine. Lambert sniffed the air, caught the scent of spices. Mulled wine, warming, soothing. She appeared relaxed, recovered from the ordeal of her flight through the night. Her dressed gaped open at the neck, exposing the smooth skin of her breasts.

The door opened and Lambert, taken by surprise, twisted to see John Carrick coming forward, steel bevor already in place around his throat, kettle helmet in the crook of his arm. Behind him, less prepared, strode the Swede, Karl Portenson. On seeing him, Lorna let out a tiny gasp and immediately put the goblet of wine down on the small dressing table beside the bed.

"Outriders have returned," said Carrick, sitting down on the bed. He gazed at her and, as if only just realising, she gathered the unbuttoned top of her dress more tightly to cover her breasts.

"What have they reported?"

"That your story is true," said Portenson, drawing closer. He stroked her hair and she did not flinch, but turned her face to his. "They have burned your home and your husband is nowhere to be found."

Carrick smiled, picking up her hand as before, but this time staring at it intensely. "It would be best you stayed here. We are taking a force of men to range out from your castle. Hopefully we can catch them and teach the bastards not to venture into our lands again."

"But the attack was led by the king," she said, turning to Portenson, eyes pleading. The Swede's hand drifted under her heavy curtain of hair, cupping her neck. "His army is too strong." Her voice grew thicker, more constrained, and the Swede leaned into her, kissing her lips as his other hand reached under her bodice, searching out her soft breasts.

She moaned and he sat back, gazing deep into her eyes. His hand remained under her dress.

"Our force is stronger still," said Carrick, standing up, his face growing red. It may have been the glow from the candles, but Lambert knew all too well it was the growing discomfort of the couple's intimacy, which caused the heat to rise. "The Earl of Douglas is moving on Annandale even as we speak. The English are camped there."

She looked from Portenson to Carrick. "You will march out between two armies? What if Douglas is defeated?"

"James is more than a match for any poxy Englishman. It will be us who has Richard squeezed. If we capture him, the bounty would be huge."

"You aim to ransom him?"

"What else would you have us do? You have not long been exposed to the vagaries of modern war, my sweet child. It can be violent, but also most rewarding."

"Most rewarding," said Portenson, returning to her lips.

Lambert watched, mesmerised as Carrick stepped away. Shuffling his feet. "I see you two need to be reacquainted. I'll..." He shrugged, forced a smile and almost ran from the room.

The Swede grinned as the door closed, then moved to return to Lorna's mouth. But she brought up both hands to ward him off, "Karl. This is not what I wished for."

Portenson cocked his head. "What are you talking about? You can't tell me you didn't enjoy our last meeting?"

"No, I'd never say that."

"Well then!" He stepped back, hands moving to his belt. Her hand closed over his and he smiled again. "Lorna, we have need of each other. Nothing more."

"Karl, the King, Richard, he ... He..." She struggled to find the words to explain the confusion which must have been running amok around her brain.

He cupped her chin. "I do not want explanations, nor excuses. All I want is your body. Tomorrow I return to my homeland and we may never see one another again."

"You're leaving? Forever?"

He smiled at her obvious disappointment. "I may come back, who knows. Life has a strange way of throwing up the unlooked for."

"Unlooked? Is that all I am to you?"

"Dear Christ, woman, you could never be anything other than the conduit for my desire." He pushed her hands away, returning to pulling apart his breeches.

She held up her hand, averting her eyes. "Karl. I cannot. It is not you, or I, but another which prevents me from continuing."

Portenson's expression changed, as did the bulge in his breeches, the fire growing dimmer. "What do you mean, *another*?"

"Please Karl. The King became so violent when he discovered my love for Devoir, I do not wish the same to happen with you."

Portenson's frown became deeper. "What the devil are you talking about, woman?"

She lowered her eyes, unconsciously drawing the neck of her dress together. "I have met another man, unlike anyone I have ever known. Sweet, kind and gentle. He is a painter and a lover of the most..." She raised her face and stared unblinking into the Swede's frozen gaze. "You showed me how much my life had become dull and fixed; you opened up a whole new world for me, one I never dared believe existed. But I knew, even as we coupled, that you could never be anything other than the most wonderful, delicious moment. You and I could never have a future, Karl."

"And that is what you desire?" She nodded. "This man, this *painter*, he can give you everything I can?"

"Yes. I did not believe another man could give me as much love as you did that night, but I was wrong. Devoir is everything I have ever wanted."

The Swede took in a deep breath, "I see. I can't say I'm not disappointed," he licked his lips, eyes rolling over Lorna's body. "By God, I want you so much, woman, it burns!" He laughed, his body relaxing, "Seems like one of the serving wenches is going to be sleeping happy tonight!" He bowed, making a sweeping gesture with his arm, "My Lady, I do not think I shall ever forget you," and with that he span on his heels and left.

Lambert glanced across to Lorna and watched as she drew up her knees to her chest, lowered her head, and sobbed.

"Andrew," she said, resting the flat of her hand over his stomach. "You saw what you needed to see."

He stared to the ceiling, his mind in disarray. "I don't understand. How can I see things from the past and yet," he clenched his fist, "they are so *real*."

"They *are* real, for their time. Do not struggle to understand, merely accept."

"But, the images, they are so *immediate*, as if I am there!" He shook his head. "Tell me, after Portenson left, you cried. Can you tell me why?"

"I will try." She laid her head on his chest, one arm draped over him. She let out a low moan, "I cried with regret, Andrew. Regret that I did not meet Karl many years before. My husband was a noble man, just and devoted to me, but his devotion was limited to providing me with fine clothes and a warm home. There was no desire. I believe he married me merely for show. He never came to me, not even on our wedding night. You understand my meaning?" She squeezed his flesh. "So, when Karl made love to me, it opened up a whole new direction. You saw how he loved me."

He smiled, but turned his head away, not wanting her to see how red he was becoming. The heat made his whole face pulse. "Yes. I did. But I saw you making love to other men too. Why did you do that if you loved Devoir?" His voice became aggressive. "What made you do so?"

She bit her lip. "What did you expect me to do? Start marauding, gathering loot and build up my strength? As you know from your history, Andrew, women were supposed to stay indoors, doing chores and feeling bored. Painting became my escape, my obsession. When I first became aware of your family, the secret they possessed about the painting, I decided to use you to gain what I wanted, because the painting links all my lives together, Andrew. That is what you need to try to understand. King Edward went to an exhibition of mine, viewed my work and became enthralled. Something stirred inside him, a memory, and he unearthed the original work Devoir created. He visited your grandfather to learn of its history. When I too went to visit him, the more I learned about your grandfather, the more feelings stirred inside me. Then, without warning, he ran away. Literally *and* metaphorically. He rejected me, tried to destroy everything about me. On the night of the accident, you somehow were able to enter into my world so I relaunched my attempts to find Devoir's portrait of me. The more I discovered, the more I realised. The Universe had its own designs on me, Andrew, right from the very beginning. All those years of searching, to find the secrets within the paint, the secrets disclosed by Devoir. I had to find it, you see. I had to possess those secrets, for myself. Through Kind Edward, I discovered your grandfather, then you. You can unearth the secrets of the painting, you can show me where it is. And, in return, I shall shower gifts upon you. You are so unique, unlike anyone else I have known. You irradiate goodness. I feel your concern. But you don't need to worry, your future is bright."

Her lips folded over his, cooling and soothing him.

He sat bolt upright, eyes wide, staring towards the far wall, heart pounding in his throat. "Jesus," he said, threw back the covers and stood up. He looked down on the bed, saw the impression of another's body and, without conscious thought, pressed his hand upon the mattress and felt the warmth.

Somewhere far below, in the depths of the house, the telephone was ringing. The world of the present had returned and he stumbled into the shower room to try to wash away the memories of the night.

No matter how hard he scrubbed, he could not.

27

Lambert took the receiver from Sinclair's grip. "Yes?"

"It's me, bonny lad."

Lambert closed his eyes. Talking to Miles right now was not his idea of fun. Perhaps he sighed too loudly; Miles sounded pissed off. "Not happy to hear from me?"

"Nothing of the sort, Miles, I'm just a little—"

"Strung out, hung over, filled with remorse?"

"None of the above."

"Sinclair tells me you look like shit."

Lambert cocked an eyebrow in the manservant's direction. Sinclair reddened and turned away. "He always did have an eye for such things."

"You mean he's observant?"

"I mean he knows a lot about shit." He gazed out of the window. The sky was darkening. A storm brewing perhaps. "What do you want, Miles?"

"You'll never guess who I bumped into this morning."

"Er, let me think ... Henry Kissinger?"

"Who?"

"It doesn't matter. Tell me."

"Evelyn."

Lambert swallowed hard. "Shit. You did?"

"Yes, and guess what – she wants to meet you. She feels pretty awful about slinking out of the party the way she did, so..." He chuckled. "I took the liberty of inviting her and Cheryl out for a drink. Tonight."

Lambert groaned. "Jesus, Miles. Why the fuck did you do that?"

"Because you need to get out of that fucking castle, Andrew! I thought the party would be a great idea, but it turned out to be a total fucking disaster. You're worse than ever."

"What do you mean?" Lambert swung around to confront Sinclair, but the kitchen was empty. "Damn him, and damn you Miles!" He disconnected and threw the phone down on the table and stormed out to confront his manservant.

He found him in the garden, kneeling on a plastic board, picking out weeds and other bits of rubbish with deliberate care, using a pair of flat tipped tweezers. He looked up as Lambert's shadow crossed his line of sight.

"What the hell did you say to him?"

Sinclair sighed, "I told him you clearly had a bad night. I changed your bed linen, Andrew."

Lambert's shoulders dropped and he blew out a loud breath. "Jesus."

"What was it this time? Medieval battles, rape and pillage, or another night of passion with the lovely Lorna."

"Fuck you! Who do you think you are talking to me like that?"

Sinclair stood up, a good head taller than Lambert. "I'm worried about you."

"You don't need to be worried. I keep telling you all, *there is nothing wrong with me!*"

"I think there is. The accident. I think it changed you."

"You don't know what you're talking about."

"Tell me about the dream."

Lambert blanched, averting his gaze. "I'd rather not."

"Tell me."

"It … All right, all right, if you must know, it was as you said. Everything. Battles, medieval soldiers burning down the castle, Lorna fleeing to the Earl of Carrick."

"Anything else?"

"What, like sex you mean? Is that the part you're interested in?"

Sinclair's eyes narrowed. "What else."

"*Sex.* Okay, happy now? Lots of wild, mad, wonderful sex."

"I mean anything historical, other than the Earl of Carrick?"

"There were scenes involving the king, Richard the Second, stealing the painting, another one of grandfather with Edward the Seventh in which they talked about the same painting. He gave it to someone."

Sinclair turned his face to the sky. "How the hell did you know that?"

"I didn't *know*. I told you, I had a dream."

"This dream, you saw your grandfather and Edward the Seventh talking about the painting?" Lambert nodded. "And you discovered where the painting is?"

"Vézelay. I told you, I'm going there."

"But you don't know where, do you."

Lambert frowned. "Are you telling me you do?"

"I convinced myself the best course was not to tell you. To let you go, root around in the dark, come home thoroughly miserable, but…" He shrugged. "At least your ignorance would have made you calmer. Perhaps."

"Calmer? If you know anything more, Sinclair, you've got to tell me."

A long silence followed, during which time a few spots of rain against the window heralded a larger downfall. But Lambert didn't care. He wanted answers. So he waited and studied Sinclair grinding his teeth, battling with some inner demon. At last, eyelids hooded, he nodded. "Very well. It's only fair. A woman visited your grandfather and afterwards he travelled to Vézelay. Those parts you already know. He went to find the painting, to buy it from the Comte de Château de Chartreuse, in Chastellux-sur-Cure in Burgundy."

"I didn't know you could speak French."

"There is much you do not know about me, Andrew."

Lambert arched a single eyebrow. "I see. Care to enlighten me?"

"Not really, but I will tell you this – your grandfather was unsuccessful because he did not look in the correct place. The Comte was no longer in possession of the painting, having sold it to someone else. He died only weeks before your grandfather's visit, so there was no way of uncovering any clues to its whereabouts."

"But you have?"

Sinclair coughed, "I think we should go inside." He hunched his shoulders as the light drizzle developed into a downpour. Both men raced to the rear entrance and huddled under the porch. Lambert laughed but Sinclair remained bellicose. "If I tell you," he said, "I have fears you will do as you say – you will choose not to return here."

"Do you want to explain to me why?"

"The same reason why your grandfather became a recluse, a broken man. This woman captured his heart, Andrew. She seduced him into helping her find the painting and in so doing, he fell in love. I do not know what power she possesses, but it is frightening in its strength. She used your grandfather to get close to Edward the Seventh, and on his visit to Edinburgh in Nineteen Hundred and Four, she was introduced to him."

"I saw the photograph."

"Yes. But when she discovered what she needed, she disappeared, leaving the King to forever wonder who she was and what she wanted. On her return here, to Castle Strythe, she begged your grandfather for help."

"And when he failed to bring the painting to her, she left again."

Sinclair sighed. "And now she is back. I did not want to tell you anything about any of this. I recognised every sign, you see. The dreams, your mood changes, your seeming slide into paranoia … Your father told me how your grandfather experienced it all and he became a broken man. She will do the same to you."

Lambert considered the story Sinclair had recounted, knowing it differed wildly from the one told by Lorna. He guessed the truth lay somewhere in the middle. He kept these thoughts to himself however, and allowed a faint smile to develop. "I don't think so. Something has changed in her." He laughed again, "I'm not my grandfather. She is nothing but a dream, something my grandfather never truly believed."

"You actually think she is a figment of your imagination?"

"If not, something very close. I don't understand any of it and I'm not going to give myself a headache trying to make sense of what's been happening. I'm going to visit Miles tonight, and I'm going to forget all about Lorna."

"Until she comes into your bed again."

Lambert smiled and shook his head. "I'm hoping it'll be somebody else doing that, somebody *real*."

True to his word, Lambert met up with Miles at a bar in Edinburgh, a lively place with plenty of pulsing music, happy people, and an ambiance charged with anticipation of what would happen next. When the girls swaggered in, Lambert's stomach lurched. Evelyn, dressed in clinging white blouse and the tightest jeans he'd ever seen, seemed to glide across the floor towards him. Long, fawn hair swung delicately as she moved, and every man's eyes followed her, locked on her round, firm bottom.

Cheryl leaned into Miles and kissed him before turning to Lambert, planting a soft kiss on his cheek. "You're looking well, Andrew," she said, a mischievous twinkle in her eye. She had to shout to make herself heard above the din, but Lambert had no interest in her. He focused all his attention on the lithe, delectable young woman standing before him. Evelyn smiled, and he kissed her cheek, as Cheryl had done to him, but the smell of her, the taste of her flesh, almost caused him to swoon.

"I didn't think you'd come," she said, lightly raking her perfect nails over the back of his hand.

"I'm sorry I missed you the other night."

"I'm sorry for disappearing the way I did."

He smiled, locking onto her pale green eyes and didn't realise Miles was talking until his friend shook his arm. "*Andrew,*" Miles shouted. "Let's find a table."

They spent a few hours there, drinking and dancing, but mainly laughing, Miles keeping them all entertained with his stories of wild adventures in Thailand with his friend Bruce. "It was only when they strapped him down on the bed he realised he was in a bit of a spot!"

Cheryl, stirring her cocktail far too much, had her tongue out, licking her lips constantly, "I can't believe he didn't know."

"Have you seen those girls?"

"Lady boys," said Lambert.

Evelyn gaped at him. "You've never been with one, have you?"

"*Me*? Christ, no! I've never even been to Thailand. Not sure if I'd ever want to."

"Why not?" asked Cheryl.

"Too scary, I guess."

"Scary? How can it be scary," continued Evelyn, taking a sip of her drink. "It's only sex, Andrew."

"Ah well," interjected Miles, "that's the thing – is it *only sex*? Not sure if poor old Bruce would agree."

"He never told you what happened?" asked Cheryl, sniggering.

"Not a word. Maybe some sort of domination thing happened, who knows."

Evelyn raised her glass in mock salutation. "Yum ... I'd like some of that!"

Lambert's eyes snapped across to Evelyn, who returned his gaze, one eyebrow slightly cocked. His stomach yawned, a horrible churning feeling growing stronger, deep inside his loins.

Miles laughed and, seemingly unaware of what passed between Lambert and Evelyn, continued with his story, "When he got back to the hotel room, he must have stayed in the shower for about two hours. He never ventured outside for the rest of the holiday, preferring to stay in the hotel bar."

"So what did *you* do?" asked Cheryl.

Miles shrugged, drank his drink, "This and that."

"Christ, Miles, I hope you used a condom!"

"Of course," said Miles.

"I haven't seen Bruce for months," said Lambert, now avoiding Evelyn's stare. "He didn't come to the party."

"The thing is," said Miles, chancing a quick look around and leaning forward across the table, "I suspected for a long time he was gay. I reckon he knew those two were really men and he went along with it because he wanted to."

"So why lock himself away?"

Miles shrugged again, "Guess it's hard to finally accept who you are, I don't know. He's always been so physical, rugby, ice-hockey, the usual stuff."

"Yeah, and being in those baths after the games," giggled Cheryl. "Imagine him, eyeing up all those lovely *big* guys!"

Evelyn's eyes settled on Lambert again and again his insides twisted. He dared not return her gaze, knowing what she wanted.

The night developed and they moved on to another, quieter place. Miles, being a member of the club, was able to gain everyone entrance to the second floor, where a live band played soulful jazz. The surrounding conversations more low-key, more refined.

"They've got private booths," said Miles, much the worse for drink.

"Are you expecting me to join you," asked Cheryl, giving her finest shocked expression.

"Yes!" said Miles and Cheryl giggled, fell into his arms and they kissed, long and hard, his hand running over her well rounded behind. He drew back, gasping, licking his lips, "God, you taste delicious. Let's go." He winked at Lambert and disappeared up a winding staircase, both he and Cheryl negotiating the steps with some difficulty.

Alone now with Evelyn, Lambert, aware of the developing heat and the terrible silence, which descended, fidgeted with his glass, avoiding Evelyn's smouldering eyes. He didn't know what to say or do but when her fingers crept, spider like over the table towards his hand. He tried, but could not avoid catching her expression, those eyes burning into him, refusing to turn away. His only escape was her mouth, and he homed in on her full, soft lips. Pure perfection they were. Everything about her. Perfection.

"What are you thinking," she asked, her voice smoky, deep.

The burning increased and he gave up a silent prayer of thanks the dim lighting did not reveal just how red he had become. "I'm, er, wondering why you, er, wanted to come out with me tonight."

"*Why?*" Her eyes danced, "Why do you think, Andrew?"

"I don't know! At the party, you seemed—"

"I'd had too much to drink, but I'm all right tonight."

"Yes, I understand, but, what I meant was, at the party you didn't appear very interested."

"Neither did you. I got the feeling your attentions were on something else. Or some*one* else."

He went to speak but then her hand seized his and she squeezed, "Andrew, Miles has been telling me about your accident, how it shook you up. He also told me about Jennifer."

Lambert breathed hard, "Jennifer? Jesus, he had no right to do—"

"But it's okay, I'm not interested in your past, even if you still have feelings for her," she held up her finger to stop him speaking, "I only want your body, Andrew. And I want it now."

His mind went into overdrive, wondering what best to do. The only semblance of sex he'd experienced these past few months had been in his dreams. He was bound to be a disappointment.

"You're sweating," she said and leaned over to run the back of her hand over his cheek, "Andrew, what's the problem? Don't you find me attractive?"

"What? Of course I do!"

"Well then. I'm not asking you to marry me, Andrew. I want some fun, that's all. Miles' stories got me horny, didn't they you?"

He gaped at her, "Well, I..."

"I'm certain they did! What is it, Andrew? Would you like to have been in Bruce's predicament?"

"Shit, Evelyn I'm not *gay!*"

"You don't need to be gay to enjoy that sort of thing, Andrew. Just be open to the experience." She titled her head, "Don't tell me it didn't turn you on, the thought of being dominated?" She raised an eyebrow, "That's true, isn't it? Domination, yes? You want to be used, don't you? Told what to do, a sex slave?"

Without thinking, Lambert ran his fingers under his collar, "Christ."

"I thought so," she smiled, still holding his hand. "Well, would you find it just as exciting to be dominated by a woman? I know you like the idea," she raised her eyes, "Christ, wouldn't we all, but ... Andrew, a woman can dominate just as well. Get you on your back, straddle you. You'd like that, wouldn't you? Have her fuck you, pin you down? Yes?"

He nodded, unable to speak, his throat dry, heart thumping.

"Good," she said softly, "because that's what I like too. Come on," she pulled at his hand, "I'll show you."

28

He came out of the departure lounge of Charles de Gaulle and went to the car-hire desk. Less than thirty minutes later he drove out of the bewildering road network of the airport, heading towards the south and Burgundy.

Lambert kept his eyes straight ahead, trying to read the signs. Too many destinations, too many numbers, nothing making much sense. He hadn't included satnav in his rental. He hated satnav, resisting the obvious advantages of using the system. Now, glancing up at the massive road signs sprawling across the highway, he wished he hadn't been such a bloody Luddite.

He concentrated on seeking out the main cities, caught the name of Troyes on the A5 out of Paris, then struck west, heading for Auxerre.

The landscape changed from flat, endless plains to the gentle rolling hills of northern Burgundy. Soon, the signs indicated Avallon and he pulled into a roadside restaurant and had his first taste of French coffee, with rolls and cheese. Under a veranda, with birds singing from the nearby trees, the general lack of traffic, he sat back, stretched out his legs, and allowed the stress to slip away.

He stayed longer than he planned, but he didn't care. Time was on his side now he had achieved so much.

Before the flight to France, he'd gone down to his office, said what he needed to say, and took a taxi to Edinburgh International. Earlier, Sinclair, noticing the bag in the hallway, blew out his cheeks. "You're going somewhere, Mr Andrew?"

Lambert kept his eyes on the suitcase. "It's something I need to do. We've discussed it."

"You know my feelings."

"Yes. And I'm sorry, but…"

A few days previously, the packages arrived. He tore them open with all the eagerness of a young child on Christmas morning, and beamed at what he held in his hand. For a long time, he sat and stared, not daring to believe their existence. Sometime later, he went into town to repost two of them. On a whim, he went to an Internet café, chose the booth furthest from the door, and typed out the words in the search engine and found the site he wanted. He leaned back and stared at the screen, lost in a world of joy, beyond anything he had ever experienced.

That afternoon, he received a phone call and the news brought tears to his eyes. From now on, the sadness and the stress were at last defeated, replaced by happiness.

Over the course of the next few days, things moved so quickly he often felt detached from it all, a bystander, not involved in the action, viewing everything from a distance. He'd stare at himself in the mirror and wondered if this too was another dream.

On the day of his departure, the doubts and the disbelief disappeared; he knew it was real. He looked at Sinclair and placed the package in the manservant's hands.

"I want you to open this, Sinclair, after I've gone. You'll find it of interest, I think. But I want you to promise me you will mention none of it to Miles."

Sinclair stared at the package and said nothing for a long, drawn out moment. When at last he turned his face towards Lambert, the fight left the old manservant's eyes. "I promise," he said, "but I still do not want you to go."

Lambert shrugged, squeezed Sinclair's arm and crossed to his waiting car. The last sight Lambert had of the manservant was of him standing in the doorway, arms folded, disapproval written into every line of his face.

A far more difficult task proved to be the email to Evelyn, which he sent from the airport. Difficult because of what had happened between them at the club.

She'd taken him into the private booth, unbuttoned her blouse and let him stare at her breasts. When she slipped off her jeans and guided his hands to her full, firm buttocks, his erection sprang up hard. She caressed him as he roamed over her silken flesh. "You have the most gorgeous arse," he breathed.

"Your favourite part, yes?"

"God yes."

She pushed him onto the bed and straddled him, as she said she would. "Hold me, as you want," she said, and he obeyed, without argument, gripping the firm flesh of her buttocks and she rode him, endlessly…

Such a memory! He closed his eyes, squeezing away the images of that moment, then he finished his coffee and stood up. On the way back to his car, he looked into the window of a *brocante,* smiling at the array of antiques on offer. At times like this, he wished he had some sort of collecting bug. A hobby would be good, he mused. Now his business was coming to its close, he needed to devote more time in finding ways to fill his days. Perhaps he had, he mused and smiled to himself.

He breathed in the air, glancing down the road which bi-sected the village. A place such as this, quiet, out of the way, he could live here. Ambition, money, fast cars, exotic holidays, none of them held any attraction for him. Some might call him boring, but to live a simple, uncluttered life, for Andrew Lambert was more than enough. He did not wish any more clutter, only clarity of thought and action, things sorely missing when he'd made love to Evelyn.

She had stood up after he came with a cry, and she gazed down on him and smiled. She swept hair from her face. Breathing hard. "I enjoyed that, Andrew. You're certainly very keen." She ran her hands over her firm breasts, bent down and kissed him, "You're nice."

"You're amazing." He stared at her in awe. The self-confidence she exhibited, her breasts so full, honey-coloured skin so smooth, legs well muscled and her arse… He could quite happily gaze upon it for the rest of his life.

"You're sweet," she said, and with those words he knew, if he hadn't realised before, there could never be any sort of future with this woman. She caught his changing mood and cocked her head, mouth turned down slightly. "Don't be sad, Andrew." She pulled on her blouse and jeans and he watched her, mesmerised, yet saddened he would never gain experience her glorious body. "Let's not make any plans, agreed?" She smiled, picking up her bag. "The dish you served was edible but, to be frank, not delicious, so I'm going back into the club, to sample the rest of the menu." She winked, swung around and left him gawping at her, incredulous.

Lambert sighed, her words smarting still, and crossed the road to his car. With the season not yet begun, he had managed to take a small rented property in the village of Asquins, only a few kilometres out of Vézelay. He unfolded the roadmap and traced his finger along the route, reassuring himself he would arrive well before evening. He gazed out of the side window, remembering how he had met Miles at the door to the club, much the worse for drink.

"Where's Evelyn?" his friend asked, words slurring, body swaying.

"God knows. Gone off with someone else I think."

Miles pulled a face, glanced back to the interior, "Cheryl is powdering her nose, as they say." He frowned. "You know for sure she's gone off with someone else?"

"She told me as much."

"Well, you should have bloody well told her to fuck off." He jabbed his finger against Lambert's chest, "You're too much of a fucking gentleman, Andrew."

"No. It's not as simple as that, Miles. Besides, you wouldn't understand – you're as pissed as a fart."

Miles leered, "Too right, mate. Cheryl is like a fucking baboon in bed! I'll need every ounce of strength to keep her satisfied."

"Yes, and a gallon of whisky will help you through I shouldn't wonder."

"I've never had any problems with alcohol and sex," he grinned. "Funny that. Don't know why. Ah, here she comes…"

Cheryl approached, makeup and hair immaculate. She certainly looked extremely fine in her cut down top and *Calvin Klein* jeans, shaped to show off her figure to best effect. "Hey, Andrew! Where's Evelyn?"

"It's a long story."

"Oh." She looked downcast, smiled at Miles, and took Lambert's arm. "Listen. She's a 'good-time-girl', you understand? She's not into relationships or anything like that. Miles should have told you, but I knew he wouldn't." Miles went to speak and she shot him her trademark scowl, designed to wither the hardest of hearts. It worked. Miles shut up. "It's nothing to do with you, Andrew, okay? God knows how many men she's gobbled up and spat out. But," her eyelids narrowed as her mouth creased into a knowing smile, "you had a *great* time, right?"

"One of the best."

"Well then," she playfully punched him, "don't be so bloody morose! She's as hot as hell, and you've had her. Lighten up!" She swung around and gripped Miles' arm. "Come on, I want breakfast. In bed."

The present slowly returned. Lambert stared at his hands gripping the steering wheel. Cheryl was right, he needed to 'lighten up', in so many ways. He understood where it all stemmed from, of course he did. He'd always known, but the knowledge didn't make the situation any easier to accept. The demons ran around in his head, scalding words delivered to belittle him, forcing him to question so much about himself.

Jennifer. He remembered the last time he'd been with her. Miles called her 'stuck-up', however in between the sheets she was like a wild thing. She loved sex, demanding it every night, and Lambert came to dread the moments he shared with her, watching the clock, knowing soon she would be wanting to go to bed. Exciting at first, the nightly gyrations became something of a chore. She yearned sex, but she was unadventurous, doggy-style being the limit of her experimentation. He dreaded the moment she would berate him over his lack of desire, but when it finally came, he reeled.

She stood next to the bed, hands on her hips, glaring. "What's wrong with you? You look like an alien. Don't you find me attractive?"

"It's not that, darling, it's—"

"We need to talk about this, Andrew, why you can't get a hard-on. It's becoming a problem."

He sat up, "A problem? Who for? You, or me?"

"For *both of us*, of course!"

"Jen, it's not you, but…"

"But *what?*"

Her accusing tone wasn't helping. He struggled with his words, skating around what he wanted to say, afraid of her reaction. "I'm not a bloody machine, okay? You can't just get into bed and expect me to want to have sex. I don't possess a switch you can turn on and off whenever you get the urge."

"No, that's not it, Andrew. It's your sex-drive. It is so bloody low! I'm not used to it, that's all. I *need* sex, okay? All of my other boyfriends couldn't get enough, but you… There's something wrong and you can't, or won't tell me."

"What do you expect me to say?"

"Actually, I want to hear your explanations. Listen," she sat down next to him, "we can work around it, okay, try other stuff, if you want."

"Other stuff… Jenny, you think… My God, don't you really want to say that I'm simply not good enough for you, is that it? I'm sick to death of trying to do my best. You're an ice-maiden, Jenny! It's got nothing to do with me, but everything to do with *you*! You lie there, with your perfect tits and your perfect legs and you think that's more than enough for good sex. Your insufferable self-esteem drives me mad! What about love? Where does that come into your bedroom philosophy?"

"Andrew, I think you need to calm down." She pulled on her clothes.

"No, I need you to understand, okay? I'm not like one of your lovers. I'm not like Clint."

"No, you're fucking not!" She bared her teeth, "He was a *man*, Andrew, a *real man*. He didn't have expectations, all he wanted was sex and lots of it. That's what he gave me and I loved it. But you, you'd prefer as nice cup of tea."

He gasped, took a moment to recover from her verbal assault. "I thought you wanted more. Like me. A relationship. Love, a future."

She snarled, "A future, with *you*?" She shook her head. "I might have done once, but you can't satisfy me, Andrew. There's nothing, no *passion*. You should take Viagra."

"Viagra only works when you're turned on!"

"Oh, and I don't turn you on, is that it?"

"If you must know, no you don't. Great body and great ass doesn't a great lover make."

"Fuck you Andrew." She swept up her bag and shoes and went to the door. "I only ever spent time with you because of your money, but now you've managed to kick all of that into touch, you're nothing but a fucking loser."

"What? You only stayed with me because of my money?"

"Well what else?" She chuckled. "Start taking the Viagra, Andrew. Or see a shrink." She tore open the door. "But do it quick." A matter of days later she delivered the bombshell – she'd been screwing an Arab businessman from Kuwait, who gave her everything she desired, including satisfying sex and a white Rolls Royce. Or so she said. For his part, Lambert experienced a curious sense of relief at her news. When she took the last of her belongings from the flat they shared, he opened up a bottle of wine and celebrated, not shedding a single tear.

But her words cut deep.

A huge lorry roared past, snapping Lambert out of his reverie and he shook himself, blew out his cheeks and wondered if Jennifer's words really had caused him problems. He remembered the night of the party, how he felt making love to Lorna. If in a dream, he could achieve such passion, such total satisfaction, why not in the real world? Was Evelyn simply the wrong choice?

He sighed. He was sick to death of thinking about it. Nobody else ever commented on his inadequacy as a lover, so why did he take notice now? And what was so very wrong in trying to find love? What had Ray Bradbury said … 'Looking back, the only thing that meant anything is love'? Something like that. Nothing more important than love anyway. Lambert believed those words, accepted their truth, knew he could never indulge in one-night-stands, which was why he felt so letdown over Evelyn. He respected himself and others too much. And Lorna? Why the hell had he succumbed to his feelings for her? And how had she seemed so real? He needed to know the answers, before he truly did sink into the abyss of insanity. His reason for coming all this way, to the beautiful Yonne valley, was to try to find those answers and perhaps, just perhaps, find a kind of peace.

29

The Golf GTi pulled up in a cloud of dust and gravel, Miles running out of the car before it had fully come to a stop. Sinclair stood on the top step, face set hard as chiselled granite.

"When did he leave?" asked Miles, panting.

"Early," said Sinclair. "There isn't another flight until tomorrow morning."

"Damn, he has a whole day ahead of us," Miles gritted his teeth, slamming a fist into his other palm. "Why the hell didn't you stop him?"

"What would you have had me do, Mr Miles? Knock him out, perhaps? Lasso him and tie him against the garden fence?"

"Don't be so bloody stupid, man!"

"Well then, you tell me. I've been ringing you all day long, I did all I could. I'm not his bloody keeper."

Miles turned away, face crimson. "All right, we'll make the best of a bad job and I'll phone the airport and—"

"I've already booked us two one-way tickets, Mr Miles, so calm down."

"*You* ..." Miles gaped at the manservant before his face split into a broad grin, "Dear God, but you're one efficient sod!" His shoulders slumped, the fight going out of him. "Okay, I'll stay here and we'll make an early start tomorrow. What time is the flight?"

"It leaves from Edinburgh at six fifteen in the morning."

"*Six fifteen*?" Miles rubbed his chin and groaned. "But we'll need to be there for ... Christ, we may as well not go to bed."

It was Sinclair's turn to look dour-faced. "If you have no objections, I think I'll pass on that particular suggestion, Mr Miles. I'll retire after I've had something to eat. You'd best do the same."

Miles shook his head, grinning, and he pulled out his mobile and began to punch the numbers. "You go to bed, my old mate – I've got much more entertaining plans in mind. Cheryl." He winked and sucked in a breath as somebody answered on the other end. "Hello my gorgeous girl! How do you fancy spending a night in a beautiful traditional castle built just for the two of us?"

Sinclair left Miles to it and retired to his room. He lay fully stretched on his bed, staring at the ceiling. After a long moment he reached for the unopened package by his side and picked it up, reading for the umpteenth time the wording on the cover, 'To my ever faithful servant and friend, I wish you every happiness for no one deserves it more than you.'

And, in the quiet of his room, after the tears had stopped, he slowly opened the package and took out the gift Lambert had given him.

Before the Sun was up, they left for Edinburgh. Cheryl, with Megan at her side, waved them goodbye before Miles took the Golf out of the drive, gunning the engine when they reached the highway. It was barely ten minutes to three o'clock on a cold, grey morning and Sinclair sat huddled up in a thick, padded overcoat, whilst Miles kept his eyes fixed ahead, concentrating hard. Sinclair sighed and closed his eyes. In an hour's time, they would be at the airport, experiencing the joys of the endless security checks. All being well, by lunchtime, Vézelay would be within reach and then the real search would begin – where to find Mr. Andrew.

Andrew Lambert stepped out into the morning sunshine and paused to take a deep breath. He walked slowly out of the front garden of his rented cottage and followed the lane towards the small crossroads, with the faded advertising hoardings on the wall of an adjacent building and, to his left, the vacant petrol pumps standing outside *Les Hirondelles*, the local café. Still early enough to catch the baker, he wandered inside and ordered a coffee and croissant from the good-looking girl behind the counter. A few other customers came crawling in, the smell of freshly baked bread a lure for them all, Lambert mused. The girl, smiling, presented him with his order. He paid and went outside, taking a seat at one of the pavement tables arranged alongside the main road.

He drank his coffee, watching a butterfly in distress on the tarmac, considered helping, then gasped as a sparrow swooped from nowhere and took the insect away. He did not know sparrows did such things.

Something else he had never considered; he could come all this way on a journey whose end seemed steeped in uncertainty. So many things he failed to consider, or attempt to understand. A lifetime putting events aside, not facing problems, hoping they would simply disappear. Time. He believed in time, the certainty that if you waited long enough, people would forget. The world would forget. Problems would become nothing more than smudged memories. His maxim. The great philosophy.

It was shit and he knew it.

He sipped his coffee and reeled back as a monster of a truck roared by, throwing up a huge gust of wind, flinging sharp bits of grit into his face. He swore, stuck his fists into his eyes and tried to clean away the debris.

"I've been watching you."

He jumped, snapping his head around and there she was. Lorna. He gripped the table edge, supporting himself, forgetting his injury, feeling as if a gaping chasm was opening up beneath him. "Dear God," he said.

She smiled. "You've made your way, Andrew," she said, taking his hand, "We are so close now, to finding destinies."

"Destinies? I've dreamt of finding my destiny, avoiding past obstacles. But what about you. Your destiny? A leap into the future, because maybe it's time to stop getting bogged down in a morass of the past. A very dark past." He jerked himself free, glaring at her. She remained silent. "What do you want from me, Lorna? You come and go from my life, leaving me breathless, exhausted, confused. I don't know anything, about you, me, or why we are here."

"Yes you do, I've told you. You have come to find my painting."

"And what happens when I find it?"

She frowned. She looked ravishing, her hair burnished at the tips by the sun, her face aglow, eyes huge and all consuming. She wore a simple floral patterned dressed, cut tight at the waist, and on the table her hat, white, wide-brimmed. "When you find it, Andrew, we will be free. We will face the truth, a chance to learn the differences between the virtual and the real world."

"You've shown me so many things, allowed me to catch glimpses of your past lives. It's been the most emotional journey of my life."

"Andrew, you must try and understand all of it is in your own mind. You were transported to the past to avoid you slipping into possible insanity. I'm aware of your concerns, of course I am, but Andrew, everyone can have another chance. You must trust me, stop worrying so much, because it is blocking your hidden possibilities."

"How can I stop when nothing makes sense?"

"Are you so sure none of it makes sense to you? Haven't you explored the inner workings of your heart, of how we are connected?"

He let out his breath slowly. "We're from different worlds you and me, from different centuries. You're amazing, in every conceivable way, but you're a dream, a figment of my imagination, frozen in past lives." He clawed at his hair. "Why are you here? Now? Are you ready to enter the modern world? This world could blow your mind. Everything about you is rooted in the past, your emotions, the words you use to express your feelings, the way you think, even your manners … You'd be better staying in your chosen past, Lorna."

"But what attracted us to one another? Maybe it is you? Maybe you live in the wrong century?"

He stared into the distance, knowing the truth of what she said. Everything that had happened confirmed he did not belong in this modern world. Hence his failed business, Jen. The life he now had, in his castle. That was his destiny now. He turned to her. "You *seem* real, but the truth is, you are as unattainable as the stars. You're a projection of my anguish, my desire to find someone who loves me."

"I could be real."

"You're not. I don't believe you."

"Then why are you here? Why come all this way if not because you believe?"

"Because I want to discover the truth for myself. I want to look into that painting and *see* the truth."

"Your grandfather did the same, Andrew. He saw the secrets and it broke his heart. He knew, at that moment he loved me more than anyone else in the entire world, but he also knew he could not leave his wife and child. So he destroyed every scrap of evidence pertaining to me, my past, our links to the castle. At least, he *believed* he destroyed everything. He forgot the letter, the one Sinclair showed you, the one which pointed you in the right direction. I needed nothing more to remain in the curious world I inhabit, the world between past and present. My world, Andrew, is now possible."

He took his hand away and pressed it over his face. "I want to believe you, I do, but…"

"You have to trust in my power, Andrew. My power is beyond measure."

"Yes." His mouth fell open, drinking her in. Her body, her words. "You're so *intoxicating*. I'm utterly under your command."

"I know. My power can be frightening some times."

"But it's so delicious."

She smiled. "Men have never dominated me, Andrew. They believed they did, but that was because I decided to make them think so. The things you have witnessed, they are projections from the past. As were my lovers. They no longer exist, at least not in the true meaning of the word. My power, however, transcends time. It is eternal."

His hand dropped. "And what of Richard? Whatever became of him?"

He caught the look in her eyes, the slight change of expression, her hesitation. "Very well. Let me tell you how it was…"

The struggle between the Scots and the English continued right along the border, raiding parties, skirmishes, peace shattered throughout the Lowland glens.

Richard returned to Castle Strythe in the early summer, his retinue riding over the hillside like a vast silver cloud, fully armoured, banners fluttering, lances poised. At their head, the King with his favourite, Robert de Vere, Duke of Ireland, haughty and assured. They cared not for the workers in the fields, who cowered, some throwing themselves face down in the dirt, and they guided their mounts across the tilled land, paying scant heed to the struggling crops they obliterated with their approach.

Jumping from his mount, Richard pulled off his helmet and strode through the open door. Lord Strythe, waiting a few paces inside, bowed from the waist. "I am honoured by your presence, majesty."

"I want you to ride with the Duke of Ireland," said Richard without a pause, wiping the sweat from his brow. "I wish you to take a message to the Earl of Carrick." He thrust a trolled up piece of parchment into the quivering man's hand. "The situation is grave. My desire is for peace, but this can never be if these raids into my realm persist."

Strythe chewed his lip. "Forgive me, sire, but I am a feared his Lordship, the Earl of Carrick, will not take kindly to any—"

"Damn your eyes, man! Take this letter and do as you are bloody well told!"

Strythe fell to his knees, throwing out his hands, "Majesty, the Earl of Carrick is preparing for war. I fear it is too late to bring him to the negotiation table."

"Who said anything about negotiating? The spineless fool will do as I heed, or I will send the hounds of hell to his door. Now get out, before my patience runs dry."

Whimpering, Strythe scrambled away, bleating like an injured sheep. Richard looked askance at De Vere. "Preparing for war he said. You think he speaks the truth?"

"If war comes, we will meet him and put an end to this sorry affair."

"I pray to God you are right."

"Do not doubt it, Richard. I've served you well these past years; I'll not fail you now."

Richard's eyes became moist and he took his friend into his arms and embraced him. "God watch over you, Robert."

"And you, my King."

Richard went outside again and watched as De Vere, with a score of riders, cantered over the rolling landscape, together with Strythe and a pair of trusted retainers. He stood until they were mere specks on the horizon, then dismissed his men and went back inside.

Lorna stood in the great hall, her pastel blue dress reaching to the ground, hair free, falling to her shoulders. Her eyes seemed to draw him in and he moved as if in a dream, forgetting everything and everyone, her presence taking hold of all of his senses.

"Oh my majesty," she said, dropping to her knees and he took her hand, lifted her to her feet, and kissed her cheek, "I have missed you so much," he said and, still holding her hand, he led her through the castle to the rear and the ornamental garden.

"Events are overtaking us, Lorna," he said. "If Carrick would seek war, then his wish will come true, but my hope is he will see sense."

"His forces are strong, sire."

"So are mine. Do not doubt my resolve, not on this, nor on my love for you."

"Sire, I cannot reciprocate. My husband is a good and just man, I cannot simply—"

"Good and just he may be, but he cannot give you what I can. I am a king, Lorna. My powers, granted to me by God, are beyond measure. I will shower you with riches, a fine house with servants, and I will love you like no man has ever done. These things I can do."

A soft footfall caused them both to turn.

Lorna gasped, stepping between Richard and the newcomer, who seemed to walk as if on some sort of cloud, his feet barely brushing across the ground. Richard frowned. "Who is this?"

"I am Devoir, and I am Mistress Lorna's closest confidant and," he smiled towards her, "friend."

"I like not the tone of your voice, sir." Richard stiffened.

"Please, sire," interjected Lorna, "Monsieur Devoir is under the employ of my husband. He has painted me, in the most wonderful setting you can imagine. Here, in Castle Strythe, next to the loch."

"Has he, by God?"

Devoir bowed deep. "Your Highness, I wish no disrespect, but my time here has allowed Mistress Lorna and I to…" He shrugged his shoulders. "Perhaps you would care to view the painting?"

Richard, a dark cast to his face, narrowed his eyes, nodding briefly, "If *Mistress* Lorna so wishes it."

They led the King through the corridors of the castle, ascending winding steps, traversing a covered walkway, finally reaching the sturdy west tower. Lorna fitted a heavy black key into the lock and released the tumblers, stepping aside to allow the king to enter.

An open window looked out across the glen to the silver streak of the loch. A cold chill filled the stark room and Richard scanned the bare walls, the darkened stonework, the simple bench seat, and there, standing on a sort of wooden support, a painting. Not large or impressive at first glance, when Richard stepped up closer, he became gripped, as if by unseen hands, unable to move, eyes bulging, mouth dropping open.

Devoir moved up next to him, running his fingers along one of the wooden legs supporting the painting. "This is what is termed an easel, Majesty. I brought it from the east, from the fair city of Constantinople. You have visited there?"

A prolonged silence was the only answer. Devour shrugged, gave a quick glance towards Lorna, then moved around the back of the easel. "The light is perfect right now, Majesty. If you look beyond the paint, into the very soul of the work you will see what only you can see."

And Richard did see.

The painting was of a mass of peonies, in full bloom, whilst in the background the castle. As the King tried to focus in on the details, the image changed, fluctuating in a wild array of colours and hues, shadows growing lighter, revealing first Lorna's face but then … Richard narrowed his eyes, holding his breath, unable to believe what lay amongst the abundance of flowers.

Lorna, bent over a simple wooden bench, her dress thrown over her back, with Devoir making long, exquisite love to her. Richard gasped as Lorna gave a loud cry. He did not know if it came from the painting, or from the woman standing not three paces from him. Nevertheless, whomever the owner of the cry, they brought him out of his daydream and he span around, the invisible fingers, which gripped him, squeezed his throat. "What manner of devilry is this?"

Devoir spread his hands, "Your innermost desires, Majesty."

"My innermost … By Christ, you believe I wish to see such things? Such debauchery?"

"It is the truth you see, Sire. What is in your heart cannot be hidden, not least from yourself."

Richard spluttered, staggering backwards a few steps, and collapsed onto the bench, wide-eyed, stricken by disbelief.

"I love him, sire," said Lorna, moving closer, with Devoir by her side, his arm around her waist. "I tried to tell you before. But every time, you chose to ignore me, dismiss my words as if they did not matter."

"I am a king," he croaked.

"Aye, you are, Majesty, but above all else, you are a man. A proud man and a wonderful one. You are a great and noble king, but I can never give you what you desire. I love another and I cannot betray my feelings."

The King leaned forward, arms on his knees, turned his face to the floor and stared, unable to speak, his defeat complete.

Lambert crossed the road and walked down a narrow path towards the river and the campsite beyond. He stopped at a bridge and watched the fish for a few moments before continuing. At the second bridge, the river was wider, faster, overhanging trees casting their shadow across the surface making water appear inky black.

"I thought Richard saw you in the garden with Devoir," he said, not turning around as she stepped up next to him. "He lost his temper, felt humiliated, betrayed even?"

"That was *his* projection, Andrew, what he chose to believe. I showed it you to try to give you some insight into the fears of inadequacy so many men experience, even those chosen to lead us. He was never able to accept I loved another, nor my rejection. Kings are proud, but Richard welcomed my power of healing. From the moment I tended to his arrow wound, he grew stronger, more *alive*. I possess such gifts, Andrew, and I imbued him with the knowledge that not only a king, but an ordinary man can develop supreme sexual power. In his past, no mistress ever gave him these feelings. They used, manipulated and cajoled, made him promises of love and devotion, but all they ever really desired was power and privilege. The same is true for his other royal courtiers.

"We met on many occasions, Andrew, often in secret. I chose not to show you them all. Throughout the moments we shared, I transferred my energy into him, brought him to a high level of insightfulness so the truth became clear, and he witnessed, as if for the first time, the lies and hypocrisy surrounding him. He also saw the truth in the painting on that final day. I developed such a sense of compassion for him as a human being, regardless of his position, yet despite this, I could never be his mistress. With that truth, he shook off everything I gave him and he returned to a darker, more violent side. He stormed my castle, my home, abused my husband and carried away the painting."

"Why didn't he burn it, along with the castle?"

"Its power proved too great. Devoir's mastery, his deep mysticism, helped transform mere flicks and daubs of paint into something otherworldly. The painting has the power to be whatever the viewer wishes it to be." She took his arm and spun him around to face her. "By tapping into its power together, we can find a world for *us*."

"And Devoir? I thought you loved him?"

"I..." She shook her head, averting her eyes for a moment, "The person I was then loved Devoir, as he loved me. That was the past. What we have now, is the present. And what I need is for the secrets to be opened, with you."

"I don't understand if you are truly talking about me, or Devoir?" He shook his head when she remained silent. "I'm confused, Lorna. However much I want to... all I need... Oh dear God..." His body shuddered and he let his head fall. "I have loved and lost far too often, and I keep going back, trying again, because I want to be loved. I'm at a stage now where I know I'll never succeed. I'm searching for something that isn't there."

"Yes it is," she said, cradling his head, drawing him closer, stroking his hair with such tenderness he wanted to scream. "And if you let me, if you trust me, I will show you exactly where it is."

He lifted his head and turned, putting the back of his hand into his eye to prevent the tears from rolling down his cheek. "I believe I know where it is," he said and turned, knowing what he would see.

The pathway, running down and twisting to the left towards the campsite, with no sign of Lorna.

30

The truck came out of the side street at an acute angle. The bend was blind, so Miles reacted too late, pulling down hard on the steering wheel, giving the other vehicle a glancing blow on the wing, but smashing his light in the process.

An angry truck driver, shaking his fist, red faced and agitated, came striding over to them as Miles sat staring through the windscreen wondering what had happened.

Sinclair got out and ducked the man's wild swing, the blow striking fresh air. He hit the man in the solar plexus, dropping him like a stone, walked around the front of the dinted hire car and, tugging hard, managed to prise open the driver's door. Miles spilled out into the road and threw up.

They were three of four kilometres out of Auxerre and the road was quiet.

Until the police arrived.

Lambert took the car down to the River Cure, parked and walked along the bank. The sunlight filtered through the overhanging branches of the abundant trees and played upon the surface of the running waters. Dragonflies and demoiselles dipped and darted and he found a tiny inlet, took off their shoes, dipped his feet into the depths and watched the fish nibbling at his toes.

The air, thick, warm, wrapped him in a comforting blanket and he stretched himself out and closed his eyes.

"This is heavenly," she said, lying on the grass beside him.

He studied her face, smooth, perfect, and he stroked her hair. A small sigh, barely audible, a slight pouting of the mouth. He turned her face and they kissed, soft lips melding as one. If this were a dream, he mused, it was the most wonderful one of all. Her scent filled his nostrils, drifted into his brain, and transported him to another plain. Her hand crept around the back of his neck, their tongues seeking out each other, sweet tasting. Lambert moaned as she surrendered under his touch, hands roaming over her pliant body.

They made love under the sun, the warmth kissing their flesh as their own lips sought out and kissed one another. He caressed her face and stared into her eyes and smiled, "I love you," he whispered.

Nothing mattered anymore except the feel of her. And when he at last opened his eyes and stared at the soft grass, his whole body shuddered, longing to experience her embrace and for her to hold him for as long as he needed to be held.

Miles sat in the tiny reception of the local gendarmerie, tapping his foot and chewing his nails. Time seemed to be irrelevant to the various police officers who drifted in and out, never pausing to so much as to shoot him a glance. The big bald man behind the desk wrote endlessly in a thick ledger and far in the bowels of the building telephones rang and metal doors clanged shut. The sound conjured images of Sinclair sat in a grotty cell, stripped down to his vest and pants, nursing his damaged pride, but other than that accepting of his fate.

The driver of the truck, who remained pole-axed as the police drove up, had lodged a complaint as soon as the gendarmes disgorged from their patrol cars. Ranting and raving like a lunatic, a detached witness might have thought Sinclair guilty of the most heinous of crimes. No amount of denials, however, prevented them both being hauled to the local station, where assault charges were levied at Sinclair and Miles forced to listen to a litany of disapproval from the officers on duty.

And now he waited and stared into nothing, wondering what he could do or where he could go. His vehicle sat in the police pound, the wing buckled. Vézelay may as well have been on the other side of the world.

Two, perhaps three hours later – he couldn't tell which – a gendarme approached Miles and told him, in faltering English, he could visit his friend for a few minutes. Led down a narrow brightly lit corridor, he ended up outside a small cell and Sinclair, sitting on a sort of camp bed, sleeves rolled up, eyes black rimmed. He looked up, caught Miles' concern, and sighed. "Mr Miles. What can I say?"

Miles pressed himself against the metal bars and grimaced, aware of the gendarme hovering close by. "You told them it was self-defence, about the car ramming into us?"

"Of course I told them. My French is good enough for them to understand everything, but they simply don't believe me. It is my word against the truck driver's."

"Where is he?"

Sinclair shrugged, "At home I guess."

"So, he gets to relax, drink wine and sit with his feet up in front of the TV whilst you—"

"There's no point going on, Mr Miles. What's done is done. All I can do is wait until I'm arraigned before the court and discover what the outcome is. My gut feeling is they'll fine me, nothing more."

"And how long will it all take, for Christ's sake?"

Sinclair shrugged, "They couldn't say. Three days maybe, but—"

"*Three days*! But that's outrageous. Can't I bail you out, or something?"

"They said because it is Friday the courts close early. We have to wait until Monday."

"Jesus, Sinclair, why the hell did you hit him?"

Sinclair arched an eyebrow, "Oh, and allow him to punch me in the face?" He shook his head. "You can still continue down to Vézelay, Mr Miles. You'll be there in an hour or two. The police told me the car can go to a garage but probably won't be ready until late this afternoon, *if* you're lucky. They don't exactly work fast around here."

The gendarme coughed and when Miles turned to him, the officer tapped his wristwatch. Miles swung back to Sinclair, "I'm going to hire another car, get down there as quickly as possible. Tell me again where this castle is."

Sinclair did so and Miles scribbled the name of the château down on a scrap of paper he had in his jacket. Miles smiled, then went to go.

"There is something more," said Sinclair.

Miles waited, not knowing whether to welcome or dread another revelation.

"Before he left, Mr Andrew received a package, he gave it to me. Inside was something which held many of the answers as to why Mr Andrew has been behaving so strangely."

"Something? What sort of something? Not more bloody nonsense concerning witchcraft or ghosts?"

"In a way. Mr Andrew discovered many things during his long hours of research, most notably his grandfather's quest to find the painting."

"I'm lost, Sinclair. What bloody painting?"

"The one Monsieur Devoir painted of Lorna in the Fourteenth century, the one Richard the Second took from the castle after he had levelled the place to the ground. Mr Andrew explained it all, including his race to the château. A race, I believe, which is approaching the final lap."

Miles' mouth opened partially as the significance of Sinclair's words drove home. "You mean, he foresaw it?"

Sinclair nodded, grim, stern-faced. "Everything."

Without another word, Miles left the police station at a run, in the hope of finding a nearby garage that hired cars. It was only when he got outside he realised he had not wished Sinclair 'good luck'. Given the manservant's revelations, when he stared back at the soulless gendarmerie building he knew luck would have very little to do with anything.

"Andrew," she whispered, head resting on his chest as they lay on the grassy bank, the only sound the gentle trickle of the river running by, "such perfect harmony. When you made love to me, I felt your soul deep inside me, and it was wonderful."

"I wish to God all of this was true."

She smiled and nuzzled in further to his body, "Persuade yourself that it's true. I have searched so long to find the painting and now, with your help, I have…" She sighed, "Your grandfather did not understand, and he refused to help me. He shut me out, tried to destroy my memory, my power, and that hurt so much. I have known other pain, Andrew, the pain of loss. When Monsieur Devoir entered my life, he swept me away, even before he began to paint me. He was handsome, talented and mysterious. He made me laugh so loud. Sometimes my husband would take my hands and stare into my eyes, asking me if something was between us, but I always denied it. I was ashamed of that lie, Andrew, for I loved my husband too. Not in the same way, for Monsieur Devoir was unlike any other I had known. On my second sitting for him, he approached me, and kissed me. A jolt of joy surged through me and although I knew I should resist, I could not. From that moment we became lovers."

"You had others. The Earl of Carrick, that big Swedish nobleman?" She giggled. "They were not the same?"

"I told you, darling, sex can be enjoyed without the complications emotions often bring. Monsieur Devoir was a caring lover, the finest I have known, unlike the rest. He almost conquered me. Almost."

"And your husband never suspected?"

"I often believed he did, but he never said a word. His attitude to me never faltered; he remained the good and gentle man he had always been. The physical part of our life was the one thing that had changed and we had not made love for many years. He had certain problems. He felt *less* than a man, despite all of my reassurances."

"So, although he still loved you, he knew you had lovers."

"I believed this to be the case, yes. As I said, he was a wonderful man. He never asked, nor condemned me, yet I knew for certain he was aware of what was happening between myself and Monsieur Devoir."

"And then Devoir left?"

She tensed, sat up and gazed out across the river. With her back to him, he could not see her expression, but something about her attitude, the tightening of her shoulders, made him realise the memory brought sadness to her heart.

"I woke up one morning and ran down to his room, as I often did. Inside his chamber, all was empty except for the painting, now complete. I went to it and saw so much within the canvas. Not only our coupling, but also the destruction of the castle, Richard's fury and you, Andrew."

"*Me?*"

She turned and her eyes were wide, lustrous, full of wonder. "Yes. I saw you and I recognised something in you, a *spiritual* connection. I believed I loved Devoir, but the more I peered into the canvas the more I came to realise Devoir fell in love not with me but with his painting. I was just a part of painting, nothing more. I understood everything at that single moment – the Universe had designs for another future for me."

"For you? But what's my role in your future? You mentioned nothing except involving me as some sort of helper."

"The Universe does not always reveal its secrets, Andrew. We are mere pawns in the game."

"I'd call what's happened a damn sight more than a game."

"Do not be angry, Andrew." She smiled and moved closer, wrapping her arms around him. "I do not know all of the answers, but I understand it is futile to resist. I believe in some way Devoir was a guide, pointing me in the right direction. The painting was the key, Andrew, the means to a new existence, beyond our wildest dreams. When I met your grandfather, he understood and—"

"Yes. My grandfather. Sinclair told me some things, about him coming here to seek out the painting. Is that true?"

"His search brought him here, yes. He uncovered some facts, knew the painting was here, in this area, so he visited a *brocante*, found an old etching."

"So why did he not root out the original?"

"Because he was much happier in his chosen life. His dreams never came true. Besides, he discovered the Comte had sold the painting."

"Yes, Sinclair told me the same."

"He learnt that from your grandfather, but it isn't true, Andrew. The painting still remains where it has always been." She leaned back and smiled.

"But why would the Comte say it was sold?"

"The Come did not."

Her smile broadened, and Andrew experienced a sudden, irresistible urge to kiss her. Instead, he stared adoringly at her lips. "I don't understand."

"He met someone in the market, an old servant of the Comte. It was her who told him." Her eyes twinkled playfully. She traced a line down his nose to his chin with her forefinger. "Thanks to that woman, your grandfather returned home without ever discovering the truth."

"You mean … the woman was you?"

"I have lived various different lives over the years, Andrew."

"I see that, but as for the rest, I'm totally lost. If you needed to find this secret, why did you send my grandfather back home? Why would you begin yet another attempt to achieve your goal?"

"All will be revealed at the end of your journey."

"So, everything you did, you did it on purpose?"

"Yes."

"And on the night of my car crash, you finally revealed your true self."

"Yes. A fissure in the fabric, I believe. The energy released, the power of my soul, piercing the membrane that separates the past and the present. Something beyond my understanding occurred that night which enabled you to see me for the first time, and from that moment…" She cupped his face and kissed him lightly on the lips, "We must trust in the power of the Universe."

"I do," he said and returned her kiss.

She ran her fingers up and down his bare arm. "We can go back to your cottage, if you like."

"But what about the painting? I've done much of what you mentioned lately, including coming here…"

Lorna tilted her head, "We will have more than enough time to go to the château."

He frowned. "Wait, you already know where it is?"

"Of course! Your father, Andrew. He uncovered much of the truth, as you know for yourself."

He stiffened. "What do you mean?"

"In the tower, in the desk? Your father was planning out a new book, before his untimely death. A book which would shed light on the secrets of Devoir's painting."

"How in the name of God could you know all this?"

"You already know the answer, Andrew. I've been with you, watching everything. Waiting."

"Waiting. Waiting for me to do what my father left undone. Is that what you mean? Is that why you didn't come here yourself to take the painting, because you needed me to guide you, bring together the past, the present, in some sort of union?"

She smiled, stroked his face and he drifted, the warmth of her caress transporting him into a state of perfect bliss. "As with most things, reasons are often so simple; I have been waiting – for you to reveal the secrets. Devoir's instructions were not complete, certain aspects of his mastery missing. Your grandfather, and your father, they assembled the jigsaw. And you, you are the last piece."

Lambert opened his eyes, the sun warm on his face. He sighed and stood up. The images were becoming more frequent and more real. He understood just how powerful the invisible forces at work all around him were, yet he still fought against them, refusing to accept such ideas. He looked down at the grass, to where she lay only moments ago, and questioned again what was reality and what were dreams. With a heavy heart, he strolled back to his car to make the short drive to the rented cottage in Asquins.

31

He stopped at Les Hirondelles and had a glass of red wine before he wandered along the back lane to his rented property. No sooner had he stepped over the threshold than the interior grew dark and hot. She came to him, slipping her arms around his waist. "I want us to make love," she said, "Slowly. To savour and enjoy."

Afterwards, he made coffee and went onto the terrace. The afternoon sun still beat down, but he noticed the clouds gathering on the far horizon. "It will rain this evening," he said.

"By this evening you will not care."

He did not understand the inference, so he quietly drank his coffee and studied her. She wore sunglasses, face turned to the sky, her white, embroidered top open almost to her breasts. His eyes locked on a thin trickle of perspiration running from her throat down to her cleavage and when he noticed her watching him, he felt the heat rise to his face and he turned away. "You're so beautiful," he whispered.

She tightened her arms around his neck and kissed him in response. "Andrew, you do trust me, don't you?"

"Of course I do. Why do you ask?"

"I don't know. A feeling. Is something worrying you?"

"No…" He placed his other hand over hers. "You still have to tell me what became of Richard?"

"The king?" He nodded. "Don't you know your own history, Andrew?"

"Not about Richard the Second, no. I know he helped put down the Peasants' Revolt, but not much else. I never knew he went to Scotland, for instance."

"That is because those episodes were not recorded. Plenty of stories of him with Wat Tyler, his being controlled by the barons, how he asserted his own authority, Henry Bolingbroke wrenching the throne from his grasp."

"You sound bitter."

"Bitter? No. Sad, Andrew. Sad he ended his days the way he did, in despair." She brought her hands to his face, her fingers pressing in on either side, making small circles around his temples. "I want you to relax, think of nothing, allow your mind to drift, Andrew."

"What is this, another dream?"

"A vision. Close your eyes and surrender to the Universe."

Lambert obeyed, concentrating on a grey mist forming at the edge of his consciousness. It filled his mind, blurring thoughts. He grew tired, a heaviness descending, and the swirling, drifting cloud simply became ... formless.

Through the misty portal to the past, Lambert saw it all. How Bolingbroke usurped Richard and threw him into the grim, cold loneliness of Pontefract castle, and of how the King died there, alone and forgotten.

Lambert peered into the bottom of his coffee cup, reflecting on what he saw. After many moments, he sat back, his voice thick with emotion, "He died broken hearted. Alone, miserable and forgotten." He drew in a ragged breath. "A sad end."

"Yes," she said, her voice distant. "I often think of him, the love in his eyes. He adored me."

"But you were not able to reciprocate that love."

"No. It is so difficult to meet someone who shares the same frequency. It is a rare thing, but once found, transcends time. Richard and I would never have achieved such a union of mind and soul." She smiled, took his hands and squeezed hard. "So many of us love but never find love in return. After the hunting accident, when we met, naturally I was aware he was a king, but at that moment, he was a wounded human being who needed not only help but much, much more. As he loved me and discovered Devoir and what such a man could do for me, Richard demanded my sincere comparison. But comparison is the greatest enemy of love. With such knowledge, he turned his heart away from me. At any other time, the situation being different, who knows what might have developed. But, we met at the wrong moment and neither of us had any control over that."

Lambert nodded, squeezed his own hand in return, and stood up. "We had best make our way to the château. I feel we still have much to do."

He looked down and saw the empty chair. No doubt, she had returned to another life and Lambert knew, instinctively, her thoughts were on Richard and the dreadful way his life, once so full of promise, simply petered out.

32

The Château stood on a hilltop, surrounded by thick woodland, allowing the occupants a level of privacy not available to many such castles in the region. Lambert took the car up the winding, twisting path to the huge gates and parked in the designated area, which seemed something of an afterthought. Broken ground, invaded by weeds, brought an air of neglect to the surrounding area. A faded sign nailed to the door denoting the opening times only fuelled the belief that here was a place where apathy had taken a firm grip.

He turned and saw Lorna standing there, smiling. She breathed in the air, thick with aroma of the encroaching vegetation. "I knew you would come."

He frowned. Hadn't everything led them both to this moment? "Of course. I had little choice."

"There is such sadness here, Andrew. Can you sense it?"

"I certainly feel something," he said, reaching for his coat, slung over the back seat. "Here, put this on."

She smiled her thanks, giggled and shook her head. "No, Andrew, that jacket will swamp me." She grew serious again, looking up to the high exterior walls. "Are you certain this is the place?"

Again, a tingle of confusion, "I thought you knew already?"

"Do I?" She shook her head, her own bemusement obvious. "Perhaps I have forgotten."

Lambert pulled out the piece of paper from the pocket of his jeans. "I wrote down what Sinclair told me. Here."

She leaned across and read the words. "Yes. I'm full of excitement, Andrew, but … I'm not sure. What did Sinclair say to you before you left?"

Lambert shrugged, tucking the paper away again. "He seemed concerned, but he didn't say much at all. I suppose he'd accepted I had to come. Why, do you think he's followed us?"

"Why do you say that?"

"I don't know. I've never seen you like this."

"No, I ... There is something. Tell me what you spoke to him about."

"I handed him something. A package."

He saw her face, the look he recognised from before. A tiny hesitation, cogs grinding in her mind. When she spoke, her voice trembled, "What was inside, Andrew?"

"In my search through Father's papers, I came across the most unbelievable set of writings. Mere scribbles, dashed off at great speed. I thought at first they were hasty, garbled notes, ideas thrown around from an over-productive imagination. Then I read them."

"They unfolded the secrets of my story, didn't they?"

"I often wonder how life would be, if you were here with me. Can we predict the future? Any of us? My father wrote down the outline of a story, which seemed to do just that, and what is more, his predictions have turned out to be true. "Andrew rested his hands on her slim shoulders, took in her enigmatic smile. " I never suspected my father wrote such things. Now I know he possessed something more than a fertile imagination; he was blessed with an incredible ability to foretell."

"He learnt it all from his own father." She leaned into him. "You wished to complete this last novel, didn't you? You resisted the urge because you believed you lacked the talent. But something guided you, and you gathered together everything your research revealed. The secrets."

He gently pushed her away and gazed into her huge, beautiful eyes. "That has been my wish ever since I came across his papers and notes. To write with passion and truth. To include every detail of us, our story. How we met, the memories of events in the distant past ... And here, in Burgundy, how we found everlasting happiness and love. That's my vision of how our life could be." Her mouth fell open and, without a pause, he kissed her. "You've ignited a fire inside me, a wonderful, raging *desire* to create. You're my inspiration, my muse."

"Yes, your passion and desire for me has created the most exciting, heartwarming story, of a love which crosses eons and never dies, and all of it made possible by the painting." She kissed him again. "I've always had such faith in you, Andrew. You think you've failed in your life and this has always held you back from achieving your greatest success. You must never fear failure so much that you refuse to attempt new things."

They fell into each other's arms, the moment swathing them with such joy Lambert grew dizzy, knowing he should tell her more, but something held him back. The time was not yet right. He nuzzled into her neck, "I think we should hurry, the afternoon is pressing." He smiled, kissed her cheeks, and took hold of her hand. "Everything is going to be just fine."

"For once that is you who are the positive one. You are almost there."

"Yes and that's your influence – your energy!" He turned his face to the sky as the rain started to fall. "Come on, let's go and have a word with the curious Comte."

Lambert eased open the latch and stepped through the doorway. He tripped on the tiny wooden step, stumbled forward and threw out his hands to maintain his balance. In so doing, he dropped his coat and he cursed as he picked it up to discover it had fallen into a patch of sodden ground. He shook it out, annoyed, and paused to take in his first sight of the château and its grounds.

He had little expectation of what he would find, but what he saw caused him to stop and gawp in wonder. An ornamental garden, beautifully laid out in a repeating pattern, flowerbeds surrounded by miniature box-hedges, narrow pathways punctuating each area. Over to the left, a lake, a profusion of reeds hanging heavy over the water's edge and everywhere the air full of butterflies. In the distance, beyond the garden, the château itself, majestic and enormous, clean lines, gleaming white walls, with roof and spires topped by steel-grey tiles.

At such moments, he despaired at not owning a camera. To capture the beauty of this place, to look back in the years to come and re-live its splendour, such an opportunity missed. He sighed, turned to tell Lorna of his regret, and an even greater despair gripped him. Once again, he was alone.

He walked along the broad path, which led to the main entrance, and the green painted cabin where he would be required to pay the admission price. A tiny, bespectacled woman, sitting in the darkness of the booth, gave him a questioning look as he stepped closer.

"Bonjour, the gallery, please" he said.

She smiled softly and gave him a ticket and a thin leaflet, which included a sketch of the château. He thanked her and continued on his way, studying the plan as he mounted a set of crude steps.

Through another door and he came into the courtyard, dominated by a large, circular fountain of indeterminate age, well worn, details blurred by age. He scanned the leaflet, the brief history of the château informing him parts of it dated back to the Twelfth Century. Impressed, he picked out the direction for the gallery and made his way straight towards it without further hesitation.

His heart pounded in his throat as he approached the entrance. All of his dreams and hopes, the many restless nights, the endless days of sitting and wondering, all of it now came together in this single point. Beyond the door lay the answer, the focus of all his desires. The painting and, hidden within its patina, the image of Lorna.

The gallery was narrow, walls and ceiling of the most serene white, almost dazzling in their brightness. Along the sides were paintings, lit by overhead lamps, and in the centre benches where visitors could sit and contemplate the wonders before them.

And they were wonders. Landscapes and portraits from across Europe, and every era of history. From early Gothic pieces with their focus on religious scenes, to lesser-known Impressionist works, here lay a rich display of artistic talent the like of which Lambert had not come across before. He gazed, awe-struck, wondering where he should go, what painting held the secrets he desired to uncover.

"Can I help you, monsieur?"

Lambert started at the sound of the voice and took a few breaths to calm himself before he answered the tall security guard who stood over him. "Sorry, I was…" He smiled self consciously, and waved his hand over the array of paintings. "I'm looking for a painting of a castle."

"A château, monsieur? This particular one, the Château de Chartreuse, or another?"

Lambert stood and cast his eyes from one side to the next, confused and anxious. He had got it into his head that all he needed to do was step inside and there it would be, the castle, painted by Devoir, vibrant and alive, so beautiful it would stand out from the rest, beckoning him forward. "A Scottish castle."

The guard scratched his chin. "I can think of only one such painting, monsieur, but its main focus is not a castle. I do know for certain it is Scottish, so let me show you."

Lambert's heart thumped again, so powerfully he felt certain the guard would notice. He did not and led Lambert towards a canvas of a small castle with a loch and a profusion of blindingly brilliant peonies dominating the foreground. Lambert stopped, took a breath and leaned forward, screwing up his eyes to get a better view. No doubt about it, the castle was Strythe, but of Lorna there was nothing. Not even a hint.

He couldn't believe it. How had things contrived to turn out this way and bring him nothing but crushing disappointment? "There is not another one, of this castle?"

"No, monsieur. This is the only Scottish painting in the collection. I believe it was donated by King Edward the Seventh."

So, this was it. Everything fitted together perfectly, except for the absence of the one person who had brought him to this place. His eyes grew blurry and his body trembled.

"Monsieur, is there something wrong?"

Lambert shook himself, forcing down the anguish and the desire to scream out at the top his voice for all the world to hear how lost, how betrayed he felt. "No. There is nothing wrong," he managed, throat constricted and he turned away and shuffled out of the gallery into the dying day, the realisation bearing down on him like a huge weight. Everything had been a dream, including Lorna. She was not real and he would never find her.

He returned to his car as if in a daze, his mind consumed by an impenetrable cloud of sadness. He leaned on the roof, remembered he had passed a little café some way down the track and decided to take a drink before leaving for home. He had no more choices left. Castle Strythe and Sinclair waited. And Miles, his best friend. No one else.

He walked down the twisting path to the café, leaving the car, needing to take in the evening air to bring some sense of equilibrium to his quaking limbs and reeling brain. At the bottom, he saw the cafe straight away, its sign already illuminated. There were a few locals in the tiny, cramped bar, none of whom paid him any heed. He made his order and waited. Sitting outside at a lonely table, he sipped his wine and reflected on his situation. He could no longer run away from the truth. Miles, for all his faults, proved true in the end – Lambert required a shrink, someone to fix his delusions, force him to face the demons and overcome them. What a fool he'd been. The accident, everything came back to that. Something shredded his common sense that night and he, like an idiot, allowed himself to be seduced. Even here, in the shadow of the castle, she had materialised from nowhere. Why had he never stopped to question the absurdity of it all? How was he ever going to live everything down?

Draining his glass, he rolled it between his hands and thought back to every incident where he had defended Lorna, her appearances, her words... How could he ignore some of the early dialogues, including the one regarding Richard II, when she pressed him over his interest in the usurped king. He focused on it, trying to recall the details.

"Why have you grown so obsessed with Richard, Andrew?" There was genuine uneasiness in her voice.

"Perhaps because I see so much of him in me." She gasped, but he plunged on, ignoring her shocked expression. "Consider for a moment how his life unravelled. From being the single most important person in the land, he ended up betrayed by everybody he ever knew. When my business folded, Jennifer left, my friends stopped calling ... I was forced to return to Castle Strythe, to start again. Richard never had such as luxury."

"Richard ended up dead. You are alive, alive and full of hope. Listen, his unswerving belief that God had placed him on the throne made him insensitive, aloof and indifferent. None of it excused the manner of his demise, but his arrogance alienated him from those whom he needed most." She shook her head. "He succeeded King Edward III at the age of just eleven so he had ample time to learn how to lie, Andrew. He was spoiled, frivolous and selfish. You are none of those things."

Now, sitting here alone, having put so much energy into uncovering the truth, her words rang hollow. He *was* like Richard. And all of it of his own making.

33

Miles managed to hire a car, but the owner of the garage offered him nothing more than a clapped out Fiat. The rate, ironically, remained unchanged. In no position to barter, Miles handed over the cash and took to the road.

The drive took him through the Yonne valley, sparkling under the sunshine in all its glory. Endless rolling fields, hyphenated by woodland and gentle, meandering rivers. He found himself wondering why he had never visited the area before now. Perhaps, living in a landscape as glorious as Scotland, he never felt the urge. Now, having seen Burgundy, he knew that here was a land equally, if not even more breathtaking than his own.

The kilometres blurred by. The radio did not work, so he entertained himself by humming old tunes, dragged up from his memory, but soon even these did nothing for the tedium he experienced. Never one for long journeys, he wished he spoke more French and insisted the gendarmerie released Sinclair on bail. Without the old retainer, he felt as if part of him were missing. The sensible, mindful part. Sinclair, forever the voice of conscience and caution, would have advised and entertained him, making this journey so much more bearable. Instead, the man sat in a cell, alone with his thoughts. Frustration was perhaps his only friend. Miles' was this journey.

He drove through a vast, seemingly endless forest, on a narrow road bisecting the centre of an ocean of trees. He glanced left and right, picking out little tracks, which trailed into the interior, and he imagined what might lie there, far from the curious eyes of the passersby. He had a mind to stop, stretch his legs, take in the glorious air, but he forced himself to continue. To give added determination, he pressed down on the accelerator and put all his concentration on the way ahead.

The highway emerged from the dense woodland, the vista opening up on either side, stretching as far as the eye could see. He spotted some boys throwing themselves off an outcrop of rock into a river and he smiled, recalling his youth when he too would do such things.

To the right, a huge crag, topped with trees, and way over in the distance he caught the first glimpse of the abbey at Vézelay. His heart thumped in his throat, anticipation rising and his hands became slick with sweat on the steering wheel. He swallowed hard and slowed down as he entered the small village of Asquins. He pulled in next to the petrol pumps to fill up the car, the dashboard display indicating the tank was virtually empty. A young girl appeared, smiling. "Twenty-five Euros worth, please," he said and cast a glance around. A curious place, the main road so close and yet, a mere half dozen paces from where he stood, the quiet of a typical French hamlet.

"You are Scottish?" the girl asked, in broken English, her smile warm and welcoming.

Miles, a little taken aback by the suddenness of her question, spluttered, "I beg your pardon?"

She made a face, "I am sorry. My English is not so good. I practise very much, but sometimes …" She shrugged, tapped the nozzle of the petrol dispenser against the fuel inlet and returned it to its cradle. "I ask as another man come to drink his coffee. A Scottish man."

"Wait," said Miles, recovering quickly, pressing more than enough notes into her hand, "What did this man look like?"

"Look like?" She considered the question for a moment, "Quite a big man, not young but not old. His hair was … How you say, brown?"

Miles fell back against the car, gaping at her. "When did you last see him?"

"He drank wine," she waved towards the table lined up outside the building, "He sat over there, and sometimes he would talk and laugh, like he was with someone else."

Miles gulped, could not find the words to speak, or the strength to move. He looked to the sign of the café. *Les Hirondelles.* The Swallows. "How long?"

"Only an hour, maybe two."

Miles put his hand over his mouth, biting back the despair threatening to overwhelm him. He looked to the sky, the blue giving way to indigo. Soon it would be night. He grunted, went around to the driver's door and got in, as the girl shouted, "Monsieur, your money!"

But he didn't care, time was moving on. With every second, the darkness grew and with the night, the possibility of gaining access to the château became less probable. He gunned the engine, swerved the car out into the main road and shot down towards Vézelay before following the route around to the left on the long, empty highway to Avallon.

He ignored the speed traps, and the outraged glares from pedestrians. He was a man on a mission and would do whatever was required to make the château before nightfall.

The road, which ran along the River Cure, was dark, unlit, and more than once he had to swerve to avoid collisions with on-coming vehicles. Nevertheless, he kept his foot pressed to the floor, leaning into the bends, using the gears until they shrieked in protest, the tiny Fiat's engine straining hard to respond. Swearing, sweating, teeth gritted, the tension mounted between his shoulders blades, turning muscles to slabs of stone. He ignored all, willing the car faster, and praying for the Sun to stay on the horizon.

He made the track to the castle moments later, slewed to a halt and scrambled out of the car, not even pausing to engage the locks. He ran to the massive double doors and cried out in despair.

They were closed. Locked.

He pounded on the woodwork with both fists, took to kicking as well before he put his forehead against the panelling and slid to the ground. He bit down the tears, unable to contemplate how close he must have been in preventing his friend, the man he loved, from falling into the clutches of whatever it was that lured Andrew to this place.

In the grey dusk, he turned his face upwards and muttered a plea, to God, to the heavens, to the invisible forces that controlled the Universe and as he did, through the veil of tears, he spied the intercom adjacent to the doorframe.

His heart leapt and he jumped up, jabbing at the 'call' button, depressing it with all his might, hoping the more force he applied the louder it would sound in the bowels of the castle.

And when it crackled into life, for a moment, the words failed him and he muttered, "Please, please help me."

"What is it you want, we are closed," came the voice, sounding chillingly mechanical through the tiny speaker.

"My friend, please. My friend came here, I am sure of it, to visit, to talk to you about a painting. I need to know where he is. It's important, I swear it. Can you help me?"

"Monsieur, we are closed, I'm sorry."

"Please, I beg you. Listen," he fumbled into his pockets, pulled out a wad of notes and waved them in front of the intercom, hoping in some way to use the force of positive thinking, or telepathy, or extra sensory perception, or anything else to convince the man on the other end to open up the damned doors. "I'll pay. I'll pay you a hundred Euros, only please, come to the entrance. Please."

The intercom clicked off and Miles stared in disbelief at the silent device. Anger gripped him, like an ignited flame, one moment lifeless, the next a huge burst of destructive power. He clenched his fist, preparing to smash the intercom to pieces. Instead, he stopped and aimed a blow at the door. It barely moved and he crumpled again to the ground and knew Andrew was lost.

For how long he sat like that in the dirt, he had no way of knowing. Soon, however, the mist cleared from his eyes. He shook his shoulders, rotated his neck, returned to full consciousness and climbed to his feet. He took in a few breaths to steady himself and made his way slowly back to the car, not knowing where he would go or what he would do. The night came on more swiftly now, shrouding the surrounding trees, the lane, the sky. He leaned against the open car door, hanging his head, and wept, despair conquering him.

The great mortise lock in the door disengaged, the tumblers making a huge sound in the stillness of that place. Miles turned, eyes wide, mouth open and there, in between the double gates, stood a small, bald-headed man, holding a torch in one hand and a walking cane in the other.

"My maid is on the telephone to the police if I do not return in one minute."

"Monsieur," blabbed Miles taking a step forward, arms outstretched. When the man shied away, Miles stopped, conscious of what this whole bizarre incident must look like. A stranger, in the night, acting like some wild, uncontrolled beast. He ran a hand across his nose, sniffed loudly, and drew himself up straight. "I'm sorry. My apologies, monsieur. I know this must seem strange, but my request is a sincere one. My friend, a Scottish gentleman by the name of Andrew Lambert, called here I believe. He may have had with him a woman, a very beautiful woman—"

"I have no knowledge of a couple, monsieur. I have visitors, but none as you have described."

Miles' throat tightened. "My God," he managed to utter.

"I am so sorry, monsieur. Your journey has been a wasted one." He switched on the torch, aiming it away from Miles, but offering up enough illumination to pick out the details. "You are his friend you say?" Miles nodded. "You seem distressed. Is your friend ill?"

"In a way."

"I see. Well, I have to tell you, monsieur, whoever your friend is, he is no longer here. I receive many guests. What was it your friend wanted? Something special?"

"A painting."

"Well, in that case, he may have gone to the gallery."

"Yes, to find it, hanging here as a gift, from Edward the Seventh of England. May I see it?"

"Monsieur, please, the castle is closed. It is night. Perhaps if you were to come back tomorrow I could—"

"I'll pay, as I said, if you would please just let me see the painting."

The man went to speak, then stopped. He stood, chewing at his inner cheek. "I do not understand your fixation with this painting, monsieur. Nor your friend's. For myself, I see nothing remarkable in it. My family received the painting as a gift some one hundred years, but as far as I can tell, any monetary value is limited. Nevertheless, my intention has always been to sell it."

"I'll buy it."

The man chuckled. "I beg your pardon?"

"I'll buy it from you. Name your price. Whatever it costs."

"But, monsieur, what you ask is nonsense! I cannot conduct business transactions in the middle of the night! The whole thing is absurd."

"You are the Comte, yes?" The man nodded. "Then don't conduct them here, in the night. I'll give you one hundred Euros if you simply show me where the painting is, then we can sit down and talk business." He dipped into his pocket and brought out the money. Then stepped right up to the Comte and pressed the note into his hand. "I'm not mad, monsieur. I'm simply determined, that is all."

The Comte stared down at the one hundred Euro note, sighed, and then stuffed it into his own pocket. "Very well," he said, "I shall show you."

They walked through the dim and silent corridors, their shoes echoing throughout the interior. The occasional electric bulb gave off a sickly glow, but there was little in the way of light. At any other time Miles would have paused to examine the treasures, the great tapestries, porcelain and gold statuettes, furniture expertly crafted dating back two or even three hundred years. Right now, however, his only thought was for the painting, drawn ever onward by some powerful and invisible force.

At last, the Comte stopped and turned. "I will light the candles, monsieur. My economising means I do not switch on the electricity in this part of the castle after closing. It is on a time switch." He went inside and Miles followed, trying to focus in on anything remotely like a painting. But he could pick out nothing. The room was in total darkness, except for the thin beam of the torch trailing over the floor, and his heart sank ever deeper, consumed by dread, even sadness for what awaited him.

A match flared, lighting up the Comte's face briefly, as he put the flame to three candles on a candelabra. Satisfied, he turned. "This way, monsieur."

Miles fell in behind him, walking slowly now, eyes glued to the wall and the paintings hanging there.

And then the Comte stopped. "Here it is."

Miles took a breath and moved closer. He narrowed his eyes. "Are you sure?"

"I am positive. As I said, it is nothing of any importance or significance. Your friend must have thought so too, for he never made himself known to me. Monsieur? Are you unwell?"

Miles, mouth half-open, shook his head and, without moving his eyes from the painting, took the candelabra and shone it upon the surface.

He gasped.

The tears welled up and rolled unchecked down his face, nevertheless he could still see what lay within the brush strokes of Monsieur Devoir, deep within the forest of blazing flowers. Standing on the hillside next to Castle Strythe, looking out across towards the shimmering silver streak of the loch, were two people. A man and a woman, their arms around one another's waists. And then, with nothing else existing for him, as if he viewed everything through frosted glass, an outsider looking into a forbidden world, Miles saw the man turn. And he saw the face, and the smile. It was Andrew, and the woman beside him, her hand raised in farewell, was Lorna.

Miles stared without speaking and knew, at that moment, his friend had found what he had been searching for his entire life.

The Comte led Miles outside, a sad smile splitting his florid face. "Monsieur, I feel you have need of a drink. Something strong perhaps."

Miles, legs weak, muscles mere elastic, allowed the Comte to escort him over to the château. Inside, a fire blazing in the grate, he sat and gazed into the bottom of his brandy glass.

"Monsieur, whatever has happened, I sense your anguish. The pain of loss."

Miles lifted his head. "Can I ask, has anything unusual happened these past few days?"

The Comte sat back, chewing at the inside of his cheek. "Unusual. Well, nothing that would…" He frowned. "There are the books, of course."

Miles shook his head, nothing registering. "Books? I don't understand."

The Comte took a sip of his drink and stood up, walking over to one of the enormous bookshelves which lined the walls. He pulled out a volume and returned. "This book. One of a pair which arrived by express delivery. I do not recognise the gentleman by the photograph on the cover."

He handed it over and for the second time Miles gazed at an image that belied explanation.

"This is Andrew," he whispered.

He turned the book over to study the cover, with its title 'The Magical Painting' and his heart shuddered. Identical to the painting in the gallery, the burst of colour from the many peonies held all of his attention.

"I do not know who sent it or why but, as you can see, the painting is there for everyone to see."

"Andrew wrote this. There's his name, across the bottom. Andrew Lambert. My God, he's emulated his father. This must have been what Sinclair was talking about before I left him at the gendarmerie. The gift Andrew gave him was this book!" His lips quivered and he drained his glass. "One of two, you said?"

"Monsieur, this may appear somewhat rude, but may I ask you your name?"

Miles frowned and told him. The Comte's expression changed to one of wide-eyed triumph. "Then I think we have an answer, monsieur." He took back the volume he had handed over, replacing it with another, identical in every way. "This one, I believe, may bring some clarity."

Miles weighed the book in his hands, then opened it. As Miles read, his eyes glazed over and his breath became ragged as the first tears tumbled down his cheeks.

The Comte moved quickly to intercept the cut-glass brandy glass, which slipped from Miles' fingers, managing to catch it before it shattered on the ground. Miles was shaking and the Comte took the book, turned it and read the words, which caused Miles such consternation: 'To Miles, my closest and dearest of friends. This book is dedicated to you.'

"It is yours, monsieur. A gift, from your friend."

Miles nodded, now mute, unable to speak. The Comte helped him to his feet and escorted him back through the corridors to the parking place and his waiting car.

"I'm sorry," said Miles at last, leaning on the open door. "I don't understand anything. Why would Andrew send this here?"

The Comte tapped the cover of the book. "Perhaps he knew you would come searching for him?" He grinned, helped Miles into the driving seat and waved him off.

34

Andrew Lambert looked up from his empty glass as a car roared past. Someone else desperate for answers, he mused, and gave a wry grin at nobody in particular. He threw some money down on the table and stood up. The long journey back held no attraction, but it was not something he could put off any longer. He pulled his coat close and began to make his way up the path, which led to the château and his waiting car.

As he approached, he patted his pockets to find his keys. He stopped. He rechecked his pockets. The keys were not there. Panic gripped him, a terrible sinking feeling overwhelming him. How was this possible? He went through every pocket again, taking his time, including the inside ones and the small zipped one on his sleeve. Nothing. Desperate now, he ripped off his coat and shook it, listening out for the telltale clink of the keys on their ring.

His shoulders slumped, defeat total.

His keys were not anywhere.

In a last, hopeless attempt, he went through his trousers, hoping against hope he had somehow inadvertently slipped them into a less familiar place.

He groaned. For a few elongated moments, he couldn't think straight. Despair raged with disbelief. What had he done, put them down in an absent moment? Slowly, after several deep breaths, he forced himself to systematically go through every place visited, every action made. He must have left them back at the café, or…

Another groan.

For the love of God, when he had first entered the château he tripped, soiled his coat, took it off and shook it dry. The keys must have fallen out at that moment. And if they did, that would mean he would have to return to the château and retrieve them. In the dark.

By now, the night had overcome the last shreds of daylight, the path to his car a barely discernible sliver of pale brown. He stepped beyond his car and shuffled over to where he believed the entrance to be, groped for the handle and pushed the door open.

This time, nothing was like before. No ornamental gardens, no lake, no château. They lurked somewhere, shrouded in the gloom. He took a single step forward and an array of security lights flared into life without warning, blinding him, capturing him in a multitude of spotlights.

He brought up his arms to shield himself from the glare, staggered backwards, hit the door and forced it back on its latch, the lock engaging. He was trapped, no way out and no hope of moving forward.

"Stay exactly where you are," came a voice.

Lambert blinked through the blaze, managing to make out three figures coming towards him, torches cutting through the darkness. He dare not move, waiting with bated breath, conjuring up any number of explanations for his entry, knowing the truth would appear hopelessly inadequate, if not downright unbelievable.

Two of the men were large, burly types in uniform, but the third was smaller, less threatening. His torch came up, bathing Lambert in yet another pool of blinding light. "*Mon Dieu*," said the small man, in a voice full of surprise, not belligerence.

The uniformed pair made to grab hold of Lambert, but the smaller one stopped them with a sharp, "No. Leave him be." He stepped closer, the torch swinging up to pick out the features of Lambert's face. "It *is* you. Dear God, how is this possible?"

Lambert, his face screwed up because of the glare, waved the man away. "Turn off those lights, for God's sake."

The man grunted, barked an order, and one of his uniformed companions turned and sprinted off. As they waited, the small man lowered the torch and gripped Lambert by the arm. "Monsieur, tell me, who are you?"

"I lost my keys," said Lambert, rubbing his eyes with his fists. "I'm sorry, I had no intention of breaking in, but the door was open."

"It was? Then it is my fault, monsieur, for I did not lock it after your friend departed."

"My friend?" Lambert dropped his hands. "What the hell do you mean?"

"I believe he called himself Miles?"

All at once, the strength went out of Lambert's legs and he crumpled, the second uniformed man reaching out to grab him before he hit the ground.

"Monsieur," said the other, bending down on his knees to move closer. "I am the Comte de Château de Chartreuse. You are not the first Englishman to have visited me this night. Indeed, you are not even the second."

Lambert groaned and the uniformed guard helped him upright. The Comte stood next to him. "I'm not English," said Lambert, running a hand through his hair, wondering how many more shocks he could take in one day. "Forgive me, I'm confused. You said my friend was here? Miles?"

"Yes. He was looking for you, I think. I took him to the gallery, to see the painting."

"The painting? But, I was here, late this afternoon. I went to the gallery and saw it. There was a security guard." He twisted round, grimacing at the one in uniform. "It was you? Do you remember?"

"I do," said the man, "You seemed upset, monsieur, as if the painting was not what you had hoped to find."

"It wasn't." Lambert turned again to the Comte. "And Miles? What happened?"

"He left, after I had given him your gift, monsieur."

"My gift…" Lambert's voice trailed away. "Damn it. It was my hope he would receive it only once the secret had been revealed."

"Secret? Monsieur, I know of no secret. The painting is unremarkable in many ways. It is old, for sure, but not a masterpiece, not by any means."

"So you've seen it?"

"Many times, monsieur. My guest, she too felt drawn to it. She arrived earlier today, but insisted on viewing the painting in the dark, by candlelight. She was most determined and, I have to say, I could not refuse her. She is there now, so I understand."

Lambert's throat closed over. He groped forward, gripping the Comte's lapel. "She is there *now*?"

"Monsieur, please," the Comte tore himself free of Lambert's grip. "If it pleases you, I will take you to her. I can see you are upset, but I am not certain where any of this will lead."

"But, she is there, now, in the darkness?"

"Monsieur, do you not listen? I have told you, she wanted to view the painting by candlelight, to help her with her own creation."

Lambert's mouth moved soundlessly.

"She is painting her own version, Monsieur. Come, let me take you to her."

The Comte followed the path Lambert had done not a few hours before, and as they approached the main gate, the spotlights at last went off and Lambert felt his shoulders relax. Tension, however, replaced now with a terrible foreboding.

He walked as a somnambulist, the beams of the torches his guide, ignoring everything else. Conflicting emotions raged within him, ranging from total despondency to simmering exultation that a chance might remain. For the Comte was leading him to the gallery and there, in the fabric of the painting as Devoir made clear all those centuries ago, the viewer can see whatever they so desire.

At the door, the Comte stopped and turned to Lambert, his face a hideous gargoyle mask in the deep and contorted shadows created by the torches. "If you will allow me one moment," he said with a smile, "I shall speak with my guest before we barge in."

He turned and went inside and Lambert stood and waited. Within a few seconds, he heard their voices, crystal clear in the still night air.

"Forgive me, mademoiselle, I understand how much you value your solitude, but I have a small question to ask."

"Certainly, my dear Comte," came the girl's voice. "How can I help?"

Lambert froze. Her voice, something about it so familiar. He craned his neck, mouth open, concentrating with all that he had on the conversation.

"I have a visitor," continued the Comte, "and, this is most unusual, but I believe his friend called here late this afternoon in search of him, and now this gentleman has returned. In so doing, he has misplaced the keys to his car."

"Oh, my dear Comte, I should have come at once to tell you…"

"Mademoiselle?"

"I found a set of keys by the outer entrance. I meant to pass them over to you, but it completely slipped my mind. Here, they are in my bag."

"Let me … Oh dear God." Lambert sensed the change, the sudden freezing of the air, the inexplicable tone of the Comte's voice, charged with disbelief, perhaps even fear.

"Monsieur Comte, what's wrong with you? Are you unwell?" The timbre of her voice moved from its light, almost playful air to one of concern.

Something had happened.

"Dear God, the painting. It has changed!"

Lambert yelped, brushed past the security guard and blasted into the gallery, charging forward with no thought of disturbing anyone. His heart pounded in his ears, throat growing dry.

Paying no attention to the Comte's cry of alarm, Lambert turned all his attention on something he never expected to find inside the gallery.

She sat behind an easel, her long hair hanging down to touch her bare shoulders, her dress a plain, floral printed design, her hand poised in the act of applying paint to her canvas. Next to her, sending out a flickering glow from three candles was a black metal candelabra. As Lambert strode forward, she turned to him and smiled.

"Andrew Lambert?" she asked and rose to her feet.

"Pardon?" The question brought nothing but confusion. Lambert stood, feet set in concrete now, unable to believe the vision he saw before him, hardly daring to breathe in case this moment became like all the rest and vanished forever.

The Comte stood transfixed, mouth gaping open, gazing at the painting Devoir created. Then he turned, his eyes glazed. "It's the same painting monsieur."

Lambert, trembling with disbelief, struggling to dampen down the hope resurfacing, merely mumbled, "A woman, surrounded by flowers. I see it. Dear God, it's Lorna ... How does she appear out of thin air?"

"I too was astonished to find her," said the woman, stepping out from behind the easel and gliding towards him, the security guard's torch illuminating her approach, the beam dancing over her in a cascade of colours and hues. Like the painting itself, the tiny flowers of her dress appeared as if in full bloom, alive.

Lambert gawped at her, mind in disarray, working far too slowly, making no sense of any of it. "But, I was here. I did not see her."

"Torchlight is the key to revealing its secrets," she said, so close now he could breathe in her perfume. "She's like halos that are sometimes made visible by the spectral illumination of moonshine."

She took his limp hand and guided him, as if he were a child, to stand before the canvas. Enraptured himself, the Comte could offer nothing more than his own bemused smile.

Lorna lay naked amongst the blooming peonies, reclining amongst them as a Hindu princess, her young body smooth and bronzed, garlands of tiny bluebell flowers around her slim neck, her wrists, her ankles. She had one arm behind her head, the right leg raised, and her smile was warm, open and welcoming. Lambert did not think he had ever seen any woman as beautiful or more alluring in his life.

"She has an uncanny resemblance to someone I have seen before," whispered the Comte again, not taking his eyes from the lithe figure. "How can it be that I looked upon this painting a thousand times and never seen anything so wondrous?"

"The secrets within the painting have to be revealed by the action of certain light," explained the woman, standing behind the two men. "Devoir knew this and painted it by candlelight, using many more hues and tones than I first supposed." Another smile, fluttering briefly across her lips. "I did not discover such meaning until this very day."

"Wait a minute," said the Comte, his face locked towards the painting, his voice trembling, incredulous. "How can this be possible? This was created nearly eight hundred years ago." He gazed at the woman when she said nothing in response. "She is ... I can't believe. She looks exactly like you!"

The woman gave a small laugh, "Really? Well, it just confirms Pablo Picasso's words: 'Art is not truth. Art is a lie that makes us realize truth, at least the truth that is given us to understand'." She went to her easel, lighting further candles arranged in a series of waiting candelabras. " If you wish to become a successful artist, your desire to create is something you have no choice over, it is what drives you on. That is what I am doing, what I have always done, looking for my own distinctive way to fulfill what lives so deep inside me. A great artist is always before his time or behind it. Your book, Mr. Lambert has opened the door to a new discovery."

Lambert did a double take, "You've read my book? But, how could you have done?"

"It seems you have no clue why I'm here." She smiled and bent down to ferret inside the wicker bag at the base of her easel. She straightened, holding the keys of Lambert's rental car. "These are yours?"

"Yes! They're the reason I came back, to find them."

"A magical and pleasant coincidence. I'm so pleased to meet you, Mr Lambert. You can't begin to imagine what your book has revealed to me."

She held out her hand and he took the keys, not daring to believe they were real. "I thought I might find some answers, but now…" He folded the keys in his fist, "I don't understand anything."

"Let me explain something. Not everything you intended to assert is true. This ancient painting has its own unique method and reason to be painted. The painting process, which Devoir used, required him to adhere strictly to the principles and guidelines of holy Śāstra. Śāstra is Sanskrit for rules, which are true and correct. In essence, the Śāstra is knowledge based on principles held to be timeless. The paint was prepared from minerals and plants, derived from the foothills of the Himalayas. They were then hand-ground into a fine powder, a process itself a Sādhanā or contemplation toward materializing the divine energy. Through this, Devoir grew more aware, enlightened if you like. He utilised candlelight as a new element of style. In his 'white phase', he blended colours in a more generous way, combining them to lend the paintings an atmosphere suffused with light. He was centuries before his time."

"But how do you know all of this?" asked the Comte, bewildered.

"I have forever been connected to her." She stepped between them, holding the candelabra aloft, its light bathing the painting, the girl amongst the peonies smiling ever more broadly. "You were so close, my dear Comte, when you said she looks like me." She turned to Lambert. "At least, I *wanted* to be her. Or, perhaps I'm her reincarnation."

Lambert gasped, his voice little more than a croak, "Lorna? It can't be true. How…"

"How do you know my name?"

"So, it *is* your name? You really are Lorna?"

"It's a miracle," said the Comte, stepping away, taking the candelabra from Lorna's grip and raising it to bring more light to the scene. "I see her … Dear God, I see *you*."

She gave a tiny laugh. "My dear Comte, it is simply what is meant to be."

Lambert stood, mouth open in disbelief, her words seizing him with all the force of a steel vice. A rush of desire surged through him, a genuine acceptance of love, brimming up to consume his entire being. He wanted to pull her to him, to crush her mouth with kisses of unbridled passion, to hold her and never let go. He closed his eyes and her arms enfolded around him, bringing a deluge of love and ecstasy to every sense, washing away all his fears, pain and doubts.

"Your book, it filled in the gaps. All the searching, trying to piece together what Devoir tried to show me. What you have done is bring all those years spent by the King, your grandfather, your father, the endless questioning, *you* gathered every clue, every hint and created the answer. I always knew you would. Destiny led me to you. And through you, the secret of the Magical Painting is revealed."

"Lorna was the light," he said, not releasing her from his embrace, "showing us the way."

"She was a goddess of eternal knowledge, a symbol of the endless human craving for the discovery of sacred secrets. And you, you were her instrument. The candle she held to light the way, through your own desires and needs, but most of all, through the words of your book."

"Monsieur Lambert, are you feeling all right?"

The Comte's voice, an intrusion into his state of bliss, nibbled away at the edges of his consciousness. He ignored it, gripping her ever more closely to him.

"We must go," she said.

"But you, you will disappear again, I know it."

"No," she said. "I am no illusion. But it is late, we must go."

He took in a breath, pulled his face from hers and opened his eyes.

And she was still there, smiling, her eyes shining and moist.

"I don't ever want to go," Lambert said, drinking in her loveliness.

"Monsieur," the Comte's hand rested on Lambert's shoulder. "I do not begin to know how to explain any of this, but I feel it is time to leave."

"We can go wherever we wish now," she said. "Destiny is in our own hands. No more looking back, only forwards."

Lambert went to take hold of her, but she stepped away. The smile lingered for a moment, gradually replaced by something else.

Filled with the fluctuating, almost magical glow of the candles, the gallery seemed to resonate with sensations beyond them both, a pulsing incandescence of pure energy. A presence emerged from the darkest, deepest corners of the room. And with it came a voice, deep and compelling yet strangely familiar.

Turning to discover who spoke, instead Lambert saw nothing but, an empty room greeting him. The Comte, the security guard, all gone, the door closed behind them. Gripped by cold, piercing dread, Lambert peered into the gloom, willing his eyes to adjust. A few seconds crawled by before he managed to pick out a tall man dressed in dark clothes, face deep in shadow, leaning against the doorframe. "Who are you?" asked Lambert, his voice small in the eerie atmosphere closing in all around.

'I've been waiting for you to work it all out,' returned the voice, a mere whisper.

Lambert strained to make out not only the words, but the features of the stranger. He thought he caught a glimpse, a shadow of the long departed painter, Devoir … but how could that be? What was real, what was fantasy? As he struggled to disentangle the confusion, the most horrible sensation of being once more alone settled upon him. He closed his eyes, and chaotic fluctuations of light and temperature blurred together, then disappeared.

"Those who search, will find, Mr. Lambert."

Who said that? Lambert kneaded his forehead, unable to disentangle the confusion, his eyes boring into where he believed the painter stood. With a final look towards the canvas, he saw within the undulating patterns glimpses of the past, of Lorna, of himself. And the more he concentrated, the more he realized the painting was a conduit, a means for him, for anyone, to see whatever the heart desired – a mirror of the universe, a vehicle for him to travel to any life, to any experience in any period of time. If he could step inside and become one with the paint … if only it were possible. Or was it already possible and what he now understood as divine energy had become reality, drawing him ever deeper into the world of brush strokes and colour. Taking a deep breath, he embraced the new worlds appearing before him and surrendered to the infinite.

THE END

Lightning Source UK Ltd.
Milton Keynes UK
UKHW041203091120
373077UK00002B/263